BABEL

BABEL

A Kathy and Brock Mystery

BARRY MAITLAND

ARCADE PUBLISHING
New York

FIRST U.S. EDITION 2003

First published in Great Britian in 2002 by Orion Books, an imprint of The Orion Publishing Group

This is a work of fiction. Names, places, characters, and incidents are either the products of the author's imagination or are used fictitiously.

Library of Congress Cataloging-in-Publication Data

    Maitland, Barry.
        Babel : a Kathy and Brock mystery / Barry Maitland. —1st U.S. ed.
        p. cm.
        ISBN 1-55970-668-6
        1. Brock, David (Fictitious character)—Fiction. 2. Kolla, Kathy (Fictitious character)—Fiction. 3. Police—England—London—Fiction. 4. Policewomen —Fiction. 5. London (England)—Fiction. I. Title.

    PR9619.3.M2635B33   2003
    823'.914—dc21   2002043928

Published in the United States by Arcade Publishing, Inc., New York
Distributed by AOL Time Warner Book Group

Visit our Web site at www.arcadepub.com

10 9 8 7 6 5 4 3 2 1

EB

PRINTED IN THE UNITED STATES OF AMERICA

To Jim

Acknowledgements

This book was written before the terrible events of 11 September 2001, at a time when the story of Islam in Britain was less widely discussed than today. I am indebted to a number of people whose knowledge and insights helped me with that aspect of the book, as well as with the workings of the Metropolitan Police. In particular I should like to thank Clare Murphy, Shiblee Jamal, Kay Suters, Rollo Clery-Fox, Ashton Nugent Cleary Fox, Scott Farrow, Anna Farrow, Akbar S. Ahmed, Philip Lewis, Fred Halliday and, as always, Margaret Maitland.

And the whole earth was of one language, and of one speech. . .
And the Lord came down to see the city and the tower, which the
children of men builded.
And the Lord said, Behold, the people is one, and they have all
one language; and this they begin to do: and now nothing will be
restrained from them, which they have imagined to do.
Go to, let us go down, and there confound their language, that
they may not understand one another's speech.
So the Lord scattered them abroad from thence upon the face of all
the earth: and they left off to build the city.
Therefore is the name of it called Babel.

Genesis, Chapter 11

Prologue

I entered the camp on the Saturday morning with the French medical team. The situation was overwhelming, devastating. Survivors were still being discovered beneath the ruins of demolished shelters, and all of the effort was going into finding them. That and putting out the fires whose oily smoke hung heavy in the air, blotting out the sun. The dead could wait. They lay everywhere, abandoned to the flies, sickeningly mutilated, dismembered, burned, hacked and shot. Nurses and paramedics accustomed to treating war victims were traumatised. They broke down in tears or stumbled from scene to scene in a state of shock. Some heroic figures with stronger nerves took charge of the situation and organised work groups and allocated tasks. I joined a stretcher party ferrying those survivors that we could find out to the gates of the camp where a queue of improvised ambulances waited, but each time we returned my feelings of fear and revulsion increased. Finally I felt so contaminated by the horror that I became convinced that the insanity of what had been done there would infect my own reason. Deep in the camp I abandoned the team and attempted to find my way out. But I became lost and disoriented in the winding alleyways, and staggered from one part of hell to another. I came to a place where limbs, torsos, heads lay scattered in my path and panic engulfed me. Then I heard a voice, the voice of a child, though I could see no one. It seemed to be reciting something rhythmical, a nursery rhyme perhaps, or a prayer. I was transfixed.

Its source lay in the dark shadow beneath a black awning collapsed close to the ground. I knelt before it and looked into a small space and made out the figure of a woman, her head cradled in the arms of a small boy. I discovered that my feelings of terror and disgust had left me. I crawled into the space. The woman was quite dead, her stomach bearing terrible wounds, but her son, a child of eight years as I later established, was unhurt. I sat with him for some time, and told him that his mother was past help. He had fallen silent when I appeared, and I never heard him utter another sound. I promised to take care of him and finally persuaded him to leave his mother's body and come with me. He was very thin and seemed to weigh almost nothing as I lifted him into my arms. I carried him out of the camp, holding his face close against my cheek so that he would not see the sights that we passed.

I

Detective Sergeant Kathy Kolla felt a great weariness overwhelm her. She didn't want to appear obstructive, but the room was warm and she hadn't slept for so long.

'It's all in my report. You've read that? I really can't add . . .'

'I've read it, yes,' the other woman said gently. 'It's very objective. It must have been extremely difficult to write. But it doesn't tell me how you felt, how you feel now.'

I feel now that my body is made of lead, she thought, heavy, dumb, grey. But she said, 'I felt mainly helpless.'

'Was that the most terrible thing about it? That you felt helpless?'

'Yes.'

'Abandoned?'

'Maybe. Towards the end.'

'That would be the time of the rape, would it?' Such a gentle, supportive voice.

'He didn't rape me.'

'No, you said that. You said he was stopped. You're quite sure about that?'

'Christ, I should know.' A little buzz of shock made Kathy sit up straight. Did they not believe her?

'Yes, of course. So the worst thing was the feeling of helplessness.'

A silence. The woman was good at silences, Kathy thought, but she had sat through enough interviews at the side of Brock, the master of the unbearable silence, to know how they worked.

Eventually the woman broke it herself. 'And feeling abandoned?'

3

she prompted. 'Did you feel let down by your colleagues for not getting you out of there?'

'No, I'd got myself into the situation. It was my mistake.'

'All the same . . . You didn't feel the least bit angry? With DCI Brock, perhaps?'

'No.'

'You've been in a number of difficult situations before, as a member of his team, haven't you?'

'Yes.'

'But this one was different?'

'Yes.'

'Because . . .?'

'Because . . . this time I really believed I was going to die.'

The woman seemed about to pursue this, then studied Kathy for a moment and appeared to change her mind. 'Yes, it must have been awful,' she murmured. 'We might come back to that later, if you like. Tell me a little more about yourself, will you? You've lost both your parents, I understand. Do you have any other close family?'

'I have an uncle and aunt in Sheffield, and a cousin and her family in Canada. They're the closest.'

'No brothers or sisters?'

'No.'

'Close friends?'

'The people I work with.'

'I mean, anyone special, a partner?'

'Not at the moment.' Kathy was aware that she was making the woman work, but she couldn't help herself.

'Recently?'

Kathy didn't answer, staring at the carpet, a neutral soft grey. But this time the woman wasn't going to give up. Finally Kathy said. 'I was living with a man in the latter part of last year. We split up just before Christmas.'

The woman gave her a careful look. 'Immediately before this happened?'

Kathy nodded.

'Do you want to talk about that?'

'No. It's got nothing to do with it.'

'You're quite sure?'

4

Another little buzz of shock. She hadn't even considered that possibility, blanking it out. 'Quite sure.'

The woman could barely disguise her disappointment. 'Well. . . Is he a policeman?'

'Yes.'

Another extended silence.

'What about girlfriends? Do you have a close friend you can confide in?'

'I have a few friends, but no one particularly close.'

'Outside of the force?'

'Not really.'

The woman checked her watch. 'Our hour is up, Kathy,' she said, with a little frown of concern. 'The next time we meet I'd like to explore a bit more thoroughly your feelings in that room, if you're up to it. Between now and then, you might like to think about how those feelings relate to the rest of your life.'

'I don't understand.'

'I mean, can we isolate what happened in that room and deal with it on its own, or do we need to consider other aspects of your life in coming to terms with it?'

She caught the look on Kathy's face and quickly added with a smile, 'Don't worry, it's just a thought.'

A bitter January east wind was blowing in the street outside. Kathy stood a moment on the front steps breathing it in as if it could scour away the sense of numbness that had weighed her down during the session. The street was crowded with people hurrying towards the evening trains and buses that would carry them back to their homes in the suburbs, and she fell in with them, glad to walk before facing the next trial.

Half an hour later she stood outside the door of the pub where the team was meeting to celebrate Bren Gurney's promotion to detective inspector. Just a quiet do, Dot the secretary had said, a couple of drinks after work. Almost three weeks had passed since the events of Christmas Eve and this was the first time Kathy had seen them all together. She wanted to let them see that it was behind her now, that she was ready to rejoin the living.

She spotted them as soon as she stepped inside, a small group clustered at one end of the bar, indistinguishable from the other knots of office workers catching a quick one before heading home. Bren was at their centre, the largest figure of the group, eyes alight, eyebrows climbing up his prematurely balding brow as he recounted some story. It was said of him that he had refused to go for this promotion, long overdue, because he had been told that it would mean his transfer to another unit. But persistence was Bren's strength, and now his patience had been rewarded. Kathy was glad for him. After Brock he was the rock of the group, the steady, soft-spoken west countryman you'd want at your side when things started going badly wrong.

Brock was sitting on a bar stool, slightly apart, contemplating his pint, and looked up as she moved forward through the crowd, as if he could sense her approach. For a moment before he spotted her she felt a tremor of panic and almost ducked and ran, but then it passed and he was beaming, waving her over, saying something to the others who turned and gave a cheer. She grinned and stuck up her chin, accepted the hugs and handshakes, and gave her congratulations to Bren.

She was pleased to see a couple of other women in the group, Dot, chuckling much more freely than usual, and Bren's wife Deanne. They were going up west for a celebration dinner, Deanne explained, their two girls in the care of a baby-sitter.

'And you, Kathy, are you really fit again? Bren told me what happened and I couldn't believe it, the things that happen to you!'

The phrase made her sound like a freak, she thought, as if she collected trouble like an eccentric hobby. 'I'm fine,' she said brightly, taking a large scotch. 'All patched up and ready to go again. No problems. And how are the girls?'

While she half listened she was aware of Brock examining her. Later he drew her aside and asked how her afternoon session had gone.

'It's a waste of time,' she said, forcing confidence into her voice. 'I've got over the shock and there's not a lot you can really say, is there? The shoulder's OK. I've been swimming and going to the gym. I'm ready to come back, Brock.'

He tilted his head, doubtful. 'Sleeping all right?'

'Yes, fine,' she lied, and wondered if it showed. Deanne had done a strange little double take when she'd first caught sight of her, as if surprised at Kathy's appearance. 'And I'm going spare sitting around at home.'

'Suzanne wanted you to stay longer in Battle, you know.'

'She was very kind.' More than that. After the hospital had released her Brock had taken her to stay with his friend Suzanne Chambers near the Sussex coast, and for a week between Christmas and New Year she had rested there, cocooned in medication and domesticity, distracted by Suzanne's two young grandchildren who lived with her. Apart from anything else, it was an extraordinary gesture on Brock's part, since he had managed to keep his mysterious woman friend private from his work colleagues until then.

After another whisky Kathy began to relax. The laughter was getting louder, the jokes about Bren's new status more facetious. He stood with his arm round his wife's shoulder complacently recounting one last joke before they had to leave. He reached the punch line, which was received with more hilarity than it really deserved, and then Deanne said that he had something else to announce, and nudged him in the ribs when he became coy. Someone called out, 'Come on, Bren! Tell us yer secret,' and he blushed happily and confessed that Deanne was expecting again, their third, another girl according to the tests. Everyone clapped, Brock at his most avuncular as he shook Bren's hand and kissed Deanne's cheek. Kathy cheered with the rest of them, and thought of how Bren had managed to hold all the parts of his life together and how empty her flat was now that Leon was gone.

As the party began to break up, Kathy headed for the toilets. A sign warned her of building work beyond the door. She opened it and found herself in a corridor of bare concrete block walls and harsh fluorescent lighting. The door banged shut behind her and the world of laughter and raised voices was abruptly cut off. The air was pungent with the smells of raw concrete and urine. Suddenly she was in that other room again. Panic, uncontrollable panic, choked her as the walls began to close in around her, crushing, and she knew that he was close and soon would come for her again.

Kathy began to stumble towards the door at the far end of the corridor, concentrating on the Fire Exit notice. She threw herself against it and it gave. She heard a cry behind her and stumbled on, out into a yard. The air was cold here but the smells just as strong

7

inside her head. An intensely bright light shone into her eyes across the darkness. She blinked blindly at it and then it was broken by a shape, a dark silhouette, striding into the light. Her breath caught in her throat as the dark shape filled her vision.

'Is she all right?'

She heard the words dimly, then blinked open her eyes. She was on the ground, two people bending over her, their breath steaming in the cold air.

'Kathy?' Dot's voice roused her. 'Kathy?'

The black sea heaved and crashed against the piles of the old pier as if aware that the structure had been abandoned, its great days gone, its stability in doubt, its entrance sealed by order of the borough engineer. Kathy turned away from the rail and continued her walk, the collar of her coat up against the north wind at her back, her short blonde hair whipping about her cheeks. There was a bright shimmer out on the eastern horizon, as if the sun were shining on the French coast and might, perhaps, edge its way towards England. Little chance of that, she decided, looking up at the weight of dark cloud looming overhead.

She came to a pedestrian crossing controlled by traffic lights. An elderly couple, faces barely visible between hats and scarves, was waiting patiently at the opposite kerb for the signal to turn green. The road was deserted, not a vehicle in sight. The sight struck Kathy as very sad. She put her head down and marched across the street, aware of the disapproving stare from the old man.

She reached the café and stepped in out of the wind. The place was empty, and she collected a cup of tea from the counter and took a seat at the front window, easing out of her coat. Someone had left a newspaper at the next table, and she reached across to pick it up and glanced idly at the front page, then looked again, transfixed. A picture of a man in a bulky black coat, cropped grey hair and beard, the familiar face staring sombrely at something away to his left, other men in black crowding round him. Brock and the team. The caption read, 'DCI Brock of Scotland Yard's élite Serious Crimes Branch, who leads the hunt for the killer'.

Kathy's eye went across to the headline, which filled most of the remainder of the page, leaving room only for the opening words of the story:

CAMPUS SLAYING

One of Britain's most respected academics was gunned down on the steps of his university yesterday in an execution-style killing. Philosophy Professor Max Springer, 66, was shot dead

(*continued page 4*)

Shot dead. And suddenly Kathy could taste the fumes at the back of her throat and feel the bile rise. She looked quickly away out of the window, fixing her attention on the bright patch of sky on the horizon. Take your time, take your time. She breathed deeply, clammy with sweat, until the panic passed.

When she turned round, she saw Suzanne standing at the counter. She went over to join her.

'Oh, Kathy, hello. I thought that was you. How was your walk?' Suzanne looked more closely at her. Brisk and to the point as always, she said, 'Doesn't seem to have done much for your colour. You look terrible. Are you feeling all right?'

'I'm fine.'

As they approached the table by the window, Kathy saw a look of consternation pass very briefly across Suzanne's face as she noticed the newspaper lying by Kathy's cup. It struck her that Suzanne had already seen the story, the picture of Brock, and also that she had deliberately kept it from her. Now she came to think about it, there had been no papers at breakfast that morning. She wondered what Suzanne would do now. They sat facing one another across the table, the newspaper lying between them. Kathy said nothing.

Suzanne sipped her coffee, then placed the cup carefully in its saucer and said, 'Not a very good picture of him, is it?'

'You've seen this already, have you?' Kathy didn't like the interrogator's tone in her voice, but couldn't help herself.

'David phoned last night and told me about it.' Suzanne was the only one who called Brock David, and sometimes it seemed to Kathy as if they were talking about two different men, Suzanne's younger and more in need of guidance than the other. 'I think he

9

was preparing the ground in case he has to cancel this weekend. Sounds as if this may be a big case. Do you think?'

Kathy thought she detected relief in Suzanne's voice, and realised that it wouldn't have been her style to deceive her. Brock then – he must have asked her to do it. She wondered again whether coming back to stay with Suzanne had been such a good idea, although at the time she'd been in little shape to argue with Brock.

'I don't know. I only just picked the paper up from the next table. I didn't get past the front page. Is it someone famous?' Her mind began to run along familiar lines – a stalker, a Yardie killing, a breakaway Irish group.

'Well, they say he was, but I've never heard of him. A philosopher, for goodness' sake, and I don't think he's ever been on TV. To be honest, if someone asked me to name a famous living philosopher, I'd be hard put to get past a couple of French names, wouldn't you?'

'Why did Brock not want me to see it?'

'Why do you think? I told him he was daft. He just wants you to forget about work while you're on leave.'

'Does he think I'm that fragile?' Kathy found herself curiously alarmed by the idea that Brock would think it necessary to hide newspapers from her.

Suzanne considered this. 'I don't think it's *that*, exactly. More that he thought you might be tempted to go rushing back to London and try to get involved, when you should be having a complete break.'

'No,' Kathy shook her head firmly, trying to sound as if she meant it. It was the first time she'd had to say this aloud, and her words sounded false. 'I'm not tempted.'

Kathy felt Suzanne's questioning eyes on her and felt compelled to say more. 'In fact, I'm beginning to think that I may not go back at all.'

'What . . . leave the police?' Suzanne frowned doubtfully.

'Yes.'

Suzanne hesitated, then spoke quietly. 'David only gave me an outline of what happened to you on Christmas Eve. But I know he's concerned that you must have enough time to get over it. Don't you think you should wait before you make any decisions?'

'Starting a new case, like Brock's doing at the moment, it's like. . .'

Kathy struggled for the image that was in the back of her mind, '. . . like standing on the edge of a deep, dark pool, having to dive in, and knowing that beneath the surface is this awful mess, everything tangled up, everything tied to everything else with lies and fear and greed, and it's your job to untangle it and sort it all out. I mean, why would you want to bother?'

'Well, if you feel like that, no, I suppose you wouldn't . . . Is there something else you'd rather do?'

'I've been thinking about that. I've been thinking how nice it must be to do something that isn't so . . . so claustrophobic and intense. Something that brightens people's lives, where they're pleased to see you instead of looking guilty or belligerent when they find out what you do. Something light and cheerful.'

'And well paid, of course. And with lots of opportunities to meet eligible members of the opposite sex in friendly and relaxed settings.'

'Yes,' Kathy grinned ruefully. 'That too. Definitely that.'

'Well, go on then. I'm all ears. What is it?'

'I don't know . . .' She fixed her attention on her teaspoon, stirring hard, wishing they hadn't got onto this.

'No ideas at all?'

'Well, I thought, maybe something to do with travel. A travel agent or a courier. Something like that.'

Kathy stared out of the window. On the far pavement the couple at the pedestrian crossing were on the return leg of their walk, the wind now at their backs and threatening to blow them off their feet.

'I feel I'm running out of time, Suzanne. Why should I waste any more of it trying to clear up the messes that other people make? Do you think that's stupid?'

'No, I don't. I don't think that at all.' Suzanne seemed to struggle with her reply, and Kathy wondered if there was another level to this conversation, as if it reflected in some way on Suzanne's own relationship with Brock, which Kathy had found hard to fathom.

'I think what you say is very sensible. When I hear some of the things that you and David and the others have to do, well, I couldn't do it. And I know that you've had some terrible experiences, especially this last time, and if I'd been through anything like that my reaction would be the same, I'm sure, to run a mile. Only . . .' She hesitated, as if struggling to force herself to be objective.

'What?'

'Well, I think it is important to understand yourself, and what you have a talent for. Like, I have a talent for what I do – I'm not boasting, I'm just saying it as a fact. I have an eye for old things, I can recognise the good stuff, and I enjoy discovering it and restoring it and then selling it to people who trust my judgement. I've known this since I was a girl, going out with my father to junk shops and flea markets. But for years I ignored it and did work that I was competent at, but that didn't really use my particular talent, because I didn't especially value it. And in the end that made me unhappy and dissatisfied.

'You ask why you would want to do police work, and I suppose the answer is, because you have a special talent for it. I know that because David's told me, and he knows. And I believe that a talent like that is something you have to recognise somehow. You don't choose it, it just is, and it may be a curse. That doesn't mean that there may not be lots of other fields where your talent can flourish just as well as police work. I don't know, but I do think you have to bear it in mind when you're thinking what you should do with your life.

'Sorry. That sounded like a sermon. Have you had anything to do with the travel business before?'

'Not a thing.'

'I know one or two people. A friend of mine runs a travel agency here in Hastings. Suppose I ask her if you could talk to her, maybe work with her for a few days to get the feel of it?'

'Oh, I don't know, Suzanne. I appreciate it, but I don't want to involve you in all this.'

'You mean you don't want me reporting on you to David? I promise. He won't hear about it from me.'

Kathy appreciated the other woman's concern, but didn't tell her that she'd got it wrong. It wasn't her talent she was worried about, but something altogether more critical. She thought of Bren in the pub, that last time she'd seen them all, and how utterly reliable he had appeared to her. That was what had gone, her reliability. She had lost her nerve, and without it she was as useless to them as a spent battery. They got up to leave, and Kathy glanced again at the photo of Brock in the paper, wondering what it was that had attracted his attention away to the left.

2

The most striking thing, Brock had thought, when he'd first arrived, was the public nature of the crime. This was no private violence in some dark corner, but a public execution staged before a large audience. The body had lain sprawled theatrically halfway down a monumental flight of steps, the image like a still from *The Battleship Potemkin*, with a trail of blood leading back up the flight, and clumps of students and police standing in immobilised groups beneath the glare of lights. He turned from his conversation with Bren to look away to his left across the curve of the Thames, towards the Millennium Dome glowing huge in the winter twilight, and at that moment a press cameraman caught him in his flash. They were practically on the newspapers' doorstep here, and the reporters had arrived quickly, attracted perhaps by this public nature of the death. He gave them a few non-committal comments, then told the uniforms to move the cordon further back.

He hadn't even heard of this university, the University of Central London East, or UCLE, nor been aware that there was a campus here in this area of the Docklands, and at first there had been confusion with the University of East London, further east in the old Royal Albert Dock. It hadn't been here long, by the look of it, one among the host of new construction projects that had blossomed eastward along the river in the past few years. The cascade of steps, the flanking cantilevered lecture theatres, the squat curved tower of the central administration, the primary colours and gleaming stainless steel panelling, all seemed to Brock to protest an aggressive claim to identity, as if compelled to compete with the brash office towers of

Canary Wharf, glittering Manhattan-like over there to the west. And for a moment, after he'd taken this all in, he'd been tempted to think that the stagey murder scene too might be some kind of pose, a publicity stunt perhaps, and that the old man sprawled so artfully on the steps might at any moment leap to his feet to the cheers of his rapt audience.

But his death was real enough, two shots to the heart, the medical examiner suggested, at very close range, which corresponded with what most of the witnesses thought they'd heard or seen.

'Inspector! Inspector Gurney!' The uniformed officer further up the steps was holding back a young woman who appeared to be trying to reach them. Bren loped up and bent to listen to what they were saying. Brock was struck by her pale elfin face, distressed, framed by short-cropped black hair, eyes wide and ringed with dark. He turned away to hear another detective's report on the assailant's description, as compiled from the accounts of a dozen students who had seen him: medium height, slim build, probably, but wearing a bulky anorak-style coat with hood covering the head, dark jeans, face obscured by a dark mask or balaclava, description of shoes too variable to be reliable. He was young, they all agreed, because of the agile way he skipped down the steps and ran off along the entry concourse towards the university entrance and the city beyond. And they all said 'he', although they couldn't say for sure why they assumed it was a male. No one could recall seeing the gun, a revolver, the police assumed, since there had been no sign of the spent cartridge cases.

Brock sighed. 'Put it out. It's all we've got for now. Let's hope the camera can tell us more.' He glanced up again at the security camera that scanned the steps. If it had been working properly they should have a complete ringside record of the event.

And there was a curious detail from just one of the witnesses, a young man who had been climbing the steps about ten yards behind the victim. He had been watching the assailant coming down the flight before he reached the old man, because he had noticed the mask beneath the hood and been startled by it. So he had his eyes on the murderer's face at the moment when he had struck, and he was convinced that he had spoken, had said something to the victim just before he closed in and put his left arm round the old man's shoulder, quite gently, and raised his right hand to his chest and fired twice, then stepped away to let him tumble back down the steps.

Bren rejoined him, a young man in a sharp suit at his heels. 'The girl was a student of his, name of Briony Kidd, didn't witness it, but says she knew him quite well. I said we might want to talk to her later. This bloke insists on having a word, Brock.'

The young man introduced himself as the President's Executive Officer.

'President?' Brock asked.

'Yes, of the university. The head.'

'I thought they were called vice-chancellors.'

The young man gave a knowing little smile. 'Not any more, at least not here. We prefer the American title. Professor Young sent me down to see if you'd like to meet with him now. You are in charge, I take it?'

Brock looked around at the activity on the steps, then nodded. 'Lead the way.'

'And the President did ask if your men could be instructed not to make any statements to the media until you've had a chance to discuss things with him.'

Brock looked coolly at him. 'They won't be.'

'Good.' Then, as if conscious that some note of accommodation might be appropriate, he added, 'This is quite shocking, isn't it? We really have no precedent for it. I'm sure we all hope it can be quickly resolved. You'll have our full cooperation, naturally.'

They walked along the dockside concourse to the foot of the Central Administration Tower and into a lobby of blond wood, stainless steel and recessed lighting, like a rather modish cocktail bar, Brock thought. A lift took them to the top floor, where a secretary led them into a spacious office dominated by a large brushed steel desk whose curved front echoed the curve of the glass wall behind, which, stretching the full width of the room, offered a spectacular night-time panorama of the Thames, from the Millennium Dome on the left to the pyramidal peak of the tower at Canary Wharf on the right. A couple of ships were visible on the black ribbon of the river, and in the distance the lights of Greenwich and South London faded into a bank of mist moving up from the south. A powerfully built man with a thick mop of fair hair rose from his seat behind the desk, and advanced forcefully towards them.

'Roderick Young,' he growled softly, fixing Brock with an intent stare and gripping his hand hard.

'Detective Chief Inspector David Brock.' The room was warm, and Brock eased off his coat which was immediately swept up by the young Executive Officer, who removed it to a wardrobe disguised behind a panel of blond veneer.

'Chief Inspector, we are very shocked by this. There really is no precedent for it. I'm sure we all hope it can be resolved quickly, and you can rely on our full cooperation, naturally.' Brock recognised the exact words the younger man had used earlier, as though over-tutored. The President waved them to seats in front of the desk while he returned to his place with his back to the panorama, as if to say, You may find this spectacular view distracting, but I am entirely focused on more important things.

'Now, would you care to brief me?' He adjusted crisp white cuffs and smoothed the faintest crease in an immaculate charcoal suit that lent an almost military style and gravitas to his bulky figure. 'I've only just arrived back on campus from a meeting in the City, and I'd like to hear the facts directly from you.'

The lights of a twin-engined passenger jet, just taken off from the London City Airport a couple of miles to the east, passed slowly across the panorama, but only the faintest rumble came through the sweep of glass wall. Without turning, Professor Young murmured, 'The 17:35 to Berlin,' and sat back in his chair.

Brock checked his watch. 'I can tell you as much as I know, which isn't a great deal at this stage. An hour and a half ago, at about four o'clock, a man, identified by witnesses as one of your staff, Professor Max Springer, was fatally shot on the main steps leading between the upper and lower concourses on this campus. The assailant escaped without hindrance. My officers have secured the crime scene and are presently interviewing the considerable number of witnesses who were in the vicinity. The body is being removed to the Whitechapel mortuary. It will be necessary to close the immediate area around the steps for some time, perhaps several days.'

'And the, er, *assailant*, has he been identified? You must have a good description, presumably, with all those witnesses?'

16

'Unfortunately not. His face was masked, and it all happened very quickly. We have very little information about him at present, though East London police have been alerted to his description, such as it is. We're in the process of examining your security camera tapes, and we're hopeful they may give us something more.'

'And no doubt there will be other evidence? Forensic?'

But Brock had had enough of this interrogation and ignored Young's question, turning instead to his own. 'Tell me about Professor Springer. We need details such as home address, next of kin, age and so on, but I'd also like a sketch of what he did, how he fitted in here. A couple of the students said he was world famous, though I have to admit the name means nothing to me.'

'Our Professor of Philosophy. Distinguished career. He's held in high regard, especially in Germany and the States, I believe. This will cause a tremendous shock.' He leaned forward to emphasise the point. 'This will be noticed, Chief Inspector Brock, *noticed*. This is not just a local matter.'

Brock took this to be a query of his credentials to handle such a case. The man was an instinctive bully, he decided. 'But not exactly a household name?' he objected. 'I mean, his fame would be confined to fairly narrow university circles, would it?'

'Not *narrow* . . . but I take your point,' Young conceded. 'You mean he wasn't a celebrity, like a television presenter, or something?'

'Yes. A philosopher . . . Did he hold controversial views, then? Did he upset people?'

'Not really. Not any more. In his heyday he did cause a bit of controversy. There was quite a lot of public debate over the views expressed in one of his books, on the Arab and Israeli question, I believe.'

'Really?'

'Yes, but that was years ago. He's in his mid-sixties now, and to be honest, he'd pretty much faded from public view. I mean, I'm sure we haven't approved any conference expenses for Max in the past three years, and there have been no research grants, or publications . . . No, the idea of a murderer incensed by his *ideas* just seems, well, bizarre, frankly.'

The President tapped on the keys of one of the two computers on his steel desk, then corrected himself. 'He was sixty-six. I'll write down the home address for you.'

'Isn't that a bit old to be still in post?'

'It is rather. Most of our older staff took early retirement several reviews ago, to clear the way for our New Model Army – that's what I like to call my new breed of academics. But a few hang on.' He gave a grim little smile, and Brock had a sudden image of old men desperately hanging on to the flanks of a great steel ship while President Young worked to prise their fingers loose.

'You were trying to get rid of him?'

'Oh no, no. Max was . . . a feather in our cap, a distinguished ornament. We can afford a few of those.' He chuckled indulgently. 'Joined UCLE nine years ago,' Young continued, reading from his screen. 'Three years before I arrived. Things were very different then. We were in a maze of old buildings in Whitechapel. A slum. He came to us from Oxford.'

'Why did he do that?'

'The previous vice-chancellor got him to come. It was quite a catch for UCLE. Put our humanities programme on the map . . . Next of kin is listed as his wife.' Young frowned at the screen. 'That's a mistake. I'm sure she died long ago. And I don't know of any other family. There certainly weren't any children.'

'Are you aware of any complications in his private life?' Brock asked. 'Anyone with a grudge?'

'You mean a jealous husband or something?' Young snorted with amusement. 'I hardly think so. I suppose you could speak to someone who was closer to him.'

'Who do you suggest?'

'Well, perhaps Desmond Pettifer.'

Brock noticed the President give a little wince, as of indigestion.

'Where can I find him?'

'Classics. His office is close to Max's.'

'Good, I need to have a look at his office. Perhaps you could get Mr Pettifer to meet me there.'

'Well,' he glanced at his Executive Officer, 'We'll try, but Dr Pettifer tends to be a bit hard to locate in the afternoons.'

The other man allowed himself a tiny smile. 'I think what the President is trying tactfully to say, Chief Inspector, is that Dr Pettifer is probably under the table in some pub somewhere, finding communication difficult.'

'And I don't suppose he has a mobile phone,' Young added. 'He'll be the last man on earth to possess one.'

Brock smiled. 'I recall that my tutor used to keep an oak cask of sherry by his bedside, for night-time emergencies.'

'Really. Well, hopefully you won't meet too many of that sort at UCLE, Chief Inspector. We've tried to eliminate that kind of eccentricity, as far as possible. It's hardly fair, is it? On the others who have to shoulder the load. Unfortunately Dr Pettifer has a propensity for intoxicating substances. He was arrested at Heathrow some years back trying to bring some cocaine into the country after he'd spent a sabbatical at a Californian university, where he'd acquired a taste for the stuff. He was treated leniently, and my predecessor chose to hush the matter up. I would have been far less tolerant, believe me.'

'Well, now,' Brock said, 'so far we've eliminated an ideological motive, a family dispute and an outraged husband, so that leaves us with the obvious, I suppose, a disgruntled student.'

Sounds of protest began to come from Professor Young, and Brock added, 'Witnesses describe the assailant as a young, agile male. The campus is teeming with them. Surely a student is the most likely candidate?'

'Ordinarily that might have been a possibility, I agree. We have had isolated cases of violence, or threatened violence from students. Last summer there was an unfortunate incident over a Chinese student who'd run out of funds and couldn't go home without his Ph.D. or he'd suffer loss of face, but his tutor refused to approve his thesis as being ready for examination and the man became very fraught and threatened her. So yes, these things are conceivable. But that is highly unlikely in this case.'

'Why?'

'Because he hasn't got any students.'

'What about . . .' Brock checked his notes, ' . . . Briony Kidd?'

'Oh, yes, I stand corrected. He has *one* student. Ms Kidd is near the end of her Ph.D., I think.'

'Isn't that rather unusual?' Brock said mildly. 'He didn't go to conferences, publish or teach? Doesn't sound very . . . productive.'

'He was an unusual case. He came here to take the chair in a fairly thriving department of philosophy, but since then we've gone through several restructurings. We no longer have departments as such, and philosophy, along with a number of other disciplines, has become incompatible with our institutional profile. We've been phasing it out, very successfully actually. We stopped enrolling new students some time ago, and most staff accepted the situation and have gone. Professor Springer was our last philosopher.'

'And Ms Kidd your last philosophy student.'

'Exactly.'

'So, do you have any thoughts as to who could have killed Professor Springer?' Brock asked.

'An intruder, clearly,' Young said decisively. 'We get them all the time, coming in here from the city. Young kids wanting to skateboard, older ones trying to deal drugs or steal the computers. Max probably ran foul of one of them, or perhaps a gang – he could be quite outspoken and provocative when he wanted to be. And they no doubt decided to teach him a lesson. I'm sure that's the answer. Our own security people should be able to help, let you have information on some of our recent troublemakers.'

He sat back in his chair as if satisfied that some conclusive point had been reached in the discussion.

'All the same,' Brock said doubtfully, 'a shooting murder?'

'You get that all the time these days, don't you?' Young said. 'You only have to open the paper . . .' Then he added, 'They told me you're with Serious Crime, is that right, Chief Inspector?'

'It is.'

'Well, I rather fear they may have wasted your time pulling you onto this one. Much more likely to be petty crime turned nasty. Can I offer you something before you go? A drink? Coffee?'

The Executive Officer, who had taken notes throughout the meeting, put his notepad aside on the edge of the big desk and got to his feet.

'No thanks, Professor Young. I'd better get back to my people.'

'One thing before you go,' the President said, leaning forward over his steel desk. 'Concerning the media. I think it would be best if all press statements, media releases, interviews and so on were processed through one office and one office only, don't you? Our Media Liaison Unit is very good. I'd like to propose that you work through them, just so there'll be no crossed wires, all right?'

'That won't be possible,' Brock replied. 'We have our own staff who handle all our media contacts. Of course you must go ahead and issue a statement of regret, how Professor Springer contributed to the university, his academic achievements and so on. But nothing concerning the murder, nothing at all. No information about the circumstances, and no speculation about motive or perpetrator. Leave all that to us.'

The President looked deeply displeased. He regarded Brock for a moment, as if for the first time sizing him up as an opponent. Brock watched Young's eyes check over his somewhat crumpled black suit, the beard in need of a trim, the shirt chosen for comfort rather than effect, the tie suffering from a small teriyaki sauce incident. 'I may have to dispute that, Chief Inspector,' he said finally, 'at a higher level.'

'Go ahead,' Brock said, getting to his feet. He turned to the Executive Officer. 'If I might have my coat?'

3

Despite the start of a fine drizzle, the crowds on the lower concourse had swollen as more students arrived for evening lectures and heard the news, and Brock had difficulty working his way through to the police line, where he joined up with Bren.

'That student, Briony Kidd, is she still around?'

'Haven't seen her for a while, chief. But we've just got word from the security people. They've set the tapes up for us to see, when you're ready.'

They moved off through the crowds, back the way Brock had come, for the security office was located close to the entrance to the Central Administration Building, a piece of defensive planning, Brock felt, that accorded well with the President's reference to his New Model Army and the military cut of his suit. The head of security looked ex-army too, deferential to Brock's rank, but guarded. His name was Truck, and Brock immediately thought of him as Regimental Sergeant-Major Truck. He showed them to seats in front of the biggest TV screen he'd been able to find, and switched on the VCR. The tape had already been wound to the moment just before Max Springer had appeared at the foot of the steps, and had been taken by the camera on the corner of the lower concourse, looking up the full length of the flight.

'He was on his way to give a lecture, Brock,' Bren explained, 'Lecture theatre U3 on the upper concourse.'

'Really? I was told he didn't give lectures.'

'Well, he definitely planned to give this one. I spoke to three of the students who were in the lecture theatre waiting for him to arrive. It was due to start at four o'clock, so he must have been running a few minutes late.'

They started the tape, the time at the foot of the screen showing 16:02.

'There! That's him. The sports jacket.'

Truck froze the image and they peered at the figure which had appeared in the bottom left of the screen, short, stockily built, shoulders stooped, head thrust forward, a bald patch in the middle of a shaggy mop of white hair, briefcase stuffed under the left arm.

'Right. No sign of the killer? No. OK, let's go on.'

The figure lurched into motion again, the gait slow and deliberate climbing the steps with a suggestion of a weak hip or leg. They watched in silence as more agile figures streamed past the old man in both directions, ignoring him. Then Bren shouted, 'There!' and pointed at someone at top right, emerging at the head of the stairs, a figure wearing a hood. 'He must have been waiting for him up there in that doorway.'

'Can we close in on them?' Brock asked.

Truck shook his head. 'Not on this, sir.'

They advanced the film slowly, watching the hooded figure come down the steps, hands in the pockets of his parka, head down. He seemed light on his feet and attracted no attention from the people who passed. The room was completely silent as the viewers watched the gap between the figure and the old man close. When they were only a few steps apart, both suddenly reacted. The old man abruptly stopped, as if fearing collision with the figure approaching directly in front of him, while the other raised his hooded head, but didn't stop.

'Springer is looking directly at him,' Brock said. 'He's seen the mask.'

'Yeah. And that bloke there' Bren pointed to a youth in a bomber jacket some yards behind and to the right, 'that's our witness who said he saw the killer speak. He's right where he said he was.'

Now the hooded figure was pulling his hands from his pockets, and they could see the right hand holding something, not a gun, surely, but something bulky, irregular, misshapen and light in colour.

'What the hell is that?'

Both police officers were down on their knees in front of the screen now, trying to make it out. Then Brock said, 'It's a bag, Bren, a plastic bag.'

'To hide the gun?'

'Or to catch the cartridges as they eject. Let's see if he keeps it inside the bag when he fires.'

They slowly advanced the film, frame by frame, as the killer moved into a weird, slow motion ballet down to the old man and embraced him as the witness had described. There was a brief burst of white smoke against the dark of the gunman's coat, then the old man, who had been motionless throughout the approach, began to crumple, his briefcase slipping out of his grasp.

'Exit wound,' Bren said, pointing to the old man's back.

'Looks like it. What about the gun?'

The killer had now pivoted away and he was presenting his right side to the camera, the plastic bag clearly visible. They watched the two figures separate and take their different courses, Max Springer to tumble back down the steps, the other running diagonally away from him and the watching student towards the lower concourse.

Brock and Bren returned to their seats. Truck ran the film through for them a couple more times, and found a magnifying glass for them to study some of the frames more closely. They got an impression of light coloured trainer shoes, but little else.

'No,' Brock said finally, 'I can't make out whether he's speaking to Springer. We'll have to see what the lab can do with it. But at least we know he still had the bag in his hand when he reached the bottom of the stairs.'

'So that means it could have been an automatic.'

'Yes, or a rifle with a sawn-off barrel and stock. Either way we've been looking for the shells in the wrong place. If they were inside the bag, which would have had a hole in it after the firing, and if he still had it in his hand as he escaped, there's a chance they may have dropped out as he ran. We should be looking on the entry concourse and out into the streets.'

He turned to the security man. 'Does any of this mean anything to you, Mr Truck? Nothing strike you about the killer?'

Truck was shaking his head. 'Unbelievable. Like something on the telly. Hard to believe it's for real. No, it could be anybody. Nimble, though.'

'Yes, I thought a student, but your boss, Professor Young, thinks it's more likely to be one of those local kids you get coming on campus and causing trouble. What do you think?'

'Phor . . .' Truck rubbed his nose, obviously not taking to that idea. 'I don't know. There's never been any violence before, only mischief. This isn't their style. I mean, it seemed . . . professional, don't you reckon? Deliberate, thought out.'

'You haven't been aware of Professor Springer being in any arguments with anybody?'

'The only trouble I know about Professor Springer was with the cleaners. He keeps his room in a bit of a state, and the girls had trouble sorting the rubbish from the rest. He accused them of throwing out precious papers so they refused to go into his room any more. I wouldn't like to cross Doris myself, but I'm pretty sure that wasn't her in the hood.' He grinned, then coughed and pulled himself together. 'I'll check with my lads, sir. See if they know of anything.'

'Thanks. And I'd like one of my people to sit down with you and go through all the incidents you've had here recently. Now, perhaps you'd take us to this untidy room of Professor Springer and let us take a look.'

But they were still there, waiting for Truck to unload the tape for them to send to the electronics laboratory for enhancement, when Bren's mobile rang. He listened for a minute, then drew Brock aside. 'Something interesting, chief. When they entered a report on CRIS just now, the computer came back with a reference on Springer. Apparently a Max Springer registered a complaint a couple of weeks ago. Offences Against the Person, section sixteen. Said he was being threatened with death.'

'Really? Where did he make the complaint?'

'The local nick, Shadwell Road station, not far away.'

They took the tape from Truck and made their way to the university entrance where they'd left their car, stopping on the way to direct a search for the cartridge cases on the lower concourse, and phoning the Shadwell Road police station to expect them.

The main entrance to UCLE was beside a station of the Docklands Light Railway, the DLR, whose elevated track formed a demarcation between the new development of the university and the

25

old buildings of the city beyond. As they walked under the concrete viaduct, Brock was struck by the abrupt dislocation between the two sides, the steel panelled university turning its back on the disordered jumble of old warehouses, workshops, derelict looking shops and tiny pubs that jostled up to it. They found their car and headed north and west into the city traffic as the drizzle turned to steady rain.

Despite the rain, Shadwell Road looked bright and cheerful, its pavements busy with people doing some evening shopping in the stores that lined its length. Beneath the umbrellas Brock noticed women in headscarves and saris, men in skullcaps and baggy pants, a Nigerian in his distinctive wide-shouldered coat, a group of Sikhs in turbans. Window posters on the shopfronts advertised cheap flights, £350 to Dhaka, £340 to Karachi, and forthcoming entertainments by Raha and Malkit Singh. Shop signs were mostly in English and one or more other languages, Urdu, Gujarati, Arabic, Hindi. They parked outside Manzoor's Saree Centre ('fabulous fashions and fabrics for all the family') next door to the police station, a converted shop in the middle of a row of small traders. Its front window was filled with posters advertising its own specials – four Wanted for Murders, five Missing Persons, a couple of Serious Sexual Assaults, one Terrorism: Postal Bombs Alert and one Prostitution. They went inside.

Their advance phone call had had some effect. The uniformed duty inspector and desk sergeant were standing together behind the counter looking as if they'd just brushed their hair and scrubbed their fingernails.

'Evening, sir,' the inspector said stiffly. 'May we help you?'

'I hope so,' Brock said, and introduced them both. 'We phoned.'

'Of course. Would you care to come this way, sir?' He lifted the counter flap and indicated a door leading through to the back of the shop, like a tailor inviting a special customer through for a fitting. They went into a small windowless interview room with a few chairs arranged around a table, some recording equipment on a side table. An extract fan rattled into life as the lights were switched on.

'The PC who interviewed your murder victim is out on the beat at the moment, sir, but we've radioed him and he's on his way. Should be here shortly. May I fetch you gentlemen something while we're waiting? A cup of tea? A bite to eat?'

Brock felt suddenly hungry. 'Anywhere round here to get a sandwich?'

'The pub across the way does a very decent sandwich. Or we could get in some take-away – Tandoori, Balti, Bangladeshi, Halal. You can get most anything here. All on our doorstep.'

'The sandwich sounds fine. And a cup of tea wouldn't go amiss.'

They placed their orders and the inspector left them to read the file copy of PC Greg Talbot's report of the complaint made by Professor Max Springer against person or persons unknown. Ten minutes later, as they were eating their supper, there was a knock on the door and the inspector showed in the young constable. He entered cautiously, as if he'd been warned he might be in trouble. As he came through the door he bumped awkwardly against the jamb with the load of kit strapped to his belt – the process pouch, quick-cuffs, first aid kit, Asp extendable baton, radio, torch, and the CS spray canister in its spring-loaded holster.

'PC Talbot, sir,' the inspector said, and the constable came to attention in front of them, eyes fixed on the wall behind Brock's head.

'Greg, isn't it?' Brock said. 'Take a seat, Greg. Don't mind us eating, will you. Fancy a sandwich yourself?'

'No, thank you, sir,' the man said stiffly. 'I'll be having my dinner shortly.' Then added, 'Hopefully.'

'Yes.' Brock checked his watch. 'You're just coming off your shift now, aren't you? But on Sunday the second you were on the morning shift, that right?'

'Sir. We were a bit short handed that day, after the New Year celebrations, and I was on front desk. The gentleman came in mid-morning, eleven o'clock. I couldn't speak to him immediately 'cos I was dealing with another person.' He glanced over at his Inspector and added, 'Mr Manzoor next door, sir. Complaining about his daughter again.'

The inspector nodded and Greg Talbot turned back to face Brock and Bren.

'Please relax, Greg,' Brock said gently, seeing how rigid the lad was. He looked too young to be in uniform, Brock thought, his face more that of a cheeky schoolboy than the stolid mask of a cop. Or maybe it's me, Brock thought, getting too old. 'We just want to get

27

your impressions of the man. You've been briefed about his murder today, I take it?'

'Yes, sir. Can I ask, sir, am I in strife?'

'Good Lord, no. I've read your report. It all seems quite reasonable.'

'But he was right, wasn't he? It happened just like he predicted.'

'The date, you mean? Yes, that is interesting . . .' Brock ran his finger down the report. 'He said that he had had a threatening phone call from a man who didn't identify himself, but said that "if he didn't stop broadcasting his views immediately, he would suffer the consequences soon, and no later than the twentieth of January", which is today. Those were his actual words, were they?'

'Yes, sir.' The policeman sounded defensive.

'I mean, precisely, Greg? "Broadcasting", for instance? That was his word?'

'Yes, sir. I wouldn't have used that word myself. I asked him what he meant, and he said he'd been making his opinions known publicly. He'd been interviewed on the radio, apparently. Radio East London. Some time towards the end of last year.'

'And did you inquire as to the nature of his opinions?'

'Yes, sir. I thought he might be a nutter. Maybe a racist. But he said he'd been speaking out against extremists of all persuasions.'

'Extremists.'

'Yes, sir. And fundamentalists. His words.'

'Hm. And he was quite specific about the date? Not "about the twentieth" or "within three weeks" or something like that?' Brock noticed the lad blink involuntarily. There was the briefest hesitation before he replied.

'The twentieth, sir. Exactly.'

'Yes . . .' Brock gave him a sympathetic smile, but held his eyes, saying nothing until the constable abruptly said, 'We worked that out, you see, sir. That's how he could be so specific.'

'Worked it out?'

'He claimed the caller had said, "within two weeks of the end of Ramadan", and we worked out that was the twentieth. I didn't put all that in the report,' Talbot said speaking faster now. 'Would have taken too long, and anyway, around here you don't think twice about Ramadan . . .'

Brock nodded understandingly. Ever since the Stephen Lawrence case and the McPherson report that followed it, condemning endemic racism in the Metropolitan Police, a tidal wave of political correctness had swept over the force. Greg Talbot had omitted the words 'fundamentalist' and 'Ramadan' from his report because they had a flavour that he would prefer to keep out of his account. He would have done this automatically, as part of a self-correcting editorial process, presenting the facts in a more neutral way, just to be on the safe side. But it did change things, by God it did. He felt Bren stir at his side.

'Greg, what I'm going to ask you to do is to write out for me as full a description as you can possibly recall, of everything that you and Professor Springer said, word for word.'

Talbot hesitated, no doubt seeing this as an invitation to weave the rope that he would be hanged by. 'I'm not sure, sir . . .' he said hesitantly, and Brock saw the lad's brain working, perhaps trying to remember where he could get the phone number of the Police Federation for help.

Brock felt momentarily helpless. He was too old, too highly ranked, altogether too heavy for this. Clearly the lad felt threatened by him. Bren on his own wouldn't have been much better, either, just another, younger version of the same. Kathy could have done it, got the kid on side, talking informally, sympathetically. He felt a little stab of pain and loss at the thought of her. She would probably see the case mentioned in the papers, on TV, and she might be tempted to return too soon. He'd have to phone Suzanne later and warn her.

'Greg, this will only be for my personal use, to further our investigation into the Springer murder, I can assure you of that. I will keep the original, and no copies will be made. As I said, I have no criticism of the way you handled this, and I take it your supervisors feel the same way?' He glanced at the inspector, who looked uncomfortable, as if wanting to keep his options open, depending on how this turned out, but he gave a nod all the same.

'He just didn't seem kosher, sir!' Talbot blurted out. 'He looked sort of weird, with his hair sticking out all over the place, and he was so bleedin' calm. He stood there for twenty minutes listening to Mr Manzoor going on about his daughter and how we weren't doing enough and he was going to go back to the justice to issue a new warrant, and all the time Springer just stood there, listening and nodding, and by the end Manzoor was talking more to *him*, appealing to him, like *he* was the magistrate! Then when finally Manzoor left, Springer told me what he'd come for, that someone had threatened to kill him, in the same, calm way, as if he was talking about someone else altogether.'

'So you didn't really believe him?'

Talbot lowered his head. 'When he said he was a teacher at the university, I thought one of his students was having a lark, winding him up, pretending to be a terrorist or something. Well, he didn't seem like the sort of man anyone would want to kill, a polite old bloke like that. And when he said how he was a widower and lived on his own, and had no close family, I thought the poor old bugger had probably had a miserable Christmas and New Year and just wanted to talk to someone. So I talked to him, and I told him his best plan was to get on to BT and get them to intercept his incoming calls, but if he got any evidence, like a threatening note or something, he should come back and we'd make out a formal report and take some sort of action. But he insisted on making a proper statement then, and that I got it recorded on file. That way, he said, if it happened again, the next person he spoke to would take it seriously. I mean, it wasn't as if he was frightened or anything. He'd have been more bothered if he'd been reporting a lost budgie.'

'I understand. We could hardly put an armed guard on everyone who thinks someone's out to get them, could we? Then something like this happens, and you think, "if only". No fault of yours, son. Just the luck of the game. But now we have to find the killer, and I do want that detailed report. We owe the old man that, don't we?'

'Yes, sir.' PC Talbot met Brock's eyes again and added quietly, 'Thank you, sir.'

'Good.' They got to their feet, and Brock shook hands with the inspector and then said to the constable, 'See us to the door will you, son?'

Outside on the pavement, with the lad on his own, Brock gave Talbot his card and said quietly, 'Call me direct if anything else occurs to you, Greg. And if they try to put any blame on you, get in touch, OK? I'll sort it out.'

The rain had stopped, and as they stood in front of the postered window one of the broadsheets caught Brock's eye. One of the Missing Persons, a picture of an attractive young South Asian woman, and the name, Nargis Manzoor.

'The same Manzoor?' Brock asked.

'Yes, sir. She's been missing now for over three months. Mr Manzoor doesn't think we're doing enough to find her. He got a warrant issued last year for us to carry out a search.'

'How come?'

'She's only seventeen. He claimed he had grounds to believe that she had been taken out of the possession of her parent for the purpose of extra-marital sex, against his will. Section nineteen of the Sexual Offences Act, sir.'

Brock smiled. 'You've been swotting up for your exams, eh?'

Talbot grinned back. 'Believe me, sir, after three months of Mr Manzoor going at us day and night, we all know the Sexual Offences Act 1956 backwards. The thing that gets me is that the abduction doesn't need to be against *her* will, only against *his*. And that's pretty much what happened in this case, we reckon. They'd been fighting, her and her dad, and we reckon she'd had enough and ran away, but he won't have it.'

At that moment a small, dapper looking man in a dark suit and tie stepped out of the adjoining shop. Seeing them he called out, 'Ah, PC Talbot. Been looking for her, have you? I do hope so.'

'Yes, Mr Manzoor. As always.'

Brock left them to it. As he got into the car Bren was finishing a conversation on his phone. On the point of giving up for the night, the searchers at the university had found a cartridge case, dropped in the area where students parked their motorbikes.

4

The following morning, Friday, 21 January, while Kathy was reading about the case in a Hastings café, Brock returned to the UCLE campus. After inspecting the area under the DLR viaduct where the student motorbikes were parked, he got Truck the security chief to open up Max Springer's room for him. It was located at the back of the university site, furthest from the waterfront in one of a cluster of old buildings which had been incorporated by the university as a temporary relief for its expanding accommodation needs. Previously workshops and small offices, the old buildings had had just enough money spent on them to satisfy the building inspector and were crammed against the DLR track, whose passing trains made their windows rattle.

Brock and Truck climbed an uneven staircase to a dark landing from which a corridor wound away. A notice board carried class lists and a few curling posters of Christmas parties and items for sale.

'This is the professor's room,' Truck said, opening one of the doors and reaching inside for the light switch.

It looked rather as if a volcano disgorging books, papers and other odd objects instead of lava had erupted in the middle of the tiny room.

'Someone's trashed the place,' Brock said.

Truck laughed. 'No, no. This is the way he kept it. Doris brought me over here to show me, when she and the prof were having their dispute.'

Standing just inside the doorway, hardly able to advance further into the room, Brock began to see a kind of pattern in the chaotic jumble. It seemed to focus on a chair, itself piled with papers, at a desk mounded with stuff, as if this were the mouth of the volcano, its source from which the debris was scattered around, and Brock guessed that, random as it appeared, the old man seated there probably knew where most things were, and could reach out a hand to find a specific book from where he had last tossed it. He could imagine how Doris' efforts to create order would completely upset this random filing system.

'See the desk?' Truck said at his shoulder, whispering as if in awe at the sight. 'When so much junk had gathered there, instead of sorting it out and putting it away, he would take that big roll of brown paper over there, see, and spread it right over the top, and pin it down at the ends with drawing pins, and start again.' Truck sucked in his breath at the sheer outrageousness of the concept. 'Then, when he'd piled up so many layers that the whole thing became unstable, he'd grab hold of one end and sweep the whole lot crashing to the floor, over there.' He pointed to a great mound of debris. 'And you wonder they have mice in here! He said he didn't mind a few mice around. Said it raised the average IQ of the university.' He chuckled.

'Had quite a sense of humour then, did he?'

'Well, to tell the truth, he wasn't really noted for his belly laughs. More a sort of acid wit, bitter like.'

'I'd better try to have a look round,' Brock said. 'You don't have to stay, Mr Truck, if you want to get on.'

'Fair enough. Just lock the door when you're finished.'

Brock pulled on a pair of latex gloves and advanced gingerly through the mess, heading for the desk. Its surface was piled with newspapers, books, hand-written notes, official memos and circulars from the university administration, pens and pencils, correction fluid, a coffee mug with some dried sediment at the bottom. A small portable typewriter was half buried in the mess. There was no computer in the room.

A DLR train passed with a loud whine and a rumble, the lower half of its carriages visible through the top of the grimy little window. Brock shifted the pile of files from the seat in front of the desk and sat down, trying to put himself in the mind of the acid-tongued, under-employed, half-famous, wild-haired, chaotically untidy old man who had spent his days here. PC Talbot had been right – a very unlikely victim of anything but a random mugging, and whatever had happened on the university steps it wasn't that. He stared at the framed pictures around the walls, mementos of Springer's past; a print map of mediaeval Oxford, a child's crayon drawing of an apartment block and a palm tree, a photograph of a much younger Springer in the company of a group of elderly men.

Brock's foot bumped a metal wastepaper bin beneath the desk, and he stooped to examine its contents. He was bent forward, eyes level with the desk top, when he noticed a piece of green paper tucked under the front edge of the typewriter. He tugged it out and unfolded it. Beneath a simplified drawing of a raised clenched fist were some printed words.

'Surely, hell lies in wait, a resort for the rebellious . . . They feared not the reckoning and utterly rejected Our Signs.'   *Sura 78: 22–31.*

Brock sat back, rubbing his beard with his knuckles as he considered this. The paper had been folded as if to go into a small envelope, and he began another search of the desk top, then the bin. Near the bottom of the bin, mixed up with a chocolate biscuit wrapping and a crumpled invitation to attend a union meeting, were the parts of an envelope that had been torn in half. The address had been hand printed in simple bold capitals, and as Brock deciphered the postmark date, ten days previous, he was thankful for the absence of cleaners to remove Springer's rubbish. He slipped the green paper and the envelope into separate evidence pouches and put them in his pocket, then considered the room again. It would have to be searched properly, and it would take a couple of people the best part of a day to do it. He got to his feet, turned towards the door and saw a man standing there, leaning against the jamb watching him.

'You look like a policeman,' the man said. He was short, balding, chin thrust forward in an expression that mixed belligerence and amusement, and he spoke with a strong Welsh accent.

'You're right,' Brock replied, peeling off his gloves as he stepped carefully through the obstacles towards him, and showed him his warrant card. 'And you look like an academic.'

'Yes, I do, don't I?' the man said, looking down at the leather

34

elbow patches on his cardigan, his baggy corduroy trousers, his old brogues, as if considering them for the first time. 'At least, a *sort* of academic. The sort that's practically extinct. Nowadays my colleagues mostly wear suits and look like used car salesmen, so that they're ready to go out and do a spot of *marketing* at a moment's notice, I suppose. Desmond Pettifer's the name. Classics.'

As he got closer to the man to shake hands Brock caught the whiff of whisky on his breath.

'What do you make of poor old Max's room, then, eh?'

'Chaotic.'

'Ha!' A speck of spittle hit Brock's face. 'No room to swing a bloody cat, is there? There's a wonderful description somewhere by Bertrand Russell, of his impression of American universities where he taught in the 1930s. He was amazed at the way the professors were crammed into tiny holes like this, while the presidents of the colleges lorded it in huge offices and behaved like the executives of big business corporations. Frightfully droll the Americans, he thought. But we're not bloody laughing now. *Stultitiam patiuntur opes*, as Horace would say; wealth sanctions folly. Russell was a philosopher too, like Max, but of course you'd know that. You went to the same university didn't you? Same college, in fact.'

'How did you know that?'

'Saw your picture in the morning papers, didn't I? Looked you up. Then I saw Max's door open and there you were.'

'When did you hear the news about Max?'

'Last night, in the pub. Noticed pictures of our noble institution on the TV news and got the landlord to turn up the volume. What a shock that was, eh? Bloody hell! It took a couple of stiff ones to calm me down, I can tell you.'

Brock thought Pettifer made the news of his friend's death sound like a bit of a lark. 'Did you have any ideas?'

'About who did it? Not a clue. It must have been some madman, mustn't it? Have you found the gun?'

'Not yet. Max didn't say anything to you about threats? An angry student? Someone he'd upset? Perhaps some extremist, opposed to his views?'

'Max? No, no. Good grief, he wasn't exactly Salman Rushdie.

And our students are a tame lot – not a radical among them. All they want is a fast degree and off to the City to earn their first million.'

'I believe he was interviewed on Radio East London a few months ago and made some controversial comments, do you remember that? Were they about the situation in the Middle East?'

Pettifer looked puzzled. 'I did listen to that, but I don't remember anything about the Middle East. I think he made some general comments about fundamentalism and people with closed minds, but he was talking more about science than politics. And he was fairly scathing about the direction universities are heading. Oh, there are a few people on the campus here who would have liked to shut Max up, but even they wouldn't go so far as to do it *that* way. At least, I don't think so.' He gave a little chuckle.

'What sort of people?'

An expression of malevolent mischief slipped over Pettifer's face. 'Have you met our great leader yet, over in the Führer bunker?'

'You mean Professor Young? Yes, I met him yesterday. He was full of praise for Professor Springer. Said he'd be sorely missed.'

'Hah! Hypocritical bastard! He's been trying to get rid of Max ever since he took over this place. Me too for that matter. We don't fit into his vision of a university for the new century, you see. Our day has passed. He reorganised the university structure when he came, disbanded the departments and lumped everybody into three divisions, two of which – the Division of Business and the Division of Science and Technology – make lots of money and are important, while the remainder, all the bits they don't really want but can't get rid of, were put in the Division of Humanities, Art, Society and Health, or HASH would you believe, which is what they've basically made of it.'

All this was said at an accelerating pace of invective. Then he stopped suddenly 'You don't want to know about all that, do you? Why should you?'

'And Max was a thorn in their flesh, was he?' Brock prompted patiently.

'Oh, yes. Not like me, exactly – I'm the bolshie little know-it-all bastard in the back row at the President's open staff briefings who asks the questions about where the money's going and how come they can recruit so many bloody administrative assistants when we

36

can't afford tutors and library books. Max's approach was more *philosophical.*' Pettifer said the word with a hint of a sneer, as if he couldn't quite bring himself to talk of anyone, even his friend Springer, without having a dig at them. 'Max attacked the principles rather than the practices. Especially those principles enshrined in the Division of Science and Technology.'

'Why them?'

'Max had a bee in his bonnet about the scientists. He thought they were dragging us willy-nilly towards a world where everything would be predetermined by technology, free will abolished. Especially here, where all their research is driven by money . . . And they make lots of that,' he added with a snarl.

'So he made enemies. Anyone in particular?'

'Richard Haygill for a start. Professor of Medical Genetics and Director of the Centre of Advanced Biotechnology. Max once described him as a latter-day Dr Mengele . . .' he smiled at the memory, ' . . . in public, in the University Senate, before the Senate was abolished.'

'That was rather strong, wasn't it?'

'Oh yes. And what made it even stronger was that Max's parents both died at Auschwitz. Mengele might even have murdered them, for all we know. And Max was dead serious, it wasn't just a bit of abusive hyperbole. Haygill blew his top, naturally, threatened to sue, but let it go in the end.'

'Was this very recent?'

'About a year ago, I think. I'm not aware of anything very recent. Since then our Great Leader has abolished the Senate and put in his own man to control the campus magazine, and generally adopted a policy of pretending that pests like Max and myself don't exist. And by and large he's been pretty successful, I must say. We rot away in this slum, deprived of funds and students and gratefully accept the package, when it's finally offered to us by some smooth little human resource consultant shit with a BMW. I probably sound very bitter to you.'

Brock smiled. 'You do rather.'

'Ah well.' Pettifer waved his hand airily. 'We all find our own forms of consolation. I might go and replenish mine now, I think, unless I can be of any further assistance.'

'No, that's fine. Do you know where I could find Max's student, Briony Kidd?'

'She shares a room just down the corridor. It's not far, I'll show you. She's usually there.'

Pettifer led him down the deserted corridor and tapped on a door marked 'Postgraduates', then stepped in. Four workspaces had been crammed into the little room, two down each side, but only one was occupied. Brock recognised the slight figure dressed all in black, the gamine looks, the large dark-ringed eyes made more dramatic now by tears and the red rims of crying. She hurriedly grabbed a tissue from a box on the little table in front of her and wiped her nose.

'All right, love?' Pettifer said breezily, not appearing to notice her distress. 'Got a visitor for you. 'Bye now,' and he left, closing the door behind him.

Brock felt immediately uncomfortable, waiting to speak while the woman drew more tissues and rubbed vigorously at her eyes and nose.

'I'm Detective Chief Inspector Brock, Briony,' he said when she finally turned in her seat to half face him. 'I'm sorry to intrude. I wanted to speak to you about Professor Springer, but I could come back.'

'No, it's OK,' she said quickly. 'I'm just very upset about it, that's all.'

'Of course. It was very shocking.'

'I should have got used to the idea of it, but I was just . . .' She looked at a sheaf of paper in front of her. 'I was just . . .' Her shoulders began to shake beneath the thick black sweater, and she began to sob.

Brock wondered if perhaps this was the only person who was really upset by Springer's death. Everyone else seemed rather enthralled by it. As he stood waiting, he wished again that Kathy were here. He wondered what another student would make of it if they walked in now and saw him, a big bear of a man standing over the weeping girl.

'I was reading his comments, you see,' she blurted out suddenly. 'What he'd written on my text. He only gave it back to me yesterday morning. With what happened, I hadn't looked at it until now.' She sobbed and wiped. 'Seeing his words . . . so normal, as if nothing has happened.'

'Of course. Look, would it be better if we went and got a cup of coffee somewhere? A bit of fresh air, you know . . .'

She shook her head. 'It's all right. I'm OK. What did you want to ask me?' There was a green Bic cigarette lighter beside her papers, and she turned it over and over in her fingers as she spoke.

'The same thing I'm asking anyone else I can find who was in contact with Professor Springer recently. Is there anything you can tell me to help us find whoever did this? Can you think of any reason why someone would do it? Did he tell you of any threats to his life?'

'No, nothing like that. The only thing . . . the thing that keeps coming back to me was something he said in his tutorial yesterday, about how it was up to "us" now. It was like Martin Luther King's last speech, do you remember, "I have a dream"? About how his people would reach the Promised Land, but he wouldn't be with them, as if he knew that he would soon be murdered. That was how Max sounded, although at the time I didn't realise. But afterwards, last night, his words came back, it was up to us now, my generation, as if he knew he wouldn't be with us much longer. I guessed he was sort of rehearsing what he was going to say later, in his lecture.'

'But nothing specific, then or earlier, about a threatening phone call, or note?'

'No.' Briony shook her head firmly and turned back to her papers, putting down the lighter and running her fingers over the pages as if wanting to feel the substance of Max Springer in his scribbled notes.

'The lecture yesterday, was it a regular thing? Only I got the impression from others I spoke to that he didn't do much lecturing.'

'No, that's right. He didn't give any undergraduate courses any more. They wanted him to teach business ethics to commerce students, but he refused. He said he didn't come here to teach budding entrepreneurs how to cheat their customers without getting caught.' She smiled wanly. 'Yesterday's lecture was a one-off, a public lecture open to everyone. The title was "The Tyranny of Faith and Science".'

39

'That sounds challenging. I shouldn't think the scientists would like that, or the Islamic students.'

She looked at him, puzzled for a moment, then nodded. 'They boycotted it. The theme of the lecture was to be that . . .' She pointed to one of a number of printed quotations, which she had stuck to the pinboard above her workspace. '*Where unanimity exists, some form of coercion is at work, whether of the tyrant or of logic.*'

'Hannah Arendt wrote that. I'm studying her for my Ph.D.'

Brock looked at some of the other quotes on the wall. Another said, '*The poor man's conscience is clear; yet he is ashamed . . . He is not disapproved, censured, or reproached; he is only not seen . . . To be wholly overlooked, and to know it, are intolerable.*'

'Arendt again?'

'She quoted it in one of her books, but it was originally said by John Adams, the second American President, the one after George Washington. It was one of Max's favourite quotations. He said that every politician should have that pinned up over their desk.'

'About the lecture, were there many people there?'

'Not many,' she said, defensive. 'There were a dozen, twenty maybe, waiting, when we heard that something had happened outside.'

'What about on your way into the theatre? Did you notice anyone then? Any strangers you didn't recognise? Maybe wearing a dark anorak, jeans, light coloured trainers.'

'That's what they were asking us after it happened, but I didn't see anyone like that.' She stared glumly at the pinboard.

'And did Max mention Islam at all in his tutorials?'

'Yes. He drew parallels between scientific methods, Nazism and fundamentalist religions, like Islam. He said he was going to discuss this in his lecture. He said it would be a revelation to some people.'

'Sounds as if he intended to upset a few people.'

She shrugged. 'It was a favourite theme of his. He was fearless in expressing his opinions.'

'OK, well I won't disturb you any longer just now, Briony. If you do think of anything, here's my phone number.'

Briony seemed preoccupied with some thought and didn't reply. Brock turned to go. As he reached the door she suddenly spoke again.

'I just remembered. At our last tutorial he said something else a bit odd. He used a phrase, "the people of the book", and said something about it being a lottery which people of the book would shut him up first, something like that.'

'People of the book? What does that mean?'

'I don't know, but I don't think he meant they were going to take away his library card or something. I asked him what he meant, but he wouldn't explain. He would do that, say something mysterious and leave you to think about it.'

'You didn't take it to mean that someone might want to kill him?'

'Not at the time, no. But now . . . well, I don't know.'

On the way back to his office in Queen Anne's Gate, an annexe of New Scotland Yard a couple of blocks away from the Victoria Street headquarters building, Brock phoned the laboratory liaison officer, Sergeant Leon Desai, and arranged for him to meet him there.

'Anything for us yet, Leon?' Brock asked when they met.

'They should be ready for a screening of the enhanced video film later this afternoon, Brock. And firearms has made a preliminary assessment of the cartridge, but verbal only at this stage, being a bit careful.' He said it approvingly, being himself a stickler for accuracy.

'Go on.'

'7.62 millimetre, probably of Warsaw Pact origin, maybe to go with something like the Russian Tokarev automatic pistol. Doesn't mean to say that's what we're looking for, of course. Could have been fired from something else.'

'Availability in London?'

'Yes, there's quite a bit of old Soviet stuff floating around. The Tokarev and its ammunition was also sold to a number of countries outside the Warsaw Pact.'

He handed Brock a list. Brock's frown deepened as he scanned it. 'Syria, Somalia, Libya, People's Democratic Republic of Yemen . . .'

He put the paper down and reached into his pocket, handing Leon the green pamphlet from Springer's desk. 'What do you make of that?'

Leon read, then said, 'It's the Qur'an.'

'That's what I thought. You're not a Muslim are you, Leon?'

Leon gave him a sharp look to see if the question was serious.

41

'No, I'm not actually, but my family used to be. They were originally Muslims from Gujarat in India who went out to Kenya, where they began to get lazy about their faith. They lost it altogether when we were kicked out of Kenya. Many of the East African Gujarati went up north to Bradford, where there already was a community of Gujarati from India who'd built their own mosques and schools, but we settled in London and never took up with Muslims here. But I was brought up on the Qur'an when I was a kid.'

It was the longest speech Brock had ever heard from Leon, normally so economical with words, on any subject other than forensics.

'Fascinating,' he said. 'You wouldn't happen to have a copy of the Qur'an handy, would you?'

''Fraid not.'

'Actually I'm beginning to think we may need the help of an expert on this. Does the phrase "people of the book" mean anything to you?'

'Yes, it's a phrase that's used in the Qur'an.'

Brock rubbed at the side of his beard thoughtfully. 'This is beginning to get worrying, Leon.' He handed him the other packet with the pieces of envelope. 'See if the lab can get anything from these. Especially the postmark. It's smudged, see? I could only get the date.'

'Is this what the green note came in?'

'That's one of the things I'd like you to find out, if you can. They were in different places, but this was the only envelope I could find. We're doing a proper search now.'

As he turned to go, Leon said, keeping his voice neutral, 'Heard from Kathy at all, Brock? Is she OK?'

'Not too bad, I think, Leon. Taking it easy, I hope.'

'Yes. Don't know how I could contact her, do you?'

'Anything urgent?'

'No, no. Just thought I'd get in touch. See how she's doing.'

'I think I'd leave it for now. Give her a bit of breathing space. All right?'

Leon nodded and left.

42

5

The officer from the Islamic Desk of Special Branch had dark curly hair and a cheerful grin. He was wearing a black leather jacket and blue jeans and had an easy, relaxed manner and an unobtrusive way about him that would suit him well, Brock thought, to the role of intelligence gatherer, which the Special Branch played. They shook hands.

'Sergeant O'Brien, sir.'

'You don't bother with ranks and sirs over there, do you? Neither do we. What do they call you?'

'Wayne.'

'I'm Brock.'

'Yeah, I know. I've heard about you, Brock. And I've heard about this place, too. Always wanted to visit the infamous rabbit warren. There's even a rumour that you keep your own pub in this place, did you know that?'

'You're not serious? A pub, in an office of the Metropolitan Police?'

'Yeah, likely, eh?' He gave a cheeky grin. 'Good story though. Adds to the myth, right? And I brought my copy of the Qur'an, like you asked.'

'Good. Tell you what, let's go downstairs and meet Bren Gurney. I've ordered some sandwiches. Come across him before?'

'Did he play rugby for the Met?'

'He did. Wing three-quarter. Put on a bit of weight since then. Follow me.'

Brock led the way through the confusing maze of corridors and flights of stairs which connected the rooms of what had once been separate terrace houses, then the converted offices of a publishing company, gradually working his way down into the basement. They passed under an arch, turned a corner and suddenly found themselves in the snug of an ancient public house.

'Struth!' The Special Branch officer stared around him at the ornate frosted glass, the tiny mahogany bar, and the huge stuffed salmon mounted in a glass case on the wall. 'It's true then! Wicked.'

'Keep it to yourself, though, won't you Wayne? Welcome to The Bride of Denmark.' He lifted a flap in the counter and squeezed behind the bar, stooping to inspect the shelves beneath. 'What's your poison, old son? Whisky, beer? No draught beer, I'm afraid.'

'Blimey.'

Bren came through the arch at that moment, bearing a tray of sandwiches, which he placed on a small table. They settled themselves around it with bottles of beer.

'Well, now, Wayne,' Brock began. 'This may be a waste of your time, but we'd appreciate a bit of advice on one of our current cases.'

'The murder down at UCLE?' O'Brien asked hopefully. 'I've seen it on TV and in the papers, of course. Choice one by the sound of it.'

'That's the one. A couple of things have come up that make us wonder if there might be some Islamic connection. Recently the victim reported that he'd received a threatening phone call which he connected with a radio interview he'd made speaking out against extremists and fundamentalists. Apparently the caller threatened to kill him within two weeks of the end of Ramadan if he didn't pipe down. Then in his room we found this . . .'

He showed O'Brien a colour photocopy of the green handbill.

He read it over, cocking his head to one side. 'The Qur'an. Let's have a look . . .' He pulled a well-worn hardback book from the bag he'd had slung over his shoulder and thumbed through to chapter seventy-eight.

'Of course, we don't know the context, how it came to be in the victim's room, but it sounds threatening, doesn't it?'

'Yes, here we go, about the Day of Judgement.'

He handed the book to Brock who read the passage, then pointed to the words that followed. '"We have recorded everything in a

44

Book." The victim apparently said something about "the people of the book". Does that mean anything to you?'

'Yeah, sure.' O'Brien took the volume back and turned to the index at the back. 'Here we go . . . Chapter four . . . "People of the Book! Exceed not the limits in the matter of your religion, and say not of Allah anything but the truth." The book it's referring to is the Bible, and the people of the Book are the Jews and Christians who follow it.'

'I see.' Brock frowned in thought. 'The victim, Max Springer, professor of philosophy at UCLE, had strong opinions about fundamentalists, apparently, though not only Muslims. He doesn't seem to have had a particularly high profile in recent years, and everyone seems very surprised that he should have been murdered, let alone in such a public and conspicuous way. He was sixty-six, at the end of his career, highly regarded for his past work, especially overseas, but not very active now. So one theory might be, if an extremist group was responsible, that it was intended as a provocative act, to strike down a figurehead. Something like that.'

O'Brien took this in, munching on his sandwich. 'He was shot, wasn't he? Anything on the gun?'

'We haven't found it yet,' Bren said. 'But we did find one of the two cartridge cases, and both bullets, one still in the body and reasonably intact. So far the best information we have is 7.62 millimetre, of East European make.'

'No hint of any drugs in this? He wasn't making a fuss about student drug use, dealers on campus, anything like that?'

'Not as far as we know.'

'I was thinking of a possible Turkish connection. Since the Turkish mafia moved into London they've cornered a big slice of the drug market, of course. I just thought, if he'd upset someone, the style of killing fits. Giving a public warning to people to keep their heads down. But I suppose the same would apply with your religious extremists. Nobody's claimed responsibility, then?'

'No, but they wouldn't necessarily need to,' Brock said. 'The timing was significant. Springer was just about to deliver a public lecture in which he was going to compare religious fundamentalists to Nazis. He was killed as he approached the lecture theatre. The killers may have thought that speaks for itself, and they don't need to risk making a further statement.'

'If it was a religious thing,' Bren said, 'you'd have to assume it was an international group, wouldn't you, not UK based? There's been nothing like this before, has there? I mean, we're not talking about our own migrant community, are we?'

O'Brien sat back and wiped his mouth. 'There's no real distinction, Bren. If your family's been settled in Brentwood for three generations, your picture of the world is London, know what I mean? But for new immigrants, with stacks of close family connections back in the old country, the world is London plus Jamaica, or Bradford plus Karachi. You can't put a wall around, say, the Mujahadin or the Tamil Tigers, and say they're foreign and far away. They've got brothers and cousins in the next street to you, like as not.'

'So you think there might be a local connection?'

'Could be. It ain't easy to walk into a foreign country and find your way around, and discover all about your victim's movements and habits, without getting noticed. A bit of local help goes a long way.'

Brock's phone burbled. He listened for a minute, then rang off. 'How would you like to have a look at our killer, Wayne? They've been working at enhancing the security video and they reckon they've done about as much as they can. They're setting it up upstairs.'

They met Leon Desai and a technician from the electronics laboratory in one of the upstairs rooms, and sat down around the screen. The small and fuzzy images which they had seen previously were now transformed, the face of the gunman filling the picture.

'Is that colour right?' Brock asked, pointing at the areas of skin that showed around his lips and eyes. They were distinctly brown rather than white.

'So-so,' the technician replied. 'I had to manipulate the colours, and that was as close as I could get, using the glimpses of teeth and tongue and the whites of the eyes as parameters. But it wouldn't be reliable enough to use in court.'

'We spent the last hour with a lip-reader,' Leon said, 'trying to make out what he was saying. Unfortunately the victim's head obscures part of his mouth towards the end. She wasn't all that happy about it, but this is her best guess.'

He looked uneasy as he handed Brock a folded sheet of paper.

Brock unfolded it and stared, his frown deepening. 'Good grief,' he murmured.

He handed it to Bren, who read out loud, '"Allan, you bastard".' He looked at Brock in astonishment. 'What does that mean? He got the wrong man? He meant to kill someone called Allan?'

'How could he?' Brock said. 'He was three feet away. How could he mistake Springer for someone else?'

'Hang on,' the Special Branch man broke in. 'Suppose he wasn't speaking in English? I'm thinking, could it be "Allah" instead of "Allan", like "Allah-u-Akbar" maybe? "God is most great". It's the traditional call to prayer, and it's also the battle cry of the shaheed, the religious martyrs. Saddam Hussein had it stitched onto the Iraqi flag during the Gulf War.'

'That sounds more like it. And that would mean that we're looking for someone who speaks Arabic.'

'Interesting,' Wayne said. 'Very interesting. I guess you want what I can give you on London activists, then, Brock?'

'I believe we do, Wayne. And let's keep this to ourselves for the moment. If we're right, this is going to be explosive.'

That afternoon Brock returned to the university campus to check on the progress of the more rigorous search of Springer's room which was going on, in parallel with a similar search of the philosopher's home, a modest semi in the Essex suburbs. While he was talking to the searchers, warning them to inform him immediately they came across anything with an Islamic connotation, there was a discreet cough at his back and he turned to see the University President's Executive Officer standing in the corridor, regarding them with a quiet smile. Brock wondered how long the young man had been there.

'Pardon me, but Professor Young heard that you were on campus, Chief Inspector, and wondered if he might have a word, when you're free.'

'I'm busy here at the moment.'

'Of course. Shall I say an hour?'

47

'All right.' Brock turned back to a pile of papers he had been studying. They were handwritten notes, in Springer's almost indecipherable scrawl, for lectures or essays.

An hour later he was shown into the President's office. Young sat in shirtsleeves in front of the broad window, the view even more distracting in daylight, studying a single document on his otherwise paperless desk. The impression given was that a vast support apparatus of filing systems and office drones must exist in order to sustain this emptiness and space, leaving the great man uncluttered, free to take decisive action. Brock thought of the contrast with Springer's tip, or, come to that, his own untidy office. Against the bright panorama it was difficult to make out Young's expression as he raised his eyes, a significant few seconds after Brock had entered the room.

'Take a seat, Chief Inspector. Thanks for coming up. I thought I'd better take the opportunity to be briefed on current progress. I'm told that you're pursuing an interesting line of inquiry.'

'Are you?'

'You're looking for Islamic connections, I understand.'

Brock didn't try to hide his annoyance. 'That's just one of a number of things we're checking on.'

'But what on earth leads you in that direction, may I ask?' he said smoothly, unfazed by Brock's obvious reluctance.

Brock began to frame a suitable phrase to mind his own damn business, then thought better of it. The man might, after all, be aware of something relevant. 'If I could have your assurance that this won't go beyond this room for the moment, Professor Young. The inquiry is speculative at this stage.'

Young waved a hand dismissively, as if the demand were insulting. 'Of course.'

'It seems that Professor Springer may have received a threatening message of some kind during the past month, possibly from someone of extreme Islamic views. And in the lecture he was about to give when he was killed, he apparently intended to attack religious fundamentalists in uncompromising terms.'

'Oh, dear. Max was prone to that sort of thing, I have to say. His lecture, eh? Yes, I've been told about that. That is very unfortunate. He didn't inform us beforehand about it.'

Brock was surprised. 'Do the professors have to get clearance for their lectures?'

Young smiled. 'Not clearance. But it was a public lecture, I understand, and they are expected to inform the administration about any public utterances they intend to make. It's a matter of the university speaking with one voice, and protecting its reputation. Max gave an interview on local radio a few months back, and some of his remarks then were intemperate. The feedback we got from the local ethnic communities was not positive.'

'Really? What form did the feedback take? Were there specific complaints?'

'No, I don't think so. Only our media people keep their ears open, and that was the impression they got. We have to be sensitive to our neighbours beyond the DLR, you see. I mean, we're the newest immigrants around here.' He chuckled. 'But there's never been any question of our staff being threatened. That does concern me.'

'We don't know where the threat, if it really existed, came from. Do you have many Muslim students at the university?'

'Ah, the deranged student theory again, eh? Well, yes, we have quite a number, certainly – Malaysians, Indonesians, Pakistanis, Egyptians . . . We depend considerably on our fee-paying international students for our funding base. But no militancy, that I'm aware of. Do you want me to inquire?'

Brock thought about that. He would have preferred to do his own investigation, but a direct police approach to student representatives might set off alarm bells around the campus. 'You must have some staff who work with student organisations, do you?'

'Several. The student ombudsman, the inter-faith chaplain, the international student counsellors. Shall I put out feelers? See if we've got any firebrands I don't know about?'

'Please. But very discreetly. Perhaps it could be done without making any connection with the Springer case.'

'Good idea. Though I'm almost sure it's a waste of time, to be frank. The more I think about it, if there is some young hothead out there, affronted by some of Max's remarks, wanting to make a name for himself and taking the law into his own hands, he's much more likely to be outside the university entirely . . . And of course, Max was a Jew. Ironic though. Max, a Jew by birth, was actually very sympathetic to the Arab cause.'

'Was he?'

'Oh, yes. He travelled there, and I'm told he's written quite passionately about their predicament. I tried to get him involved in our marketing effort in the Arab countries on the strength of it, but he wasn't interested. Well now . . .' He glanced at his watch. 'Good hunting, Chief Inspector. Do keep in touch, won't you?' His attention returned to the document on his desk, as if Brock had already left.

As Brock got to his feet he decided that he hadn't been unfair in his first assessment of the man. He thought he knew the type, the little boy who discovered a craving for dominance in the primary school playground, and had changed only in developing more subtle and effective techniques than fists. He had met versions of Young among businessmen, lawyers in the courtroom, and in the police force, but never, until now, in a university. But then, it had been a very long time since he had been in a university, and why should it be any different from the rest of the world?

On his return to the lower concourse he thought he should get a better picture of the whole place, and began to walk along the waterfront towards the part of the campus that lay beyond the administration tower. Buildings that he hadn't seen before appeared, like gigantic versions of the simple primary coloured blocks their designer might have played with at nursery school – a red cube, two yellow cylinders, a green pyramid and, most spectacular of all, a circular tiered ziggurat, stepping skyward in blue mirrored glass. He followed a cluster of students towards doors in the stone wall that formed a giant podium for some of these toy shapes, and stepped into a huge cafeteria. He bought a cup of tea and a Chelsea bun at the counter and sat at one of the hundreds of tables, eyeing the other customers, and was surprised by their variety, young people of every shade of skin and hair colour and dress. Listening carefully he was able to pick up many languages too, Swedish from a group of enormous blonde youths at one table, Spanish from a passing cluster of beautiful black-haired girls. Two wiry black women were clearing and wiping the adjoining tables and were talking in some dialect that sounded even more exotic, until he realised that it was broad Scouse, from Liverpool.

His stomach felt vaguely queasy, and he knew it wasn't just the Chelsea bun. He felt unsettled, adrift, unexpectedly indecisive, although he knew that time was short. If the Islamic line was a false trail then he was wasting valuable time in a case whose notoriety and public interest seemed to be ballooning with every newscast. If it was true, on the other hand, he wouldn't be able to keep it from public knowledge for long, and the killer, if he hadn't already done so, would be on the first flight back to whichever state would shelter him. And soon now there would be the inevitable call to share this with the Anti-terrorist Branch, SO13, or, more likely, hand the whole thing over to MI5.

But the problem was more personal than that. Something vital was missing, and he recognised, reluctantly, what it was. Kathy. He wanted her here, covering the parts of the ground that he couldn't, making him think more clearly, giving him energy. Bren and the rest of the team were completely dedicated, of course, and highly competent, but somehow they didn't fill the gap. And he didn't like the notion that he might, over the years, have come to rely on her too much. Suzanne hadn't said anything directly, but she'd dropped a couple of hints, as if preparing him for the possibility of losing Kathy. Well, one thing you learned in an institution like the Met was that everyone was dispensable and everyone, at some point, moved on. Whatever relationship he had built up with her had arisen from the work, that was all. The idea that the reverse might have become true, that his taste for the job might now be dependent on her, was more than a little disconcerting.

6

The smell comes from the bucket in the corner of the room, that and
the all-pervading reek of cold concrete. Her right wrist is handcuffed
to the bed frame and she has begun to give up hope. He is bending
over her, silent, and she realises that something she has said has made
him angry. She watches his doped smile fade and black fury flare in
his eyes. He bends down and grabs her left arm and leg, lifting her up
and throwing her bodily across the bed. Her right arm jerks taut and
twists on the handcuff, and she screams as she feels the muscles in her
shoulder tear.

Kathy sat up, gasping for breath, fumbling for the bedside light
switch. 'He's dead,' she said out loud. Dead, but he keeps coming
back to her, night after night, at about the same time, when the
effect of the sleeping pill begins to wear off. She reached for a small
notebook and pencil and wrote the date, 23 January, the time, 2:36
a.m., and the words, 'Silvermeadow, again'.

Later that morning she sat in a pool of unexpected sunshine in the
conservatory at the back of Suzanne's house, leafing through the
Sunday papers. She poured herself another cup of coffee and opened
one of the news review sections. They were all full of the Springer
murder, as if everyone recognised in it some special public
significance or dramatic quality that made it irresistible. In retrospect
it had been absurd for Brock to try to hide it from her, for it
dominated every news report, and Brock himself could be seen on
TV, his voice punctuating radio reports. She felt remote, watching
their activity as from a great distance, no longer a viable member of

the team. That at least was clear to her, and probably to the rest of them by now. She had no choice but to move on.

She was alone, Suzanne having taken her grandchildren off to her sister's for Sunday lunch, and Kathy was glad of the solitude. She'd been grateful for the distraction of the children and the company of Suzanne, but she knew she must soon leave. She had spent Saturday morning in the travel agency watching, and occasionally trying to help, Suzanne's friend, and had been amazed at her patience. Customers changing their travel plans for the umpteenth time, airlines in confusion over their special fares, hotels double-booking, computers crashing, none of it ruffled Tina. And Kathy had come to realise how sheltered she had been working in a big organisation with specialists to back up on everything. Tina had to do it all herself, looking after her staff, getting the computers fixed, negotiating with her bastard of a landlord, working out the cash flow, getting the weekly ad in the local paper. On Monday Kathy was to help her with the next quarter's VAT returns, but more importantly she was to meet a rep for a tour operator who would tell her about their tour guides and put her in touch with a London agency that specialised in travel jobs.

She turned the page of the newspaper. Despite the number of column inches, the actual information contained in the reports was thin, and she could imagine the pressure on the Met press office to give more. The editorials and commentaries went on about freedom of speech, or violence on campuses, or the inadequacies of gun controls, but in the absence of hard facts about either motive or culprit, they were diffuse and unsatisfying. The most informative article, she thought, was an obituary of the victim printed in the *Observer*.

Max Springer was born in 1933 into a prosperous German-Jewish merchant family in Hamburg. In 1939, following the Kristallnacht riots, he was sent to stay with distant relatives in England. He never saw his family again, all of whom perished in the concentration camps. From 1952 to 1956 he studied philosophy at the University of London under Sir Karl Popper, then Professor of Logic and Scientific Method, and went on to the University of Chicago as a doctoral student and then lecturer, where he came under the influence of the

53

philosopher Hannah Arendt. It was there also that he met and married the classical pianist Charlotte Pickering. In 1965 he returned to England to a lecturer position at Oxford, there working under Sir Isaiah Berlin, who was Chichele Professor of Social and Political Theory. In 1978 Springer published his book *The Poverty of Science*, in which he questioned the assumptions underlying the principles of scientific logic and method. This work established his reputation as a radical and independent thinker, and he was elected to the Wyatt Chair of Modern Philosophy at Oxford.

As an extension of his studies of scientific method, Springer investigated what he termed 'blinkered thinking systems' and became interested in fundamentalist religious and political modes of thought. This theoretical interest was transformed by 'the electric shock of reality' as he later described it, during a visit to the Middle East in 1982, when he personally witnessed the atrocities committed at the Shatila Palestinian refugee camp in Beirut. He subsequently gave help to Palestinian relief organisations, especially for the support of orphaned children, and wrote of his experiences in his 1985 work *The Origins of Fundamentalism*, which aroused much controversy, especially among apologists of the state of Israel, much as his mentor Hannah Arendt had provoked outrage by her work *Eichmann in Jerusalem*, debate about which was at its height when Springer worked with her in Chicago in 1963.

In 1990 Charlotte Pickering, Max Springer's wife of thirty-two years, died, and in the following year he published an autobiography *A Man in Dark Times*, which was marked by passages of extreme pessimism. Upon its publication, stating that he wished to renew his life with fresh challenges, he resigned his chair at Oxford and accepted the position of Professor of Philosophy at the recently established University of Central London East. However, and despite a hopeful beginning, this move failed to fulfil its initial promise. His book *Totalitarian Science* (1996), which took up his earlier themes questioning current scientific thinking, was poorly received, and was widely condemned for the way it drew parallels between what he saw as the authoritarianism of science on the one hand and of fundamentalist religion on the other. In recent years he was perceived to be out of step with current movements in philosophy, and with the policies of his own university, which he publicly criticised.

While Max Springer's life may have appeared to have lost its relevance, his death has transformed that assessment, by demonstrating in the most dramatic and tragic way the significance of the principles for which he stood. He died a martyr to those principles, steadfast in his opposition to extremism, totalitarianism and authoritarianism of all kinds.

The following morning, while Kathy was adding up strings of Tina's VAT figures on a calculator, her mobile rang. A female voice said, 'Hello? Is that DS Kolla?' Kathy's heart gave an involuntary thump of panic. It was almost a month since anyone had addressed her by her rank. She didn't recognise the voice, and she tried to remember who at Headquarters had her mobile phone number.

'My name's Clare Hancock. We've met a couple of times and you gave me your number. I'm a crime reporter for the *Herald*.'

Kathy could place her now, an intelligent, deceptively mild-looking woman, whom Kathy had once seen reduce a Chief Superintendent to a trembling jelly at a press conference with a few very well-researched questions. But that wasn't her problem. With relief she got ready to deliver the magic phrase, 'I'm not working on that case'.

'I wondered if we could meet. It's about the Springer case, as you might expect. I have some information I think you'd be interested in. Frankly, I want to trade. Are you at UCLE? Where would suit you? It is rather urgent.'

'I'm afraid I can't do that, Clare. I've got nothing to do with that case.'

There was a moment's hesitation, then the voice doubtful, as if not sure to believe Kathy. 'Really? I understood that Brock has you with him on all his big cases now.'

'Not this one. I'm on leave, as it happens. I'm not even in London.'

'Oh, dear. Bad timing. I'll bet you're kicking yourself.'

'You'd better ring him instead. Do you have his number?'

'I don't want to do that. Brock gave me a hard time once, when I was new to the job. Grumpy old bastard he was. I'm hoping I can work with you, Kathy. Can't you drop everything and get back here? You won't be sorry. Brock will thank you for it, believe me.'

Kathy felt a jab of resentment. The rep from the tour operator was due in any minute and she didn't want anything to do with this.

'I take it you've seen our coverage this morning?' the reporter said suddenly.

'No, I haven't.'

'Well, go out and buy a copy. The Yard's busting a gut about it. They've been hammering my editor all morning, wanting to know where we got our information. Well, what I've got for you may be better than that. Have a look, go on, and ring me back in half an hour.'

Kathy had no intention of playing this game, whatever it was. She reluctantly wrote down the phone number. 'If I don't get back to you, Clare, speak to Brock, or to Bren Gurney.'

'You'll ring me, Kathy. I know you will.'

Kathy looked up from her pad and saw Tina greeting someone at the door of the travel agency, then waving Kathy over to join them. I don't think so, Clare, she thought.

All the same, as she chatted to Tina and the tour operator rep, she couldn't help wondering what could be so compelling on the front page of the *Herald* that morning. After half an hour the other woman said she had to go. It appeared that Kathy's lack of proficiency in another language would be a handicap, and she should probably get to work on her schoolgirl French as soon as possible. On the other hand her police experience would be a plus, coping with difficult people and situations, knowledge of first aid and so on. They'd rung the contact at the London agency and made an appointment for Kathy for the next day, but afterwards she felt deflated, feeling for the first time the insecurity of looking for work, and the fear that this way of escape might be more difficult than she'd assumed. She excused herself from the shop and went round the corner to a newsagent's and bought the paper. The headline read, 'FATWA DEATH OF SPRINGER: SENSATIONAL NEW POLICE THEORY'.

She skimmed the lead article: new information suggesting prior death threats from Islamic fundamentalists, speculation from experts on possible terrorist groups, guarded comments from university sources, terse 'no comments' from the British Council of Muslims in Bradford and the Islamic Research Centre in London. Inside an editorial invoked the Rushdie affair and called for calm until more facts were known.

OK, Kathy thought. So what? It was intriguing, shocking perhaps, but did Clare Hancock really expect her to drop everything for this? Then it occurred to her that MI5 would want to get their hands on something like this, and might well be trying to take it away from Brock at this moment. And again, if Kathy wouldn't talk to her, the reporter might go to them instead. For Brock's sake then, she realised she'd have to ring the woman back.

They had spent the weekend working through the Special Branch leads that Wayne O'Brien had fed them, rating his suggestions according to his private scale of adjectives, this one being 'cool', that one 'ripe', another one 'the real McCoy'. This steady but so far unproductive progress was thrown into disarray by the *Herald* story. Now resources were being thrown at the case from all sides, SO13 had joined in, the Diplomatic Protection Group, SO16, was demanding participation, as was SO10, Covert Operations, and, as expected, MI5 was circling hungrily in the background. Action, not discretion, was the order of the day, and Brock found himself at the centre of a turmoil of activity.

And in the middle of all this, he had found himself entangled in an absurd industrial relations fiasco. They had decided to interview PC Talbot once more, with O'Brien present, to see if they could tease any new information out of the young constable's memory of his interview with Professor Springer. But when Brock had phoned Shadwell Road police station and spoken to the inspector he had been met with the stiff information that PC Talbot was currently under suspension, pending review of his conduct in not keeping his superiors properly informed of the approach of a member of the public at serious risk, namely Professor Max Springer and his appeal for help. Brock smelt some frantic retrospective fireproofing on the inspector's part and tore into him, demanding that the constable be reinstated immediately and sent up to Queen Anne's Gate. After some token protest, Brock having asked him how he thought his action would appear to a hostile press and to the Metropolitan Police at large, the inspector relented. Ten minutes later he phoned back with the news that PC Talbot was being advised by his union, the

Police Federation, to stay at home, speak to no one and leave future negotiations to them.

And so Brock was in a car with O'Brien, stuck in traffic on their way to the East End, when Kathy phoned and said she'd like to meet him to talk to him about something important and in private. It was a hell of a time to try to talk to him about her future, he thought, but he tried to sound calm and reassuring and told her to take the Blackwall Tunnel and meet him at Shadwell Road.

When she got to the police station, Kathy found that Brock was locked away in conference in the back room, and the desk sergeant told her he couldn't be disturbed. She showed him her warrant card and he reluctantly agreed to inquire. While he was away a young man in a leather jacket and jeans who had been lounging against the far end of the counter came over and introduced himself as a Special Branch officer.

'Call me Wayne.' He gave her a friendly grin.

'Kathy.'

'I'm waiting for him too,' Wayne said. 'Some stuff-up with the local boys.'

The sergeant reappeared and said that DCI Brock had asked if she would give him another ten minutes, discussions having reached a critical stage. Wayne suggested they get a cup of coffee across the road, and they went out together.

Kathy hadn't been in Shadwell Road before, and as she looked more closely at the shops and people she became increasingly fascinated. What she had at first assumed to be an ordinary high street meandering through an old area of the East End, now seemed more like a bit of the Indian sub-continent, not transplanted so much as grafted onto the root stock. The brick building over there, with an unpretentious attempt at a classical portico on its gable, which might have been a modest old non-conformist church, was in fact a mosque. The girl behind the coffee shop counter was wearing a headscarf and track pants, and the CD she was playing was, according to Wayne, Billy Sagoo's *Bollywood Flashback*, which Kathy liked but he said was only OK, and he preferred the likes of ADF. He was entertaining in an unforced sort of way, and he told her something of the Springer case and why they were here, Springer's visit to Shadwell Road and the present predicament with PC Talbot. 'A right cock-up.'

On their way back Kathy stopped to examine a rash of exotic-looking fly-posters on a section of brick wall, when Wayne suddenly cried out, 'Oh, Christ Almighty!' doubled up and dropped to his knees. Kathy thought he'd had a heart attack, then realised that he was tugging at the loose corner of one of the posters. Beneath it, partly obscured by it, was another poster, green, printed with a black symbol of a raised fist and some writing in an unfamiliar script.

'You little beauty!' Wayne murmured, then got to his feet, eyes shining with excitement. 'Your guvnor's going to love this.'

They hurried into the police station to find Brock emerging, grim-faced, from the back room with a group of men, both uniformed and plain clothes. He nodded to Kathy, then noticed Wayne's excitement.

'Got something to cheer us up, Wayne? We certainly need it.' The other men in the party shuffled their feet, lowering their eyes.

'I think so, Brock. Something choice, I think. Fancy a bit of the old fresh air?'

'Can yours wait a bit longer, Kathy?'

Kathy said yes, then watched from the doorway of the police station as Wayne led Brock down the street towards the posters. This time he seemed to show no sign of special interest in them, though their pace slowed as they went past, and Brock took a long look. His eyes too were bright when they returned. He spoke to the station Sergeant and Inspector, asking them to take a discreet walk with Wayne, then turned to Kathy.

'Right, then, Kathy. Your turn. How are you, anyway?' He peered at her in the dim light of the corridor and she caught a small frown pass over his face. 'You're looking good.'

He was lying, but she ignored it and said, as brightly as she could, 'Oh, I'm just fine.' The truth was that the interior of the seedy police station, the voices and smells and worn furniture familiar from dozens like it, had made her heart sink. 'Suzanne's treating me like an honoured guest.'

'Good, good. So what can I do for you?' They went into the interview room and sat down, Brock bracing himself for whatever revelation was coming. Whatever it was, it wouldn't be good, he thought, but he was startled as she began to tell him about the reporter, and the conversation which she had just had with her.

'You see they've got this problem, Brock. They've gone full-tilt for this religious assassination story, and they've got their campaign all planned. All these actors and novelists and people are lined up to sign a petition about free speech and religious intolerance, and the paper thinks it will run for weeks.'

'I'm sure they're right,' Brock said gloomily. 'What's their problem?'

'She thinks there's a possibility that they may be completely wrong about this, and she's worried they may end up looking irresponsible and stupid.'

'*She's* worried?'

'It's her story. She thinks she'll be in the firing line if it all goes wrong.'

'So she knows where the story came from, then? She knows who told them we were working on this in the first place? I'd very much like to know who that was.'

'She won't tell us that. She was adamant about it.'

'So what has she got to offer?'

'She says that the paper has something else, something that seems to contradict the fatwa theory.'

'Hell's teeth, Kathy! If they've got something they've got to give it to us.'

'Yes, well, she thinks the paper will deny they have it if we press them. Apparently it's a bit embarrassing to them in some way. Only Clare thinks that if she can do a deal with us, they may agree to it.'

'What sort of a deal?'

'She lets us have this other piece of evidence, and then, if it turns out to be solid, and the fatwa looks like a false trail, we give them early warning, so they can ease out of their corner with whatever dignity they can, and with a lead on the new story.'

'Let me get this straight, Kathy. They want us to reward them for not withholding crucial evidence in a major murder investigation?'

Kathy smiled. 'I knew you'd like it. *She* wants us to do this, not *they*. They don't know about this at the moment. She wants your promise and mine that we'll play ball, and then she'll approach her boss.'

Brock rubbed his beard thoughtfully. She smiled to herself at the familiar gesture, the bear ruminating.

'Let me think about it,' he said. 'If young Wayne out there has really found what I think he has, then the fatwa line is looking increasingly solid. We may not need Ms Hancock's special deal.'

He got to his feet and opened the door, calling the others in. The inspector and the sergeant both shook their heads. Neither remembered seeing the green poster before, or knew who might have put it there. There were so many fly-posters, no one took much notice. And no, they couldn't point to any particular religious groups or individuals who'd been giving trouble lately.

'What about PC Talbot? Might he know? He seemed to know his way around here pretty well.'

With great reluctance they agreed that he might know, except that he wasn't talking to anyone.

Brock dismissed them and turned to Kathy. She caught the calculating look in his eye and guessed what was coming before he opened his mouth. 'Why me?' she asked.

'Because I've met him, and I think he might respond to you. He's a good lad who's been shafted by senior officers who should have been looking after him instead of their own backs. I promised him it wouldn't happen, but it did, and now he doesn't trust me either. It's important, Kathy. You can see that.'

It suddenly occurred to Kathy that Brock was testing her, trying to see if she was ready to go back to work. She felt the flutter of panic in her chest, and was surprised at how calm her voice sounded when she replied. 'Is it really worth trying to push him if he's got the Federation telling him not to cooperate?'

'He knows all the locals and their stories. Like the Kashmiri next door whose daughter's run away. He was telling me all about it. That's the sort of person we need.'

'What approach do you suggest?'

'He's an honest, decent bobby. Make him see that it's his duty to help us. And impress on him that we haven't time to muck about.'

Greg Talbot's home was a little rented flat about a mile from the police station. Kathy rang the doorbell and waited. Eventually it was opened a couple of inches to reveal a young woman's face. It looked as if she'd been crying.

61

'Mrs Talbot?' Kathy said brightly, trying not to sound like a dodgy salesperson.

'Are you from the Federation?'

'No, I'm a detective, working on an important murder investigation . . .'

First lie. The door began to shut.

'We're not speaking to anyone,' the woman said, sounding faint.

Kathy put her hand up to the edge of the door and slipped it in, so that the woman would be obliged to crush her fingers if she slammed it. 'Please, I know the background to this. I just need ten minutes with Greg. It is very important.'

'I don't want him to speak to you.'

Another voice, a man's, sounded behind her. 'Who is it, Shirl?'

'A copper. Don't talk to her.'

The door opened tentatively and PC Talbot peered out at Kathy, who explained who she was.

'The Federation have told me not to talk to anyone.'

'I know, but something's come up that you may be able to help us with. No one else can, Greg. It's really important.'

He hesitated, then finally stepped back and let her cross the threshold. His wife, who was in a dressing gown, glared at her, and Kathy had the impression that there had been a quarrel. In the background a baby began to cry, and the woman turned and marched away.

'Shirley's just come off her shift,' Talbot explained. 'She's a nurse.' He led Kathy through into a cramped living room where they sat down.

'Look,' she began, 'I'm really sorry about what's happened. My boss, DCI Brock, is very angry. He knew nothing about it.'

'Yeah, well.' He sounded very tired. 'I'm thinking of jacking it in, anyway. Shirley wants me to, and I reckon she's right. Her young brother is earning twice what I am, and he gets home regular at six each night, and he doesn't 'ave to put up with people wanting to poke him one, or trying to stick a syringe in 'is face.'

'Yes, I understand. I'm looking to get out myself.'

'Are you?'

'Yes. And I have nothing to complain about my boss. That must

62

have been the worst thing for you, was it? Not having a boss who'd back you up.'

'Yeah, that didn't help. So why are you quitting?'

Quitting. She wished he hadn't used that word. 'I had a rough time on my last case. It wasn't the first time it's happened. I think I've had enough.'

He nodded sympathetically. 'Yeah. We had a sergeant that happened to. Great bloke. Got attacked one night by three guys. He reckoned that was the end for him. Just couldn't stomach it any more.'

And that was what they'd say, she presumed. Couldn't stomach it any more. Lost her bottle.

'What exactly do you want from me?'

Kathy took the photocopy of the green handbill from her pocket and handed it to the constable. 'This was found in Springer's room. We think it may have been intended as a threat. We haven't been able to trace where it came from until we noticed one like it on a wall in Shadwell Road, not far from the police station. No one at the station knows who might have put it there. We wondered if you might.'

Talbot handed it back with barely a glance. 'None of them know? The sergeant? The inspector?'

'Right.'

He smiled bitterly. 'No, well, they don't get out much. Not on the beat, talking to people.'

'Do you know, Greg?'

'Yeah, I know who made this.' He sat back as if he might say no more, then said, 'They're a crew calling themselves Islamic Action. Sounds impressive, but it's really just three young lads who are pissed off with everything. Maybe I should join them. The leader is Ahmed Nathaniel Sharif. He gets real annoyed when you call him by his middle name. Left school two or three years ago. Quite bright really, but hasn't got a job. People don't like his attitude and the way he looks. He's got dreadlocks and a feeble attempt at a beard.'

'Arab?'

'No, Paki, I suppose. Or Bengali. English anyway. He lives somewhere on the council estate east of Shadwell Road. The mosque will know. That's the Twaqulia Mosque, just up the road from the police station. Speak to the imam, Mr Hashimi.'

Kathy wrote it all down, checking the spelling. 'Thanks, Greg. I appreciate that. Brock said you know the local characters, like the Kashmiri with the runaway daughter.'

'Mr Manzoor? Yeah, well, I didn't tell him the worst part.'

'What's that?'

'Old man Manzoor reckons his daughter's humiliated him in the eyes of his family, and people say he's sworn to kill her when he finds her, and the bloke she's with. He and his two brothers are out most nights after they close up shop, cruising the East End looking for her. They think she's still around there somewhere. That's the main reason we're still keeping an eye open for her, to get to her before her dad does something stupid.'

'Nasty. You know this young Sharif lad then, do you, Greg? Has he been in trouble?'

'About six months ago he attacked The Three Crowns – that's the pub on Shadwell Road, just across the way from the police station.'

'Attacked it?'

'Yeah. Marched in one Saturday lunchtime and announced that the pub was an offence in the eyes of God, or something, and started to smash the place up. The landlord and a few of the customers managed to restrain him after a bit, but not before there'd been a good bit of damage, both to the pub and to him.'

'What did he get?'

'Twelve months good behaviour. He wanted to be a martyr, see, and go to jail, but the magistrate wouldn't oblige.'

'So he can be violent?'

'You mean, shoot Springer?' PC Talbot rubbed his nose doubtfully. 'I never thought of him as bad, really, but he fills his head with these crazy religious ideas. Maybe it makes him feel important, part of something.'

'Greg, I think you should speak to my boss about this yourself. He tells me your inspector and sergeant have agreed to cancel your suspension and give you a private apology.'

Greg nodded unhappily. 'Yeah, I know. But the Federation want a public statement printed in *The Job*. Apparently there've been other cases like this, and they want to make an issue of it.'

Kathy felt sympathetic. Through no fault of his own, circumstances had conspired to make life difficult for PC Talbot. 'Yes, it's hard. I suppose that's up to you in the end. But meantime, we need your help. Will you come back with me and speak to Brock?'

He stared gloomily down at his feet, then said, 'I'll talk to Shirley.'

Kathy waited by the front door to see what the answer would be. She heard Shirley's voice, angry, and wasn't optimistic, but eventually Talbot appeared, pulling on a coat, and they went out to the car.

He directed her to a lane running behind Shadwell Road, from which they turned into a yard behind the police station. Another vehicle was there, a van from which men were unloading folding screens. Kathy spotted Leon Desai among them, and guessed they were a forensic team, preparing to retrieve the green poster from the wall. Wayne O'Brien was with them, talking to Leon, and she said hello to them as she and Greg Talbot passed, avoiding Leon's attempts to catch her eye.

After they'd gone inside, the Special Branch man, who had been watching Kathy meditatively, turned to Leon and said, 'What do you reckon on her, then? Know her, do you?'

'Yes, I know her,' Leon replied, but didn't offer more.

'Well, I reckon she's dead gorgeous. I go for that arctic blonde look, and just a hint of haggard, like she had a heavy night last night, know what I mean?'

Leon turned away with a discouraging frown. 'No, can't say that I do.'

But Wayne wasn't going to be put off. 'Come on, old son. You must know something about her. Is she hitched?'

'She's not married, no,' Leon said, his disapproval beginning to sound pompous.

'Going steady?'

Leon hesitated before replying. 'You're wasting your time,' he said softly.

'How come?'

'Just believe me, OK? Leave her alone.'

But Wayne loved a challenge, and he hadn't got where he was by taking things on trust.

Inside the police station Brock shepherded the reluctant PC

Talbot towards the interview room, ordering coffee and cakes from the reluctant desk sergeant. He turned to Kathy with a beam of satisfaction.

'I knew you could do it, Kathy. Well done. I'm just sorry I had to involve you. You on your way back to Suzanne now? Give her my best.'

He was in a hurry and she was being dismissed, she realised.

'I've got one or two things to do in town,' she said. 'I'll probably stay at my place tonight. What about the reporter, Clare Hancock?'

'Do nothing. If she contacts you, tell her I'm thinking it over. Say it may be a day or two before we can give her an answer.'

'Is that a good idea? Suppose she takes her material to someone else?'

'I think she's already worked out that we're her best hope. At the moment it's still our case.'

He gave her a reassuring nod and turned away. Kathy dug her hands in the deep pockets of her coat, feeling suddenly dispensable and at a loss.

'Hi there!'

She turned to face Wayne O'Brien, a big infectious grin on his face. 'It's my lunchtime. How about you? Fancy another expedition into the Hindu Kush?'

She smiled back, grateful. 'Don't they need you here?'

'They can spare me for an hour. Come on.'

7

Brock walked alone to the steps which led up to the front door. It was unlocked, and he stepped inside without pulling on the iron bell handle. When he closed the heavy door behind him the noises of the street abruptly ceased. Inside was silence.

Immediately in front of him, laid out on the cheap blue vinyl floor covering, were several pairs of shoes. He bent and removed his own, placed them alongside, and padded forward in his stockinged feet. The place smelled musty, as if years of irretrievable dust had settled in the cracks around the old skirtings and wooden floor boards whose irregularities his feet could feel through the vinyl. A stair with a heavy wooden banister rose steeply against the wall to his left, while ahead lay a corridor running to the head of another flight, leading downwards. He went that way, picking up the sound of dripping water as he approached the stairs and descended.

He came to a white-tiled ablutions room, with taps and duckboards running along each flank and on both sides of a low central dividing wall, three or four dozen wash places in all. He was taking this in when a cough behind him made him turn. A man was watching him suspiciously from the stairs.

'Good afternoon,' Brock said. 'I would like to speak to the imam. Can you tell me where I might find him?'

The man considered him without speaking for a moment, then said, 'Follow me,' and turned on his stockinged heel. Brock went after him, back up to the entrance, then up the long flight of stairs to the first floor, where the man told him to wait while he went through a door in a partition nearby. He was standing in the corner of a hall, surprisingly large, with timber-fronted balconies cantilevered around three sides, and half a dozen elaborate chandeliers suspended from the high ceiling. It was bare of all furniture, as if it might be used for dancing, except that the whole floor was carpeted. The pattern on the deep green carpet was a repeated motif of the yellow outline of a shape like a small pointed archway, or an artillery shell, and the disconcerting thing was that, instead of pointing towards one of the walls, in line with the geometry of the room, the carpet had been laid with the motifs all pointed at a skew angle, as if some great hidden magnet had swung them all off course.

After a few minutes the man returned to the doorway and waved Brock through. In a small office, amid filing cabinets and the clutter of stationery, a small black-bearded man in a white skullcap and black gown looked up from the desk where he was writing.

'Mohammed Hashimi,' he said cautiously, unsmiling through his spectacles. 'I am the imam. How may I help you?'

Brock thanked him for seeing him, and asked if he might speak with him in private.

The imam frowned, then nodded to the other man who had remained waiting at the door. He left, closing the door behind him, and Brock then explained who he was.

Imam Hashimi invited him to sit, and said, 'Our relations with the local police are excellent. What kind of help do you want from me?'

'I'm working on a serious case. You may have read about it. The murder of a Professor Springer, at the university near here.'

A tremor of alarm crossed the imam's face, and he slowly bent to a side drawer in his desk and drew out a copy of that morning's *Herald*, as if he were producing something dangerous or dirty that he hadn't wanted to leave out in public view.

His fingers touched the headline. Brock nodded confirmation.

'But surely, we can't help?' The man's Pakistani accent was modified by a soft nasal Yorkshire twang.

'We're trying to eliminate people from our inquiries. And we want to do it without barging into a community and causing unnecessary alarm. I believe you may be able to help us with some local people we'd like to speak to.'

'You've got lists of people in our community?'

'Not *lists*, no, no. Nothing like that.' Brock tried to sound reassuring. 'Just three lads who've been expressing some rather extreme views, I understand. I dare say that's all it is, youthful exuberance, but I'd like to speak to them anyway. These are their names.' He handed the imam a piece of paper.

'Oh, Islamic Action,' he murmured wearily.

'Sharif has been in a bit of trouble in the past, hasn't he, expressing his views in a fairly violent way?'

The imam sighed. 'A very stupid incident. Ahmed gets carried away by ideas and expresses the impatience that all young people feel from time to time, but in a most intemperate way. It's good to see a young man taking a passionate interest in his religion, of course, but there was always something excessive about his piety. It would distress me very much if he's done anything really bad. He is a bright, impressionable boy. The other two follow him for their own reasons.'

'Where does Ahmed get his ideas from?'

'Ideas are everywhere, Chief Inspector. He reads books, watches satellite TV programmes from the Middle East, and follows the web sites.'

'I was thinking more in terms of human contacts. Is he in personal touch with any groups, here or overseas?'

'If so I'm not aware of it. He probably wouldn't tell me anyway. He's always respectful to me, but I think he believes I'm too ready to accommodate and compromise. He is what the people back in Pakistan call a BBCD, a "British Born Confused Desi". BBCDs have a problem with their cultural tradition, basically. They either reject it totally and try to become more English than the English, or they go to the other extreme and embrace it with a fanaticism that is embarrassing to those back home who still actually live in it.'

'What about his family?'

'Ah, yes. He lives with his mother who is a good, mild-natured woman who cannot control him. His father was white, and left them years ago. You can make what you want of that. Ahmed took his mother's family name when he was a teenager and refused to answer to his father's, whatever it was, I forget.'

'What about this man Springer? Would Ahmed have known of him do you think?'

'I can't imagine how. I've never heard of him. As far as I know

I've never heard his name mentioned. That's what seemed so improbable when I read this story in the paper. I said to myself, a fatwa against *whom*? Surely this is nonsense. But dangerous nonsense.'

'Exactly. Now, Imam Hashimi, can you tell me where we can find Ahmed and his friends?'

The imam sighed. 'I suppose I can. It wouldn't be hard to find out, anyway.' He referred to a thick office notebook filled with names and addresses in alphabetic order, and wrote three down for Brock.

On the way out they stopped for a moment in the main hall of the mosque, where Brock asked about the carpet pattern. 'It points to Mecca?'

'That's right.' Imam Hashimi handed Brock a small publication about the history of the building. 'In the nineteenth century it was used as a Methodist Hall for sailors and dock workers, then it became a synagogue, and now it's a mosque. But the joke is that it was originally built as a brewery.' His eyes twinkled behind the glasses and he lowered his voice. 'That's been left out of the official history. I dare say Ahmed would be offended.' Then his face became serious again. 'The trouble is that people don't take care with words. It's so dangerous. This word "fatwa", for example. A fatwa is simply a ruling on some question or in a dispute, issued by a specialist in Islamic law, a mufti. In a Muslim state, for example, the judge in a court of law would be assisted by such a mufti who would issue fatwas for his guidance in a case. But now, you see, in the newspapers a fatwa means the insane death-lust of fiendish Islamic *fundamentalists* – another dangerous word. It's all so dangerous. That is why I will do what I can to help you, Chief Inspector. To restore calm and good sense.'

They shook hands, and Brock padded down the stairs to retrieve his shoes.

If Ahmed Sharif still had dreadlocks, as PC Talbot had described, they were now hidden beneath a grubby-looking strip of material wound round his head in the style of a Taliban guerrilla, a look reinforced by his unkempt wispy beard, his pinched, underfed build, and his large unblinking eyes.

70

'Again, what's your real surname, sunshine?' Bren asked. 'Nathaniel what?'

Ahmed's eyes grew marginally larger and wilder.

'Nathaniel being your correct *Christian* name, right?'

Brock wondered whether Bren intended being quite so offensively crass. It wasn't his real nature, but he was doing it very convincingly. He decided to stop him. Apart from anything else, it seemed to be counter-productive, since the boy had said nothing since Bren had started on him, and had progressed from rigid to trembling.

'Em . . .' Brock interposed gently. 'I'm sure Inspector Gurney didn't mean that quite the way it sounded, Ahmed. We know you're a devout Muslim. And I'm sure Ahmed Sharif will do very well for the record just now, Bren. You are a regular at mosque, aren't you, Ahmed?'

The lad looked at Brock suspiciously, but still said nothing.

'Only, if you don't want the services of a solicitor at present, I wondered if you'd feel more comfortable if we had someone here from the mosque while we interview you? Imam Hashimi, perhaps? Or someone else?'

'I object to that, sir,' Bren said, in his best imitation of recalcitrant constabulary.

'Overruled, Inspector,' Brock said firmly. 'What do you say, son?' He looked at his watch. 'Only I may be called away soon, and I may have to leave you and Inspector Gurney to battle on without me.'

Ahmed blinked, the first time for some while, and then spoke. 'How long's this going to take then?'

'Up to you, son. As long as necessary, I suppose.' Brock glanced at his watch again. At least the lad had spoken. The thought of being left alone with Bren clearly didn't appeal.

'Yeah, all right. Imam Hashimi.'

'Fine, fine. In point of fact, we may not even need to trouble the Imam, who I imagine is a very busy man, with a big flock to tend to. If you'd just answer the inspector's questions, we could get this over very quickly, eh?'

He nodded at Bren who said, 'Where were you on the afternoon of last Thursday the twentieth of January, between four o'clock and six?'

Ahmed gave this some thought, then answered suspiciously, 'With two of my friends, at my place.'

'Did your mum see you there?'

'No, she was at work.'

'Anyone else see you there?'

'No. Where am I supposed to have been? And who am I supposed to have threatened, anyway?' He turned to Brock angrily. Now the silence had been broken, the words were coming out fast and angry. 'He said I was under suspicion of issuing a threat. Well, who did I threaten? This is crap, this is. This is your kafir justice, this is. You're just trying to stitch me up, 'cos I'm not white, 'cos I'm a Muslim!'

Brock raised a calming hand. 'No, no, Ahmed. We're not trying to do that. Tell me, do you know anyone down at the new university in the docklands, UCLE?'

There was a slight but definite reaction, Brock thought, but then Ahmed might well have been following the Springer case. 'You do?'

'No, I don't know anyone there. I wouldn't want to.'

'Why not? You're a bright lad. You'd get on with the students, I should think. In fact I'm surprised you didn't go there yourself.'

'They're stuck-up kafir trash!' Ahmed burst out. 'They just learn error and lies in that place.'

'Do they?' Brock said softly, beginning to feel close to something at last.

'And they wouldn't let the likes of me in anyway, on account of their prejudice and discrimination.'

'But I thought they had quite a lot of Islamic students there, from many countries . . .'

'Oh, yeah! Paying fees! Of course they take them if they pay! The greed of Satan knows no bounds!'

'No, no,' Brock shook his head sceptically. 'I'm sure that's not true. They wouldn't be allowed to have a discriminatory policy, surely?'

'It's true! They speak lies and favour their own. I know. They turned me away.'

'Really? When was that, Ahmed?' Brock was aware of Bren sitting very still.

'Four years ago! Before I took my A levels. I went for an interview, but they wouldn't offer me a place, because I was a Muslim.'

Brock shook his head, looking shocked. 'That's hard to believe, these days. What subjects were you interested in, as a matter of fact? What did you apply for?'

'PPE. But they wouldn't have me, a Muslim from the East End.'

Brock sat back and nodded at Bren. 'PPE. That's philosophy, politics and economics, isn't it? You'd have been one of Professor Springer's students, only they closed down his undergraduate course. Was he the one who interviewed you?'

A look of confusion slowly filled Ahmed's face, as if something had just surfaced in his mind. 'I'm not going to say any more. Not until Imam Hashimi gets here.'

'Actually, I've changed my mind about that,' Brock said. 'I really would advise you to accept a solicitor. As I said, it won't cost you anything.'

'I don't want a Christian lawyer speaking for me.'

'Well, we can see if a Muslim one is available. But you really do need the advice of someone who understands the law. Shall I arrange that? And while we're waiting for that to happen, can we just confirm one little matter . . .' He reached across to open the file lying on the table in front of him. Inside, in a plastic bag, was the green leaflet from Springer's study. 'This is one of yours, isn't it, Ahmed?'

The young man looked carefully at it, then nodded defiantly. 'Yeah, that's ours.'

'And you sent it to Professor Springer, didn't you?'

'Eh?' Again the look of confusion, turning into alarm. 'I don't know what you're talking about. Who is this Professor Springer?'

Brock smiled. 'If you don't know, Ahmed, you must be just about the last one left in the country who doesn't. You sent him this as a death threat, didn't you?'

Ahmed's mouth snapped shut, his eyes startled and wide.

'One of the interesting things about making a death threat, Ahmed, is that you're guilty of a crime even if you don't actually intend to carry out your threat, so long as the victim *believes* you do, and we know that Professor Springer believed the threat was a genuine one, because he told us about it. But then, you did intend to carry out your threat, didn't you? You weren't playing games.'

8

After the event, Kathy found it hard to work out exactly how she ended up sleeping with Wayne O'Brien.

After their lunch in Shadwell Road, a fish kebab at the Banglatown Balti House, they had arranged to meet that evening for a meal at what Wayne described as his favourite curry palace, Chutney Mary's in Chelsea. Then Kathy had strolled along Shadwell Road, wondering at the number of travel agencies advertising flights to places she'd never heard of, and she'd bought a few unfamiliar goods along the way, including jackfruits and some black seed oil, irresistibly promoted as 'able to cure every disease but death'.

She was putting these goodies in the back seat of her car when her mobile rang. It was Clare Hancock.

'Well, have you discussed it with Brock?' she demanded.

'Yes, Clare.'

'And?'

'He's not sure. He wants to think about it. Maybe a day or two.'

Silence for a moment, then, 'He didn't buy it, did he? He thinks it's a waste of time.'

'It's not that, but he's got a lot of other pressing things at the moment, and you haven't given us much to go on. He has no idea how credible your other lead might be.'

Another silence while the reporter thought it over, then she came back with, 'All right. I'll let you look at it, Kathy, or at least a photocopy of it. I won't give it to you, because I'm not supposed to have it, and if you put me in a corner I'll deny I ever did have it. But you can read it, and judge for yourself.'

'Clare, you really would be far better dealing directly with Brock.'

'No way. Where can we meet?'

She said where she was, and Kathy agreed to drive to a place nearby where she could park. It wasn't really taking her far out of her way home to Finchley anyway. When she rang off, Kathy wondered at this insistence on dealing with her. Not just sisterly solidarity, surely. Did Clare think she would be more easily persuaded than Brock? Or was it something more devious? If she but not Brock viewed this piece of evidence, might that put her credibility or judgement on the line at some future date, when everybody was denying its existence? The same way Clare Hancock seemed to feel that her reputation was at risk. Kathy decided to ring Brock and let him know what she was doing, but she was told that he was interviewing a suspect and wasn't available.

She spotted the reporter standing in a doorway as soon as she turned into the street. The woman was talking into a phone, but snapped it away as soon as she saw Kathy's fair hair and ran over to the car and got in.

'Well . . .' She took a deep breath, like someone bracing for a big jump. 'I hope I'm not going to regret this.'

Kathy waited, unable to offer any comfort.

'OK. The reason my paper's being coy is that we got a letter from Springer two weeks ago, and did nothing about it. He claimed, among other things, that his life was at risk. The letter was obviously libellous and unprintable, and the sub-editor who read it didn't even bother to run it past the lawyers. He put it in the reject box and it didn't get entered into the computer or anything. Then he went skiing. When he came back on Monday morning and read the fatwa story, he remembered the letter, dug it out of the box and showed it to my boss, who showed it to me. The letter didn't seem to support the fatwa idea, and we were in a spot. Here we were pursuing this murder theory when the victim himself had tried to get in touch with us with a different story, and we'd ignored him. We'd look stupid. My boss decided we'd best pretend we never saw the letter, and just hope it hadn't been sent to any other paper too. So far that seems to be holding up.'

She handed Kathy several photocopied sheets of paper. The letter had been typed, badly, on what looked, from the irregular letters, like an old manual machine, on UCLE letterhead.

The Editor

Dear Sir,

In recent years it has become commonplace to read letters to the newspapers complaining about the current state of our universities. These refer to inadequate government funding, overcrowded lecture theatres, low staff morale, and so on. Rarely however do they discuss the fundamental issue underlying these symptoms, which is the extent to which the whole ethos of the universities has been corrupted and betrayed by those who were its guardians. The purpose of the university is scholarship and the cultivation of diverse and creative thought, not the enlargement of the gross national product or the private incomes of its senior managers.

Among those centres of learning which have led the charge into prostitution of their talent, my own university, UCLE, is an outstanding leader in whoredom. On the one hand it adopts a breathtaking promiscuity in soliciting commercial funding for research which distorts and corrupts genuine scholarly activity, and on the other it ruthlessly stifles dissent and debate among its academic staff, who are reduced to the role of intellectual harlots, required to service the needs of whichever drooling customers their glossy senior management mesdames can lure off the street.

The glamorous star of our particular bordello is a siren by the name of CAB-Tech, the Centre of Advanced Biotechnology, a model of its alluring kind, whose groping assignations with commercial interests are not open to public scrutiny, which has produced no tangible benefits for its host university, and whose prime purpose appears to be the enrichment of its sponsors.

All this would be merely distasteful were it not coupled with an arrogance which elevates it to the level of tragedy. For CAB-Tech is so driven by the greed of its clients as to pervert the very nature of human inquiry and human life itself. Under the guidance of its Svengali-like director, Professor Richard Haygill, the whore aspires to the role of God, with results that will surely be catastrophic for us all.

One cannot say these things within the university, which has

76

shut down its forums of debate, yet there comes a point where they must be said, and the intolerable hubris of fundamentalist science exposed. I do not do so lightly, knowing full well the risks involved. Those who speak out against tyranny must offer their very lives to the cause.

Yours sincerely,

Professor Max Springer

'I can see why you couldn't print it. It sounds mad.'

'Yes. When the sub-editor first read it he thought it was one of those crazy feuds you hear about among academics who are supposedly very bright but have no common sense. Like the old joke, "Why are disputes in universities so bitter? Because the stakes are so low." Only the stakes here aren't necessarily low, at least as far as CAB-Tech is concerned. From what little I've been able to find published about it, it seems to be a very successful outfit, and this Professor Haygill is a highly respected scientist. My editor's reasoning was that we hadn't published the letter, and as far as we knew Springer hadn't denounced CAB-Tech anywhere else, so why would he be at risk from them?'

'Yes.' Kathy thought about what she knew about Brock's case, and about him already interviewing a suspect. 'I think he's right.'

'Do you?' Clare Hancock looked at Kathy hopefully.

'Well, the idea of sinister scientists bumping people off to protect their research . . .' She smiled, and Clare grinned back.

'That's what I hoped you'd say. And they wouldn't do it like that anyway, would they, have him shot in public? They'd put some fiendish chemical in his tea or something, wouldn't they?'

They both chuckled. 'I don't know,' Kathy said. 'It just all sounds so hysterical and unlikely. I'll tell Brock about this if you like, but I really don't think it's going to interest him.'

'Good.' The reporter took the sheets of paper back from Kathy and turned to open the car door. 'No one would have given this a second thought if Springer hadn't died like that. And . . .' she paused with the door half open, ' . . . I suppose I also had a lurking worry that we'd been given the fatwa story to put us off this, if this was for real.'

Kathy didn't really follow that, but waved goodbye and drove on to Finchley where she collected the bills and junk mail from her letterbox and took the lift up to her flat. It seemed hollow and cold when she opened the door, the first time she'd been there for over a week, and the view from the twelfth floor window of suburbs stretching into the distance seemed sodden and bleak. She remembered with regret the bustle and warmth of Suzanne's house with the children. That was a home, she thought, while this was just a filing cabinet for lonely people. She had two rooms, and her heart sank at the thought of the other, the bedroom, almost filled by the big bed she'd bought when Leon had moved in, briefly, before Christmas. Now that bed seemed like a big, bad, empty joke she'd played upon herself. This is just self-pity, she thought. She made herself a cup of tea, sat at the little dining table and wrote down a paraphrase of Springer's letter, together with a brief report for Brock, and put it in an envelope which she gave to Wayne later that evening.

He filled her in on Brock's progress, and she asked him one or two questions about the case. It had occurred to her that it shouldn't be hard to confirm Springer's obvious obsession about the scientists at UCLE and his mental state when he'd written the letter to the *Herald*. Wayne told her that, as far as they'd been able to gather, Springer was a solitary man with few friends. Brock had said that he'd found only one person who seemed genuinely upset by his death, his sole student, Briony Kidd.

'And this Muslim gang that Brock's arrested. What are they like?'

'Three kids. Well hard, or thought they were. In a panic now though. I didn't think they could have done it until we discovered that one of them had met Springer, and believed that he'd refused him a university place. The tragic thing was that it wasn't Springer who'd done that, it was the university closing down Springer's course. There certainly never was a fatwa – that idea was always crap. Just some kid in a rage, lashing out at injustice and the fact that nobody would take him seriously. We reckon he acted alone. I'd sure like to know what bastard sold him the gun though.'

'He hasn't confessed?'

'No, and his two mates are sticking to his alibi. At the moment Brock's staying with the death threat charge, but if he needs more time he can use the Prevention of Terrorism Act and hold them for forty-eight hours, or five days with extensions. Forensic are going through their clothes, looking for gunshot residue. I reckon the kid'll crack when they find that.'

Kathy also tried to find out more about his undercover work in Special Branch, but he was gently evasive. Neither of them wanted to dwell on work, it seemed, and they turned to other things. Wayne had travelled a good deal, and Kathy encouraged him to talk about the places he'd visited. He was entertaining and good company. They began with a drink in a pub in the King's Road, then went on to the curry, which Kathy confirmed was the best she'd ever tasted, thinking as she did so that it was ironic that the last man she'd been out with had been Leon, an Indian, who had never, to the best of her recollection, bought her a curry. Come to think of it, she wasn't even sure if he liked Indian food. The thought of him still hurt, but less so as the evening passed. The two men weren't at all alike, Leon seeming even more cool and taciturn in her memory the more relaxed and jolly Wayne made her feel. And of course *that* was the root of her problem, she decided with the clarity of revelation, as they continued to a little night club Wayne knew, and another bottle of wine took its effect. She simply hadn't had enough experience, of life, of men, of the world, to know what suited her best and what would make her *really* happy.

And in the light of this understanding, and the spirit of openness and experimentation it engendered, it perhaps wasn't necessary for Wayne to spin her the line he did. At least she assumed, when she thought about it the next morning, that it was just a line, but subtly spun, in fascinating little tit-bits of information dropped during the course of the evening, so that by the end of it she was thoroughly taken in. His girlfriend, it seemed, was going through a crisis of the heart. Basically she wasn't sure whether she loved him or someone else called Kim, who turned out to be a woman. Kathy could imagine, could she not, what that did for Wayne's sense of self-worth, although in point of fact Kathy hadn't noticed him at all deficient in that area. The crux was that the girlfriend was meeting with Kim that very evening, in the flat that all three shared, in order to resolve things one way or the other, and Wayne had promised to stay away. So he couldn't go home. Regardless of what his girlfriend decided however, Wayne had realised that things could never be the same between them again, which made him feel pretty sad, although again Kathy hadn't noticed that.

So she had taken him back to Finchley, to sleep on her sofa, except that it didn't work out that way. After he'd slipped away the next morning, with a kiss and a cup of tea brought to her in bed, she ran her hand over the warm rumpled bedding at her side and told herself, through her hangover and without complete conviction, that she had done absolutely the right thing, and was on the road to building a new, happier, freer Kathy Kolla. And there was something else − for the first time in weeks she hadn't dreamed about that room, and had to face its terrors. It was a sign, surely, that she could escape for good, and the first step was her interview that day. Her appointment with the agency wasn't until the late morning however, and she decided that in the meantime she might have a look at this glitzy university in the docklands, and, if she was around, have a quick word with Springer's only student. Clare Hancock's parting comment had stayed in her mind. No matter how mad his rantings in the letter seemed, Springer's prophecy had come to pass. Kathy thought she probably owed it to Brock to do this much.

Briony Kidd was again at her desk, and again the only postgraduate student in the little shared study, which today was blue with cigarette smoke, despite the 'no smoking' sign that someone had pinned to the door. The others, if there were any, had perhaps found more congenial places to work. She barely glanced at Kathy's identification and seemed distracted and low. Her eyes kept returning to a blank sheet of paper on her table. Kathy had trouble getting her to talk at first.

'Is this a bad time?'

Briony shrugged, her eyes straying back to the blank paper.

'I mean, if you're busy working . . .'

Briony took a deep, exhausted breath. 'I can't work. I haven't written a word since Max . . .'

'A thing like that is bound to upset your concentration,' Kathy offered, pulling up a chair.

'I've got to finish it this year, but I don't think I can, without him. It was all going so well.'

'What's it about?'

'Hannah Arendt's theory of action,' she said reluctantly, sounding as if any kind of action would be too much for her.

'She was a philosopher?'

'Yes. A German Jew, like Max. She escaped from Germany before the War, and worked in France helping to get Jewish children out of Germany for a time, then she went to America.'

'Ah yes. Max met her there, didn't he? I remember reading that.'

Briony nodded and lapsed into silence. She looked very pale and frail, and Kathy suspected she wasn't eating much. That's probably how I looked to Suzanne in the café that morning in Hastings, Kathy thought, and realised that something, her night with Wayne perhaps, had lifted her out of that, at least for the time being. The thought of it aroused a tingle of pleasure.

'So, what was her theory of action?'

The student looked round at her slowly. 'You don't really want to know.'

'Is it too complicated for me to understand?'

'No, but . . .' She shrugged, as if the effort of arguing was too much. 'She believed that there are essentially three modes of human activity. The most basic mode she called "labour", satisfying the necessities of life, in which individuals are submerged in a common task, behaving according to patterns, playing pre-ordained roles, becoming members of classes.' Her voice, becoming more lethargic, trailed away.

'Right. So that's number one.'

'Mm. The second mode is called "work". That's where the individual is able to express himself through his activity, as a craftsman or creator of something. This mode has greater freedom, but the individual is still subordinate to the end product. Arendt believed that capitalism is intent on turning all work into labour, and that almost the only true work left is that of the artist.'

'And the third?'

Briony roused herself a little. 'The third and highest mode of activity is "action". This means initiating undertakings and interacting with other individuals who are also capable of action. It's only in action that people are able to realise their individuality and reveal what they personally are. Even they themselves don't know what this is until the event they precipitate reveals them to themselves and to others. They cannot know in advance what kind of self they'll reveal by their actions.'

'Oh. I think I see. Vaguely. And her life, was it one of action?'

'Yes, it was. Through her books and arguments and the expression of her ideas.'

'And mine is one of labour, I should think.'

She said it as an attempt at a joke, but Briony didn't smile. 'Yes. Most people's are.'

'What else did she believe?'

'Lots of things. That there's a conflict between truth and freedom, for instance.'

This was said with some sharpness, and Kathy wondered if it was aimed at her, the police. 'You'll have to explain that. I kind of thought they supported each other.'

'She was repelled by the uniformity of the truths of religion, and now of science. She believed in the constant struggle of ideas and opinions against one another, rather than the inevitability of ideologies.'

Kathy grasped at this. 'I've heard that Max was antagonistic to science, and I couldn't understand why. Is that the reason? He thought like Arendt?'

'Yes. He believed that the whole project of science is to construct a single unified truth that will exclude all other views of the world. In that sense it is like a fundamentalist religion, and he hated it.'

'What about the scientists here on this campus? Did he hate them?'

'*Especially* them, and they hated him for challenging their "truth".'

'Are they particularly bad here, then?'

'Oh, God, yes. Haven't you heard of the CAB-Tech research project? That's the ultimate obscenity. They don't just want to find perfect truth, they want to create the perfect man.'

Kathy smiled as if this was a joke, then realised that she was serious. 'What, they say that?'

'That's what it amounts to.'

'Really?'

'It's true! They're getting all this money to make everybody's genes the same.'

'That's how Max described it, was it?'

Kathy couldn't keep the scepticism from her voice, and Briony abruptly turned away. 'What did you come for, anyway?'

'Oh, I was just trying to establish what Max's state of mind was like over the past three or four weeks. I thought you might be a good person to ask, working closely with him.'

'State of mind?'

'Yes.' Kathy really wanted to ask if he was normal, but was beginning to suspect that normal wasn't quite the term for Max Springer. 'Was he at all agitated, would you say, under stress?'

'Oh, you mean, did he feel threatened by the people who did this? No, not at all. He seemed very calm and normal to me. Almost . . . well, serene.'

Kathy nodded and began to get to her feet. 'All right. Well, I won't—'

'I don't understand why you didn't know about CAB-Tech. Aren't you investigating them? Surely you must be? I read in the papers . . .'

Kathy hesitated. She hadn't picked that up from either Brock or Wayne. This was what happened when you blundered uninvited into other people's investigations. Feeling foolish she said, 'What did you read?'

'About the Islamic extremists. I thought that was what you were looking for.'

Feeling even more confused, Kathy said hesitantly, 'Islamic . . . Yes, but I thought we were talking about CAB-Tech?'

'But, that's them, isn't it? They have lots of Islamic fundamentalists working over there. That's what's so absolutely *right*, isn't it? The two old gangs seeking after one truth working together. Max thought it was bitterly funny if it weren't so bloody tragic.'

'Islamic fundamentalists?' Kathy wondered if she was really following this.

'Yes. Have they told you about the Christmas e-mail yet? No? Well, ask them, go on. You ask them about that.'

9

When she left UCLE Kathy realised that she was running short of time to get to her interview in the West End, and of course it was impossible to find a car park. Eventually she arrived half an hour late for her appointment, a lapse that the woman interviewer, middle-aged and severe, obviously found both significant and annoying.

'You see, being on time is one of the absolutely basic require-ments for a courier or tour guide. We run to timetables, schedules. What are you going to do with your party of twenty pensioners from Pontefract at Moscow airport at ten o'clock at night when you've just missed the last flight back to the west because you turned up half an hour late, eh?'

'Yes, of course. I'm usually very prompt. In the police—'

'Yes,' the woman leapt in, the reference to the police obviously touching another nerve, 'but in the police you can just say you were tied up with something important, and people just have to put up with it.'

Kathy's heart sank. Probably the woman had just been given a speeding ticket, or the cops had failed to turn up after she was burgled.

'. . . whereas in a service industry like tourism, there simply is no acceptable excuse for letting the customer down. You do understand that, don't you? I mean, why exactly do you want to change from the police anyway? You don't have some romantic notion of exotic travel at someone else's expense, do you? Because it's not like that at all. It's not *glamorous*, it's hard work, sometimes extremely tedious, and often dealing with people who are boring and annoying.'

While she tried to keep up with this, occasionally offering a conciliatory few sentences that only seemed to irritate the woman more, part of Kathy's brain kept returning to Briony Kidd's outburst. Kathy hadn't tried to contact Brock, because she had been in such a rush, she told herself, but also, she knew, because this time she wanted more than a quick thanks and goodbye from him.

'And apart from the languages problem, it doesn't sound as if you've actually had a great deal of experience of travel, Ms Kolla, have you? I mean, a school trip to Paris . . . Excuse me, have I said something? What's the matter?'

The matter, the reason why Kathy was staring so disconcertingly at the woman, was that Clare Hancock's final throw-away remark had just come back to her, the comment she hadn't understood at the time, the reporter's 'lurking worry' that they'd been given the fatwa story in order to put them off Springer's feud with CAB-Tech. And with it had come the blinding realisation that this remark was very important, for with it the reporter had told her, inadvertently or not, who her informant for the fatwa story was.

'Oh, golly,' Kathy said, and blinked. 'Sorry, where were we?'

The woman stared at her with a mixture of alarm and incredulity, then looked hurriedly at her watch. 'We were just coming to the end, I'm afraid. I have other clients waiting. I suggest you fill in the questionnaire in the reception area outside and leave it with the girl at the desk. We'll be in touch.'

Kathy left the place flattened. She went into the café next door and sat with a cup of short black in front of a mirrored screen in which she saw a reflection of a drained, unemployable female. 'Well done,' she muttered. 'So what exactly can you do right?'

'Kathy! Come in, come in!' Brock seemed genuinely pleased to see her as he waved her to a seat. He looked tired and rumpled, and his secretary Dot had warned Kathy on the way in that he was short of sleep. She had done this, Kathy guessed, because Dot assumed Kathy's visit was about some personal matter Brock could best do without.

'I got your note from Wayne. Many thanks. Helps to paint a clearer picture of Springer's state of mind, if nothing else. Obviously had his knickers badly in a twist.'

'Yes, but suppose there was something in his claim that people at CAB-Tech might want to silence him?'

Brock looked puzzled. 'Oh, I don't see how that's possible, Kathy. You said yourself, in your report, that you didn't believe it.'

'Yes, but still . . . You're positive that this Muslim lad is the killer?'

'Looks pretty convincing, Kathy. I believe we can make a solid case that he had met Springer and had a grudge against him. He's admitted that the green pamphlet was his, and forensic have established that the torn envelope was posted to Springer from the East End, somewhere within a mile of Shadwell Road. So we have evidence of a threat, a motive, and, when we crack his buddies, an opportunity.'

'Is that enough?'

'Well now . . .' Brock considered Kathy carefully, his hand going up to rub the side of his grey beard. 'I'd like more, of course. I'd like the gun and its source, and I'd like residue traces on Ahmed's coat . . . That's why I haven't released any information yet, despite the best efforts of our press office, who are desperate to dampen this fatwa story that's flaring up everywhere now. You've seen this morning's papers? Yes, so . . . what is it, Kathy? I've seen this look before. You've thought of something.'

'Have you worked out where the *Herald* got the fatwa story from?'

'No, wish I had.'

'Could it have been anyone at the university? Did anyone there know that you were working on the possibility of an Islamic extremist?'

Brock thought about that. 'Only one person to my knowledge. The University President. I told him myself.'

Kathy explained about Clare Hancock's puzzling final comment. 'I realised afterwards that it made sense only if she knew that her source might have some interest in suppressing Springer's accusations against CAB-Tech.'

'Someone at the university . . .' He pictured the man sitting in his shirtsleeves at his steel desk in front of his great window, and his desire to control the information that went out to the media. 'Yes, it's possible.'

'And there's something else.' As she told Brock about Briony's claim of Islamic fundamentalists in CAB-Tech, he slowly stiffened upright in his seat with what Kathy thought was the look of someone who'd just discovered that he'd missed his flight, with twenty pensioners from Pontefract waiting at his back.

Professor Haygill's secretary explained that the professor was currently on a plane from the Gulf, and that he wouldn't be returning to the university that day. Could someone else be of assistance? If the Chief Inspector would like some information on CAB-Tech, Professor Haygill's Principal Research Scientist, Dr Tahir Darr, might be able to help. Brock said that would do fine, rang off and raised his eyebrows at Kathy. 'The Gulf!' He looked thoughtful, then added, 'I know you're on leave, Kathy, but since you've been taking a bit of an interest, and since two heads are better than one . . . fancy coming with me?' Again Kathy sensed that she was being gently tested, like an invalid. And on the road out to the East End, Brock went on, in a tone of casual vagueness which Kathy thought contrived, 'So, how are you, anyway? Everything's all right at Suzanne's?'

'It's very comfortable, thanks. She's been good to me.'

'Yes, yes. And you were coming up to town anyway, were you? Only I wouldn't like to think that I'd broken into your leave . . .'

'Clare Hancock did that. But I didn't really mind.' That wasn't true, she thought. At the time she'd minded a lot, like a patient being forced to get out of bed. 'Yes, I had one or two things to do. Nothing serious.'

'Ah. And you met up with Wayne yesterday evening, he tells me. Nice lad.'

'Mm.' Kathy didn't feel inclined to encourage this line of inquiry, but the interrogator had a supplementary.

'Leon was asking after you. He wanted to contact you earlier, but I thought it best you be left in peace for a while. Was I wrong?'

'No, you were right. I couldn't have faced him. Not sure I can now.'

'Ah. And this . . . being out on a case with me again, Kathy. Can you face that I wonder?'

She frowned to herself, both of them keeping their eyes strictly on the road ahead, and she wondered if Suzanne had said something to him.

'To be honest, I'm not absolutely sure.'

'Ah. Because I may not have mentioned it before, but it's always a pleasure to work with you, Kathy. Even if, in this case, it's only temporarily.'

No, she didn't think he had mentioned that before, not in so many words. She waited until he'd negotiated the next lights, then quietly said, 'Thanks.'

Brock was surprised to see the security chief waiting for them at the entrance to the university.

'We didn't need a reception committee, Mr Truck,' he said.

'Don't want you getting lost now, do we, sir?' Truck replied, in the jovially menacing tone that Brock associated with prison warders and drill sergeants.

Brock recognised the blue mirrored ziggurat glinting like a stepped iceberg in the wintry sunlight. 'Is that all CAB-Tech, Mr Truck?'

'It is, sir. Built with Arab money that is. You can sort of tell, don't you think?'

Brock looked around at the other architectural prisms and didn't think he could.

A tall, very dignified South Asian in a spotless white lab coat was waiting for them in the foyer, and introduced himself as Dr Darr. He had the same colouring as Leon, Kathy thought, and the same coolness, but older and not as good looking. As they waited for a glass lift to arrive, he pointed to the plans of the building on an information board, like a series of pineapple slices of diminishing size.

'The central core of the building contains all of the services, electrical, telecommunications, hydraulics, fresh and exhaust air, which are, as you can imagine, very sophisticated in a research facility such as this. From the core the laboratories radiate outward . . .' he paused to emphasise the poetic simile, '. . . like the petals of a flower.'

'And I suppose Professor Haygill's office is at the top?' Brock asked, pointing to the smallest, crowning plan level.

Dr Darr gave a thin smile. 'Actually, no. The Director was emphatic that the top floor, with the best views, should be devoted to the staff relaxation area. It was a functional decision. You see, the staff like to go up there for the views, and there they mix and discuss their work freely and often ideas are sparked between teams who normally wouldn't be working together. We are not a particularly hierarchical organisation. People contribute to the limit of their ability and are rewarded accordingly. Professor Haygill's office is only on the next level up in fact, with the meeting rooms and administrative support.'

The meeting room they were shown to was simply furnished, with a view out across the river to the Dome. The most surprising thing about it was the man sitting at the head of the conference table, the University President, Professor Young.

'They alerted me to your visit,' Young said, and Kathy imagined frantic phone calls and alarms. 'And I thought I'd take the opportunity to keep in touch. Professor Haygill's secretary misinformed you, as it happens. He landed a short time ago. He's on his way here to meet you now.'

Kathy was even more impressed. Had they got a message to Haygill on the plane, or hit him on his mobile while he was queuing for immigration? Young gave no indication of panic, unless it was in the overly languid way he strolled forward and shook their hands. Kathy noticed a small pile of glossy brochures on the table.

'So in the meantime, if there's anything about CAB-Tech's role in the university that I can help you with, be my guest.' He turned to Dr Darr and murmured, 'I think we might leave any technical matters until Richard arrives, Tahir. So we won't detain you.'

Darr nodded and withdrew. From another door a woman looked in.

'What can we offer you?' Young said. 'Tea, coffee?'

Brock shook his head. Turning his back on them, he walked over to the window, staring out at the view. He clasped and flexed his hands behind his back and Kathy realised that he was angry.

The woman left, closing the door silently behind her.

'All right, then.' Brock turned. 'Tell us about CAB-Tech.'

'It's one of our research centres,' Young said, casually easing back in his chair and crossing his legs. 'A particularly successful one. As its name suggests, it works in the field of biotechnology, which of course is a particularly dynamic area of scientific research at present.'

'And it is part of the university, is it? Its staff are your staff?'

'It is semi-autonomous. Its Director, Professor Haygill, is a professor of the university, and Dr Darr there is a senior lecturer. Other research staff are appointed directly by CAB-Tech.'

'From its income which comes from where?'

Young examined his nails. 'Can I ask what this has to do with your inquiries, Chief Inspector?'

'Just interested.'

'Well, it's not a secret. CAB-Tech attracts the major part of its funding from private sources.' He reached forward and slid the brochures across the table to Brock.

'Overseas?'

'Largely.'

'From the Gulf?'

Young nodded.

'And the staff, are they from the Middle East?'

'Oh, good Lord, they come from all over I should think. Stepney to Singapore.'

'But specifically, they include a number of Muslims?'

'Professor Haygill has links with several Middle East universities and his connections in that region make it natural that he should attract staff from there.'

Kathy noticed that both his phrasing and his body language were becoming more guarded.

'Are they militant?'

'Oh, really, what does that mean? I dare say they practise their religion, but they haven't tried storming the Administration Building with Kalashnikovs as far as I've noticed.' His laugh was a sarcastic bark.

'What about the business with the Christmas e-mail?'

That shook Young. 'You've heard about that? What gossip merchants have you been talking to, I wonder?'

'What really happened then?'

'It was simply a storm in a teacup. One of the secretaries on this floor sent out an e-mail to all staff, quite innocently, wishing

90

everyone a happy Christmas, and some of the Muslim researchers objected on the grounds that it was discriminatory and insulting.'

Brock frowned sceptically. 'And?'

'And we instituted conciliation procedures and everything was resolved amicably. End of story.'

'Did you leak that fatwa story to the press, Professor Young?'

Young didn't move, his face lost all expression. He said softly, 'Now, why would I do that? It has the potential to be extremely damaging to us. Already, this morning, Haygill phoned me to say that his partners over there had got wind of it and were disturbed. If I were you, Chief Inspector, I'd concentrate on the job at hand. Find the maniac who killed Springer and let us get on with our work.'

At that moment the door opened and a man bustled in. He had thinning sandy hair, glasses, a slight stoop made worse by the heavy black hand luggage he was carrying, and he wore a lightweight cream suit that seemed exotic in the darkening English winter afternoon.

Young got to his feet and said, 'Ah, Richard. You made it. Let me introduce you.'

Professor Haygill shook hands, slightly breathless, a worried frown on his face. 'I only heard about the dreadful business with Springer on Sunday. And then this report in the papers. I can't believe it. And . . .' he peered more closely at Brock, '. . . you're interested in CAB-Tech? How come?'

Young checked his watch. 'I'd be fascinated to hear the reply to that, gentlemen, but I'm ten minutes late for another meeting. I must go. I'll speak to you later, Richard.' He shook Brock's hand abruptly and walked out, ignoring Kathy.

The side door opened again as Haygill and the two detectives sat down, and the secretary glided in with a mug of coffee that she placed in front of the scientist. 'Ah, lifesaver,' he sighed. 'Will you . . .?' he asked Brock, also ignoring Kathy. Brock shook his head and the woman left once more.

'Two things,' Brock said. 'Much of what you'll have read in the newspaper reports is speculative, but it is true that we have information that suggests that Professor Springer may have been murdered by someone with an Islamic background.'

Haygill looked sombre as he sipped at his drink. 'Extraordinary.'

'So we're interviewing such people who may have had a connection with him, through the university, for example. We understand that a number of your staff are Muslim.'

'Well, that's true, but I doubt they ever had any contact with Springer. But you're welcome to speak to them, of course.'

'The second reason for us coming here is that we'd like to talk to you about the dispute you had with Professor Springer. We understand it was fairly acrimonious.'

Haygill set down the mug wearily. Kathy had the impression of someone weighed down with difficulties.

'On his part, not mine. I have enough real problems to deal with without indulging in misguided philosophical wranglings with the likes of Max.'

'That's what it was, was it? Philosophical? Nothing personal?'

Haygill pursed his lips with exasperation. 'He framed his objections to what we do here in high-flown philosophical terms, but, yes, he frequently expressed himself, publicly, in a very personal and offensive way. It was paradoxical, I thought, that someone supposedly dedicated to clear and objective thought should be so emotional and subjective. But that sort of thing does happen in universities sometimes. I've been around long enough to know that.'

'You didn't respond?'

'As little as possible. From time to time I had to set the record straight and refute his wilder and more slanderous suggestions. I wasn't bothered for myself, but I couldn't let some of the things he said go unchecked, for the sake of my team here, as well as our sponsors and my family.'

Haygill frowned intently at his coffee as if trying to puzzle out some truth hidden in its depths. 'To begin with there were some solid and practical reasons why Springer and I might find ourselves in opposite camps in this institution. Things to do with resources, university policies, academic standing and so on. But after a while those things ceased to matter.' He narrowed his eyes and nodded as if he'd found what he was looking for. 'The real tragedy in all this, the root of the matter, was that what we are doing here matters, and what Max Springer was doing doesn't. That was the plain fact that, at the end of the day, he simply couldn't face.'

Brock said, 'And what is it that you do here, Professor, that matters?'

'I suppose you could say that we're editors . . .' Haygill regarded him with a weary little smile, and Kathy got the impression that he was using an explanation that he'd trotted out many times before, ' . . . editors of the most important book of all, the book of life.'

'The *book*?' Brock asked softly, so innocently that Kathy glanced at him to try to make out what had alerted him.

'The human genome,' Haygill replied, then added quickly. 'You've heard of it, of course. It's had so much publicity lately.'

'Yes, although, I have to admit, I haven't been following it all very carefully. I think I got lost somewhere after the double helix and DNA. I don't remember it being called a book, though.'

'It's a useful metaphor. Almost every cell in your body carries a copy of the "instruction book", if you like, of how to make you and maintain you. If you think of it like that it's easier to understand the way the scientific terms fit together. Shall I stop there, or do you want me to go on?'

'Please. I'm very ignorant. Kathy here probably knows all this stuff. I'm interested in the idea of the book.'

'OK.' Haygill got stiffly to his feet and went over to a whiteboard on the wall and took up a black marker pen. 'The genome has a structure like any ordinary book. It's broken down into twenty-three chapters, called *chromosomes*.' He wrote the word.

'Each chapter contains several thousand paragraphs, or *genes*. And each paragraph is made up of sentences, *exons*, separated by spaces, *introns*, strung in a sequence along a DNA strand. Some paragraphs are long, like the dystrophin gene, and others are short, like the β-globin. The sentences are made up of words, or *codons*, which are composed of just four letters, or *bases*, which we know as *A, C, G* and *T*. OK?'

Brock looked impressed if not enlightened. Haygill put down the marker and returned to his mug of coffee.

'It must be a very long book to hold all the necessary instructions?' Brock asked.

'Oh yes. It has about a billion words, so it's the equivalent of eight hundred bibles long, and it's so compact that it can be carried inside the nucleus of each of your cells. You'll have read about the human genome project, of course. It's the most important scientific frontier at the present time. Teams of people all over the world are studying and deciphering its parts.'

'So you could be described, all of you, as "people of the book", yes?'

Haygill shrugged. 'I suppose so.'

'And how does CAB-Tech fit into this?'

'Our interest is in gene therapy.' He saw the blank look on Brock's face and got to his feet again. On the whiteboard he circled the word *gene*. 'Sixty per cent of these paragraphs in the book are fixed and the same for all humans, but forty per cent are polymorphic, differing slightly from person to person. These variations in the polymorphic genes are what make us unique as individuals, hence genetic fingerprinting, which you people are familiar with, of course.

'Now the book is extraordinarily clever. It's able not only to read itself, but also to copy itself, so that new cells will be able to acquire its information. But in the process of copying a billion words, some, just a few each time, get miscopied with each edition of the book. This is an important natural process, because it allows species to change and evolve, but it also means that harmful errors can happen, which will be damaging to the parent body and cause genetic diseases. Up until now, medicine has hardly been able to deal with these. Until now almost all of the advances in medicine have been concerned with combating diseases and other factors originating outside the body. But now, for the first time, we are able to look inside the book and correct the errors that accumulate in there in the form of genetic diseases. That's what gene therapy is all about, editing the book of life.'

'That's like genetic engineering, then, is it?' Brock asked.

'That's right.'

'Therapy sounds gentler I suppose, less intrusive.' Haygill shot him a questioning glance, and Brock smiled back benignly. 'A massive project, though?'

'Oh, yes. We're looking at just one group of genetic disorders, and even then we have to focus on a small part of the problem at a time. But that's how we move forward.'

'You mean you're looking at one group like, what, cancer?'

'Not exactly. I suppose, from what you've told me, that the most interesting aspect of our work to you would be that it relates to a specific cultural region of the world. Predominantly, to the Islamic regions of the Middle East and South Asia.'

Brock looked puzzled. 'A cultural region? Do you mean, a racial group?'

'The more I learn of human diversity, Chief Inspector, the more convinced I am that the term "racial" has no meaning except as a cultural category.'

'But surely genetic disorders aren't cultural?'

'The ones we study are.' He reached across the table to the glossy brochures and flicked through one of them until he found what he was looking for. He handed it to Brock, pointing to a map of the world on which certain regions, principally in North Africa, the Middle East and parts of South Asia, were shaded pink. The title read, 'Global distribution of areas where consanguineous marriages exceed 10% of total. *Source*: World Health Organisation'.

Haygill said, 'The custom of cousins marrying has been entrenched in some societies for thousands of years. There are sound practical reasons for it, strengthening family structures, stabilising relationships within clans, and so on. Unfortunately it also leads to a much greater frequency of errors in the copying of the human book. The risks of stillbirth and serious congenital malformation are approximately doubled for the offspring of couples who are first cousins. This wasn't especially noticeable when external factors such as malnutrition and disease resulted in high infant mortality, but when living and medical conditions improve, as they have through-out these regions, congenital malformations and chronic disabling diseases in children become more and more apparent. That is our project, Chief Inspector, to find gene therapies to offset the effects of consanguineous marriages.'

It was said, Kathy thought, with an enormous dignity and exhaustion, as if the task and the responsibility were both so noble and so vast that any individual would risk being crushed by it.

'How could Max Springer object to that?' Brock asked.

'How indeed. How indeed.'

'And naturally, the countries that suffer from these diseases would want to fund the work.'

'Yes, through various agencies, the Arab World Bank, the Islamic Health Foundation, and so on. They're listed in the books there. They support a number of teams, some in the Middle East and Pakistan and some in the States, one in France, and us in the UK. We each have particular paragraphs of the book to study, and are developing our own techniques for interventions.'

'And you've made a point of recruiting staff from those regions also, have you?'

'As far as possible, yes.'

'They form a close-knit team, I imagine? Strong sense of loyalty to you and to the project?'

'Yes.' Haygill frowned at him. 'You have a point?'

'Oh, it's just the story we heard about the Christmas e-mail problem, Professor. It made me think that your Muslim team members must feel rather isolated here, somewhat embattled, perhaps, to react in that way?'

'It might seem a trivial matter, but they had some justification for feeling that they had to make a point. This wasn't the first incident. But I'm sure we'll resolve it all in due course.' He passed a hand wearily across his eyes.

'I thought it was resolved.'

'Not yet. An arbitration committee has been appointed, but it hasn't heard all the evidence yet. But Springer had nothing to do with this.'

'And the earlier incidents?'

'Oh, some of our laboratory technicians had a somewhat unfortunate sense of humour. They dubbed our project . . .' he winced and lowered his voice, '. . . the "super-wog project". They even had a scurrilous newsletter that they produced. You can imagine the kind of offence that caused when it got out. There was a disciplinary committee, and the university wanted to dismiss them outright, but the union fought that as an excessive penalty. In the end they were kept on, but moved to another part of the campus. It left a great deal of bitterness all round. Hence the sensitivity to the Christmas e-mail.'

'I see. And again, Springer had no involvement in any of this?'

'Absolutely not. As I say, I'd be very surprised if any of my team, beyond Tahir Darr perhaps, has ever heard of Max Springer. And if you have the slightest reason to doubt it I'd be very much obliged if you'd interview my people as soon as possible and clear this up, because these rumours of some kind of Islamic fatwa against Springer are potentially enormously damaging to us. Do you see that? The reports were causing untold consternation in the Gulf when I left. They're wondering what the hell is going on at UCLE, and I want to distance ourselves absolutely from whatever has happened.'

'I appreciate your cooperation, Professor Haygill. As a start I'd like a complete list of CAB-Tech staff, preferably with some information on their background.'

'That's easy. We keep profiles of our research team updated on file for our funding submissions. I'll get a copy run off for you.'

A giant blood-red sun hung low on the western horizon as they left the CAB-Tech ziggurat, its light glinting on the dark surface of the Thames, shimmering off the prisms of the university buildings.

Kathy turned her collar up against the cold. 'This place is weird, isn't it? What's it trying to be, Disneyland? And the people! The editor of the book of life; a girl wasting five years of her life writing about a theory of action that no one will ever read; a mad old man shot dead on the lecture theatre steps . . . Only the students seem normal.' She watched a group of them hurrying towards the doors of the cafeteria, a couple kissing in the shadow of an overhanging balcony, a youth whistling past on a bike.

'Got time for a drink?' Brock said. 'Somewhere normal.'

IO

The warm fug, the smell of stale beer, the dimly lit browns and creams of the saloon bar of The Three Crowns were all reassuringly normal. Around the walls were old photographs of it in its heyday as a watering hole for the dockers, shipwrights and sailors who had once populated Shadwell Road. From her seat by the window Kathy could see out between the red velvet curtains to the evening crowds of turbaned and saried shoppers who had taken their place, but with rather less patronage for the pub.

Brock sipped his pint thoughtfully as he worked his way through the sheaf of staff biographies Haygill had supplied, each helpfully provided with a photograph in the top corner. He set aside six, which Kathy considered. There were two Pakistanis including Dr Darr, one Egyptian, two Iraqis and a Lebanese. All had impressive academic pedigrees from a mixture of Middle East, UK and US universities, and all had doctorates in the biological sciences with the exception of the Lebanese, who was the team's systems analyst and chief computer programmer.

'You see, what I'm thinking, Kathy . . . well, it's obvious, isn't it?'

'That one or more of these might have put the gun in your wild young tearaway Ahmed's eager little fist.'

Brock nodded. 'Not a conspiracy, necessarily, but something like that. We have a tightly knit, somewhat paranoid group, devoted to their great cause and to Haygill, who is being unjustly harassed by some mad old coot who just won't shut up. And maybe, at the end of another long, hard day, Haygill says, in that weary way of his,

"Who will rid me of this meddlesome priest?" or words to that effect. Not seriously, just out of exasperation.'

'So you'd be looking for someone with some connection to Shadwell Road.'

'Yes. Someone who lives around here, or worships at the Twaqulia Mosque across the way perhaps. Someone who heard about Ahmed beating this pub up, and knows what a charge he'd get from a real mission. Something really important, part of a jihad, involving a real gun, brought in from the Middle East with some shipment of scientific equipment or something.'

'Sounds plausible.'

'Mm. Pity.'

'What?'

'I was just thinking that you would have been the ideal one to tackle these lads, Kathy.'

'Me?' Kathy looked with surprise at the pictures of the swarthy men scowling from the corners of the file sheets. 'Surely a woman would be the last person to put onto them . . .'

'No, no.' Brock waved this aside, taking another swig of his bitter. 'They admire strong women, Kathy. They're disarmed by them. Think of Benazir Bhutto, Hanan Ashrawi . . . er . . . that rather attractive Turkish ex-Prime Minister. Did you know there are more women deputies in the Iranian parliament than women MPs at Westminster?'

'Isn't that a bit of a caricature? *They're* disarmed by strong women?'

Brock smiled. 'Well, the truth is, we all are.'

'Wayne would be ideal, wouldn't he?'

'Special Branch don't interview suspects for us, Kathy. And anyway, I don't agree. I think these boys are far too smart to be taken in by Wayne's hail-fellow, how's-your-father patter, don't you? I mean it might work with some dumb mug down the pub, but these blokes would see through Wayne right away.'

Kathy felt her face burning and reached quickly for her glass.

'But anyway, no matter. It can't be helped. We'll find someone else. Do you want to give it to me now, or do you need another whisky first?'

Kathy blinked. 'Pardon?'

'Whatever it is you've got in that bag that you've been clutching like a live hand-grenade ever since we met.'

'I wasn't aware that . . .'

'Oh, yes. Another whisky then.' Brock got up and ambled over to the bar. He stood chatting to the barman for some time before he returned with her glass refilled. 'He remembers Ahmed's assault on the pub well. Bit of a lark, he thought, once they'd realised that the boy wasn't armed.'

Kathy looked over at the huge character pulling a pint behind the bar, twice Ahmed's body weight. It had taken three of them to subdue him.

'More worrying is that he's heard rumours that the coppers have arrested three Pakistani lads from the estate behind here for the murder of a white professor, and he says he's had a few skinheads dropping in last night and this lunchtime, asking about it. He smells trouble. You've heard about the firebombing of the mosque in Birmingham overnight? We'd better warn the local boys here.' He checked his watch. 'I've got to give a combined briefing to Home Office and Foreign Office staff this evening. That's why this is so important, Kathy.' He tapped the papers Haygill had given them. 'No matter what the reality, if anyone else was involved with Ahmed, it will be seen as a conspiracy, a deliberate attack by a group of Islamics on British lives and freedoms, and all hell will break loose. That's what everyone on both sides is so worried about.' He shook his head gloomily and took another sip before rousing himself. 'So, better let me have it, eh?'

Kathy reached into her bag and pulled out an envelope. 'I wasn't sure whether to give it to you just yet.'

Brock nodded, took out a neatly folded handkerchief to wipe some froth from his beard. 'I have one just like it in my desk drawer in the office. It's dated the fifth of September 1976. My marriage was breaking up at the time, things getting on top of me. I gave it to my boss, and he opened his desk drawer and took out another one just like it, dated 1957. He took mine and put it with his own in the drawer and said he'd keep them there together for a while, to see what happened. After a month I went and asked him for it back.'

Kathy stared down at the envelope in her fingers. 'Suzanne told you?'

'Absolutely not. No need. Goodness, Kathy, it would be unnatural if you hadn't done something like that.'

'But maybe . . .' Her voice dropped to a whisper. 'What I'm thinking is that I've lost my nerve, Brock.'

'Hm.' Brock scratched the side of his beard. 'How did it feel, returning to Queen Anne's Gate to see me this afternoon?'

'Strange. I felt detached.'

'Physically uncomfortable?'

Kathy shook her head.

'And did the thought of interviewing these blokes tomorrow make you feel sick in the pit of your stomach?'

'No.'

'Kathy,' he leaned forward intently and covered her hand with his big fist, 'I'm not a psychiatrist, but I've seen people who have lost their nerve. Whatever it is you've lost, or temporarily displaced, it isn't that, believe me.' He glanced up and saw the publican looking at them. The man grinned and gave him a big wink. Brock hurriedly took his hand from Kathy's and leaned back against the padded pub seat.

Kathy sat in silence for a while, head bowed. Then she said, 'If I interview these men, I have a condition.'

'I wasn't serious about that, Kathy. I only raised it to see how you really felt. There are lots of people I can put onto it. You get back to Suzanne and take the rest of your leave. Decide what you want to do about that letter.'

'Maybe it would be easier to do that if I was here. I mean, pacing up and down the Hastings sea front in January doesn't necessarily give you a clearer perspective on anything.'

'Well, that may be. What was the condition?'

'I'd want PC Talbot with me.'

Brock's face dropped. 'I'd hoped I'd spent enough time on PC Talbot. You know the Federation's getting quite militant about his case. Why him?'

'Because he's the most likely to recognise any of them if they've shown their face around Shadwell Road.'

'That's true.' He thought for a moment, then came to a decision. 'All right, Kathy, you're on. We'll get Special Branch to check these characters overnight, and you and PC Talbot can get started first thing in the morning, even if it means risking the first police strike since World War One.'

'What's wrong with now?' Kathy said, snapping the clasp on her shoulder bag. 'According to the list they gave you, most of these men are living in hostel accommodation on the UCLE campus. We might get to them all tonight, while Wayne does his stuff on their past records.'

'What about PC Talbot?' Brock said, looking worried as he tried to work out which point in the hierarchy to attack first.

'Can we get him a baby-sitter? His wife's on nights at the hospital. I'm sure I could talk him into coming out with me for an evening if we can take care of his kid.'

Brock grinned with relief. 'Kathy, I don't know what I did without you. Anything else?'

'Well, if these blokes are as touchy as they sounded over the Christmas e-mail, and if they are involved in some way, we're going to need back-up, maybe armed, and on campus.'

'Yes. As discreet as possible.' He drained his glass and got to his feet, slipping Kathy's envelope into his pocket. 'A race riot *and* a police strike. Now that would be something for one night. I hope you're not going to make me regret this, Kathy.'

She swallowed her whisky. 'Not losing your nerve, are you, Brock?'

They started with Dr Tahir Darr, the senior researcher of the team, and the oldest. He was still working in one of the laboratories in the CAB-Tech building when they arrived, and he recognised Kathy from their earlier meeting. He glanced dismissively at Greg Talbot, who stood back, saying nothing, looking very junior and inoffensive out of uniform, and clearly Darr felt unthreatened as Kathy worked through the first set of questions she'd prepared. He'd been with Professor Haygill for over three years now, and when he talked of the team 'we' had built up, the work 'we' were engaged in, he was referring to Haygill and himself as the prime movers of CAB-Tech.

It was only when she went on to more personal matters that he began to look at her more quizzically and measure his answers more carefully. Yes, he was a practising Muslim, and attended the East London Mosque in the Whitechapel Road, the oldest in London, and why was that any concern of hers? Kathy explained that, with all the loose and inflammatory speculation recently concerning the Springer case, the police were anxious to be able to protect people who might come under unjustified attention, especially those on campus.

'But isn't that the excuse that police have always used, for collecting dossiers on everyone?' Darr exclaimed, with a ferocious flash of his brilliant white teeth. 'You're doing it for our own protection! How very kind!'

'My boss, Detective Chief Inspector Brock, whom you met, discussed this with your boss, Professor Haygill, very carefully this afternoon,' Kathy smiled back, playing what she assumed to be her best card. 'Professor Haygill was in complete agreement, in fact very insistent, that we speak to you. But if there's any question you'd feel uncomfortable about answering, then please don't.'

'Oh, but then I'm being uncooperative, which is only a small step down from being a trouble-maker, no?'

Kathy struggled on, mentally striking off her list the questions she'd prepared on the Christmas e-mail saga. Yes, Dr Darr had been aware of Professor Springer's attacks on Professor Haygill. Springer was a very foolish, irrational old man who had lost touch with the realities of life, quite beneath contempt, more to be pitied. No, he couldn't recall the CAB-Tech team ever discussing Springer before the murder, why would they? He may have raised the matter with Professor Haygill at some stage, he wasn't sure, but Professor Haygill had no wish to talk of such foolishness. At the time of Springer's death he, along with all the other members of the team, was working here in the laboratories, naturally. And he had no theories to explain why anyone should want to kill the old man.

At the end of it, Kathy felt as tense as if she'd been stepping through a minefield, though Darr seemed rather pleased. 'Have I satisfied you, Sergeant?' he demanded, beaming.

'I believe so. Do you know where I can find the other members of the team, Doctor?'

Darr's good humour abruptly evaporated. 'The others? But I have spoken for everyone. It will not be necessary for you to interview them. I cannot agree to it.'

'Professor Haygill was quite specific, Dr Darr. We have to speak to everyone. You could talk to him if you want to check.'

After a tense little negotiation Darr relented. The two Iraqis were working in another lab on the floor below. The others he wasn't sure about. As they made their way there they marvelled at the equipment they passed, ranks and batteries of gleaming machines stretching away in all directions, all looking new and well maintained. Greg Talbot compared it to the dismal state of the technology available at Shadwell Road police station.

'Ah, but you're not editing the book of life, Greg,' Kathy said. 'You're just trying to stop it nicking cars.'

Talbot hadn't recognised any of the photographs on the staff information sheets, but they had made an arrangement that he would pull out the purple handkerchief he carried and blow his nose if he thought he knew them when they were interviewed, and he confirmed that he'd never seen Darr before. When they found the two Iraqis the purple handkerchief remained in his pocket. They had none of the confidence and bluster of the senior researcher, and Kathy wondered what experiences they'd had with police in the past as each in turn answered her in low monosyllables, eyes on the floor. They also worshipped at the East London Mosque and denied having heard of Springer before his death.

They moved on, leaving the warmth of the CAB-Tech building and hurrying through the cold night to the extreme east end of the campus developments, where a series of serrated-roofed zigzag blocks along the waterfront provided dormitory accommodation.

'They're like monks,' Kathy muttered as they followed the colonnade behind Block A towards Block C. 'Haygill's team. They're all either single or they've left their families behind. They toil by day in the labs and retire at night to their cells to pray.'

The stairwells and corridors were spartan, clean and free of graffiti and the two police met no one, although from time to time they would hear the sounds of music or a TV behind a closed door, and smell cooking. The Lebanese computer expert answered their knock at room C-210 and Kathy knew as soon as she registered his face, and even before Greg Talbot started loudly blowing his nose, that he was the one.

Afterwards she tried to work out how she had been so certain. He had been warned of their coming, that was obvious, and no doubt Darr had been on the phone to all of them as soon as they'd left his lab. But it wasn't that he had mentally composed himself for their arrival. It was something to do with the look and body tension beneath the composure, a mixture of fright and exhilaration and relief, as if he'd been preparing himself for much longer than the half hour Darr would have given him for this first bold stare into the eyes of his fate. It radiated from him and she felt it instantaneously, and knew, as soon as she met his eyes and smiled at him, that he knew she had picked it up.

Without a word he stepped back into the room to let them in. A monk's cell it was, Kathy thought, with barely enough possessions to fill a small suitcase, and cold, as if to test his resolve and his faith.

'Mr Khadra?' Kathy asked, continuing to smile at him. 'Mr Abu Khadra?'

He was an extremely attractive young man, she thought, lean and svelte like a colt, with delicate, sensitive features and large dark eyes. His hair was cut short, his ears tight against his skull emphasising the impression of intense alertness, and he was wearing a white T-shirt, black jeans and a pair of old trainers, once white but now worn and grey. Behind him, on a small wooden table, a book lay open.

He answered her questions with barely more words than the Iraqis had used, but with a calm that brought back to Kathy the word that the student Briony Kidd had used about Max Springer, 'serene'.

He went to mosque in Shadwell Road, he said, and Kathy wasn't in the least surprised. She was about to ask him if he'd ever met a Pakistani boy there, by the name of Ahmed Sharif, when her phone began to ring. She frowned with annoyance and turned away to answer it. It was Brock, sounding tense and short of time. She excused herself and went out into the deserted corridor.

'Kathy, how far have you got?'

'We're on number four, the Lebanese.'

'Anything?'

'This one's promising. Definitely a possible.' She was conscious of her voice sounding loud in the empty corridor.

'Nothing more concrete?'

'Not yet.'

'Well, we've got a problem. Just had a call from Haygill. Dr Darr's been onto him, complaining that your questions are personal and intrusive and insulting to their faith, and now Haygill's denying that he gave us permission to interview his staff individually. Says he'd meant for him to approve the questions first and to be present. Darr's obviously put the wind up him, told him he's got another Christmas e-mail situation on his hands, and he says he'll get the University President to kick us off the campus if we don't stop what we're doing immediately and wait for him to come over to mediate.'

'How long will that take?'

'He's at home in Enfield, in his pyjamas. Darr caught him just as he was going to bed, exhausted from his trip. He's very agitated and wanted us to leave it until morning. When I refused he said I'd have to meet him at the university to negotiate with him, but I'm tied up with this bloody meeting for at least another half hour.'

'What do I do?'

'Leave.'

'Can I take this one with me? I think . . .'

'Definitely not. If Haygill gets too stroppy we'll go back in with warrants, but for the moment we'll do it his way. I promised him you two would get off the campus right away.'

Kathy returned to room C-210 where Abu Khadra and Greg Talbot were standing exactly where she had left them, in silence. She gave the Arab a big warm smile. 'Well, that'll be all, Mr Khadra. We'll leave you in peace now.'

'You're going?' He looked mystified.

'Yes, we're quite satisfied, thank you.' Her eyes met his and she knew immediately that he didn't believe it for a minute. 'If I have forgotten anything, will you be staying here for the rest of the evening?'

He nodded, still mystified, and they left. When Greg started to say something outside in the corridor she put a finger to her lips and led him away. Not until they were well clear of the building did she explain what had happened.

'That's too bad,' he said, 'I was beginning to enjoy it. That last one was promising, I reckon. I know I've seen him around.'

Kathy nodded agreement. More than promising, she thought, trying to put aside her sense of misgiving. She wondered how Wayne O'Brien's research was going, but couldn't reach him on her phone and left a message. Then she and Greg bought some fish and chips and settled down in her car beneath the track of the Docklands Light Rail to wait for Brock's instructions.

They got Brock's call to meet him at Haygill's office at 8:15 p.m., sooner than Kathy had expected. Darr had adopted a defensive position behind the director's right side, and scowled at them as they entered the room. His boss looked grey and exhausted, and it was this that got things moving. Once the initial conciliatory sentiments had been expressed, Haygill and Brock quickly agreed that they should jointly witness the remaining interviews, and when Darr began to repeat all his grounds for objecting to Kathy's questions Haygill silenced him by asking him to get Abu Khadra.

While they waited, Brock passed Kathy a note. She opened it and read the fax, from Wayne O'Brien to Brock.

'One result only so far. Abu Khadra was arrested by Israeli army in south Lebanon under emergency powers in 1989. Then aged fifteen years. Held for twenty-one days. No further record.'

Darr returned shortly to say that Abu wasn't answering his phone, and that he'd sent the two Iraqis over to his room to fetch him. They rang back a few minutes later with the news that there were was a light on in C-210 but the door was locked and there was no response to their knocks.

'He's probably just popped out to visit someone,' Darr suggested huffily, but Kathy knew otherwise and Brock saw the look on her face and said quietly to Haygill, 'Maybe it would be wise to go over there, and get security to meet us there with a key. What do you think?'

For a moment Haygill looked confused and uncomprehending, then Brock's tone registered and anxiety brought him to his feet. 'Yes . . . Yes, you're right.'

They hurried across the windswept campus, heels clattering on the wet concrete paving slabs, to find the corridor to room C-210 now filled with people. Other CAB-Tech team members had joined the Iraqis, and a number of residents had been attracted out of their rooms by their shouts and the banging on Abu's door. Two of Mr Truck's security men were there too, bulky in thickly padded jackets and military style caps. Haygill exchanged a few terse words with them, and the gathering fell silent as one of them pulled out a bunch of keys.

Whatever worse fears the spectators might have had didn't just evaporate when the door swung open and they saw into the empty room, for although there was no Abu lying unconscious on the little bed or slumped with a rope around his neck, there was still something immediately disconcerting about the room's bareness which gave an almost supernatural dimension to his vanishing. There were no postcards on the pinboard, no creases on the bedcover, and no curtains on the window to hide the sinister blackness of the river beyond. Only the book lying open on the bare table confirmed that he had once been there.

Brock stepped forward to examine it. No one else seemed inclined to follow him into the room. After a moment he called back over his shoulder, 'Dr Darr. Do you or one of your colleagues read Arabic?'

'Yes, sir,' Darr declared, and waved one of the Iraqis to step with him to Brock's side.

'It is the Qur'an, sir.'

'Yes. He's underlined one of the verses, here. What does it say?'

The Iraqi stooped to read, then straightened and stared meaningfully at Darr and murmured something. Darr whispered in return, then took a deep breath.

'It concerns the fate of martyrs, sir,' he said at last, reluctantly, clinging to the formal mode of address like a shield.

'Could you translate it, please?'

Darr muttered to the Iraqi, who began to recite.

'"Don't think that those who are slain in the cause of Allah are dead. They are alive and in the presence of their Lord, who looks after them and heaps gifts upon them. They are happy that those they have left behind suffer neither fear nor grief. They rejoice in Allah's grace and bounty . . ."'

A murmuring broke out among the people in the corridor as they picked this up, and phrases were repeated for those who hadn't heard. Some men began to press forward into the room to see the book for themselves. Brock spoke to the security guards, asking them to clear the crowd, which they began to try to do, with some difficulty. He turned to Darr and the Iraqi again. 'Where could he have gone?' he demanded.

They shook their heads. Abu was always the outsider in the team, Darr explained, because of his work, in computers rather than the science. He worked to a different pattern, a different timetable. He attended a different mosque.

'In Shadwell Road? Why there? Did he know people there? Friends?'

They shook their heads, uncertain.

''Ang on.' PC Talbot spoke up. 'I've got 'im now. He drove a motorbike, didn't he? A little yellow Yamaha.'

They nodded, yes. His pride and joy.

'Yeah, I can picture 'im now. With a black helmet. I've seen 'im down the Road a lot. I thought he lived there.'

Brock turned to Haygill, who was hovering just inside the door to the room as if he wanted to be anywhere but there. 'Anything you can add, Professor?'

The scientist cleared his throat. 'Er . . . Excellent worker. Good computer people are like hen's teeth these days, and Abu is outstanding. A brilliant young man. He's had offers from other places, but he's stayed with us. Believes in the work.'

'Any relatives in this country?'

'Not to my knowledge. His family is all in Lebanon, I understand. He went to the Gulf to study. University of Qatar.'

That seemed to be all that they knew of Abu, or were prepared to tell, and Brock asked them to leave while he and Kathy carried out a search of the room. Its emptiness extended into all its corners, no hangers in the wardrobe, no fluff beneath the bed.

'I don't think he did live here,' Kathy said finally. 'He didn't have enough time to clean it out this thoroughly.'

Only the book seemed to bear any signs of vital human life, its pages interleaved with small fragments of Abu's past, an old postcard of the Roman ruins at Ba'albek in the Beqa'a Valley of Lebanon, some letters in spidery Arabic, some photographs, an elderly smiling woman wearing traditional headdress, a family group at a table, two little girls, a middle-aged European.

'Bloody hell,' Brock said, lifting up the last picture for Kathy to see.

It had been cut from a glossy printed page, and the face was younger by ten or fifteen years, the unruly bush of hair thicker and darker, the face plumper, but it was certainly him.

'Springer?' Kathy asked.

'Springer,' Brock nodded. 'Our victim.'

He turned the paper over but the back was blank. 'Looks like it's come from the dust-cover of a book,' Brock suggested. 'His autobiography maybe.'

He put the picture back between the leaves and stared at Kathy. 'The book of his life.'

11

They went first to Shadwell Road police station and made arrangements with the duty inspector to call in additional officers from surrounding divisional stations. Soon they were joined by Bren Gurney and a carload of people from Serious Crime, including Leon Desai.

Bren cornered Kathy soon after he arrived. 'Leon insisted on coming over with us, Kathy. What do you want me to do? Send him off somewhere?'

Kathy's heart sank. So her break-up with Leon was common knowledge. And she had fondly hoped that people didn't even know they'd been having an affair. Some hope.

'Doesn't matter,' she said, aiming for total indifference but hearing herself sound snappy. 'Not an issue.'

Leon himself appeared shortly after. 'Kathy, can I have a word?'

'I'm very busy, Leon,' she said, although embarrassingly she suddenly found herself with nothing particular to do.

'Yes, but why?' He was pressing too close to her, trying to keep his voice low as people passed by in the narrow corridor.

'Why what?'

'Why are you involved in this? You're supposed to be on stress leave. Did Brock make you come back?'

She turned on him then. 'It's none of your bloody business, Leon. Just bugger off and leave me alone.'

'Kathy, I'm concerned!' He choked off whatever he'd been going to add as two men newly arrived from the Divisional Intelligence

Unit called out a greeting to a small black woman from the Race Hate Unit at Rotherhithe.

'You were told to take time off. And you shouldn't be involved in this,' he hissed under his breath. 'This Special Branch stuff, it's not even your area. I'm going to speak to Brock.'

'You'll do no such thing!' Her yell startled the others, who turned to see what was going on.

'Let's talk about it, then.' He was pleading now, and she hated it more than his high-handedness.

'Leave – me – alone,' she said, slowly and deliberately. 'I don't want your advice. Do you understand?'

He stared at her, and she saw his dark eyes filled with hurt, and understood finally what was going on. *This Special Branch stuff . . .* She thought, some undercover man Wayne O'Brien turned out to be. I should start my own 'Kathy's love-life' website, just in case some distant outpost of the Met isn't quite up to date.

Brock padded up the stairs, Bren at his shoulder, wondering if anyone had actually made an arrest before in their stockinged feet. No doubt they had, and in frogmen's suits and tails and long johns too, but there was something peculiarly subversive about being made shoeless, as if the whole ominous dignity of the occasion might be punctured by a pin dropped on the carpet. His hope was that the place would be as quiet as the last time he'd come here, but his optimism began to fade as he picked up sounds filtering down from the upstairs hall, and died altogether when they reached the top and opened the doors. There were maybe two dozen men on their knees in prayer, another dozen in small huddles squatting on the carpet, and one larger group, like an adult class – nearly fifty men in all, enough to start a riot or a massacre.

He scanned their faces, aware of a number of them looking suspiciously at the two of them in their coats and socks. He couldn't spot anyone resembling Abu, but he did recognise Imam Hashimi, who appeared to be leading the adult education group. The imam caught sight of him at the same instant, and a look of alarm appeared on his face. He gave some kind of instruction to his group, jumped to his feet and hurried over.

'What do you want here?' he demanded, voice low.

'Your help, Imam Hashimi,' Brock said.

'No!' the man said, agitated. 'Please go at once. You are not welcome here.'

At the same time another man came sidling over, trying to hear what was being said. He must have caught the tone of anger in the imam's voice, for he said, 'Is everything all right? Are you in need of assistance, Imam?'

'No, no. Everything is fine.'

Several more men approached, and Brock recognised Manzoor, the owner of the clothes shop next to the police station, looking particularly dapper in dark business suit and silk polka dot tie. Manzoor recognised Brock too and hurried forward eagerly. 'This is the police, Imam! This is Scotland Yard!'

'It's all right, Sanjeev!' Imam Hashimi anxiously flapped both hands at him in an attempt at a calming gesture. 'They want my assistance. I will have to talk to them.'

But Manzoor wasn't ready to be put off. 'Is it about the Sharif boy, Superintendent? Have you arrested him? Did he murder the professor?'

A small crowd was gathering now, and the men who had been at prayer were beginning to sit up, looking round in bewilderment.

'No, Mr Manzoor,' Brock said firmly. 'We haven't charged anyone in connection with that case. I want to speak to the Imam about a private matter. There's no need for concern.'

Manzoor looked disappointed and the imam took advantage of his hesitation to guide the two policemen away to the door to his office, which he shut firmly behind them.

'You see? You see how troubled they all are? You shouldn't have just walked in here. You should have phoned.' He spoke in a kind of strangled whisper for fear of ears at the door, but his extreme agitation needed an outlet and he paced back and forward in the small space, gesturing with his hands. 'You should have made an appointment!'

'I'm sorry, but there hasn't been time for that. This is a very urgent matter we need your help with.'

'No! No, no, no! I helped you once and what happened? Three of our young people are in your hands for over twenty-four hours now, and you say you haven't charged them with any offence? How is this possible? Their families come and ask my advice, and what can I say to them? That I was the one who delivered them up to you?'

'Everything is being done according to the law, Imam Hashimi. Tell them to get legal advice.'

'Do you think I don't do that? But what happens when they find out that I supplied the addresses?'

'I haven't told anyone that, and I have no intention of doing so.'

'All the same, you were seen here, before the boys were arrested . . .'

'Look, I'm sorry, but time is very short. We came here to try to prevent a death, Imam. One of your parishioners has disappeared and we fear the worst. He left us a message. I think you will understand my concern when I tell you what it was.'

The imam stopped pacing and faced Brock. 'Yes?'

'A verse from the Qur'an, Chapter Three.'

'The Imrans? Yes?'

'Verse one hundred and seventy.'

He frowned in thought, and then his eyes widened and he whispered, '"Do not account those who are slain in the cause of Allah, as dead" . . . Who is this person?'

'A young man by the name of Abu Khadra, a Lebanese, who works at the university. He worships here with you.'

The imam shook his head slowly, frowning, 'No, I don't know the name.'

Brock handed him a copy of the photo from Haygill's files, but still Hashimi shook his head, then went to the record book on his desk and searched for some minutes before looking up. 'No, he is not one of our people.'

'Perhaps he just comes unannounced, without introducing himself, or under another name. He is devout, I believe, and he has been seen in Shadwell Road. We think he may have a room in the area, and friends.'

'What has he done?'

Brock hesitated. 'We're not sure. But we think he can clarify whether your three young men are innocent or not.'

'You mean he may have led them astray?'

'That's a possibility. I wonder, if you were to ask some of your

114

most faithful and regular worshippers, they might tell you if they have seen him here?'

Imam Hashimi thought about that, then nodded agreement and went to the door. He returned ushering in half a dozen of the more senior men and a couple of younger ones. Manzoor was among them, shouldering his way to the front. The imam explained in English Brock's request for information about the man whose picture he passed round and whose name he told them. Someone then asked a question in another language, and some discussion followed in what Brock took to be Urdu. From time to time the men would glance at him, as if his appearance might clarify some point. Finally Manzoor spoke up. He seemed agitated, striking the air with his fist to emphasise what he said, and giving Brock a look of veiled cunning. The others seemed to agree, and the imam then returned to English to announce to Brock that no one had ever seen this Abu Khadra in the mosque, although some thought they may have seen him in the Shadwell Road in the past. As they filed out of the office, Brock reflected that it had taken an awful lot of discussion to arrive at this conclusion, and wished that he'd been able to understand Urdu. Imam Hashimi patted the last departing man on the back and closed the door again.

'No, he is not from our congregation,' he said firmly.

'That's disappointing. He specifically mentioned coming to the mosque in Shadwell Road.'

'Well, now, that is possible. There is another mosque, though strictly speaking, we do not consider them to be Muslim.'

'I don't follow.'

'They are Shia. You are aware of the five pillars of our faith, are you, Chief Inspector? They define the necessary steps to be a Muslim. First the shahadah, the profession of faith; second the ritual of worship and prayer, salah; third sawm, which is fasting during the month of Ramadan; fourth is Zakaat, or almsgiving; and fifth is the pilgrimage to Mecca, the hajj.'

Brock tried to interrupt, but Hashimi wouldn't be stopped. His voice rose and he went on, 'The most important of these is the first, the shahadah, which is a form of words which must never be changed. The Shiites however, in their misguided error, use a different form of words. Therefore they are not true Muslims. You see?'

'And where is their mosque?'

'They call it the Nur al-Islam mosque. A miserable affair. I have never been to it, of course, but I am told it is a very inferior place. They are mainly Yemeni, you know.' He shook his head. 'A primitive, desert people.'

'Is it on Shadwell Road?' Bren asked.

'In Chandler's Yard. You know The Three Crowns public house? Well, it stands on the corner of Shadwell Road and Chandler's Yard. Go down there. There is a café, the Horria Café, run by a man called Qasim Ali. You might ask for him. He is what they call a "muwasit", what you might call a "Mr Fix-it". If your man is down there, he will know of it.'

They thanked him and left, aware of the eyes that followed them in absolute silence across the hall, and then the murmur that began as soon as they reached the stairs. Out on the street a soft drizzle had dispersed most of the pedestrians, and Brock spoke into his phone for a moment, then they crossed the street and made towards The Three Crowns and beside it the narrow entrance to Chandler's Yard.

After twenty yards the narrow laneway broadened into the cobbled square that had once formed the focus of the local candle-making industry from which Chandler's Yard had taken its name. The jumble of old workshops and storehouses which stood around the yard still bore the marks of their old occupation, their brickwork blackened and door jambs scarred, like veteran craftsmen irretrievably gnarled by a lifetime of labour. Among them, as flamboyant as a belly dancer, glowed the bright shopfront and garish red neon sign of the Horria Café.

Inside, four old men played cards at a table beneath a silent TV showing a soccer game, while an ancient juke-box at their side throbbed with Arab music. A very fat, dark-skinned man behind the counter wiped fingers like sticky pork sausages across a grubby apron and then flicked at his bushy moustache. He narrowed his eyes at the newcomers suspiciously, and Brock wondered if he was going to need an interpreter to communicate with these 'primitive desert people'.

After due consideration, the fat man spoke. 'Yes, gents. What can

I do for you?' he said affably in a broad cockney accent. 'I got a fresh load of chips on. Stewed lamb's the speciality of the house, if yer interested.'

'It smells very good,' Brock said, feeling suddenly remarkably hungry. 'Maybe later. Right now we're looking for a Mr Qasim Ali. Know where we might find him?'

'Who wants 'im?'

Brock showed him his warrant card.

The man peered at it, then nodded and held up his fat hand. 'I'm Ali.'

Brock took the hand, warm, smooth and with a surprisingly hard grip.

'We're wondering if you can put us in touch with someone we need very urgently to talk to, Mr Ali. A young Lebanese man, twenty-six, name of Abu Khadra, rides a yellow Yamaha bike.' Brock showed him the picture. Ali gave no sign of recognition as he studied it and slid it back. He reached beneath the counter, produced a pack of Benson and Hedges and a Bic lighter, and slowly lit up, wheezing a long draw.

'How come you came to me then? No, let me guess. Was it them wankers out there?' He jerked a hand in the general direction of Shadwell Road, the gesture making the flesh of his arm wobble. 'The Pakis? Yeah, that'd be right. Any shit they don't want, they pass it on to old Ali, eh?'

He tipped his head back and exhaled towards a fan slowly beating time with the music. His head began to rock with it. 'Umm Kalthoum, that is. They don't make singers like that any more. You heard of Umm Kalthoum?'

'I believe I have,' Brock replied. 'Egyptian?'

'Yeah. The greatest. This place is named after one of her biggest hits. Horria. That means "freedom", see? Very important, yeah? We all value our freedom. What's he wanted for, this Abu Khadra?'

'We just want to talk to him. But there's some concern about his state of mind. So there's some urgency . . .' Brock could sense Bren stirring impatiently at his side.

'Lebanese. What, is he an illegal? Is that it?'

'No, no.'

'No, it'd 'ave to be something more serious than that, wouldn't it?

They wouldn't send two big blokes like you out looking for one little illegal, would they?'

'The person who suggested we come to you, Mr Ali, said that you were the one man who would know what was going on around here. However, if you can't help us . . . There's a mosque in Chandler's Yard isn't there? Where can we find that?'

Ali stared at Brock, then crushed his half-smoked cigarette in a saucer on the counter. 'I didn't say I couldn't help. I just resent those newcomers strutting around, throwing their weight around like they own the place.'

'Newcomers?'

'Yeah, the Pakis.' He thrust his two forearms like hams onto the counter and leaned forward to make his point. 'Tell me, you'd consider yourself a Londoner, would you? 'Ow long's your family been 'ere? One generation? Two?'

Brock took a deep breath, trying to remain calm, and replied, 'Two, I suppose. They came from up north.'

'Yeah, and what about your friend there, who's lookin' so impatient? How long 'as your family been 'ere, squire?'

Bren answered stolidly, 'I'm the first.'

'Right. So you're like them out there, newcomers. Did you know that the Yemenis are the oldest Muslim residents of London? My great-grandfather was 'ere when the old queen died – Victoria that is. We came 'ere 'cause the Merchant Navy made an 'abit of picking up engine-room crews everywhere they went. Sixteen men to a crew – twelve stokers, three greasers and one donkeyman – all the same race, no mixing. Sixteen Chinese from Singapore, sixteen blacks from the West Indies, sixteen Yemenis from Aden, see? And when they got back to England they dropped them off wherever they landed, Newcastle, Cardiff, London.'

'That's very interesting, Mr Ali, but . . .'

'I 'aven't finished yet. My point, you see, is that as Londoners of such long standing, we may feel a certain obligation to shelter a stranger of our own faith, cast ashore among us, without necessarily knowing all of his circumstances.'

'I understand.'

'I 'ope you do. 'Ave you got a search warrant?'

'No.'

Ali lowered his head, pondering, then said quietly, 'The mosque is up those stairs.' He nodded towards stairs at the back of the café. 'The kid's praying. He's been 'ere for over an hour.'

'Thank you. Is there anyone else up there with him?'

'No.'

'And would you know if he's armed, by any chance?' Brock asked mildly.

The fat man looked startled. 'Blimey. I dunno about that. Are you expecting trouble?'

'Thanks very much for your help, Mr Ali. Tell me, would it be very disrespectful if we kept our shoes on, under the circumstances?'

Qasim Ali gave his dispensation, then hurried over to get the four elders, protesting, to their feet.

The young man kneeling on the middle of the carpet in the little room which served as the Shiite mosque of Shadwell Road looked slight and vulnerable in his white T-shirt and jeans. In the lobby outside, above his grey trainers, a dark coat hung from a peg. It looked to Brock very much like the coat they had seen on the assassin in the security film, but there was no weapon in its pockets, or on the person of Abu, who submitted to his arrest without surprise or resistance.

Umm Kalthoum's song throbbed plaintively in the deserted café as they led the young man out into Chandler's Yard. The rain had stopped, leaving puddles on the cobbles. There was no one in the dark square or laneway, but beyond they could see many figures moving about under the brighter streetlighting of Shadwell Road.

'Let's make this quick,' Brock said, and they hurried forward, each gripping one of the lad's elbows, his wrists cuffed together at his back. It wasn't until they were practically out into the main street that they realised that the people there were waiting for them. They stopped abruptly as the crowd recognised the detectives and cries went up, 'Here they are! Here, here!' Brock recognised faces from the Twaqulia Mosque, eager, excited, among the people pressing forward to see who they had brought out of the yard.

'Let's keep moving,' he murmured, and they stepped forward again, holding Abu tight between them. As they passed the corner entrance of The Three Crowns they saw the doors were open, a group of pale-faced young men standing against the light, shaved heads. One of them shouted, 'Hello, Abu!' and Abu twisted between the detectives to try to see who had called his name. Others from the doorway joined in, right arms raised, their yells becoming a chant, 'Aaa–booo, Aaa–booo.' Brock saw alarm growing on the faces of the crowd from the mosque as the chanting youths fell into step behind them. The crowd wavered as Brock and Bren pressed forward, stepping out into the roadway, then they heard a scream and a running of feet from behind a group of turbaned men ahead. The men turned and began to scatter and in a sudden clatter of boots more skinheads were bursting through from the front. One was swinging something, an axe handle or a baseball bat, others throwing punches and now everyone was shouting and screaming and running. Bren swore, his arm raised to block a blow as they charged on, almost lifting the man between them off his feet in their effort to keep their momentum. Brock felt a numbing blow to his knee, hands grabbing at his arm trying to drag him down, a boot flailing past. Then more shouts and he glimpsed the entrance to the police station ahead and uniformed men running out, batons in their hands. A scream of pain very close to his left ear, then a surge as they stumbled clear and hands were hauling them inside. Bren was shouting something. 'Made it . . . bloody made it . . .' But Brock was too winded to speak, his ears singing, and it was a moment before he realised that their prisoner was lying face down on the floor between them, not moving.

They rode together in the ambulance, the three of them, Brock, Bren and Abu, but the young Lebanese was dead before they reached the hospital, two deep stab wounds in his back. Apart from these almost invisible wounds he was unblemished, in contrast to the other two who were battered and bloody.

It was several hours before Kathy was able to see either of them. She sat in the casualty waiting room, watching the staff process a motor-bike accident case, an asthmatic child, two men hurt in a pub fight, a coronary victim, and decided that there were worse things than being a copper. It was exactly a month since she'd lain on a bed in a place just like this, waiting to be treated. The harsh lighting, the smells, the sense of an invisible but relentless process, all seemed designed to bring home the reality of the fragility of life. Here all the comforting little props and reassurances of normal routine were stripped away. You came here damaged, hoping to be saved and put together again.

She had seen it all from an upstairs window of the police station, from an office where they had the computer link to CRIS, the Crime Report Information System, which she was trying to trawl for information about Abu Khadra. In truth she'd gone there to keep out of the way while Leon Desai was around, an absurd and unnecessary reaction since he'd made himself scarce immediately after their encounter. The fact was that his vulnerability and her reaction to it had shaken her. She had never seen him off-balance like that before, and her response had been so hostile because she had felt herself being touched by it. She realised that she was tempted to think back again over the time they had spent together before Christmas, to pick over the memories of what for a few short days had seemed euphoric, to find new, more forgiving interpretations of their split. And she was resolved not to do that. She had decided on a fresh start, and that was that.

So she'd bashed another spelling of 'Khadra' into the machine and sat back and stared out of the window at the unexpectedly crowded street. Then she'd seen Brock and Bren emerge at the corner of the pub with the slender young Arab held tight between them. She saw him raise his head just once and turn towards some men who were following them, skinheads dressed in army fatigues, who seemed to be chanting and waving. Then he turned back, his head bouncing as the two big men broke into a jog, and the crowd parted in front of them, people scattering in all directions, and six or seven men, looking almost like a single flailing animal, charged directly at them from the front. For a second the impact brought the three of them to a halt, but then they recovered and heaved forward again, lashing out with fists at their attackers who slithered round their flanks.

A nurse finally called Kathy and led her down a corridor to a small ward where she pulled back a curtain to reveal Bren sitting looking glum and alone. His right eye was covered by a large gauze pad, his mouth swollen and bruised, his right hand bandaged and in a sling.

'Oh, hello, Kathy,' he said disconsolately.

'Bren! How are you?'

He shrugged. 'I'm fine. Nothing worse than a match against the All Blacks.'

'That's a miracle. I thought you'd both be dead.'

'You saw it?'

'Yes, from the office upstairs at the station. You were both fantastic.'

Bren looked down at his bandaged hand and sniffed modestly. 'We'd have been kebabs if we'd been twenty yards further from the station or the lads had been slower coming out for us.' He grinned reluctantly. 'The boss did all right, though, didn't he? Like an old warrior. He clocked the guy with the pickaxe handle, did you see that? Knocked him out cold.'

'Where is he?'

'They're worried about his left knee. It took a bashing. They're doing some more X-rays. But that's not what's pissing him off. It's what happened to the Arab kid. He's dead, Kathy.'

'I know.'

Bren shook his head in disbelief. 'When we got him into the station I couldn't believe our luck. He looked completely untouched. It must have been those bastards behind us, from the pub. Did you see it happen?'

'No. I wasn't aware of anything like a knife. They're hoping a street camera might have picked something up.'

'How did they all appear like that, out of nowhere? And how did they know his name, Kathy? That's what I can't fathom.'

'What do you mean?'

'Those fucking Nazis, they knew Abu's name. They were chanting it as they came out the pub.' He wearily rubbed the unbandaged parts of his face with his good hand. 'On the way here in the ambulance, Brock was going on about how he's never lost a prisoner. He's really cut up about it. Hell, me too.'

'Yes.' She could imagine the feelings of outrage and dismay the two of them must feel at having failed to protect the helpless Abu. And there would be ramifications. While she had been sitting outside in the waiting room, Kathy had recognised a plain-clothes officer who had come in and stood waiting at the information desk. At first she couldn't place him, and had assumed he must be following up on one of the other cases, the motorbike accident or the pub fight. But as he turned from the counter and walked away she remembered him, an inspector in the Crime Support Branch, which watches over the performance of the other specialist operations groups, such as their own Serious Crime Branch. And it had come home to her how completely Abu Khadra's death changed everything. Now Brock and Bren were no longer simply investigating officers, but were themselves witnesses and participants in a murder. Herself too perhaps? Would she now be isolated and corralled while a new major inquiry squad took over? Then again, she was on leave. Strictly speaking, in this investigation she didn't exist at all.

12

The sense of being invisible grew in Kathy during the following days. As she had anticipated, a new major inquiry team was rapidly established to take over both the Max Springer and Abu Khadra murder investigations, but, although Kathy remained in London in case she was needed, she was not interviewed or contacted by them, presumably because neither Brock nor Bren mentioned her participation. In any case, it was soon clear that the new team would be so inundated by information and advice that its problem would be focusing on the material issues. Abu's murder had occurred just in time on the Tuesday night to make the first editions of the Wednesday morning papers, and the morning radio and TV news bulletins were dominated by the 'Shadwell Road Riot' and its fatal outcome. National and international news services headlined the story for days afterwards, and by the weekend, when interest might have begun to wane, the arrest of half a dozen members of a right-wing white supremacist group brought it back to the front pages.

Throughout these days Kathy was in touch with the unfolding developments, and even pursued some inquiries of her own, yet she felt curiously distanced from them, neither touched nor noticed by the storm of legal, media and political activity, flitting almost like a ghost across the scene, or an unseen shadow in the wake of the new investigation team.

She saw Brock regularly, acting as a kind of domestic help in his first days of incapacity. Apart from a host of relatively superficial wounds to his upper body, arms, head and pride, his knee was badly bruised and had suffered a fracture, probably as a result of a blow from the same thug with the pickaxe handle that he had subsequently felled. Although Suzanne tried to persuade him to come and stay with her in Battle for a while, he had refused on the grounds that he could be needed at short notice in London, which wasn't true. Kathy had interpreted this as a kind of pride, or perhaps vanity, not wanting to be seen in his battered state, like some veteran boxer staggering from the ring. She could sympathise, especially in view of Brock's uncertain relations with Suzanne's two resident grandchildren, but his stubbornness was inconvenient, for whereas he might have had a ground floor room at Battle, in his own house the main rooms were at the top of a winding stair up from the front door, with his bedroom another floor above. Although he wasn't completely immobile, being able to stomp around on a crutch, in practice he came to rely on Kathy bringing him daily supplies and generally making life more tolerable. She made up a bed for him on the sofa in the living room, and rearranged his key possessions so that he could survive in that room, the kitchen and the bathroom.

He told her that the new team was headed up by a Superintendent by the name of Russell, an experienced, sound detective, he said approvingly, then added, with less enthusiasm, that he was unlikely to be distracted by divergent evidence. Russell had interviewed Brock early on the morning after Abu's murder and was already fully conversant with both cases. He seemed convinced that forensic evidence would prove decisive in the end.

'He's riding Leon hard,' Brock had said. 'And who knows, he may be right.'

Kathy just nodded dumbly, feeling even more disconnected from events.

It wasn't the possibility of bumping into Leon that took her back to Shadwell Road on the late afternoon of that Wednesday, or at least that's what she told herself. Rather, it was Bren's perplexity, repeated by Brock, over how the skinheads had known Abu's name.

After all the media attention she had expected the street to be alive with activity, but instead it was eerily deserted, as if people were ashamed or embarrassed to be seen there. Police barriers had been erected at each end to stop vehicles entering, and many of the shops were closed, some freshly boarded with plywood sheets, the owners apparently afraid of some new outbreak of trouble. Kathy walked to the front of the police station, then retraced the route diagonally across Shadwell Road that Brock and Bren and their prisoner had followed. The road surface and gutters seemed unnaturally clean, and Kathy guessed that the whole area had been vacuumed and scraped by scene of crime teams, though their barriers and screens and tapes had been removed.

The Three Crowns too was deserted. Stan, the same hefty barman who had served her and Brock when they had been there the previous evening, complained that he had only just been allowed to reopen the pub. All day the street had been teeming with thirsty coppers and reporters, and he hadn't been able to sell a single drink.

'I suppose they were interested in where the skinheads were sitting, were they?' Kathy asked, ordering a glass of wine.

'Yeah. They were over there by the games machine most of the evening, and hanging around the door.'

'It was a bit cold to have the door open, wasn't it?'

Stan nodded. 'They came and went, not all together. I had to ask them at one point to close the door, they were letting all the heat out.'

'Do you mean they looked organised?'

'Not organised, exactly. More like they were on the lookout for trouble. And it made me nervous, I tell you. We don't usually get types like that coming down Shadwell Road unless they're looking for trouble, and like I told your guvnor yesterday, we've had groups of them drop in the last couple of nights, getting bolder, talking louder, drinking more.'

'When there was the trouble last night, some of the lads reckoned that the skinheads knew the name of the bloke we'd arrested – Abu. Did it look like that to you?'

'The other coppers asked me that. What I think is that they picked it up from the Pakis out there in the street. See, what happened was that we all began to realise something was going on about ten fifteen or thereabouts. The bovver boys left the machine and gathered round the front window there, looking out to the street where a crowd was building up. Then one of them, a little bloke with a furry parka hood, came running in through the front door, all excited like, and they went into a huddle, and then the bloke went out again. I wanted to see what was going on, so I went after him to the door and looked outside. There was quite a crowd milling around in the street there, some looking down the lane, and I saw the skinhead talking to them.'

'Talking to the local people?'

'Yes. Most didn't like the look of him and turned away, but others spoke to him. That old busybody across the street, Mr Manzoor, he was one. Then the bloke came running back and I got behind the bar again. It was soon after that that they all started to hang around the doorway, and then the trouble started. I gave their descriptions to the other coppers. And I'll tell you what, they had a mobile phone.'

'You saw them using it?'

Stan nodded. 'Several times.'

Kathy finished her drink and went back out into the street. Across the way an illuminated sign advertised Yasmin's Finest Asian Sweetmeats, next to the deserted window of Bhaskar Gents Hairstylist. V & K International Discount Travel on its other side gave Kathy a small squirm of guilt. She should have spoken to Tina to tell her how her interview had gone, and to Suzanne, too. She had avoided telling Suzanne what her plans were for returning to Battle, simply because she'd avoided making any. She knew she must get in touch. Tonight, for sure.

Next to the travel agent was Manzoor Saree Centre, its lights bright, though, like everywhere else, doing little business. She crossed the street and opened the shop door to an accompanying tinkling of a bell. The interior was dazzling, bolts of multi-coloured fabric stacked and cascading everywhere over counters, mannequins and rails. Mr Manzoor himself, in a dark suit, formed the only note of sobriety in all this exuberance. He smoothly closed the order book he was studying and glided forward to greet Kathy with a little bow, his eyes examining her critically as his head dipped.

'Good evening, madam. How can I be of assistance? You would like a silk business suit, perhaps? Or something for evening wear?'

'I'm with the police, Mr Manzoor.'

'Ah.' He sighed regretfully. 'But still, the police need affordable clothes of excellent quality just like everyone else. I have given away many cards today. I expect many orders in the fullness of time.' He offered Kathy a business card.

'Thank you. I'm just following up one or two loose ends from the day. You were interviewed, weren't you?'

Manzoor gave a modest little bow of assent. 'Like all my fellow traders in Shadwell Road, I did my best to assist the officers to reconstruct the shocking events of yesterday.'

'Because you were there, weren't you, in the street at the time the man was killed?'

'Sadly so, although I saw nothing of it, with such a crowd . . . I am not a tall man, as you see.' He smiled deprecatingly.

'And before that, you actually spoke to one of the skinheads, I understand.'

Manzoor looked momentarily startled. 'Why, yes! You know, I had forgotten that until you reminded me. The riot, the fighting, it was so terrifying that what happened before had faded in my mind. Did the skinhead tell you that?'

'Another witness mentioned it. What did you talk about?'

'Well . . .' Manzoor thought for a moment. 'The man was coming through the crowd, asking people what was going on, why we were there. Most people looked away and pretended not to hear him. He was about the only European among us, but more than that, he was a skinhead, an ugly little fellow. People didn't want to talk to him. He approached me, and I said that we didn't want any trouble. I have to confess that I was thinking more of my shop windows. I had no idea that anything worse than that might happen.'

'He mentioned Abu by name, did he?'

Manzoor looked vague. 'I don't recall that.'

'But you knew of the name Abu?'

'Oh, yes. I was at mosque when the two officers came to speak to Imam Hashimi. He called several of us in to ask if we knew of this Abu Khadra.'

'Did he say what he was wanted for?'

'Not in so many words, but we assumed it was to do with the murder at the university.'

'And did the crowd in the street learn about this?'

'The imam asked us to be discreet, and to keep it to ourselves, but pretty soon I gathered that the story was going round. Probably the younger men had spread the word.'

'What story was that?'

'Why, that the two detectives had gone into Chandler's Yard to arrest someone called Abu.'

'For murder?'

'I would say so.' The draper shrugged regretfully. 'It is hard to keep such things quiet. People are such gossips, don't you know? Now, tell me, before I show you some of my finest cloth, specially discounted in honour of our fine police force, tell me where this Abu lived. I am curious. Some say it was in the university, and others that it was in Chandler's Yard itself. What is the truth?'

Something greedy, almost prurient about Manzoor's interest in the details of the tragedy disturbed Kathy. 'The university,' she said quickly, and turned to go.

Kathy reported this conversation to Brock that evening over a companionable couple of steaks.

'Makes sense,' he nodded stiffly, shifting his weight with a wince. 'Word travels fast. By the time we got Abu out of Chandler's Yard half of the East End must have known.' He thought of the minutes they'd wasted listening to the café owner's history of Yemeni settlement in Britain. 'Maybe if we'd been a bit quicker, or told them less at the mosque . . .' Or been able to understand Urdu, he repeated to himself.

'It probably wouldn't have made much difference. The skinheads had been gathering for days, ever since Springer's murder and the arrest of Ahmed and his mates. They were spoiling for trouble. If it hadn't been Abu it would have been someone else.'

'All the same . . .' Brock reached for a bottle of pills on a shelf at his elbow, then pushed them away. 'What's so frustrating is that Springer's murder remains a blank. I was itching to sit down with Abu and find out what the hell he thought he was going to achieve, if he was the killer. Come to that, Springer himself remains pretty much a blank. His death kicked up a storm, but the man himself, at the centre, remains a void, at least to me.' He dropped his fork from two thickly bandaged fingers and sighed with frustration. 'It seems as if what's happened almost vindicates what Springer was going on about. Maybe I should make some use of my time sitting here and read some of his books.'

Kathy didn't like to say that, since he now seemed completely shut out of the Springer inquiry, there didn't seem very much point. 'If they're anything like what his student was trying to explain to me, they're probably a good cure for insomnia. But I'll get them for you, if you want. I could go over to the university tomorrow.'

'Ah, talking about that,' Brock said, pouring them both another glass of red wine, 'I was speaking to Suzanne on the phone this afternoon, and she was asking how you were, and when you were going back down there.'

'Yes, I must ring her. The thing is, I don't feel I should leave London just at the moment, with all this going on, and you laid up and everything . . .'

'Mm,' Brock nodded. 'Take your point,' he murmured carefully. 'Better not make me your reason though. You're sure, are you? You feel OK about staying?'

Kathy stared into the deep purple of the wine, as rich as the colours of Mr Manzoor's fabrics, and nodded. 'Yes. Yes, I do.'

Thursday, 27 January was one of those bright, windy, glittering wintry days that remind you that spring will come. When she reached UCLE Kathy parked her car under the viaduct, buttoned up her coat and strode down to the river's edge of the university concourse where a few other brave souls were sitting on the steel benches, getting some sun on their pale faces and wind through their hair. She made her way along the concourse thinking that she might quickly pick up the books from the library and then get a cappuccino at the student cafeteria. She followed signs to the library, which was vast and circular, with inquiries at the centre. Kathy managed to access the computer index, and track down two of Springer's books that were on the shelves. She took them to the central checkout point, and tried to explain, as a queue grew restive behind her, that she was from the Metropolitan Police and just wanted to borrow them for reference purposes for a few days. The librarian looked at her as if she must be slightly simple, and explained that if she didn't have a staff or student number and identity card, well, she'd better apply to the Head of Data Resources. She found the Data Resources inquiry desk and was given a form to fill in, but the assistant seemed to feel that it might take some time, weeks probably, before she would hear.

She decided on another tack, and found her way to the scruffy old wing in which Springer and his doctoral student had their rooms. As always, Briony Kidd was at her desk. She looked up as Kathy knocked and stepped into the little room, and Kathy had the immediate impression that the bright and cheery approach she had been framing wouldn't be a success. Briony looked terrible, her eyes red, skin blotched around her throat and wrists as if she had been scratching herself raw.

'Yes?' she said, as if she expected the effort to earn her a blow.

'Er . . . Briony, hi,' Kathy said, suddenly uncertain. 'How are you?'

The woman's eyes narrowed. 'Why?'

'You look . . . tired.'

'Oh, I wonder why?' The sarcasm was heavy, too forced to be anything but painful.

Kathy was at a loss, but Briony saved her the problem of finding appropriate words.

'How could you have been so *stupid*!' she said, spitting her despair. 'Of all the unlikely people in the world, you had to pick on *Abu*! God!'

'I don't understand,' Kathy said cautiously.

'Well, I don't think that will surprise anyone!' Briony wailed and turned away.

Kathy took a deep breath and tried again. 'Briony, *you* were the one who told me we should be talking to the Muslim members of Professor Haygill's staff.'

'But not Abu!' the woman spun back, tears pouring from her eyes. 'Not Abu!'

'Why not?'

'Because he would never, *never* have hurt Max!'

The intensity of her conviction was baffling. Kathy took another deep breath. 'You knew Abu?'

'Yes, yes.'

'You didn't tell me that, Briony. How well did you know him?'

'Oh . . .' She made a wild gesture with her arm. 'We met . . . in the cafeteria, and places. He was a gentle, caring man. I can't believe what's happened. First Max and now Abu! I think I'm going mad.'

'Did he and Max know each other?'

'Yes . . . Maybe . . . I don't know . . .'

'Which?' Kathy insisted. 'Yes or no? Did they know each other?'

'I . . . I . . .' Briony seemed caught in some kind of confusion. 'I don't know. But that's not the point, is it? The point is that you charged in with your great jackboots and arrested him and dragged him out into the street and let those Nazis kill him!'

Kathy remembered the expression on Abu's face when she had first seen him, the look of recognition and acceptance. Could it have meant something else? Had she completely misjudged him? She felt a chill of panic and defensiveness and guilt as the possibility occurred to her that she might have engineered Abu's arrest and murder on the strength of some misread signs from Briony and Abu himself. And then it occurred to her that the source of Briony's distress was precisely the same as this, the guilt of having inadvertently betrayed her . . . her what? Friend? Lover even? She tried to picture the two of them together, and found it difficult, but certainly not impossible. The over-serious, lonely, passionate English girl and the Arab with the shining eyes. Both slender, fragile, ready to be broken by life . . .

She stopped her imagination running away with her.

'Briony, we all feel terrible about what happened, but I can tell you that neither you nor I am responsible for Abu's death. The people who are will be caught and punished.'

Briony swung back at her. 'You are responsible!' she cried. 'You killed him!'

The force of her accusation was almost physical, and Kathy felt herself backing away, shaking her head. She found herself outside in the corridor, and realised that she was trembling. She turned and walked slowly away and almost stumbled at the next corner of the corridor into a man whose breath smelled strongly of whisky.

'Oh, easy there!' he breathed and squinted at her. 'You all right?'

'Fine, yes.'

'Lost?'

'A bit, yes.'

He gave her a roguish leer. 'Well, let me give you a helping hand. Pettifer's the name. Desmond.'

Kathy remembered Brock mentioning him. 'Oh. You were a friend of Max Springer's, weren't you? I work with DCI Brock.'

Dr Pettifer checked himself. 'Ah. Interesting developments, eh? Anything you need?'

'Well, maybe there is something you could help me with. I'm trying to get hold of some of Professor Springer's books.'

'What, short of door-stops at the Yard, are you?' He tried out a wink and a chuckle. 'Don't intend to try reading them, do you?'

'That was the plan. Only the university library say I can't borrow them without a proper pass. I was hoping to find a friendly academic who would borrow them for me.'

'What about Max's own copies, from his room?'

'The room's sealed. We're not supposed to remove anything.'

'Well, I can do better than the library. I can lend you my own copies. Don't normally do that, mind. I've lost too many of my books to students to ever lend to them any more. But a police woman should be beyond reproach, or am I being naïve?' He twinkled at her boozily.

'Absolutely,' she said. 'I'd be most grateful. Just for a week or two.'

'No hurry. And in return, you can slake my curiosity. *Curiosis fabricavit inferos*, eh?' He led the way down the narrow corridor, speaking back at her over his shoulder. At his door he drew a ring of keys on a chain from his pocket and let her in. There was an unpleasant sweetness in the musty air of the room.

'What I wondered,' he said, pulling books down from his crowded shelves, 'was whether this Abu chap had the weapon on him when you caught him. I'm having a bet with a fellow in Sociology. He reckons that they always throw the thing away down a drain or something after they've done the deed, but I feel he would keep it as a kind of security. So which of us is right?'

'I'd say that usually your friend is right, Desmond, but in this case I couldn't comment.'

Pettifer looked put out. 'Oh, come on,' he wheedled. 'Just a hint. Which of us would you put your money on?'

'I really couldn't say.'

'Oh, well.' He turned away in a huff, and after a moment's search found the last of the books. 'Was it a big gun? Heavy to carry around?'

Kathy took the books and handed him her card. 'I don't think so. Many thanks for these.'

He looked vaguely cheated as she turned and left, wondering why people were so fascinated by the gory details.

She crossed the river, stopping on the way to buy some sandwiches for lunch and a few other supplies that Brock needed. In Matcham High Street she turned through the familiar archway into Warren Lane and parked in a space between other cars in the yard behind the shops. The wind picked at the skirt of her coat as she carried her bags under the dark skeleton of the horse chestnut tree towards the irregular terrace of houses that faced the lane that ran along the top of the railway cutting. She glanced up at the bay window that projected from an upper floor, and thought she recognised the shadow of Brock in the window seat in which he now spent most of his time. She fitted the key he'd given her into the front door, and stepped into the warmth of the small hallway calling out 'Hello'. There was no reply, but as she climbed up the stairway she thought she caught the sound of a murmur of voices. Perhaps the radio, she thought, and turned from the landing towards the kitchen that overlooked the small courtyard at the back of the house, setting her bags down on the table.

Kathy recognised Suzanne's perfume a moment before she heard her step on the wooden kitchen floor behind her. She turned and smiled, 'Suzanne, hello,' and immediately took in two very strong impressions. The first was that Suzanne had gone to some trouble to look good for her visit; her hair looked recently styled, in a slightly darker shade of her natural auburn, and her clothes had been selected from the more expensive and classy side of her wardrobe. The second was that she was very angry and upset.

'You OK?' Kathy said carefully.

'Why didn't you tell me he was like this?' Suzanne's voice was low and tight. 'I had no idea, no idea at all that he was in such a state.'

'He's coping pretty well.'

'He's a wreck,' Suzanne's voice rose. 'He could barely get down the stairs to let me in.'

'We didn't want to worry you,' Kathy said, and immediately knew that the 'we' was exactly wrong. She saw the look of betrayal on the other woman's face, and thought of the phone calls she'd meant to make to her. 'He looks worse than he is,' she added unconvincingly.

Suzanne took a step nearer, angry. 'Don't patronise me, Kathy. I thought you were a friend. How could you have kept me in the dark?'

Kathy hung her head, feeling defeated by Suzanne's passion. 'I'm sorry. He felt he had to stay here for the time being, so then it seemed better not to alarm you. His leg's the main problem. The doctors say the rest will mend quickly.'

Suzanne shook her head in exasperation. 'It's ridiculous! He's too old to be fighting in the street like a twenty-year-old.'

'It just came out of the blue. No one expected something like that. He and Bren were caught. It could have happened to anyone. He was rather heroic, actually. You'd have been proud of him.'

But Suzanne wasn't ready to listen to that. 'He should never have been in that situation. He shouldn't be in that job at all.'

Kathy looked at her in surprise. She hadn't heard this from her before, but she remembered the oddly stilted conversations she had had with Suzanne about her own career choices, and guessed that this was a long-running issue.

'He should have moved on like everyone else, into senior management. Or if he doesn't want that, he should get out completely.' She wasn't offering a point for discussion. She said it with absolute certainty, as a fact that would be obvious to any right-thinking person, and Kathy felt she was seeing for the first time the underlying tension in the strangely on-off relationship between the two of them. She imagined them at some point putting their cards on the table, two people of determined views, and, finding that they couldn't agree, settling on a kind of mutual half-life together. It made her feel vaguely stupid, as if she ought to know how to help, but couldn't. She'd lived with Suzanne for a couple of weeks, after all, during which time Brock had stayed overnight two or three times, and yet she still didn't know for sure if they were sleeping together.

'You don't agree, of course.' Suzanne said it flatly, a demand to know if Kathy was an ally or an enemy.

'I wouldn't like to say what's best for him, Suzanne,' Kathy said cautiously. 'I don't think he would be happy in senior management, to be honest. As for doing something else . . . I don't know.'

Suzanne turned away, as if Kathy had confirmed her suspicions.

'Why does he have to stay here, exactly?' she asked coolly. 'Someone else has taken over the case, surely? He's invalided out, isn't he?' There was a note of suspicion in Suzanne's voice now, as if she suspected Kathy of some duplicity, or felt threatened by her professional relationship with Brock.

'Yes, but the new people have been consulting him—'

'There's an invention called a telephone, I believe.'

Kathy hadn't heard this sharpness from Suzanne before. She was obviously very hurt, and not stupid. 'There's also an internal inquiry been set up into what happened. Brock hasn't said to me, but I think he's worried about it. It wasn't his fault, but he's taken it badly, that the man they had arrested was killed in their charge.'

'All the more reason he shouldn't lie around here moping while he waits for things to happen.' Suzanne turned back to face Kathy. 'And what about you?'

Kathy felt herself flush, suddenly aware that all this time she'd been holding Brock's front door key in her hand. 'Me? I've just been looking in from time to time, and doing a bit of shopping for him.'

'I meant, what are your plans these days? I've hardly heard from you since the weekend. Tina wanted to speak to you, but she couldn't get you at your flat. She had some news about your interview. You should contact her.'

'Yes, of course. Since I came back up to town, everything's moved so fast . . . I'm sorry, I'll do it straight away. Look, Suzanne, I think you're right about Brock getting away from here for a while. I can keep my ears open for him here, and there's Bren and the others. Why don't you have another go at persuading him to go back with you to Battle?'

'So you're staying in London, are you?'

'I think I will. I've got so much to catch up on here,' she lied. 'The break with you was fantastic, just what I needed, but I feel OK now.'

Suzanne sighed. 'Maybe you should tell him. I don't seem to be having much success at telling him anything at the moment.'

The tension had ebbed from her voice, and Kathy said, hanging the key on a hook above the worktop, 'Let's have some lunch. We can both work on him.'

13

Kathy's sense of detachment intensified in the days following Brock's departure to Battle. Over lunch he had bowed to the inevitable and accepted Suzanne's invitation to stay with her for a while with good grace and even, Kathy thought she detected, some relief. When he asked how the two grandchildren, who had on a previous occasion found his presence around Suzanne threatening, would deal with it, Suzanne had said grimly that everyone would have to cooperate and make compromises. He didn't try to argue. She added that his crutch and bandages would probably do the trick, and if not he could try a parrot on his shoulder. So they had packed a couple of bags of clothes, books and Brock's laptop and set off for the coast, leaving Kathy to return alone to her flat in Finchley.

In her mail was a letter reminding her that, under the terms of her sick leave, she was required to attend a further session with the staff psychologist before she could obtain clearance to return to work. Kathy had come to regard her reluctance to make arrangements for these sessions as symptomatic of her disillusionment with her job, and again she hesitated, put the letter aside and opened the next. This one was from the agency in the West End, informing her that she had been accepted as a client subject to completion of the enclosed contracts.

She thought about that for a while, then rang Tina the travel agent in Hastings, who told her that she had herself spoken to the woman who had interviewed Kathy.

'But I thought it went so badly,' Kathy said. 'I turned up late and had no languages.'

Actually the woman had been impressed, Tina said, but made a habit of never showing it. She should do something about the languages, and there were some other courses she should do, but yes, they thought she could make a go of it.

Kathy replaced the receiver and stared out of the window for a while. 'Hell,' she said at last, and dialled the number on her first letter and made the appointment with the psychologist. She was told it would be at least a week before she could report back to duty. Another week of limbo.

She thought often of Leon Desai over the following days, but didn't ring him, nor did he try to contact her. But in a moment of weakness she did ring Wayne O'Brien and suggested they try another Indian. He sounded regretful. That would be magic, he said, and he'd like nothing better, but things were a bit dodgy. His girlfriend had miraculously recovered from her imagined infatuation with the third member of their household, who had now departed. And despite his earlier doubts, Wayne had found it in his heart to forgive and make up, so it didn't look as if he'd be able to manage a return match with Kathy. Much to his regret, incidentally, but he wasn't that sort of guy. Kathy said that was fine, in a tone that suggested she had so many competing claims on her time that she hardly knew which way to turn. And was he still involved with the Springer/Khadra case?

He hesitated, the way an undercover man might, weighing up how much to say. 'The case is dead as a dodo is what I hear, Kathy,' he said finally. 'No conspiracy, no terrorist plots. It was never really one for Special Branch, as it turned out. Shame really. I understand there's been some new forensic evidence. Your lab liaison, Desai, has been working on it. You should talk to him.'

Kathy didn't, but she did ring Battle. Suzanne answered, sounding out of breath and happy. Everything was going well, she said. As she had predicted, Brock's bandages and crutch had given him an heroic status with the grandchildren. In the background Kathy heard the cry of children and felt a twinge of regret.

'But how are you, Kathy?'

'Oh, busy, busy.'

'Good! That's the way to be. You are coping all right on your own? I've been worried about you.'

'I'm not an invalid,' Kathy laughed. 'I was in your last batch of lame ducks, remember? All patched up and ready to fly again.'

'Tina said she'd been talking to you. Sounds promising?'

'Yes. I'm learning Spanish.'

'Terrific! Well, you know you're always welcome here, any time. Did you want to speak to David?' Suzanne's voice dropped to a whisper. 'Only he's got someone with him at the moment. A policeman. He came down from London specially. They've been talking for almost an hour now. Shall I get him to ring you when he's finished?'

'Thanks. Do you know the man's name?'

'Russell, it was. Superintendent Russell. I just hope he's offering David a nice job off the streets. Doing research into police methods in warm and sunny locations, or something. Then you could do the travel arrangements for our extended overseas trips.'

Kathy didn't spoil Suzanne's fantasy by telling her who Russell was. If the man who'd taken over Brock's case was interviewing him at length now, he probably needed a lawyer more than a travel agent. Instead she asked to say hello to the children, then rang off and made a cup of coffee.

The phone rang before she had finished it. She heard Brock's voice and quickly said, 'How did it go with Russell? Is it a problem?'

He said, sounding relaxed, 'No, no. He came down to go through his conclusions for his report to the coroner, partly out of courtesy, he said, but mainly to check that I couldn't see any obvious holes. I'll tell you if you promise to keep it to yourself.

'It seems his faith in a forensic outcome has been justified by three new pieces of evidence that weren't available to us. First, and most important, they found traces of gunshot residue on Khadra's coat and gloves that matches that on Springer's clothes, so there's little doubt that Abu was the gunman. So then there's the question of whether he acted alone.

'The second forensic success concerns the bullet. They've been able to match it with another that was used in a drug-related shooting in North London eighteen months ago. Both were fired from the same gun, and there seems to be no connection between the two crimes. In other words the gun appears to be just one of those floating around the underworld black market, and Abu probably bought it from a bent dealer. Therefore no indication of the involvement of foreigners or of some larger organisation.

'And thirdly, the three kids we picked up, Ahmed Sharif and his mates, appear to be in the clear. The saliva used to lick the stamp and the gum on the torn envelope I found in Springer's study doesn't give a DNA match with any of them, nor with Abu. In fact it was Springer's own saliva, presumably from a self-addressed envelope used for something else entirely. Springer could have picked up the green leaflet at any time – we know he went to Shadwell Road, and the three kids were handing them out to passers-by. So that was all irrelevant.'

Brock paused as if skimming notes. 'So, three bits of forensic evidence that seem to simplify the picture a good deal, supporting the view that Abu Khadra murdered Max Springer, and acted alone.'

'What was his motive?'

'There we can only speculate. It seems he was a private, serious young man, not socialising much with his colleagues at work, a computer fanatic and very religious. You've also got to remember that he grew up in Lebanon at a time when violence was seen as an obvious solution to any problem. The hypothesis is that he regarded Springer as a blasphemer who was attacking a project that aims to alleviate the lot of the faithful. However that won't go into the report. It smacks too much of religious fundamentalism, which everyone's keen to avoid mentioning. It'll be up to the inquest to speculate about motive.'

'You sound unconvinced, Brock,' Kathy said after a pause.

'No, no, it's not that. It makes sense, and if I'd been in Russell's shoes I'd probably have come up with the same answer. Just my natural scepticism, I suppose. Russell made it clear that everyone's looking for closure on this one, and that's exactly what he's offering – no conspiracy, no fatwa, no jihad, just a disturbed loner with no one to speak for him now.'

Kathy was immediately reminded of Briony Kidd's outburst at the university about Abu's innocence, and remembered that she hadn't had a chance to tell Brock about it. She mentioned it now. Brock wasn't much impressed.

'That woman seemed very emotional about Springer's death, Kathy. The forensic evidence looks pretty conclusive, I'd say. Abu killed him all right. I think Briony Kidd needs to put it behind her now and move on. Reading stuff like Springer's books all day won't do much to cheer her up, either.'

'Are they hard going?'

Brock groaned. 'Very. I'm extending my vocabulary though, if nothing else. Have you ever heard of the word "psittacism"?' He spelt it.

'No.'

'It means the mechanical repetition of ideas or words, parrot-fashion. I might use it the next time I give evidence in court. "But isn't that simply psittacism, your honour?"'

'He'll probably give you three months for contempt,' Kathy laughed.

'There was one interesting thing that Springer pointed out in one of the books, about the nature of martyrdom, which I thought was relevant to what happened to him, ironically enough. He said there are two quite different traditions of religious martyrdom, the Christian and the Muslim. The Christian martyr is passive, suffering death as a victim for the sake of his faith, whereas the Muslim martyr gives up his life in an active attack on the enemies of his faith. It occurred to me that Springer and Khadra exactly demonstrated the two traditions. You might say that they were each an example of a type, and each suffered a martyr's fate.'

They hadn't been able to see Springer's face on the security tape at the moment of his martyrdom, but Kathy had seen Abu's face later, and after she rang off she wondered if that look of expectancy might have been the look of a martyr who knows his time has come. But that made no sense, for no one, least of all Abu Khadra, knew that a bunch of skinheads would take his life later that night.

Kathy felt at a loss. The case was over, as Wayne O'Brien had said, dead as a dodo. Like her private life. There was only one thing to do; she went shopping. She bought a Spanish language course of tapes, a Walkman and a new pair of joggers, and took them all for a run through the suburban back streets of Finchley and out along Dollis Brook and Woodside Park, abandoning herself to psittacism in the rain.

14

Through circumstances that nobody designed, but nobody resisted, both the memorial service for Max Springer and the interment of Abu Khadra were arranged for the same day, the first Thursday in February. By then Brock had been away from London for a week, and Kathy drove down to Battle to collect him and to act as his driver for the day. She found that he had dispensed with most of his visible dressings by this time, and substituted a walking stick for the crutch. She felt that the air of an old warhorse that he projected as he rejected offers of helping arms and stomped to the open car door, wounded but unbowed, was entirely right for the occasion. They waved goodbye to Suzanne and the children, and headed north. It was a bright cold winter's day, freezing and sunny, the most appropriate of weather to face the reality of death.

Aware of how marginalised Professor Springer had become within his university, the two detectives wondered how many people would turn up for his service. But as they found a parking space in the back streets some distance from the university entrance they became aware of a host of black-coated figures all moving in the same direction as themselves, towards the university gates and the entry concourse beyond. Uniformed security staff stood at intervals to direct them towards the venue in lecture theatre U3, which meant that each sombre visitor followed the route of Springer's last moments, the stations of Springer's cross, passing beneath the security camera which had recorded his last moments, and up the great flight of steps on which he died, to the upper concourse where they inevitably stopped to gaze back at the view across the river towards the Millennium Dome, before continuing on to the entrance doors of the auditorium in which he had planned to give his final lecture.

Brock waved aside Kathy's suggestion that they take the handicapped persons' lift to the upper concourse, and, grey-bearded chin thrust forward, he grunted his way up all fifty-two of the broad steps with the help of the handrail and his stick. When they reached the lecture theatre they discovered that Springer had attracted many more people in death than in life. Looking at the size of the large hall, Kathy could see how pathetic the twenty or thirty audience for his lecture would have appeared, and how impressive the present turnout was, both in numbers and range of the university hierarchy. Even Richard Haygill, the subject of Springer's venom, was there, accompanied by a rather glamorous looking blonde several inches taller than himself.

A small, elegantly printed leaflet on each seat explained that this would be a secular celebration of Professor Max Springer's life and achievements, in accord with his creedless philosophy. Despite this, the service began with the stirring opening of the Fauré Requiem, the haunting lines of the Kyrie reverberating through the auditorium, *Kyrie eleison, Christe eleison*, Lord have mercy, Christ have mercy.

After the notes had faded away, the University President, Professor Roderick Young, moved to the simple lectern in the centre of the stage and delivered an eloquent eulogy on what he described as his 'most highly esteemed colleague'. He spoke in a commanding, sonorous voice of the irremediable loss to the international community of scholars and to the 'UCLE family'. After several minutes of this, Brock began to stir and make noises of either discomfort or disgust, Kathy couldn't be sure.

Young was followed by an elderly man introduced as Springer's cousin, speaking on behalf of the family. He seemed rather overwhelmed by the occasion, and spoke in a wavering Midlands accent, mainly of his recollections of their shared childhood in Solihull during the War. Kathy got the impression that there hadn't been so much contact in more recent years, and she imagined that Max had probably had little in common with the English family into which, an intellectual cuckoo, he had been introduced in 1937.

Other speakers followed. An American academic and a leading member of the London literary scene both spoke powerfully about the values Springer stood for, to the accompaniment of much flash activity and note-taking from the press contingent which occupied the rear third of the raked seating. Perhaps the most surprising contribution, and for Kathy the most moving, came from a reasonably sober and clean looking Desmond Pettifer, who took the lectern and announced that he would recite his friend Max Springer's favourite poem, which henceforth, he believed, would carry redoubled meaning for all present. With an accent becoming more pronouncedly Welsh with every syllable, he then spoke the lines of Dylan Thomas' 'Do Not Go Gentle into That Good Night'. Tears rolled down his cheeks, and began to appear around the hall too, as he intoned the final words with a fierce passion, 'Rage, rage against the dying of the light'.

The contrast with the interment of Abu Khadra that afternoon could hardly have been greater. After a light pub lunch, Kathy drove them to a large public cemetery near Tooting in South London. The morning sun was now hidden by a sullen grey cloud mass, and as they turned in through the gates and slowly wound their way through endless silent lanes of death the prospect became more and more grim, and, it seemed to Kathy, Dylan Thomas' defiance more and more forlorn.

In a bleak corner most distant from the entrance, a small area had been set aside for those of the Shia Muslim faith. They were early, and reversed the car and parked at the roadside on the fringe of the area, with a view towards the newly excavated hole visible at the end of a desolate row of stones and markers inscribed with Arabic characters, a few freshly delineated in gold, the majority old and faded. As she stared out through the misting window at the scene, it occurred to Kathy that this was an appropriately terminal backdrop to the final moments of what looked to be her last case.

To avoid any possibility of fresh disturbances, there had been a strict news blackout on Abu's burial. Only the imam of the Nur al-Islam mosque had been consulted over the arrangements, and he had been entrusted with inviting only the closest intimates of the dead man, in strictest confidence. Shortly before 3:00 p.m. a black hearse approached, followed by a single car, a battered red Toyota. They stopped just beyond the grave, steam coiling from their exhausts. Two men got out of the front of the Toyota, and Brock pointed out the heavy bulk of Qasim Ali, proprietor of the Horria Café, as he eased himself with difficulty out of the driver's seat. He didn't know the other man. Both wore overcoats and were holding black Homburgs which they arranged carefully on their heads before moving forward to the hearse, where two attendants in black suits were opening the rear door. Together the four men slid a plain casket out of the vehicle and gripped its side handles. Another man got out of the front of the hearse, wearing the black robe and headdress of a cleric, and led the way towards the grave.

Now the back doors of the Toyota swung open and three women emerged. All had covered heads, two wrapped from head to foot in loose black chadors, the other in a quilted coat and black headscarf. The last hesitated and stared curiously at Kathy's car before following the men.

'That's Briony Kidd, isn't it?' Kathy pointed at her. 'I was looking out for her at Springer's service.'

'You're right. What about the other two?'

Kathy shook her head, unable to recognise them. They walked together, comforting each other, heads bowed, handkerchiefs held to their eyes. 'They look like Arabs, don't they? Maybe Abu's relatives?' It was impossible to tell their ages.

As the group gathered around the grave and began the rites of interment, Brock nodded towards the far end of the road along which they had travelled, where it emerged through a cluster of extravagant Victorian sarcophagi. Another car had appeared there, dark blue or purple, and had come to a halt in a position where it could observe the proceedings, though without switching off its engine. A light drizzle had begun, and its wipers began to beat very slowly across its windscreen.

'The next funeral?' Kathy suggested, but they had seen no other freshly dug graves at this end of the field. As she spoke the dark car began to creep forward, as if trying to maintain its view in the diminishing visibility.

'Probably Russell's boys,' Brock said. 'I thought they'd be here. Like us, unsure whether to show their faces or not.'

The other car had moved forward into a dip, its windshield

visible, but not its grille and numberplate, like a half submerged crocodile, watching.

For a while nothing moved, the rain becoming heavier. Then the graveside party began to stir. The officiate spoke to each in turn, then the whole group began walking back to the cars, flanked by the two men in suits, now carrying umbrellas.

There was movement on the road ahead, too, the windscreen glinting as the dark purple car slid up out of the dip and came forward, steadily putting on speed. Puzzled at first, and then alarmed, Brock and Kathy watched as it accelerated towards the back of the Toyota. The funeral party was unaware of it at first, then Ali and the other man jerked up their heads and suddenly began shouting. With a squeal of brakes and skidding rubber the dark car juddered to a violent stop inches short of the Toyota, boxing it in against the back of the hearse. Its doors flew open and three men jumped out, waving clubs as they dived for the women.

'Bloody hell!' Kathy and Brock swore in unison, then Kathy ducked forward to the glove compartment, groping inside for the Asp extendable baton that she kept there. She hurled her door open, flicking the baton out as she jumped.

As she ran forward Kathy saw that Ali and his companion had closed with the attackers, the big café owner giving a great roar as he pitched himself on top of one of them. Another one turned, raising his club to strike Ali, but was pulled down too with a flying rugby tackle from Ali's mate. The third attacker didn't pause, charging on, his attention fixed on the two cloaked Arab women. He ripped the headdress off one, then thrust her aside and turned on the other, grabbing her round the neck, club arm raised, just as Kathy reached him. She lashed at his upper arm with her baton and felt it connect with his elbow with a crunch, then heard his wild shriek echo across the rain-soaked cemetery as he released the woman and stumbled backwards.

She yelled at the men struggling on the ground, 'Police! Don't move! Stop fighting!' but they took no notice whatever of her. They were punching furiously, arms and legs flailing.

Briony Kidd ran to Kathy and grabbed her sleeve. 'Do something! They want to kill her!' she screamed. 'They're crazy! Save her! Get her away!'

Kathy looked quickly around. The hearse was on the move, bouncing across the burial area as it turned in a wide arc and back onto the road heading in the direction of the exit. The three women, wide eyed and terrified, were clustering around her. The man she'd struck was bent over, cursing as he nursed his arm, and his companions seemed to be getting the better of the fight on the ground.

She said, 'Come on, quickly,' and started ushering the three women towards her car. As she hurried them along she looked back and saw the man she had disarmed pointing at her with his good arm. He was yelling something in a language she didn't know, and his two companions were struggling to their feet, disengaging themselves from Ali and his friend who lay on the ground.

Kathy bundled the women into the back of her car and jumped in behind the wheel, tossing the Asp to Brock. The blood was pounding in her ears. She felt elated and thought, *I did OK, I didn't blow it.* But no sooner had she formed this thought than it was overwhelmed by a wave of nausea that flooded through her. She gripped the wheel tight, fighting to hold it down. Her skin felt icy and she began to shake.

'Let's go, shall we?' She heard Brock's voice, incredibly calm, at her shoulder, and half turned to see his eyes on her white knuckles. She nodded stiffly and dragged one hand off the wheel to ram the gear stick home. As the car jumped forward the three attackers stumbled to a halt, gasping for breath, then the injured one screamed something and they turned and began running for their car. As she passed them Kathy was startled to recognise the man she had struck as Sanjeev Manzoor, proprietor of the Manzoor Saree Centre on Shadwell Road. And at the same moment he clearly recognised her, for he let out a great cry of fury and began shaking his good fist at her.

Kathy drove as fast as she dared along the cemetery road, watching her mirror for any sign of the purple car behind.

'Are any of you hurt?' Brock was asking, stretching back over his seat at the three women in the back as he pulled out his phone. The most distraught was the shrouded figure in the middle, sobbing steadily while the other two tried to comfort her. 'Is she hurt?' Brock repeated.

'She's pregnant,' Briony said, glaring at him as if it were his fault.

'How much?'

'I don't know.' She looked questioning at the other woman wearing the chador. 'Fran?'

'Six or seven months,' Fran offered, looking worried.

Brock turned back to Kathy. 'We'd better get her to a hospital. I'll call for assistance.'

'No!'

The cry from the back was so loud and firm that Brock swung back with surprise and saw the weeping woman in the middle staring at him.

'I don't need the hospital! I'm all right. And anyway, he'll find me there.'

'We're police officers,' he said reassuringly. 'We'll protect you.'

But this information only seemed to distress the woman more. She looked pleadingly at Brock and sobbed, 'No, no. No police, please. No hospital.' She turned to the women on each side of her and began whispering frantically. As he watched them, Brock's uncertainty grew. Although the pregnant woman had the dark eyes and brown complexion of an Arab or Asian, she had spoken with a broad London accent, and, looking more closely at her, she seemed very young, no more than a girl. The other woman wearing the chador, Fran, had the same white complexion as Briony Kidd, who looked the oldest of the three, and also the most decisive.

'Look,' she said to Brock after some whispered conversation, 'all we need is for you to get us away from here and drop us somewhere. A tube station or somewhere. We can look after ourselves after that. We don't want to press charges against those men or anything.'

Brock was about to reply when Kathy muttered 'Damn!' and brought the car skidding to a halt. They had reached an older part of the cemetery and the roadway was narrow and meandering, hemmed in on each side with stone obelisks and angels and dripping yew trees. Ahead the road crossed an ornamental stone bridge, now blocked by a funeral procession coming sedately towards them. Kathy was forced to pull hard over to let them through. The leading hearse slowly passed, then one by one the long cortege of following cars came rolling over the bridge.

Kathy was still watching her mirror. After a while she murmured to Brock, 'Company.'

He looked back through the rear window and saw the purple car approaching in the distance. It slowed as it saw them and the other procession, but didn't stop, creeping steadily forward.

Briony caught the expression on Brock's face and looked back over her shoulder to see what he was looking at. When she turned back she was frowning with doubt, biting her bottom lip.

'Briony, back there you told me they wanted to kill your friend,' Kathy said. 'Was that a lie or the truth?'

'It could be true,' she muttered. 'I don't know.'

'I don't think you've got any choice but to let us help you.'

She said nothing. The other two had seen the purple car now and were whispering together in agitation.

Brock said, 'Let's do a deal, Briony. We'll get you somewhere safe and listen with an open mind until you've explained to us exactly what this is all about. Otherwise we're heading straight for Tooting police station and I'm going to charge the lot of you with affray.'

The three women looked at each other, then the pregnant girl wiped her eyes and said in a whisper, but with firmness, 'Yes,' then added, 'please.'

Brock nodded and turned away and started pressing buttons on his phone. The last car of the cortege finally cleared the little bridge and Kathy drove off just as the purple car came up behind. Together they accelerated away, driving fast enough to attract disapproving looks from mourners leaving the chapel near the cemetery entrance. At the gates Brock told her to go right and they turned into the general traffic, their tail sticking close behind for over a mile until first one, then a second police patrol car joined their progress and pulled the other car over. The women watched through the back window until they were out of sight.

'What'll happen to them?' Briony demanded.

'We'll start with carrying an offensive weapon in a public place, and see where we go after that. It rather depends on you, and your other two friends.'

'Yes, what about George!' Fran cried. 'What about George and Qasim!'

'Qasim has a mobile phone,' the pregnant girl said, and reeled off a number.

Brock made her repeat it, dialling as she spoke. After several rings a hoarse voice said, 'Hello?'

'Is this Qasim Ali?' Brock asked.

'Who wants to know?' This seemed to be Qasim's habitual greeting.

Brock offered the phone to the women in the back and Fran grabbed it. 'Qasim? It's Fran. Are you all right? Is George all right?'

She listened anxiously for a moment, then said, 'No, no, we're safe. They were the police. We're with them. We have to talk with them. We're all fine. You're sure about George?'

Brock took back the phone and spoke to the café owner. It seemed that Qasim and George were only bruised from their fight, and were currently driving aimlessly through the South London streets trying to find the missing women. Brock told them to go home and wait for him to ring again, then turned and spoke quietly to Kathy. 'Well, now, we're almost in Dulwich. Where's close, private and comfortable, where we can sit down with a nice cup of tea?'

Kathy glanced over at him, eyebrow raised. 'You're not thinking . . . Warren Lane?'

'It did cross my mind.'

'Is that wise?'

Brock shrugged and checked his watch. 'I'm sure it isn't. But time may be short. And I very much want to hear what all this has to do with the deaths of Abu and Springer.'

Kathy said nothing, but turned the car in the direction of Matcham High Street. Within ten minutes they were in the courtyard at Warren Lane. She parked under the horse chestnut tree near Brock's house.

Brock led the way to his front door, limping on his stick, and led the women inside.

'Is this what they call a "safe house"?' Briony asked. She seemed fascinated, scrutinising everything, the pile of mail waiting inside the front door, the titles on the spines of the books lining the upstairs landing, the computer in the living room.

'Something like that,' Brock grunted, lighting the gas fire and getting them seated in the armchairs around it.

'Pretty classy,' Briony said, studying the little Schwitters collage hanging in one corner. Her eyes were still red and puffy from the tears she had shed at the funeral, and her interest now seemed like a front.

'Come and sit down, Briony,' Brock told her. 'You can make us some toast on the fire, OK?'

He assembled food and tools, Kathy brought in a tray with the tea and they settled themselves, awkward at first, then gradually more relaxed and calm.

'Well, let's begin with your names,' Brock suggested. 'I know Briony. What about you two?'

'I'm Fran Said, George is my husband.'

'George Said,' Brock said. 'And he's a friend of Qasim Ali's, is he?'

'They're cousins. We live with them, in Chandler's Yard. We're all part of the same family, see?' She took a bite of the slice of toast and honey that Briony handed her. She seemed hungry after all the drama.

'I see.' Brock frowned, tentative. 'Forgive me for sounding personal, Fran, but you don't look . . . well . . . Yemeni.'

'My mum's from Middlesex, and she says my dad was Irish, but I couldn't say for sure.' She said this with a note of defiance, then took another mouthful of toast.

Brock didn't pursue this, but turned to the pregnant girl. 'And are you part of the Ali family too?' he suggested gently, but from the way he said it Kathy guessed he already knew the answer.

The girl lowered her eyes, and for a moment there was silence and her two friends paused in their chewing. 'No,' she said at last. 'My name is Nargis Manzoor.'

'Ah yes. The missing daughter of the man who has the shop in Shadwell Road.'

The girl nodded.

Kathy said, 'That was him, at the cemetery . . .' but everyone else seemed perfectly aware of that.

'How old are you, Nargis?' Brock asked.

'Seventeen,' she whispered.

'I've heard a little of your story, but I'd like to hear it properly, from you.'

Nargis took a deep breath, the oval of her face all that was visible of her in the black habit.

'My dad is very old-fashioned,' she began. 'It's not his fault. It's just the way he is. He grew up in a place called Mirpur, in Kashmir, which is big on dust and religion and not much else. He followed his uncle out here in the seventies, and after a few years he went back and brought my mum out. She's been here for twenty years, but she doesn't speak any English. She doesn't need to, 'cos she never goes outside. Dad takes care of everything. She might as well still be in Mirpur. What dad values more than anything is respect, from his family, and from the people he goes to mosque with and does business with.

'At school I was good at maths, and at first dad was pleased, 'cos I could help him doing the books in the shop. I got good O levels, and I told him I wanted to become an accountant, or something like that in business. Maybe, if I was good enough at the maths, even an actuary. He didn't like that. He told me that just wasn't possible. I was a woman, so my future was to be someone's wife. That above everything else. Meanwhile I was sixteen, and I wanted the same as all the other girls at school, a boyfriend and clothes and some fun. I was friends with one of the Ali girls from Chandler's Yard, even though my dad said they were Shia rubbish, which I thought was stupid. Through her I met Qasim and their family, who I liked because they were Muslim but relaxed about it, and then George and Fran, who were at the university, and then Abu.

'Abu and I became friends because of his computers and my maths. He helped me with my homework, and told me about what he did. He was very gentle and shy and I liked him a lot, although I knew he was too old for me – he was twenty-five then. Despite that, we fell in love. I was very innocent and knew nothing about sex really, and my ideas of love were very romantic and unrealistic.'

Brock guessed she was repeating a phrase her father had used.

'On my seventeenth birthday my dad told me he had something important to tell me. He said that someone had asked for my hand in marriage. I was surprised, but also thrilled. I thought Abu must have spoken to my father, and although the age difference might worry him, Abu was a devout Muslim boy, and I began to prepare what I would say to persuade him, like how we would wait until I was a bit older or something.

'Only it wasn't that at all. Apparently my dad was talking about one of my cousins in Mirpur, who I'd never heard of. He said that he was sending me and mum over there for a few months to meet our family there, and to prepare for my wedding. I tried to argue with him, but he wouldn't listen. I asked him at least to delay the trip until I'd done my A levels, but he got angry then and told me I wouldn't be doing any more exams, because there wasn't any point.'

Nargis paused to take a sip of tea. Although the youngest, it now seemed to Kathy that in some ways she appeared to be the most composed and perhaps the strongest of the three women. Briony had stopped toasting the bread slices in front of the hissing gas fire, their appetites gone as Nargis told her story.

'So mum and I went to Kashmir. It was like going to the moon, honestly. After two months I was told to prepare myself for my wedding. I was given a present from my future husband, who I'd still not seen. This was a shalwar khameez and scarf embroidered with gold. It was very beautiful, but heavy and it scraped my skin. The wedding ceremony lasted all day, and throughout I had to keep my eyes on the floor and wasn't allowed to look at my husband who sat beside me, and the heavy veil and jewellery stopped me when I tried. In the evening I was taken to my husband's house, and when the last of the guests left the other women led me into the bedroom, where I put on pyjamas and sat and waited. Eventually this man came into the room. He had grey hair . . .' she glanced apologetically at Brock, '. . . and was quite fat and old. He told me that he was my husband. When I said that I didn't want to sleep with him he beat me up and forced himself on me.'

Briony had folded her arms tight round her chest and sat forward, hunched, frowning angrily. Fran was expressionless.

'Later, I told my mother, and she said that it was for a husband and wife to work out how they would live. She said that dad would often take his hand to her, and she accepted his punishment as just.

'My husband now began to make preparations for us to return to the UK, which for him and my father was the main point of our marriage, and about three months after the wedding we travelled to

Islamabad for him to get papers and travel documents. There we discovered a problem with my British passport, which had expired, and me and mum had to fly home immediately, before my husband had got clearance. He saw us off at the airport like a devoted husband, promising me a wonderful married life in London with no more beatings. He emphasised that it was essential that my father immediately take charge of the documents that he gave my mother, so that dad could finalise my husband's British passport application. On the flight home, when my mother fell asleep, I stole the documents from the envelope he had entrusted to her and replaced them with the in-flight magazine. I was sorry to do this, because I knew my father would be very angry with her. He met us at Heathrow with a great welcome and drove us back to Shadwell Road, and that night I escaped from the house and ran down to Chandler's Lane and begged Qasim and George and their family to take me in. They gave me a room next to Fran and George's flat and I've been hiding there ever since.'

All this time, Kathy thought, just fifty yards away from her father. Nargis lapsed into silence, head bowed. Eventually Brock prompted, 'How long ago was it that you returned to London?'

Kathy had been wanting to ask the same question, calculating the time when she must have become pregnant.

'Last September,' she said.

'And your father has been searching for you ever since?'

She nodded. 'He was very angry of course. I had disgraced him in the eyes of the world and his family, and he felt humiliated. He searched for me everywhere, him and my uncles, and he went to the police. He even offered a reward for anyone who would betray me to him. Two thousand quid.'

'And your husband,' Brock asked, 'is he over here now?'

'I don't think so. I think things went wrong for him because I had the papers he needed. But I think he'll get a second chance. I've heard that my father has announced that he is engaged to my sister Yasmin, who is fourteen.'

'Do they know about your baby?'

Nargis shook her head, folding her arms across her tummy. 'You want to know about Abu?'

'Yes.'

'It wasn't long before I met him again in Chandler's Yard. He would often come to the Horria to eat, and he was almost like part of their family. At first it felt very awkward seeing him again after what had happened, and me being pregnant, but he didn't seem to mind. After I'd been there a little while I decided to try to finish my A levels and he encouraged me. I started a correspondence course, and he became sort of my tutor.'

Kathy remembered the unlived-in atmosphere of Abu's spartan room at the university, and her feeling that he had really lived somewhere else.

Brock said, 'I understand that your father told the police that you had been abducted by a man.'

'Yes. He had to say that so the magistrate would issue a warrant.'

'But did he believe it himself?'

'Yes, he did. People told him that I had had a boyfriend before I went to Mirpur, an older man, and he became convinced that this man must have helped me to run away and stay hidden. He and my uncle asked questions everywhere about this man, but nobody outside of Chandler's Yard knew about me and Abu.'

'Then how did he know to come to Abu's funeral today?'

Nargis shook her head in despair. 'I don't know,' she whispered. 'I just don't know.'

'Someone must have told him,' Brock insisted. 'Someone must have decided that they'd collect the two thousand.'

Nargis bowed her head and began to weep. Brock looked in turn at the other women, but each seemed lost in her own thoughts. He glanced at Kathy, then got to his feet with a grunt and limped over to the long bench that ran along one wall of the room and reached to a row of reference books on a shelf above. Kathy gathered the plates onto the tray and carried it out to the kitchen.

After a few minutes she heard someone pad in behind her. Fran had brought in the jar of honey and packet of sliced bread. She was the enigmatic one, Kathy thought, and was pleased that it was her.

'Thanks.' Kathy wiped off some plates in the sink. 'Poor Nargis. She's very lucky to have friends like you. It makes all the difference.'

'They're not all like her dad,' Fran said defensively. 'Muslims I mean.'

'No, of course not . . .'

155

'He's just very traditional, from a place where life is hard. He can't help it.'

'So you married a Muslim too, Fran?'

She didn't reply and Kathy thought she'd been too direct. Then the woman said, 'Yeah. I suppose I've done the opposite of Nargis, and we've both ended up in the same place. Funny, init?'

Fran got a drying cloth and began to take the plates Kathy was stacking on the draining board. Leaving home and coming to UCLE had been traumatic for her, she explained. An eldest daughter, like Nargis, she had helped her mother, a single parent, raise her three brothers. At university she couldn't identify with the other girls who just wanted to party and have a good time with boys, and the boys who were only interested in getting pissed and screwing the girls. She became friends with a Muslim girl from the East End and their family, and began to go to classes in the Qur'an. Before the end of her first year she went home and told her mother that she wanted to convert to Islam. Her mum was horrified, and threw her out when she insisted on wearing the chador to go out to the shops. When she returned to London her Muslim girlfriend said that her family would like Fran to meet her cousin George. She realised that they were arranging a marriage, but she didn't mind. George turned out to be a very nice young man, very hard working and serious. Fran felt very secure in her marriage, because she knew George was devout and wouldn't drink alcohol or gamble or look at another woman.

'I suppose,' she added, still defensive, 'you'd say I was just reacting to the way I was brought up, with a new "uncle" in the house every six months, and Mum getting pissed and slapped around.'

Kathy thought about that, then said, 'It sounds to me as if George and his family are good people, Fran. I think it sounds as if both you and Nargis have been lucky to find them.'

Fran nodded. 'Yeah. And I reckon it would have worked out for Nargis and Abu too, even with the baby, if people had left them alone. I still can't believe that Abu hurt anybody. He just wasn't like that. Qasim used to say he was too gentle for his own good. If he really did do it, then someone else must have made him.'

'How could they do that? And who would want to?'

'I don't know. Maybe he was conned. Maybe they told him the gun was loaded with blanks.'

In the living room, Brock was thumbing through an old, well-used copy of *Butterworth's Police Law* when Briony sidled up alongside, scanning his reference shelf.

'I don't know about you,' he muttered, 'but without offence to our Muslim friends, I always took it to be an absolute tradition to have at least one stiff drink after a funeral, and today I've been to two. Where do you stand on that?'

'I wouldn't mind a drink,' she said.

'Fine.' He reached under the bench, producing a couple of glasses and a bottle of whisky. 'I noticed that Professor Springer favoured Scotch. With water?'

'He drank it neat, but I like mine with water.'

'I'll get some.'

He heard Kathy deep in conversation with Fran in the kitchen and went instead to the bathroom, returning with a small jug of water that he splashed into each glass. 'Cheers.'

She gulped, giving no reply, then pointed at one of the books on the shelf. It was one of Springer's books that Kathy had got for him.

'You're reading Max?'

'Trying to. Haven't got to that one yet. I'm afraid I'm finding them tough going.'

'Try it,' she said peremptorily, jutting her chin at the book.

'*A Man in Dark Times*,' Brock read the title. 'That one's easier, is it?'

'Probably. It's his autobiography, written just after his wife died, so it's a bit gloomy in parts. But moving too. His experiences in the camps for instance.'

Brock frowned, puzzled. 'I thought it was his parents who were in the camps . . .'

'Not in Germany – in Lebanon. He understood, you see? He experienced it. It gave him the right to talk about it.'

'About what?'

'About the struggle between truth and freedom.'

Brock sipped his drink, none the wiser. 'You haven't told us how you fit into all this, Briony. How come you know these people?'

'I met George at uni, and through him I met Fran and Nargis and Abu.'

'That puts you in a rather special position, doesn't it? You must be one of the few people who knew both Max and his killer.'

She flinched at the word and glared at him. 'I still don't accept that Abu did it,' she hissed fiercely, keeping her voice low so that Nargis wouldn't hear.

'I'm afraid the forensic evidence is pretty overwhelming. Both his gloves and his coat were impregnated with the same gunshot residue that was on Max's clothes.'

She stared at him in disbelief, as if genuinely unable to reconcile this with something else in her mind.

'Why do you doubt it so strongly?' Brock pressed her.

'Because . . . because I *knew* Abu. He wasn't a mad fanatic. And he didn't hate Max.'

'How do you know that? Did he know Max?'

Her eyes shifted away. She sipped her drink. 'We discussed Max, as my tutor, and because he'd attacked Abu's boss, Haygill. Abu thought it was rather silly, that's all. I couldn't even get him to have a decent argument about it, you know, the ethics of what they're trying to do and all that.'

'Sometimes people are very good at not showing what they really think, Briony. Especially if they've had painful experiences in the past. Did you know he was detained by the Israelis for a time when he was a teenager? Did he ever talk about that?'

Briony shook her head, the same frown of bafflement on her face.

'And Max was Jewish, wasn't he?'

'But not practising. He didn't even support a lot of what the Israelis have done. That's what I'm saying. You should read the book.'

Brock said, 'OK,' and reached up for Springer's book. 'And how's your work going now?'

'Nowhere.' She turned away. 'It's impossible without him.'

'But wouldn't he want you to finish it? Surely that would be the best thing you could do to honour his memory?'

'It doesn't work like that. It has no meaning now, like empty labour. I just feel sick when I think about it. Each day I go in there and sit at the table and hope that he'll tell me what I should do.' She pushed the glass aside and walked away.

15

Brock made some phone calls, getting the address of a refuge in East London where he could take Nargis. He also spoke to the duty inspector at Tooting police station, and was advised that Mr Manzoor and his companions had been interviewed under caution, then released pending further inquiries. They had claimed to be mourners who had become involved in a minor scuffle when Mr Manzoor had attempted to make contact with his runaway daughter whom he had recognised at the scene. The so-called clubs they were carrying were in fact traditional Kashmir walking sticks. Manzoor demanded that the police execute the warrant issued by the magistrate for the return of his daughter and prosecute anyone who attempted to obstruct it. In particular he wished to make a complaint against a woman police officer at the scene who had made a racist attack on him, injuring his right arm.

'That's nonsense,' Brock said. 'I was a witness to the whole thing.'

'That may be so, sir,' the inspector said, 'but I've had to follow procedure and notify CIB.'

Brock's heart sank. The Complaints Investigation Bureau would follow up any accusation of racial abuse against an officer with vigour. 'Where is Manzoor now?' he asked.

'He was given a medical examination here, sir, then taken to hospital for X-rays and further treatment. He had quite a bit of swelling and bruising, and he'd worked himself up into a fair old state. You say you were a witness, sir? Maybe you could come over and give a statement.'

'Yes, yes,' Brock shook his head impatiently, wishing now that he'd used some other way to shake off the purple car.

'And what about the daughter, sir? Any information on where we can find her?'

'I think you'll find that the warrant he referred to covered the East London area,' Brock said vaguely. 'You might speak to Shadwell Road. They have the details.'

'Very well . . .' Brock could hear the caution in the inspector's voice as he tried to pick his way through what was becoming a minefield – a race complaint against an officer, a DCI from Serious Crime, a warrant for an abducted girl . . . 'You won't be approaching Mr Manzoor yourself, will you, sir? Only, if you're a witness it might be . . .'

'Thank you, Inspector,' Brock said tersely and rang off. All the same, he knew the man was right.

While the three women sat huddled together around the gas fire, discussing what they should do, Brock took Kathy into the kitchen and told her what he'd learned. She went pale when he mentioned CIB.

'Now, look, you've got plenty of witnesses, Kathy. You used minimum force to prevent a serious assault.'

'I don't know for sure he was going to assault her,' she said, feeling her heart thumping, adrenalin flushing through her as surely as if the assault on her was a physical one. 'I didn't know it was him, or his daughter.'

'Exactly.'

'And I can't remember if I identified myself before I hit him.'

'There was no time. It all happened too quickly. I saw it very clearly, Kathy. You acted quickly and properly.'

She looked at him directly. 'But then, you would say that, wouldn't you? You're my DCI. That's what CIB3 will say.'

There were three complaints departments. CIB1 was administrative and advisory, while CIB2 investigated serious allegations. The third department, CIB3, was different. Its task was to search for police corruption and racism in an undercover, proactive way, even without complaints. The case against Kathy might be investigated by CIB2, but Brock and the others might be tainted by it and become a target for CIB3.

'Let's not get carried away,' Brock said. 'Manzoor's putting up smoke, covering up his hurt pride. But maybe he's got more than that to hide.'

'Like what?'

'If he came to the funeral in the hope of catching his daughter, then he must have known that Abu Khadra was her boyfriend, right? So when and how did he make this discovery? If someone at Chandler's Yard tipped him off that she was there, why didn't he just tell the police and get them to execute the warrant? Why wait till the funeral?'

'I don't know . . .' Then something kicked in Kathy's memory. 'When was it . . .?' she said slowly, thinking. 'On the day after Abu was killed, yes, the Wednesday afternoon, I went back to Shadwell Road, just to sniff around.'

'What? You were supposed to be on leave, Kathy. Russell had taken over the case.'

'I know, but Bren had been going on about how quickly everything had happened, and I was curious. That's when I met Manzoor – that's how he recognised me this afternoon. The barman at The Three Crowns had mentioned that he'd seen Manzoor talking to one of the skinheads, so I went into his shop and asked him. He said he'd just tried to persuade the man not to make trouble. Then, when I was leaving, he asked me kind of casually if I knew where Abu had lived. Was it in Chandler's Yard, or was it the university?'

'You're thinking that he must have known then that Abu was the boyfriend? And if he knew on the Wednesday, why not earlier, before Abu was killed? But how?' Brock thought about that. 'It'd be a terrible irony if I told him, wouldn't it?'

'How do you mean?'

'Well, suppose he knew the boyfriend's name, but nothing else. Then Bren and I turn up at the mosque looking for someone of that name and with a picture as well, and one of the other men there says they think that man goes to the mosque in Chandler's Yard . . . What would Manzoor do?'

'Tell the skinheads?' Kathy asked softly. 'Deliberately get Abu killed? Is that possible?'

'It felt as if we were set up,' Brock furrowed his brow, thinking back. 'As soon as we stepped out of the alleyway. The crowd waiting for us, the skinheads in the pub doorway falling into step behind, the flying wedge from the front, the sneak attack from the back. Yes, it did feel like we'd been set up, but I put that down to my paranoia at having failed to bring Abu in alive.'

He reached for the phone again, flicking through the pages of his notebook until he found a number that he dialled. 'Superintendent Russell, please,' he said. 'This is DCI Brock, in connection with the Springer/Khadra inquiry.'

He waited, both of them tense. Kathy began pacing the couple of yards from one side of the kitchen to the other, chewing her lip.

'Cyril!' Brock said at last, crouching forward over the instrument as if he could focus himself down the line.

'Evening, Brock. Saw you at the service this morning.'

'Yes. I went to the Khadra interment this afternoon, too.'

'So I understand. I gave clearance. You must have been about the only one there, weren't you? We kept it very quiet. Unfortunately our crew was called away on another matter just beforehand. Everything go off all right?'

'I'm afraid not, Cyril. Some outsiders followed the mourners to the cemetery and caused a bit of bother.'

Russell swore softly, then listened as Brock told him what had happened. Despite the silence from the other end of the line, Brock could imagine quite clearly what was going through the other man's head. He was within a year of retirement, Brock knew, after a highly distinguished career. The Springer/Khadra case was a potential minefield and his rapid closure treatment of it may have been precipitate, wishful thinking. They had gone to pains to keep the arrangements for Abu's burial confined to the few people involved, but the absence of a police escort had been, in retrospect, a serious lapse, and uncharacteristic of Russell, normally a punctilious manager.

'I hope I don't presume too much, Cyril,' Brock said, having painted the bleak picture, 'when I say that I regarded ourselves as being your representatives, even though technically both DS Kolla and I were on leave at the time. We felt our earlier involvement made it appropriate for us to play such a role, in the absence of other police presence.'

Silence, then, 'I see.'

Brock knew that Russell was perfectly well aware that if he was being offered, not a life raft perhaps, but at least a life jacket, then there was a price tag attached.

'We've been going over a few ideas about Manzoor and his role in all this, Cyril, and we've got some thoughts we'd like to share with you, which might even impact on your report. If you thought that would be proper.'

Russell cleared his throat, then said, 'I think it would be essential, Brock, if they have a bearing on my inquiry. What sort of thoughts?'

'I wonder if you could tell me if any of your skinhead suspects mentioned anything about being helped, or even encouraged, by the Asians.'

'One of them, a little thug by the name of Wilson, said he talked to some of the Asians in the crowd and they told him about Abu and what he was being arrested for. He said he passed this on to his friends in the pub, but of course denies having anything to do with what followed.'

'Nothing more specific than that? About a particular Asian, perhaps, egging them on?'

'I don't recall anything specific, but I can check the transcripts of his interviews. You think Manzoor played a more active role?'

'It's a possibility. However, I'm constrained by the fact that we had to call for back-up from the local force, with whom Manzoor has now laid this complaint against my DS, and being myself a witness to what happened, I can't be seen to be hounding the man.'

'Ah.' Russell was beginning to get the picture. 'Well, let me say, Brock, that although I can't interfere in any way with what CIB may do, I will certainly lend every support to my people on the ground, including, on this occasion, you and your sergeant. And if either of you have further information . . .'

'Not information, Cyril. What I'm suggesting is that it may be necessary for me to participate with you in having a closer look at Manzoor's involvement in all this. Not Sergeant Kolla, of course. She can't possibly be involved while there's an outstanding complaint against her.'

'Ah, yes. Well, if you're fit for duty, Brock, I can't see any obstacle to that proposal. None at all. Sounds very reasonable.'

Brock replaced the phone as tenderly as if it were made of fragile porcelain. 'Good,' he said. 'Good. Now let's get these people off our hands and get down to work.'

'Brock,' Kathy said cautiously. 'Suzanne was expecting me to get you back to Battle in time for dinner tonight. Do you think you should phone her?'

'Oh, Lord. Yes, yes, of course. What the hell do I say?'

'Why don't you tell her I beat up a suspect and now you've got to save me from the CIB.'

Brock winced and turned back to the phone. Kathy tactfully left him alone and returned to the living room to check on the women. They seemed remarkably comfortable, even Nargis, who was sipping at a weak whisky and water, presumably prescribed by Briony. Both she and Fran had pulled their scarves back, letting their hair fall free, and in the glow of the fire the three of them looked like students comparing notes on boys or movies rather than women grieving the dead.

From time to time Kathy went to the door and picked up phrases from Brock's conversation, 'Knocked him flying with her baton . . . Not a scratch . . . Now that's unfair, Suzanne, Bren and I were surrounded by dozens . . . She may well be fitter than me, but . . . Anyway, I've got to get her out of this mess . . . But you know I can't drive with this leg . . .'

Kathy returned to her armchair before Brock appeared at the door, looking more drained than after his conversation with Superintendent Russell. 'Well, now, ladies,' he said wearily. 'Let's get you sorted, shall we?'

After they dropped Nargis and Briony at the refuge, Kathy drove on towards Shadwell Road with Fran who was anxious to get back to her husband George. She directed them to approach the area through the neighbouring back streets, parking the car at the end of a short lane that connected with the far end of Chandler's Yard. By this way they were able to arrive at the illuminated front of the Horria Café without going into Shadwell Road itself. As Kathy kept pace with Brock's limping steps, Fran ran ahead into the café. From the darkness of the yard they watched her joyful reunion with her husband inside. There was a crowd this evening in the Horria, and they saw Qasim enthroned in the centre, a bandage round his head like a turbaned potentate.

Brock pulled the door open, was hit by warm smells of cooking and a hubbub of noise, and hobbled in. Immediately the noise died away and he found himself standing there facing a wall of implacable faces. For a moment he felt like the clown who opened the wrong door and found himself inside the cage of man-eating tigers. Then someone shouted something and pointed, and the faces immediately lit up and a great roar of approval echoed round the café walls. Only they weren't looking at him. He turned and saw Kathy at his shoulder, grinning at them, and then they were clapping, the claps falling into a chanting rhythm, and Qasim hoisted himself off his seat and lumbered forward and grabbed her hand and led her into their midst.

Ignored, Brock stood by the door watching as George and Qasim demonstrated with flashing arm gestures the way in which Kathy had felled Manzoor. They urged her to produce her weapon and demonstrate it before them all, but she modestly declined, and murmured a few words to Qasim who reluctantly waved Brock over and seated them both at what was apparently the table of greatest status in the Horria. Here was already seated an old man whose leathery features were embellished with a magnificent large moustache and an embroidered skullcap.

'This is my grandfather, also called Qasim Ali,' Qasim explained. Grandpa Qasim was the patriarch, the doyen of merchants and wisest of men. He gracefully welcomed his guests while Qasim junior explained that, when he was a boy, before the Pakis had become so numerous, his grandfather had owned several shops and warehouses on Shadwell Road and had been the principal businessman in the neighbourhood. He had also been the king of the trade in qat, a narcotic leaf chewed by Yemenis, which Grandpa Qasim flew in twice a week to London from Ethiopia and Kenya, and stored in fridges that used to fill the rear storeroom of the Horria, freshness being of the utmost importance to the connoisseur of qat.

'Those days are gone,' Qasim junior said sadly. 'In those days any man foolish enough to interrupt a family burial would have ended up in a grave himself. But look at us today, shamed by those Paki cowboys. Only Kathy came out of it well.'

'I know what you mean, Qasim,' Brock nodded, rubbing his knee.

'Oh, but yours was a great battle, two against hundreds. You couldn't help what happened to Abu.'

'How do you think Manzoor knew that Abu and his daughter were close?'

'I don't know, but I can tell you that nobody here, in Chandler's Yard, told him. If they had, he'd have known that she was here . . .' he pointed up at the ceiling, 'all the time.'

'Her room is up there?'

'Top floor, in the attic above the mosque, across the landing from George and Fran.'

'And Abu spent a lot of time with her there?'

Qasim shrugged. 'It's not something the imam would approve, perhaps, but they'd both experienced suffering, and who were we to say they weren't good for each other?'

'I know about Nargis' story, but what suffering had Abu experienced?'

'I don't know all the details, but he came from a poor family in Lebanon, and they went through some very bad times and he got into some kind of trouble. But he was lucky, he said. He might have become a kid of the streets or maybe a terrorist, but instead he got a sponsor who helped him get an education. He went to university in Saudi or the Gulf, and when he was qualified he got a job from this professor who brought him over here. He said he owed this man everything. He said he was like a father to him.'

'Professor Haygill?'

'I don't know his name. He just said this English professor had saved his life.'

They were interrupted by several women from Qasim's kitchen who began to bring dishes to the table, containing stews and loaves of flat bread. 'A feast for the heroes!' Qasim announced, and then, in an undertone to Brock, added, 'This is yer classic Yemeni *asid*. But I can do you steak and chips if you'd rather, eh?' Brock said he'd stick with the stew, and everyone began to eat.

After they'd wiped their plates clean, and Qasim relaxed with a contented grunt and lit up, Brock said, 'The room that Nargis lives in upstairs, who owns it?'

'Grandpa Qasim owns the whole building.'

'And did Nargis pay rent?'

'No. She hadn't a bean. She came with nothing.'

'That was good of you.'

'Why do you ask?'

'I want to have a look in the room, with Sergeant Kolla. You can come along too, if you want.'

'You want to search Nargis' room?'

'Yes. I'm entitled to do that if I believe that Abu occupied the room too, and may have left something there. I'd like your cooperation. Would you ask Grandpa Qasim for me?'

Qasim tilted his weight back dangerously in his chair and drew on his cigarette, pondering. 'You still 'aven't got the gun, 'ave you?'

'That's right.'

'I don't like the idea of you poking around in their room.'

'No, neither do I, but I'm afraid it's necessary. Fran could be a witness too if you like.'

'Blimey.' Qasim blew a puff at the ceiling fan. 'It's not that big a room.' He leaned forward and spoke to Grandpa Qasim for a moment, then turned and nodded to Brock and got up to lead the way.

They climbed the stairs at the back of the café which led up to the lobby of the little mosque where Brock had found Abu's shoes and coat, then continued up another, narrower dog-leg flight to the attic floor. There was no lock on the door of Nargis' room, and Fran and Qasim looked on with disapproval as Brock and Kathy put on latex gloves and went inside.

It was a small space, once perhaps a maid's room, largely filled by an old iron-framed bed, and the belongings it contained were pathetically few. As they studied it, their backs to the others at the door, Kathy murmured to Brock, 'Are you sure this is a good idea?'

He gave her a sidelong look, then nodded. 'You're right. Go back outside with the others. I'll take care of it.'

She hesitated, then shook her head. 'Come on. Let's do it quickly.'

The clothes that Nargis had brought or been donated were hung behind a curtain in an alcove in one corner, and Kathy started there. Brock turned to a backpack in another corner, which held some of

Abu's things, his motorbike helmet, some socks and underwear and sweaters, a folder of documents.

They both finished at the same moment and turned together to the bed, approaching it from opposite sides, and began feeling swiftly under pillows, blankets, mattress as the witnesses watched them dolefully from the doorway. Beneath the pillow they found a folder of documents that appeared to belong to Nargis, her passport, birth certificate and medical papers, as well as a number of documents in foreign script that they assumed related to her period in Kashmir. They put these back and continued working down towards the foot of the bed where they raised the tail of the mattress and found a plastic bag.

Brock lifted it up, immediately disappointed that it didn't seem heavy or hard enough. More documents, he guessed, and confirmed it by pulling out Abu's passport and a number of documents in Arabic. Wrapped inside them was a plastic pouch, sealed with a strip of tape. He carefully pulled it away and looked inside, and as he did so his face lost all expression. He handed the pouch across to Kathy, who felt inside and slid something out of one of its pockets. They all recognised immediately what it was, a wad of money.

Kathy examined it and said softly, 'Hundred pound notes. A pack of fifty.' She laid it on the bed and slid five more identical wads out of the pouch.

'Thirty thousand quid,' Qasim breathed.

Brock took the pouch back from Kathy and held it up to the light of the lampshade hanging from the centre of the ceiling. 'BCCD,' he read. 'What's that?' Then he squinted more closely at some small print. 'Bank of Credit and Commerce Dubai.'

He replaced the money in the pouch and the pouch in the plastic bag and they continued with their search, under the carpet, behind the mirror, beneath the little table and chair, until they were satisfied that there was nothing more.

Sanjeev Manzoor bustled in looking belligerent and aggrieved. He was dressed in a smart dark suit as usual, against which the white triangle of the sling supporting his right arm looked particularly conspicuous, like a banner signifying 'victim'. His solicitor was an older Asian with greying hair and a look of permanent scepticism on his face, as if he'd seen everything and heard every possible explanation for it. He carried a bulging, battered leather briefcase that seemed to require all his strength to hoist onto the table. They waved aside the offer of tea or coffee, and nodded curtly as Superintendent Russell introduced himself and Brock. They were in the scruffy setting of the interview room of the Shadwell Road police station, where Brock had found a fax awaiting him when he finally arrived after leaving Chandler's Yard. The fax had comprised a cover sheet from Russell together with a copy of a single page from an interview with the skinhead Wilson.

A   (NO AUDIBLE REPLY)

Q 37   Well, why would they want to help you?

A   . . . . be surprised, wouldn't you?

Q 38   No but—

A   Like there was this one, a little Paki in a flash suit, what was fucking wetting himself. He said the Arab the coppers had gone to fetch had topped a white man. He said there was only two coppers.

Q 39   You thought he wanted to help you?

A   He only tried to give me some fucking scissors, didn't he?

Q 40   What? Say that again.

A   A pair of fucking great scissors. Said if he was younger he'd use them himself.

Q 41   What did you think he meant by that?

A   He wanted me to stick them in the Arab, didn't he?

Q 42   Why?

A   Well, they all hate each other, don't they, Arabs and wogs and stuff.

Q 43   What did you do?

A   I told him to fuck off.

Q 44   What did he look like, apart from the suit?

A   They all look the same, don't they? Middle-aged, my height, dotted tie.

Q 45   Dotted?

A   Yes. White dots.

Brock set his chair slightly behind and to one side of Russell's, so that there would be no doubt as to who was in charge. He eased himself down, hooked his stick on the seat and gazed benignly at Manzoor who, he was delighted to see, was sporting the same silk polka dot tie he had been wearing at mosque that night.

Russell cleared his throat and began, pressing the start buttons on the recording machines and identifying those present and time and date. He thanked Manzoor for his cooperation and emphasised that he was not under arrest and was under no obligation to answer questions, but cautioned him nonetheless.

'One moment, Superintendent,' Manzoor's solicitor, by the name of Versi, interjected, wrestling a fat file out of his briefcase. 'My client has asked me to make it plain that he will refuse to answer any questions unless and until he has an explanation of why the police have not yet taken steps to return his daughter to him under the terms of the magistrate's warrant dated the sixteenth of October last, of which this is a certified copy . . .' He plucked a sheet of paper from the file and slid it across to Russell. 'His cooperation is also conditional upon the arrest of the officer, Sergeant Kolla, who obstructed him in speaking to his missing daughter and who caused the serious injuries to my client this afternoon.'

Russell studied the paper for a moment, then said, 'I'm afraid I can't help you with either of those matters, Mr Versi. Since Mr Manzoor has lodged a formal complaint against Sergeant Kolla, that matter will be taken up by the department that specialises in such cases. But I can assure you that they are taken very seriously indeed. As for the matter of your daughter, I believe that is in the hands of the local division. We are here purely in connection with investigations into the arrest and death of one Abu Khadra, about which we believe you may have information that can be of assistance to us. This is a very serious matter, Mr Versi, a murder investigation, and we cannot accept conditions upon your client's cooperation.'

Versi and Manzoor put their heads together for a moment, then Versi straightened and said, 'My client is a very prominent and public-spirited citizen, Superintendent, and will be glad to provide whatever assistance he can. He only wishes to draw your attention to the extreme emotional and physical stress these other two matters are placing him under.'

'That is understood.' Russell nodded and turned to Brock. 'Chief Inspector? Anything you'd like to add?'

Brock gave a mild little cough and said, 'No, no . . .'

Russell turned back to address Manzoor.

'. . . except . . .' Brock smiled apologetically, 'well, since Mr Manzoor mentions those other two matters together, there is one curious feature, although as you say, Superintendent, it has nothing to do with our case . . . May I?' He reached over and picked up the photocopy of the warrant. 'Ah, yes. Issued under Section nineteen of the Sexual Offences Act 1956, relating to the abduction of girls, on the basis of a statement on oath provided by the father.'

'Yes?' Versi looked at him curiously. 'So?'

'And witnessed by yourself, I see, Mr Versi.'

'Certainly. What is your point please?'

'Well, you're the lawyer, so correct me if I'm wrong, but I understood Section nineteen of the Act related to the abduction of *unmarried* girls under the age of eighteen.'

Brock was aware of Manzoor giving a little start.

'That's right.' Versi nodded.

'Well . . .' Brock beamed, 'of course, Mr Manzoor, of all people, will know the marital state of his daughter Nargis. It's only that the very same Sergeant Kolla whom he refers to happened to mention to me only today something about getting a translation for a wedding certificate issued to a girl called Nargis in Kashmir. And if that were the case, of course, the issue of a fraudulent warrant on the basis of a perjured oath would be an extremely serious matter. But probably I'm getting confused with another Nargis, eh? Just a curious coincidence?'

Manzoor was rigid in his seat, staring at Brock. Versi turned to him, puzzled.

'Anyway,' Brock went on cheerfully, 'this is all completely irrelevant to what we're here for. Those investigating the complaint against Sergeant Kolla will no doubt be interested in clearing up the confusion, if there is one, but we are not.' He turned to Russell with an apologetic smile. 'Sorry, I'm wasting time.'

Russell frowned, 'Yes, I think we'd better stick to the point here, Brock.'

'Em . . .' Versi was glancing back and forward between Manzoor and Brock with a look of perplexity. 'I wonder if I might have a moment with my client?'

But Manzoor roused himself abruptly and said, 'No, no. Let's get this other thing out of the way and then we can be gone. I don't feel well.'

Versi said, 'Mr Manzoor was given pills at the hospital.'

'Of course,' Russell conceded. 'I have only a few simple questions to ask Mr Manzoor. It shouldn't take long. Firstly, how long have you known the man Abu Khadra?'

'I have never met him. The first time I heard of him was when he—'

'You're indicating Chief Inspector Brock?'

'Yes, when he came to the mosque and asked for our help in finding this man.'

'That was the Twaqulia Mosque in Shadwell Road on the evening of the twenty-fifth of January?'

'Yes.'

'You'd never heard Khadra's name or seen him before then?'

'That's right.'

'Then why did you go to his funeral today, Mr Manzoor?'

'Out of curiosity, that's all.'

'How did you find the way? The burial was deliberately kept confidential.'

'I . . . I saw the others leaving Chandler's Yard. I followed them.'

'You saw some people leaving Chandler's Yard and you thought, "Ah, they're going to a funeral, I'll just tag along", eh?'

Manzoor said nothing.

'At the funeral you attempted to confront one of the mourners, your own daughter, as you have yourself just said. How did you know she would be there?'

Versi said, 'Superintendent, you have just said that Mr Manzoor's daughter is another matter.'

'But in this point she is relevant to my inquiries. I put it to you, Mr Manzoor, that you followed the funeral party because you knew that your daughter had been friends with Abu Khadra, and you expected her to go to the interment. Is that true?'

Manzoor shook his head and said nothing.

'You refuse to answer? Then let me also put another obvious

conclusion to you, and that is that if you knew of Abu Khadra this afternoon, the second of February, then you also knew of him on the twenty-fifth of January, when DCI Brock came to the mosque.'

'No!' Manzoor snapped.

'Oh, I think you did. You believed him to be her lover, didn't you?'

Versi had no idea where the policeman's questions were leading, but it was clear to him that his client should say nothing until they did know, and he interrupted to say as much. But Russell could see that Manzoor was boiling with fury and frustration, so he merely nodded and said, 'Yes, yes. I can imagine how difficult it must be for you, Mr Manzoor, with a runaway daughter and all that. I dare say you thought you were doing the right thing . . .'

'The right thing!' Manzoor exploded, banging a fist on the table. 'Don't you patronise me, sir! Don't you talk about my daughter to me! You're just trying to protect your own kind! I am attacked and humiliated in front of my brothers and my daughter by a racist policewoman and you do nothing but try to spin webs to protect her.'

Russell snapped back hard, 'But suppose you were wrong about Khadra, Mr Manzoor? Suppose he was nothing but a good friend to your daughter, and you got yourself worked up over nothing?'

Manzoor's eyes bulged with outrage at this sidestep. 'No! He was her seducer! He corrupted and debauched her, my daughter, my beautiful Nargis.'

'You've got no proof of that,' Russell said dismissively.

For a moment it seemed that Manzoor was tearing at his clothes, pulling off his jacket prior to a fight, but then he jerked a leather wallet out of an inside pocket and plucked out of it a colour photograph which he waved at the two policemen. 'Proof?' he yelled. 'I have proof!'

It was taken in a public swimming pool, Brock guessed, the background all black heads bobbing against blue water. In the foreground, leaning on the tiled edge, were Nargis and Abu, both dripping wet and grinning widely at the camera. She was wearing a bikini, and he had his brown arm round her shoulders, holding her close. They both looked very young and very happy.

173

Russell and Brock examined it carefully while Versi argued in an agitated whisper with his client, trying to get on top of all this.

'When was it taken?' Russell asked.

'I don't know. Before . . .'

'Before she was sent to Kashmir,' Brock nodded, recognising the differences between the girl in the picture, softer, plumper, and the one who had drunk tea in his living room that afternoon.

'Is that why you sent her away?'

'No, no. I didn't know then about this man.'

'So how did you get this picture?'

The rage had gone from Sanjeev Manzoor. He lowered his head and began to weep bitterly. 'It came in the post.'

'When was this?'

He pulled a crisp white cotton handkerchief from his pocket and wiped his eyes and nose. 'The day he came to the mosque.'

'You are indicating DCI Brock? So that would be Tuesday, the twenty-fifth of January. Do you know who sent it?'

'No. There was nothing else, no letter, nothing.' He shook his head in despair. 'It was the first sign I had had of Nargis in three months. It broke my heart.'

'And you felt very angry towards the man in the photograph, Abu Khadra?'

'I didn't know his name, only that picture. Of course I was angry. I wanted to kill him.'

'And that evening, after DCI Brock came to the mosque and showed you a picture of the same man and told you his name, you had the opportunity to do that, by telling the skinheads what to do. You stage-managed it didn't you, Mr Manzoor? You directed the murder of the man you thought had corrupted your daughter.'

16

Kathy felt a new energy as she drove back to the women's refuge that night, as if the discovery of the money under Nargis' mattress had awakened some instinct for the hunt that had been missing until then. Perhaps it was the amount of the cash, *thirty* thousand as in thirty pieces of silver, that seemed so telling, but for the first time she felt a sense of reality about the crime and their dead suspect, as strong as if they had found the gun rather than money in the pouch. In fact more so, because the gun would have simply sealed Abu's guilt and finished the story, whereas the money opened new questions and trails. About Nargis, for example, the beautiful, innocent Juliet mourning her killer Romeo. Even if she hadn't pried into Abu's belongings when he was alive, he had been dead now for ten days and it seemed inconceivable she hadn't known that she was sleeping on all that cash. Kathy just hoped she could find out before the CIB caught up with her.

Nargis and Briony were washing up some plates in the kitchen when Kathy arrived. She told them that she had to ask Nargis a few additional questions, and explained that she would have to do it in the formal setting of the local police station, where a proper record of their interview could be made. Briony began to object that her friend had gone through enough that day, but Nargis said it was OK. She seemed quite calm and answered Kathy's questions about the refuge in her soft little voice as they drove.

Since Nargis was still a juvenile, Kathy had arranged for a social worker to be present for the interview, and when the three of them were seated in the small interview room, Kathy cautioned the girl and explained her rights, then began to ask her about her relationship with Abu.

'You first met him how long ago, Nargis?'

'A year ago, this time last year.'

'And you became close friends?'

'We went out together.'

'You were his girlfriend?'

'Yes.'

'And then, six months ago, your father sent you overseas to be married, and when you returned last October you ran away from your home and went to live in a room in the house of Mr Qasim Ali in Chandler's Yard?'

'Yes.'

'Did you have any money then?'

A crease appeared between Nargis' dark eyebrows at this question. 'No. Mr Ali's family took pity on me. They helped me.'

'And you began to see Abu Khadra again? When was that?'

'Yes, soon after I arrived there.'

'You became lovers?'

Nargis looked startled, glanced at the social worker, then down at her lap and didn't answer. You're right, Kathy thought, tell me to mind my own business.

'What I mean is, Nargis, that you couldn't go outside for fear of your family, and so Abu came and spent time with you. A lot of time.'

She gave a meek little shrug.

'In fact, he pretty well lived with you in Mr Ali's house, didn't he?'

Again she said nothing, and Kathy went on, 'So you were very close. Did he tell you about what he had to do? To kill Professor Springer?'

'No!' The girl shook her head firmly. 'Never. I don't believe he did that.' Yet the words lacked force.

'But he did, Nargis. There's very strong scientific evidence. And since Abu died, you must have thought about that a lot, haven't you? About what signs he gave? For instance, do you know where he was that afternoon that Springer was killed? Just over two weeks ago, the Thursday. You must have thought back to that day.'

Nargis' eyes slipped away. 'I don't know,' she said softly at last. 'He came home that evening . . .'

'To Chandler's Yard?'

'Yes, at about eight. He said he'd been working, at the university.'

'Didn't he seem agitated, worked up about something?'

She didn't reply, head bowed to her hands clutched over her tummy, and Kathy was again struck how self-possessed she was, as if she had determined to let nothing further intrude on her private meditation with her unborn child.

'You see, I'm wondering if someone forced Abu to do this terrible thing, Nargis.'

'How could they?' she said simply.

'Perhaps he needed money for something?'

Again Nargis seemed to focus at mention of the word. 'Money? No, he had a good job.'

'He didn't seem anxious at around that time? Under stress? Did he talk about other people? People at his work, perhaps? Or new people he'd met?'

But Nargis only shrugged and said nothing. Kathy began to feel that she was wasting her time against this implacable artlessness.

'Where did he keep his gun?'

'I never saw a gun.'

'What about the money?'

'The money?' Nargis' head came up and she stared at Kathy, fully engaged.

'Yes, Nargis. The money under the mattress in your room.'

'You've been in my room?' She seemed more astonished than upset.

'Yes.'

'That money belongs to my baby and me. Abu gave it to us.'

'When did he do that?'

She hesitated, then said, 'About . . . about two weeks ago.'

'When exactly?'

'I don't know. He just showed it to me one evening and said that it was for me and the baby, if anything should happen to him.'

'"If anything should happen to him"? You must have thought that was very strange, didn't you? Didn't you ask him what he meant?'

'No.'

'Where did he get it from?'

'I don't know. It was his.'

'It's a lot of cash.'

'Thirty thousand pounds.' Then she added fiercely, 'You'd better not have taken any. He said it was for the baby and me.'

Kathy eventually left her in the care of the social worker who wanted to talk to her about her benefit entitlements, and returned home. There were two messages on her answering machine. One was from Tina the travel agent, sounding bright and cheerful; the other, guarded and ominous, was from an inspector of the Metropolitan Police Complaints Investigation Bureau, CIB2. Both asked her to return their call. Despite having anticipated it for the past several hours, Kathy still found her hand trembling when she pressed the button to replay the second message. Together, the two calls seemed to sum up her choices, the fork in the road. She had a bath, went to bed, and didn't sleep.

When she reported to Queen Anne's Gate the next morning she discovered that the CIB inspector had left a message there too. She found an empty room, and without putting on the light, sat at the unfamiliar desk and stared at the phone. Then she realised that she was behaving as if she were guilty, hiding herself away as if deserving to be separated from the others. So she got up and returned to the office she shared with Bren and another detective, and picked up her phone.

The inspector informed her curtly that a serious complaint had been made against her by a member of the public, a Mr Sanjeev Manzoor; that she was not under any circumstances to approach Mr Manzoor or any member of his family or acquaintances; and that she should consider herself suspended from duty until a preliminary interview had been held some time in the following week, to which she would be entitled to bring one adviser.

She cleared her throat and said, 'Superintendent Russell has asked me to make a report on a related matter at a case conference he's holding this morning, sir. May I attend that?'

The inspector considered this, asked her a couple of questions, then agreed.

Again that trembling hand when she replaced the receiver. She swore softly under her breath and took some deep breaths. She became aware that Bren and the other man, a DC on secondment from SO8, were looking questioningly at her.

'CIB,' she said.

'Shit!' Bren breathed.

'Shit!' the DC echoed.

'They didn't take long. What'd they say?' Bren asked.

Kathy explained and both men swore again. It seemed to be the only adequate word. Kathy found their anxious sympathy even more scary than the CIB inspector's curtness.

'This happened to one of our blokes last year,' the DC said. 'He's still on suspension, eight months later.'

'We had a DI suspended eighteen months,' Bren said gloomily.

Kathy was wishing she'd made the call from the empty office. Then Brock put his head round the door to check they were all available for the conference, and Bren, nodding at Kathy as at someone who'd just been diagnosed with something terminal, said, 'CIB, chief.'

'Oh, they've been in touch already have they, Kathy? That was quick. What's the story?'

She repeated it and he nodded, point by point.

'Just the usual, then.' He didn't seem particularly dismayed.

'We were saying, boss,' the DC chipped in, 'how long the process takes. What do you reckon?'

'Opening a book on it, are we?' Brock asked. 'Put me down for a fiver. Let's see . . .' He rubbed his beard contemplatively, then took out his wallet and pulled out a note. 'Forty-eight hours. No, make it twenty-four. Five quid says they'll have dropped it within twenty-four hours.' He winked at Kathy and limped out of the room.

The DC shook his head sadly. 'Got to hand it to him, though, haven't you, Bren? He knows how to do the right thing. For morale and that. That's leadership, that is.'

Kathy left them to work out their own doom-ridden forecasts and went back to the empty room to nurse her morale and make her second phone call in private. Tina had exciting news, she said. She'd heard of a group that had just lost an assistant tour guide, and were looking for a replacement at short notice. If Kathy had a current passport and could get leave, she could have two weeks in the tropics seeing how the system worked, all expenses paid.

Kathy cupped her forehead in her hand, trying to come to terms with this. She thanked Tina but explained that she was caught up in something where she'd have to be available over the next few weeks.

'Oh, too bad. I thought it'd be right up your street. Can't you just tell them to take a jump? I mean, if you're getting out anyway?'

'I really appreciate it, Tina. I'm sorry, it's a legal thing. I can't get out of it.'

Was that really true? She sat for a while after she rang off, her head in her hands, wondering if she was thinking straight.

The case conference was held in a meeting room in the main New Scotland Yard building on Victoria Street. Most of the people there were from Superintendent Russell's team, with the addition of half a dozen of Brock's. Russell began with the announcement that a decision had been made at senior level that the Springer/Khadra inquiry would be split between two groups, under his general direction. One, led by Brock, would focus on the murder of Springer, and the other, comprising Russell's core team, would continue with the case against the skinheads involved in Abu's murder. Everyone seemed pleased with this decision, especially Russell's team, whose investigations had revealed an orchestrated campaign of actions by a number of linked right-wing groups culminating in the Khadra murder, and there was optimism that these investigations would trap a number of leading neo-Nazis in conspiracy if not murder charges.

After hearing a detailed summary of these ramifications, illustrated by complicated diagrams prepared by Special and Criminal Intelligence Branches tracing a web of extremist associations in the Greater London area and further afield, Brock presented a summary of the Springer case that seemed very modest in comparison. The outstanding question really, he said, was whether Khadra had acted alone in killing Springer, or whether some wider conspiracy was involved. Had he been compelled or induced or supported in any way? Where had the gun come from, or the money? And was it possible to clarify his motive, or the choice of victim? There was little discussion at the end of this, and Kathy had the impression that, like the media which was now focusing exclusively on the skinhead angle, most of the police were no longer much interested in why Max Springer had died.

When the meeting broke up Brock came over to Kathy and asked if she was free for lunch. She took this to be another little morale-boosting gesture, and said he didn't need to worry, if he had more important things to do.

'No, no,' he waved that aside. 'This is work, Kathy.'

They walked a couple of blocks down Victoria Street and turned off, coming to an Italian restaurant favoured, Kathy knew, by lawyers from the Crown Prosecution Service. Inside the climate was suddenly hot and crowded and noisy, and they were shown to a table at the back of the room, squeezing between diners most of whom seemed to know Brock, to where a man sat alone, nursing a glass of white wine. They shook hands, and Brock introduced Reggie Grice, a man of dignified bearing, well barbered silver hair and a beautifully cut charcoal grey suit.

'Reggie's one of our scientists,' Brock explained. 'He used to be a sort of "Q" for MI6, didn't you, Reggie, brewing untraceable poisons and so on.'

Reggie screwed up his nose with distaste. '*Please*, Brock. You know I hate to dwell in the past.' He cast an imperious gaze across the restaurant. 'Why have I never been here before? It seems rather jolly. They can't be coppers, surely?'

'They're lawyers, Reggie.'

'Oh, well, that answers both questions.' He turned to Kathy. 'When you've been divorced as often as I have, you tend to avoid the haunts of lawyers.'

'I heard there was a new Mrs Grice in the offing, Reggie. Is that true?'

'Pure rumour and speculation. And what about you? You look as if someone's been giving you a hell of a battering.' He peered at the traces of bruises on Brock's face, then looked with interest at Kathy.

Brock picked up the menu and said, 'I can recommend the veal.'

Reggie inclined his head to Kathy. 'Brock is *so* secretive, Kathy. I wonder if you and I could get together and swap information on the old goat.'

'I should warn you,' Brock murmured, 'that she's currently on suspension for beating up a member of the public with her Asp.'

Reggie looked entranced. 'You hit someone with a snake? How perfectly splendid. Doesn't that make her a sort of Cleopatra to your Mark Anthony, I wonder, Brock?'

It gradually transpired that Reggie Grice was no longer a practising scientist, but rather, in the manner of poacher turned gamekeeper, chaired various Home Office committees concerned with the regulation of scientific and medical research.

'And you want to know more about Richard Haygill and CAB-Tech?' he said, consulting the menu. 'I've been following the case with great interest, of course. It was one of his boys who bumped off the mad philosopher Springer, wasn't it?'

'I suppose, to get to the heart of it, Reggie, we've been wondering what possible threat Springer could be to someone like Haygill and his operation. From what I've been able to gather, Haygill seems to have a great deal of credibility. I'm not sure that the same can be said for Springer.'

'Oh, we're all vulnerable, Brock. I came across Springer once, at a conference on ethics and science, ages ago, and although they dubbed him Mad Max behind his back, he struck me as very shrewd. Of course he could have gone gaga since then. He was one of those people who instinctively take a contrary point of view, just to see what will come of it. We need people like that, of course. My God, we could do with a few in my neck of the woods! And you'd think that scientists would particularly welcome them, since scientists are supposed to constantly question everything. But in practice it doesn't necessarily work like that. We got quite ratty with Springer at the conference, as I recall. He unsettled us, made us feel vulnerable.'

Reggie turned his attention to the wine-list. 'I should warn you, Brock,' he said, 'that I have absolutely no appointments this afternoon, and presumably Kathy doesn't either if she's on suspension. Which means that we can get stuck into the reds, while you nurse your mineral water.'

'Be my guest, Reggie.'

'Thank you, we shall. Have your researchers dug up an article in

Nature of last May about UCLE and CAB-Tech?' He reached for a slim document case on the floor beside him and selected a photocopied sheet which he handed to Brock. The page was headed 'NEWS' and contained several short articles on current events. The one circled in yellow marker was titled, 'UNIVERSITY DENIES RIFT WITH BIOTECH RESEARCH CENTRE'.

Brock read the article while Reggie consulted with Kathy on her tastes in wine.

UCLE President Roderick Young has issued a press statement denying rumours that the university's Centre of Advanced Biotechnology might move to another institution, possibly overseas. The university has recently been embroiled in a race discrimination case involving staff of the Centre, which receives much of its funding from Middle East sources. Describing CAB-Tech as the flagship of UCLE's research effort, Young said that earlier problems had been exaggerated, and that both parties were committed to the partnership.

Kathy suggested a wine on the list, but Reggie turned it down on the grounds that it was far too modest for Cleopatra's taste. He stabbed a finger at the article. 'A bit like me issuing a press statement denying rumours that my wife was leaving me, eh?'

'So there have been domestic problems at CAB-Tech,' Brock nodded. 'We heard about some of them.'

'Bound to happen. You put a high-flying operation with bags of money like CAB-Tech inside a cash-strapped university and it's bound to attract hostility and jealousy. Haygill's position in particular would be sensitive. Who is he really answerable to, and who is his real paymaster? The university or his overseas backers? There have been several cases recently of universities suing academics with strong external consultancy funding for a share of their outside earnings. You could imagine the mischief someone like Springer could create in that sort of atmosphere, if he wanted to.'

He indicated to Brock his selection from the wine list. Brock suppressed a wince and called over the waiter.

'So Haygill could be vulnerable to Springer on the home front,' Reggie went on, snapping a bread stick. 'But more interestingly, he could be equally vulnerable on the foreign and scientific fronts too.'

'How come?'

'There's no doubt Haygill's science is top-drawer stuff in a highly visible and competitive area, but it's a tricky field, gene therapy. Bucketfuls of cash have been poured into it, but so far results have been sparse, and in at least one case – the Jesse Gelsinger case in the States last year – fatal. The American authorities have examined several hundred gene-therapy protocols involving thousands of patients, but so far we've been very cautious about approving experimental programmes involving humans in this country.'

'Your committees would have to clear what Haygill does, would they?'

'What he does in the UK, yes, which is mainly laboratory work on genes and gene vectors. He's said to have gathered an extraordinary amount of material for his analysis, genetic material from over a million women from around the Middle East.'

'What?' Kathy looked up, startled. 'In that building of his, a million women?'

'A few cells from each, yes . . .' Reggie's attention wandered to the menu. 'The veal, you reckon, Brock? What about the pollo?'

'I've always found it quite edible, Reggie.'

'Yes . . . but you don't really care much about food, do you? Not really . . .' He mused over the alternatives, then ordered the chicken liver crostini, Brock some grilled pigeon. Kathy didn't feel hungry, and ordered a small risotto and green salad.

'Anyway,' Reggie went on, reaching for another bread-stick, 'we have to approve what he does here, but we don't monitor whatever experiments or applications of his basic research he or one of CAB-Tech's commercial affiliates may do overseas, right? And that's where things become sensitive.'

'What sort of things might he be doing?' Kathy asked, still thinking of the million women's cells inside that ziggurat, and wondering if she really wanted to know.

'Well, let me give you an example. A few years ago the Ashkenazi Jews in the United States became concerned about the incidence of cystic fibrosis, a genetic disease, among their people. So they decided to screen their schoolchildren's blood. Each child was given an anonymous code number, and when they reached marriageable age and a match was considered with another young Jew, the two code numbers were examined, and if both were found to be carriers for the disease the Committee for the Prevention of Jewish Genetic Diseases advised against the marriage.

'It was an extremely successful campaign, and as a result cystic fibrosis has been pretty well eliminated from the American Jewish population, but it was also controversial. The *New York Times* attacked it as being eugenic, and there was considerable debate. Since the Nazis, the word 'eugenic' is the big bogey word, of course – the deliberate attempt to breed certain characteristics into, or out of, the human population. But before them it was a quite respectable idea. We'd been improving cattle and wheat that way for thousands of years, so why not people? In the first few decades of the twentieth century lots of respectable people, from Theodore Roosevelt to Winston Churchill, thought eugenics was the way to go, and lots of countries passed eugenics laws for the compulsory sterilisation of inadequate citizens who might be weakening the gene pool, Sweden and many US states, for example, apart from Germany.

'In the end, you see, science is a political and a philosophical matter. It was the *compulsory* nature of the eugenics laws that we now consider repugnant, the state enforcing an idea against the free will of the individual. And for that reason the campaign of the American Ashkenazi Jews was felt to be acceptable, because it merely screened and advised the individuals concerned about the possible consequences of their actions. But in other circumstances there might be social or cultural reasons why people might not follow that advice. And what if some form of gene therapy became available which would allow a government to actively interfere in the passing on of the defective gene?

'So, that brings us back to Haygill. Let's say you have some incurable genetic disorder like, say, Duchenne muscular dystrophy, which is more prevalent in certain regions of the world because of patterns of intermarriage which, for social and cultural reasons, you don't want to interfere with. And let's say someone like Haygill comes along with some kind of therapy for a specific gene, let's call it BRCA4, which will eliminate the disease without restricting people's intermarriage choices, provided it's applied systematically according to some government-controlled protocol. Is that eugenics?

And if it works for that disease, why stop there? Why not clean up all the genetic typos in the book of life?'

Reggie paused as lunch arrived.

Brock, who had been making notes, looked up. 'And is there such a project?'

Reggie shrugged. 'We don't know. We know that Haygill has done work on BRCA4 in his labs over here, and we've heard rumours of a trial for an ambitious BRCA4 protocol, but it's never been submitted to us.'

'When we first met Haygill he gave us a dumb copper's guide to genetics, and he used the same metaphor, about the book of life.'

'Oh, yes. He must use it all the time. His clients and paymasters will like that, the idea of an authoritative, true book of life, kept free of error. But that's where Springer could make trouble, you see, where science becomes philosophy. Is it blasphemous to tamper with the human genome, with God's book of the human being? Springer would probably argue that it is. And Haygill's clients would be susceptible to that. They've been brought up to believe in a Book which records Divine revelation in the actual words spoken over a twenty year period by the Prophet, and preserved over the following fourteen hundred years by continual repetition without error. They would be sensitive to the suggestion that Haygill's project might be heretical and blasphemous.'

Reggie stopped talking for a while to eat. His lecture seemed to have given him an appetite, and he tucked in vigorously. Kathy, on the other hand, had become less and less hungry as he'd gone on. She knew that the kind of work that Haygill was doing might prevent much suffering, but since she'd formed the image of the glass ziggurat and its vast collection of female cells the idea of it had seemed increasingly insidious, as if the whole production had made the human patients it was meant to serve completely passive and even irrelevant.

Brock didn't seem very hungry either, and appeared preoccupied. His phone began to ring, and he murmured an apology and put it to his ear. He muttered something and slipped it away, checking his watch.

'Don't tell me you're going to run away,' Reggie said, mouth full.

'No, no. I was just checking the time. I was badly out with my estimate, Kathy. Only five hours. I said twenty-four.'

She looked at him in surprise. 'What's that?'

'Mr Manzoor has decided to withdraw his complaint against you. CIB have closed the case.'

'Just like that?' She felt numb for a moment, then relief flooded through her. 'I can't believe it.'

'That means you're not on suspension any more, so you'd better lay off that wine.' He smiled and poured some from the bottle into his own glass and raised it. 'Congratulations.'

Reggie joined in. 'How did you wangle that, Brock?'

'Upon reflection the complainant realised that Kathy would have revealed some inconvenient facts about him, if the matter had been pursued.'

'But I didn't know any,' Kathy objected.

'You would have done, Kathy. You would have done.'

She shook her head, grateful but not understanding, and it occurred to her that it might not be too late to ring Tina and tell her she could go on the trip after all. It wouldn't be difficult to arrange it. All she needed to do was excuse herself and make a couple of calls. But then she thought about Brock's intervention with Manzoor, and imagined him quietly pulling strings in the background, preparing the way for her return to duty. She thought about it, working through the options, and still she didn't move.

She became aware that the two men were talking about something else. Reggie had asked about Abu and his place in Haygill's team.

'Odd,' he said eventually. 'Seems all very clumsy and incriminating.'

'How do you mean?' Brock was taking another sip of the wine, reluctantly acknowledging Reggie's excellent taste.

'Well, he must have been a real loose cannon, this Abu. I mean, what he's done must be a tremendous embarrassment to Haygill, the very person he was trying to protect.'

'Presumably he didn't expect to get caught. Perhaps he knew that Springer was planning something to get at Haygill, along the lines you've suggested, and felt he had to act. Apparently he regards Haygill as a kind of father figure.'

'I see . . .' Reggie didn't seem convinced. 'All the same, you'd think he would have talked it over with someone else on the team. You know, with a group like that, tightly knit, strong sense of themselves as outsiders, I would have expected a pretty strong pressure for people not to fly off and act on their own.'

'He was an outsider within the group, Reggie. The computer man, not a scientist like them.'

'Still, he shared their beliefs . . . I'll tell you something else I would have expected, too.'

'What?'

'Well, think about it from the investors' point of view. They're putting money into a tricky research project being undertaken miles away, in a foreign country and led by a foreigner. Of course there will be all sorts of agreed procedures for Haygill to report to them and keep them informed, but he will obviously present things in the best light, and he's a foreigner. But then there are the Islamic team members, who share the investors' culture and values. Wouldn't you expect one or more of them to be acting as inside agents for the investors, their commissar, keeping tabs on the others and sending back the inside story?'

'And maybe trying to cover up anything that could be embarrassing to them,' Brock said. 'Muddying the waters if necessary.' He thought of the way in which Abu's death had seemed to be set up. Could his guilt also have been contrived in some way?

As they came to the end of the meal, Brock thanked Reggie for his ideas.

'Hope the cost wasn't too excessive.'

'You're always good value, Reggie.'

'Well, I haven't completely finished yet. There are things you hear at the bar, after a long day conferring with one's fellow scientists, after one has exhausted the exalted topic of how life works and turns instead to what the bloody hell it all means. Have you met Mrs Haygill?'

'Seen her. We haven't spoken. Blonde, big hair.'

'That's it. The whisper is that she's a bit of an embarrassment to her husband. Likes the booze a bit too much to be allowed to accompany him on the Gulf trips. Also rumoured that she likes to play around while he's away on his trips, possibly with Haygill's boss.'

'His boss?'

'Yes, at the university. The head man, Vice-Chancellor or whatever.'

Later that afternoon Brock's team met at Queen Anne's Gate to plan the next steps. All of the employees at CAB-Tech would be interviewed or reinterviewed, and inquiries into the source of Abu's money were proceeding at the Bank of Credit and Commerce Dubai in the City. Brock had asked Wayne O'Brien to attend, and now asked the Special Branch officer to comment on Reggie Grice's thoughts on the dynamics of Haygill's group, particularly the Middle East scientists. He went through them in turn, sketching the information they had been able to find on each.

'The key man is Haygill's deputy, Dr Tahir Darr, without a doubt. At thirty-eight he's the oldest of them and he's always at the centre of things. He also seems to have the most interesting private life and access to money. He's got a wife and kiddie living in Shepherd's Bush, but he also likes to go out clubbing on his own or with male company. When their sponsors come over from the Gulf it's Darr gets the job of taking them out to see the sights. A favourite nightspot for the visiting Arabs is Thoroughbreds in Mayfair, a drinking and gambling club where Darr is a member. One of the staff there is a friend of ours and knows him as a regular.'

'Do we know who these visitors are?' Brock asked, and Wayne produced a list.

'All respectable businessmen, venture capitalists, scientists.'

'And Darr knows them all.'

'Probably better than Haygill does. He speaks Arabic as well as Urdu.'

'It'd be interesting to get inside his head, but not easy,' Brock said. 'From the way he reacted when we spoke to him at CAB-Tech, I reckon he'll be a difficult nut to crack in interview.'

'Yes, I was wondering about that,' Wayne said. 'Whether we could get closer to him.'

'What about your friend at the club he goes to?'

Wayne shook his head dubiously. 'Rupert? He's one of the

189

barmen, keeps us informed who's passing through, especially the known drugs figures. But he wouldn't be right for a job like this.'

'Sounds one for you, Wayne,' Bren suggested. 'Undercover's up your street, isn't it?'

'I don't think he'd come across for me, either. I reckon it needs someone he can relate to, another Asian, maybe with a science background, to catch him at a weak moment in his cups. We've got a couple of good Asian guys in my section, but they're up north at the moment, working on a case in Bradford. You don't have anybody like that, do you?'

Bren shook his head, pondering. Kathy didn't speak. There was someone, of course, but she waited, expecting one of the others to say the obvious. Finally, when no one did, she said, 'Well, there's Leon.'

They looked surprised. 'He's not even part of our section, Kathy,' Bren objected.

She shrugged, not wanting to pursue it. It was a stupid notion, really, and she could see Brock thinking the same.

But Bren was having second thoughts. 'He is Asian, though, and he's got scientific knowledge, with his DNA and all that, and he's very familiar with the background. Maybe it's not such a bad idea.'

'I met him, didn't I? At Shadwell Road?' Wayne said. 'Yeah, he might be spot on.'

'He's forensic liaison, Wayne,' Brock objected. 'He's not an undercover detective. This isn't his line of work at all.'

'You never know,' Bren pursued, enthusiastic now, 'he might jump at the chance. Why don't we ask him? I saw him downstairs ten minutes ago.'

He jumped to his feet and went off in pursuit, returning after a few minutes, Leon Desai following.

Brock said, 'Leon, sit down. We've been talking around a problem, and a suggestion came up . . .'

He spoke diffidently, as if they were discussing the unlikely plot from some new movie, and as he went on, Kathy could see exactly why. Watching Leon sitting there, listening carefully with his polite but sceptical, rather distant, expression, she could understand why he was completely wrong for the task, and she kicked herself for ever suggesting it. He was the opposite of Wayne, lacking small talk, keeping himself to himself, not inviting confidences. As an undercover operative he might just manage to extract an opinion on the weather.

Leon heard Brock out in silence, giving nothing away from his expression. Then his mouth formed a little smile and he said, 'What idiot dreamed that one up?'

They all laughed, and glanced over at Kathy, and Leon followed their looks, still with his little smile, until he realised it was her. For the briefest of moments his expression registered a small shock, then clouded and turned away. It was enough for Kathy to read, however. He believed she had done it to humiliate him, to make him a joke among her friends, the real detectives.

Bren, oblivious to all that, was enthusiastically beefing up Brock's sparse outline, suggesting approaches that could be tried, and getting Wayne O'Brien to offer his ideas.

Leon listened until they were finished, then turned to Brock and said, 'None of it would be admissible in court, would it?'

'That's right.' Brock looked uneasy. 'It would purely be a matter of giving us background, Leon. But look, I've already explained to Wayne that your expertise lies in the forensic area. You haven't been trained for this sort of thing. I really think . . .'

'Well, we could give it a try,' Leon said calmly, 'if you think it'll help. I'll need to be properly briefed.'

'Great!' Bren beamed and clapped Leon on the back. Brock smiled reluctantly, and Kathy wanted to crawl under the table.

She tried to catch him alone as the meeting broke up, but Wayne intercepted her and Leon slipped quickly through the door.

'I thought I might take you up on that offer of a return match,' Wayne said with a cheeky smile. 'If you're free tonight.'

'How come? What about the girlfriend?'

He raised an open hand, palm down and wiggled it from side to side. 'Bit dodgy. I think the wheels are falling off again.'

She felt a sudden spurt of irritation with the glib grin. 'Well, I'm sorry about that, Wayne. Only I don't much fancy being a stop-gap for when your girlfriend's wheels come off.'

He began to protest, but she brushed past him after Leon. He had gone.

Later that evening she rang his home number and left a message with his mother, but he didn't phone back.

17

It was the weekend, but Kathy couldn't let the case go. She lay awake through half the night turning it over in her mind, and the next morning she still couldn't shake it. She kept returning to the photograph that Manzoor had produced, of his daughter and Abu together in the pool, and the image haunted her. Innocence before the fall, before marriage in Kashmir and murder on the university steps. Someone had sent it to Manzoor, and Abu had died.

Unable to settle to anything else, she drove into central London and managed to find a parking space near the office. A few people were working in the building, but the room they had set up for their discussions the previous day was undisturbed. The photograph in its evidence pouch was still pinned to the board, and she assumed that no one had yet followed it up. She made a couple of colour photocopies, then left, continuing on to the refuge where Nargis was staying.

When she got there it was mid-morning, and the house was filled with the comforting sounds of domesticity, women talking over coffee, some children playing on a swing in the back garden, a washing machine rumbling. Kathy asked for Nargis and was surprised when Briony Kidd appeared.

'Nargis is at prayer,' she said, sounding hostile. 'Can't you leave her alone? She was upset after that grilling you gave her last time.'

'I'm sorry about that, Briony. I have to do my job.'

'That's what the Gestapo said too, wasn't it?'

The words blurted out, angry, and Kathy waited a moment before she replied. 'That's not fair. We were the ones who brought her here, remember?'

Briony flushed. 'Sorry. This is all just so awful. I wish it would all be over. Do you . . . do you want a cup of coffee?'

They sat at the kitchen table and Briony explained that she had been to Chandler's Yard that morning to collect Nargis' clothes for her. 'She's too scared to go anywhere near Shadwell Road yet. But the social worker has put her in touch with people who can stop her father from stalking her.'

'Where do you live?' Kathy asked.

'In Bow. I rent a house with a couple of other grad students. It's damp but convenient.'

'Did Max mix socially with his students much?'

'You mean me, don't you? I was the only one.'

'There were others before though. I just wondered if he was a very sociable person.'

'He wasn't a hermit, if that's what you mean. We'd go to the pub sometimes for our tutorials, sometimes Dr Pettifer would come along too.'

'So you must have been as close to what he was working on as anyone, I suppose? Did he talk about that? Things he was writing about?'

'Sometimes.'

'Do you remember if he said anything about a "protocol"?'

'A what?'

Kathy checked in her notebook to get the term right. 'Something called a "BRCA4 protocol"?'

Briony picked up a pencil and wrote it down on the tail end of a shopping list. 'I think I do remember him using the word "protocol" once or twice.'

'Can you remember what he said about it?'

'Not exactly . . .' Briony screwed up her nose, thinking. 'He was being scathing about scientists, I think, "with their evil protocols", that sort of thing. I don't remember a specific number like that.' A light dawned in her eyes. 'This is something CAB-Tech is doing, isn't it? Yes, I do remember he referred to a specific project they were involved in. And it had a code number, like this. I didn't take it in at the time.'

'OK.' Kathy nodded and went to put her notebook away, but Briony gripped her wrist and said fiercely, 'You are investigating them, aren't you? I knew you would. It's them, isn't it? They're responsible for what happened to Max.'

Then her eyes skipped up over Kathy's shoulder and she got quickly to her feet. 'Nargis!' she cried, and Kathy turned and saw the other girl standing in the doorway watching them.

'Sergeant Kolla wants to speak to you again. Are you up to it?'

Nargis came silently to the table and sat down. 'I was praying,' she said softly. 'For Abu.'

Kathy said nothing, thinking of the grief she might cause when she showed her the photograph, and wondering whether to let it go. But she knew she had to ask.

'I'm really sorry to intrude again, Nargis, especially with this. I just need you to identify something for me, a snapshot of you and Abu.' She took one of the copies from her bag and placed it on the table. But the girl wasn't distressed, only puzzled. 'That looks like one of mine. How did you get it?'

'Yours?'

'Yes, I'm sure it is. It was last spring, wasn't it, Briony? In the pool at Thamesmead.'

'Who took it?' Kathy said gently.

'Why, it was Briony. Wasn't it? With Abu's camera.'

Briony shrugged. 'I remember the day we went to the pool. George and Kasim came too, didn't they?'

'So it was Abu's film. Do you know where the other pictures are?'

'Abu gave them to me. They're in my room in Chandler's Yard. Why?'

'It was just a loose end we had to tie up.'

'I suppose somebody else might have taken pictures that day. George or Fran maybe. I can't remember.'

Nargis stared sadly at the image. Kathy said, 'Keep it if you like,' and got to her feet before the girl could ask her again how she'd come by it.

When she returned to Queen Anne's Gate Kathy retrieved the inventory that had been made of things in Max Springer's room. She eventually found what she was looking for in a long list of items under the general heading 'Files and papers'. Number 1076 was listed as 'File marked "BRCA4 Protocol": empty'.

They had arranged a schedule of interviews with CAB-Tech staff through the Monday, booking interview facilities in a modern divisional police station just across the river from the UCLE campus. Brock kept Darr and Haygill until last, hoping that some discrepancies would emerge in the statements of the others, but his hopes faded as they went on. Of course, yes, they knew Abu very well, as a colleague and friend; they saw him every day, prayed with him, shared their meals with him; he was universally liked as a quiet, sincere, loyal and competent workmate. And no, he had given no indication that he was planning any violence to anyone; he had never spoken in anger against Professor Springer; he had never spoken about firearms. The whole thing was incomprehensible.

After several hours of this, Bren sighed with frustration. 'The same story every time.'

'Psittacism, Bren,' Brock grunted. 'Pure psittacism.'

'What's that on a clear day, chief?'

'Repetition of words and ideas parrot-fashion. Did you notice how the same phrases kept coming up? They've been taking classes.'

'And we can guess who the teacher was.'

'Yes. Let's have him in, shall we?'

Dr Darr didn't repeat the exact phrases of the others, but the ideas were much the same. Abu simply wasn't an unpredictable or highly emotional type, and it was impossible to imagine him doing anything so terrible. From there Darr went on to gently challenge his questioners. What would Abu have to gain? Were the police absolutely confident about their evidence? Could it not be a case of tragically mistaken identity? Or even, a deliberate attempt to discredit CAB-Tech through Abu, by a rival organisation perhaps? He couldn't suggest any specific names, but theirs was a cut-throat research area, and it was well known that certain American companies could act ruthlessly when their commercial interests were at stake.

Richard Haygill was accompanied by a solicitor from a firm that represented the university, and appeared even more tired and drawn than the first time they'd met. He sat down and rubbed a hand across his eyes. Brock asked him if he was all right, and if they could get him anything, and he apologised.

'Sorry, I had to fly out to the Gulf again over the weekend and I'm a bit behind in my sleep. This business has been incredibly disruptive, you understand. It's been very hard for us to focus on our work.'

'Yes, I can imagine that your overseas partners would find it a little disturbing.'

Haygill raised his eyes. 'More than a little, Chief Inspector, I can assure you. The sooner we can put it behind us the better. Incidentally, may I ask something? I felt very bad that we weren't represented at Abu's interment. I understand that there was a young woman there, and that there was some kind of incident. Is she all right?'

'She's fine now.'

'Good. Is she a relative?'

'I understand she was a friend of Mr Khadra's.'

'Really. I didn't know he had a girlfriend, you see, and I wondered if I should get in touch with her, express our regrets.'

'If you wanted to send a note to me, Professor, I'll make sure she gets it.'

'Oh . . . thank you. I wrote to the address we had for his family in the Lebanon, but I haven't heard anything.' He sighed. 'It's so hard to know what to say.'

Brock began the formal interview. 'Professor Haygill, there is strong forensic evidence to suggest that Abu Khadra was the man who murdered Max Springer, but we are puzzled by his motive. Why would he have done such a thing? Have you any idea?'

'I'm afraid not.'

'But you must surely have wondered about this. What possibilities did you come up with?'

Haygill hunched forward slightly, frowning through his glasses at Brock. 'I don't think I quite understand. Are you asking me to speculate?' He turned to the solicitor at his side, who gave a small shake of his head.

'I don't think that's appropriate,' the solicitor advised.

'I think it's inevitable,' Brock retorted, 'if not with me then with a wider public. People *will* speculate, Professor, and I'm asking for your informed help.'

Still Haygill didn't offer anything, and Brock went on.

'Well, let me put this to you, just as an example. Max Springer was an extremely hostile critic of you and your work. On one occasion I believe he compared you to the Nazi Dr Mengele, am I right?'

Haygill took a deep breath and made a weary gesture with his hand. 'Yes.'

'That's a pretty drastic kind of criticism, isn't it? Especially coming from a man who lost his parents in the concentration camps.'

'It was a preposterous, outrageous remark for which he was censured by the Chair of the University Senate.'

'But you didn't pursue it, Professor? You didn't consider suing him?'

'I did consider it, but on reflection I felt that would only give his absurd opinions the public exposure he craved. He wanted me to sue him. He wanted a forum and publicity to present his idiotic ideas. He didn't care that he would have lost. So I declined to give him that opportunity.'

'But it must have been extremely frustrating and upsetting to you and the members of your team at the Centre of Advanced Biotechnology?'

Haygill regarded Brock impassively, then wiped a hand quickly over his sandy hair and replied, 'I think we regarded it with the contempt it deserved.'

'You regarded him with contempt?'

But Haygill wasn't going to be caught like that. 'I regarded his *statement* with contempt. I had no particular personal feelings for Max Springer, except to wish that he would calm down and have a bit of common sense.'

'But your staff are younger people, less mature than you, less able to take a detached, scientific view of Springer's remarks, perhaps. They must have been outraged, surely?'

'Well, you can ask them. But my impression was that they took little notice.'

'Come on, Professor! I'm told they practically caused an international incident over some Christmas e-mail! If they took

198

offence at something like that, they'd hardly accept Springer's taunts calmly.'

'That was completely different. They saw that as an attack on their religious convictions.'

'Hm.' Brock consulted his notes. 'On another occasion I believe Springer described your role in CAB-Tech as "Svengali-like".'

'Really?' Haygill looked mildly surprised. 'I haven't heard that one. But no abusive remark attributed to Max would especially astonish me.'

'That particular remark has a specific meaning, though, doesn't it? It suggests that you hold a dominating influence over the people under you at CAB-Tech. Isn't that right?'

'Nonsense. We operate on teamwork and cooperation between team members, just as in a hundred other scientific establishments around the world.'

'But your team is unusual, isn't it, in the way you've recruited a group of Middle Eastern staff with a common religious outlook and strong personal loyalty to you.'

'You find it questionable that our staff should include some Islamic scientists?' Haygill said coldly, straightening in his seat. 'Maybe you should examine your own attitudes, Chief Inspector. Maybe there's some prejudice lurking in there that we should know about.'

The solicitor leaned over to make a comment, but Haygill shook his head impatiently. 'I'd like to hear where they're going with this.' He glared at Brock. 'You're implying that Abu was so upset by Springer's insults, and so loyal to me, that he went off and shot the man dead? Is that it?'

'Is that possible?' Brock asked mildly.

'It's laughable.'

'I understand Abu felt that he owed you a great deal for advancing his career, and looked up to you almost as a father.'

Haygill looked doubtful. 'I think that's putting it far too strongly.'

'So you don't see much merit in the idea that he did it for you?'

'As a theory, I think it's feeble.'

'Well . . . would it be stronger, as a theory, if you'd encouraged him to do it?'

Haygill swivelled away in his seat and laughed, shaking his head.

'Perhaps half-joking, a few hints that things would be a lot easier if someone could make Springer shut his mouth. That kind of thing?'

'No.' Haygill swung back and leaned forward across the table at Brock to make the point. 'Not half-jokingly or in any other way. I did not encourage him or anyone else to do·anything to Max Springer.'

'Very well.' Brock scanned his papers as if running out of questions.

'Is that all?'

'Er, not quite. Does CAB-Tech do business with the Bank of Credit and Commerce Dubai?'

Haygill looked stunned. 'Yes.'

'How many accounts are there?'

'Why on earth are you asking?'

'How many?'

'There are several individual research project accounts, a reserve deposit account, a general working account . . . Probably eight or nine in all.'

'What about you personally?'

'Me?'

'Yes, do you have a personal account with the bank?'

'Yes, but what has this got to do—'

'We would like your authorisation to examine all of the accounts for the period of, say, the last twelve months.'

Haygill said, 'Absolutely not! They are commercially sensitive . . .' His face had gone pink, eyes blinking rapidly. 'This is absolutely outrageous!' He turned to his lawyer who took up the objections.

'There is no question of my client agreeing to such an examination, Chief Inspector. We would maintain most vigorously that his business and personal financial records are excluded material under the terms of the 1984 Act.'

Brock shrugged and went on. 'Do you or does anyone else associated with CAB-Tech, either here or overseas, to your knowledge own a hand-gun of any kind?'

'No! Certainly not!'

'What is the BRCA4 Protocol, Professor Haygill?'

Once again the scientist looked stunned, as if physically struck by

some blow from a totally unexpected quarter. He shook his head, 'I
. . . I don't understand what all this . . .'

'What is the BRCA4 Protocol, Professor Haygill?'

Haygill pulled himself together, spread his fingers wide on the
table and stared at them as if counting to check they were all there.

'Chief Inspector Brock,' his solicitor said, 'I would like to speak in
private with . . .'

'No, it's all right,' Haygill said. 'The BRCA4 Protocol is a
proposal for a research project originating from our laboratories.
One of dozens.'

'Could you describe it to me?'

'No, no, I couldn't.'

'You have some kind of proposal document, describing it?'

Haygill frowned. 'Yes.'

'I would like to have it examined by our staff.'

'No. It is commercially sensitive.'

'Secret?'

'If you like.'

'Then how did Max Springer know about it?'

'Springer?' Haygill looked horrified. 'Are you sure?'

'There was evidence in his room at the university that he had
information on it.'

'I'm astonished . . . How could he?'

Into Brock's mind came an image of Springer's room when they
had first opened its door, and the impression of it having been
ransacked, countered by the security guard's assurance that it always
looked like that.

'If he had, it would have been very sensitive, would it?
Commercially?'

'Well . . . it's only a proposal for a feasibility study at this stage . . .'

'So not especially valuable commercially?'

Haygill shrugged doubtfully.

'How about ethically? Would it have been ethically sensitive, in
the hands of an opponent like Max Springer? Something that could
have been used to embarrass you if produced in a public lecture, for
example.'

Haygill lowered his eyes to his spread fingers and didn't answer.
Looking at him, Brock knew he didn't need to. Reggie Grice had

been right – despite all the differences in their power and influence, Haygill was vulnerable to the kind of trouble that the wayward Springer could stir up, and he knew it. There was something here, something Haygill had kept hidden, which he now felt that he could almost smell.

'Thank you, Professor Haygill.'

'What? Is that all?'

'For the moment. Are you planning any more trips abroad?'

'Er . . . The next is scheduled for the end of the month, but as things stand, it may be necessary—'

'Don't make any arrangements without consulting us first, will you? Here's my contact details.'

Brock handed Haygill a card and got to his feet.

Leon Desai left his coat with the cloakroom attendant and strolled through a pair of large panelled doors into a bar lounge, trying to appear confident and relaxed, as if he came to places like this all the time. It wasn't at all to his taste. A cross between an old-fashioned gentlemen's club and a Turkish brothel, Wayne O'Brien had said, and he could see what he meant. The furniture was too amply stuffed, the carpet pile too thick, the port and burgundy colour scheme too livid, so that the effect was bombastic. The theme of the decorations was horsy, in keeping with the club's name, with large Stubbs reproductions of thoroughbred champions framed around the walls, and bronze horse heads mounted on pedestals. Leon found it all both contemptible and thoroughly intimidating, especially in view of O'Brien's estimate of the amount of money that passed through here each night.

The place seemed quiet, a few people embedded in the plump furniture around the room. The opulent mahogany bar that formed one end of the lounge was deserted, and Leon walked to it and eased himself onto a leather barstool. The doors in the far wall opened as a couple passed through, and he glimpsed more people in the gaming room beyond.

The barman returned with a silver tray of empty glasses. 'Good evening, sir. What can we do for you?' He was as smooth and glossy as the brandy balloons glistening against the mirror at his back.

'My name's Desai. I'm a friend of—'

'Mr O'Brien, sir. Why yes, of course. I'm Rupert. How are we this evening?'

Actually he wasn't feeling too bad now. Earlier he had been petrified with what he took to be a form of stage fright, his mouth so dry that he could hardly speak, his stomach aching. But now that things had begun, he felt much better. 'Fine, just fine. I might have a glass of champagne.'

As he poured it Rupert leaned forward a little and said, confidentially, 'The gentleman you're interested in is behind you, Mr Desai, in the far corner, talking to a blonde lady. They've been there for twenty minutes.'

'Ah, right.' Leon glanced at the mirror behind the bar and just managed to make out two figures in the distance.

'Don't know who she is. Haven't seen her here before. Let's hope he sends her packing and comes to the bar, eh?'

While they waited Rupert chatted on about what a great bloke Wayne O'Brien was, a real card, while Leon tried to make appropriate noises. He had a tape recorder in the pocket of his suit, but he didn't switch it on. He had no intention of recording praise of O'Brien if he could help it.

The barman left to service the seated drinkers and an American came and sat at the bar for a while, resting, as he said, between bouts of losing his children's inheritance. He went on at some length about his ungrateful children, and Leon began to feel depressed. Finally the American slid out of the stool and lurched away, and Rupert returned, with a wink for Leon.

'He's getting her a taxi. I think we're in luck. Another champers?'

'Why not?' Leon reached into his pocket and clicked on the machine.

After a few minutes Leon sensed Darr's presence behind his right shoulder, and caught sight of him in the mirror. He had an impression of a tall, sombre figure. The hands that rested on the edge of the bar wore heavy gold rings.

'Another of the usual, Rupert, please. And one of my cigars.'

He watched the barman fixing his order without turning to look at Leon. Rupert lit his cigar and let him draw on it before saying, 'And have you met Mr Desai, Dr Darr? He's in the science game too, aren't you, sir?'

Darr turned slowly and eyed Leon for a moment before offering his hand. 'Tahir Darr.'

'Leon. What sort of science are you into then, Tahir?' Leon thought his words sounded fatuous and utterly false as he said them, and his confidence ebbed away.

Darr eyed him as if he really didn't want to get into a conversation, but then replied, 'I work for a research company. Biotechnology.'

'Oh, right. Important area.'

'And you?'

'We do testing. DNA, that sort of thing.'

Darr nodded but didn't seem inclined to pursue it. He puffed his cigar and raised the glass to his mouth, then cleared his throat. 'Pakistan?'

'What? Oh, no. Liverpool. You?'

'London.'

Rupert obviously sensed that they didn't seem to be hitting it off, and said brightly, 'And what sort of a day have you gentlemen had, then? Good start to the week?'

'An abomination of a day, Rupert,' Darr pronounced with grim relish. 'And if this week's like last week, and the one before it, it will be an abominable *shit* of a week.'

'Oh.' Rupert was a little taken aback by the vehemence of Darr's words, and turned to Leon. 'And what about you, Mr Desai?'

Leon watched the smoke curling from Darr's nostrils and caught his mood. 'Awful,' he said morosely. 'My boss has given me a pig of a job to do and my girlfriend's run off with a bloody copper.'

It seemed rather lame to Leon, but Darr turned to him and a smile spread slowly over his face. 'Join the bloody club, old chap.'

Afterwards, when she came to hear the tape, Kathy realised that she had been wrong in doubting Leon's ability to get Darr talking. Someone with O'Brien's breezy style would only have alienated Darr. In his dark mood, Leon's laconic misery touched a chord. And much of this, it seemed to Kathy, was due to the fact that Leon's gloom was quite genuine, and his tales of woe absolutely true. She felt his real pain when he told Darr about the misunderstanding he had had with his girlfriend, and how she had gone off with someone else, a smooth-talking police bastard who had no soul. She felt it, and responded in kind.

'And tell me, Leon,' Darr had said, 'is this a white girl you're talking about by any chance? Yes, I thought so. These English women are total bitches, believe me. It's the way they're brought up, indulged, spoilt.'

'You talk from experience, Tahir?' Leon had asked, and the reply had come,

'Oh, yes . . . Oh, dear me, yes.'

They had bought each other further drinks, warming to their theme, turning from the treachery of women to the injustices of work. Darr didn't go into details, but he was clearly discontented with his lot.

'We are in the most unenviable position, you and I. Those below us need us to guide their every step, while those above expect us to make their business work. We are under pressure from both ends. We have maximum responsibility without commensurate reward.'

'You're right. Does your boss make unreasonable demands on you?'

'Oh, does he not!'

'Did you see that psychological study of bosses of British companies, how one in six fulfil the diagnostic criteria for psychopaths?'

'Hah! Only one in six?'

'I suppose you're expected to control everything your staff do, are you, Tahir?'

'Absolutely. And if they do something, if something goes wrong, then it's as if it's *your* fault. As if *you* did this stupid thing!'

'Has somebody done something stupid, then?'

'Oh, I can't talk about it. It's all a disaster. And then, on top of all that, I'm expected to drop everything to write some phoney report, which no one will ever use, to cover my boss's unworthy backside. As if I didn't have a mountain of real work to do!'

'Yes, yes. He's English, is he, your boss?'

'Yes, very pukka, quite the English gentleman. "Just get it done, Tahir. Just see to it." Hah!'

'And what about *Mrs* Haygill. What is *she* like?'

This had been a line that Brock had suggested, following Reggie

Grice's hint. But for some reason the question seemed to throw Darr completely. There was a long silence, and then he asked, '*What* did you say?'

Leon repeated the question, not sure what had happened. 'I just wondered what his wife was like. Do you know her well?' Darr was staring at him fixedly, and Leon began to ramble. 'If she's anything like my boss's wife she treats the staff like private servants, you know? A chauffeur, a secretary . . . What's wrong?'

Darr turned to his drink and didn't reply for a moment. He looked at his watch, then at Leon, 'Oh, I could tell you a few interesting tit-bits about her, don't worry. But I must get going now. I'm late for another appointment. How long are you in town?'

'A few days.'

'Tell you what, if you're stuck for something to do, I could meet you for another drink tomorrow night, and continue our conversation.'

'Yes, great. That would be good.'

'Do you have a card?'

Leon reached for his wallet, then stopped and said, 'Oh, I ran out today. I need to get some more.'

'I see. Well, let's say nine o'clock tomorrow. All right?'

They shook hands and Leon breathed a huge sigh of relief and switched off the recorder.

'Go all right, did it?' Rupert asked as Leon got to his feet.

'Excellent, yes. We're meeting again tomorrow. See you then.'

'Give my best to Mr O'Brien.'

And it was O'Brien, as they listened to the tape the next morning, who spotted what had gone wrong. 'You said "Mrs Haygill", you berk.'

Leon flushed. 'What do you mean?'

'No one had mentioned Haygill's name until then. Darr had been careful not to give you any names, of CAB-Tech or UCLE or anything. He's rumbled you.'

There was a deathly silence. Then Leon said, 'Rupert could have told me, while we were talking before Darr came over.'

'How would Rupert know the name of Darr's boss?' Wayne objected scathingly.

Brock said, 'Is it possible that Haygill has been to the club,

Wayne? Maybe you could speak to Rupert, and discuss our problem.'

They waited in uncomfortable silence while O'Brien tried to get hold of the barman on the phone. Kathy felt sick in her heart. Leon hadn't looked once at her since they had come together, and she'd had a couple of quizzical looks from Bren as they'd listened to Leon's voice on tape complaining about his faithless girlfriend.

Wayne returned, looking worried. 'I can't get hold of him. But look, I've been thinking, it's just too big a risk. We should stop this now. If Leon doesn't turn up tonight, Darr will never be sure and no harm will be done.'

'But nothing will have been achieved, either,' Bren objected. 'We didn't learn anything concrete, except that Darr's pissed off with his boss. I think he'll start getting down to specifics on a second meeting.'

'It was intriguing what he said about writing a phoney document,' Brock said. 'That could be the protocol I asked Haygill for.'

'Brock, my priority has got to be to protect Rupert,' Wayne O'Brien protested. 'There's a lot of dodgy people go through that club, and he's a very useful source. If Rupert tells Darr that he knew his boss's name was Haygill, and Darr knows for a fact that he couldn't have, then Darr will know that Rupert is as fishy as Leon here. He's a regular at that place. If he spreads the word that Rupert spies for us, then Rupert's finished.'

Brock nodded. 'Yes, I see that, Wayne. Pity.'

He seemed about to debate it further, but Kathy broke in, agitated. 'Apart from that, I think it would be wrong to go ahead with the second meeting anyway. For all we know, Darr may well be the one who engineered Springer's murder and Abu's death. It's far too dangerous for Leon to keep this appointment now. The whole thing was a mistake in the first place. I was wrong to suggest it.'

They looked at her in surprise and she flushed, feeling that she'd been a little too vehement. 'I just think it's risky and a waste of time. We should get Darr in again and question him formally, so we can use whatever he says.'

Leon looked at Kathy for the first time, and as their eyes met she read the doubt, as if he couldn't make her out.

Bren said, 'Seems a shame. I thought Leon was doing pretty well. What do you think, Leon? You're the one in the firing line?'

He hesitated, then said, 'I think I've been wasting my time if I don't go back. Yes, I think we should go on with it.'

He had to say that, Kathy thought. He felt he had to redeem his mistake, and probably thought that she'd said otherwise only so as to support O'Brien.

But Brock settled the matter. 'No, Wayne and Kathy are right. The risks are too great. We'll play this by the book. Thanks anyway, Leon. You did very well. I'm sorry to cut short your promising undercover career. Sounds as if you got a taste for it. Maybe you'll be applying to join Special Branch, eh?'

Kathy caught Leon's half-hearted attempt to smile at that, and watched him leave.

18

Kathy was on her own in the office later that day when her mobile phone rang and the reporter, Clare Hancock, came on.

'Hi, back on Brock's team again are you, Kathy?'

It was a question that Kathy had postponed thinking about.

'Only I was down at UCLE this morning, and I heard that you're reinterviewing Haygill and his staff, is that right?'

'Clare, I can't discuss it with you, I'm sorry.'

'Oh, come on, off the record. You're talking to them, right?'

'Yes.'

'Does that mean you don't buy the lone gunman theory any more?'

'Sorry, Clare. Are you running out of ideas or have you got something for me?'

'Oh, I've got lots of ideas, and trading with you didn't do me much good last time. But let me run an idea past you, free of charge, and if you feel inclined you can give me a theoretical, off-the-record opinion. You remember how we were torn between the fatwa and Haygill for Springer's murderer? Well, why not both?'

'How do you mean?'

'I mean, Haygill orders the fatwa. He's got some pretty heavy friends overseas. Maybe he decided Springer had to be stopped, and they obliged.'

'Why would Haygill be so desperate to stop Springer?'

'Yes, that's the puzzle, isn't it? No suggestions?'

'No suggestions.'

'Well . . . suppose Springer had found out that Haygill was doing something scandalous.'

'Like what?'

'Oh, I don't know, practising human sacrifice, or eugenics or something.'

Kathy hesitated, then said, 'You'd need to have some solid evidence before you printed anything like that, wouldn't you, Clare?'

'Well, it's only an idea. What do you think of it?'

'I couldn't say.'

The reporter laughed and said, 'That's better than saying it stinks.'

'Look,' Kathy was losing patience, 'instead of inciting another race riot with wild guesses, why don't you let us finish our investigations?'

'Because there's something else here that hasn't come out yet. I can smell it, and so can you. Why did Khadra kill Springer? You tell me.'

'We're working on it. I'll let you know as soon as we're ready to say anything.'

'Trouble is, Kathy, I've always been so impatient. I don't like waiting for other people to tell me when to move.'

Afterwards Kathy wondered what the call had been all about. A bit of fishing no doubt, but perhaps a warning too. She rang the media office to see if they'd heard anything, but they weren't aware of anything brewing in the pages of the *Herald*.

Leon emerged from Bond Street tube station and began walking south. It was a fresh night, the streetlights glistening on pavements wet from a recent shower. The crispness of the breeze blew away any lingering doubts and he marched forward confidently. Perhaps he was doing this for the wrong reasons, because O'Brien had called him a berk in front of everyone, because Brock had kidded him about joining Special Branch, and, most of all, because Kathy had got him into this in the first place and then changed her mind and got it stopped, as if he were some kind of obedient pet to be redirected at will.

No, that wasn't exactly it. He shook his head angrily, and an oncoming pedestrian stepped warily out of his path. It would be puerile to act simply because he felt goaded. He tried to tell himself that he was doing it for his own sake, because it was unfinished and unresolved and he didn't like leaving things that way. Soon he would move up to Liverpool, begin his masters degree, and forget about the lot of them. But first he wanted to tie this up. And if he did turn up anything juicy, the look on their faces would be a bonus.

He turned a corner and an easterly blast of icy wind sucked his breath away. Who was he kidding? He was doing it because she seemed to hate the sight of him now, and he couldn't stand it.

He pushed that painful thought away and strode faster towards the next corner, from where he could see the front door of Thoroughbreds lying ahead.

Towards ten that night Kathy was doing some ironing in front of the TV, only half-listening to the current affairs programme, when she heard them mention Max Springer's name. She looked up and saw images of troops on the streets of some city. It was night, their vehicles and helmets and riot shields silhouetted against bursts of flame, and she searched for some clue as to where it was, without success. It might have been Belfast or Seattle, Colombo or Jerusalem. Then she realised that the programme was about Springer, with the commentator illustrating his points with news clips. She still wasn't very sure what Springer's philosophy actually said, but it did seem to have acquired a sudden currency. You could hardly open a newspaper or turn on a newscast these days without hearing some reference to 'Springer's Syndrome' or 'Springer's Nightmare', whenever some example of extremist violence was being discussed.

Her phone rang, and she flicked off the TV and picked up the receiver. It was Brock.

'Kathy? You haven't heard from Leon in the past hour or so have you?'

The tone of his voice made her stomach tighten. 'No. What's wrong?'

'Wayne's had a call from Rupert, his contact at that club, Thoroughbreds. Apparently Wayne had phoned him earlier to say that Leon wouldn't be keeping the appointment, and had asked him to give Darr a message that he'd been called back up north. Rupert did that when Darr arrived. Then a few minutes later Leon turned up.'

'At the club? He kept the appointment?'

'Yes. I don't know what the hell he was thinking of. Rupert was serving other customers when he walked in, but he saw him quite clearly. Leon chatted with Darr for a couple of minutes, then they both left.'

'He didn't tell anyone?'

'Not a soul. He didn't say anything to you, then?'

Kathy thought, I'd be the last one. And then, *but he's doing this because of me.*

'Rupert has no idea where they were going?'

'No. He gave Wayne the names of some other clubs that he knows Darr takes his guests to, and we're just starting to check those. But . . . Rupert said something else, Kathy. He said, before Leon arrived he was talking with Darr, and Darr asked him if he'd ever met his boss, Haygill. Rupert hadn't, and Darr then asked him if he'd even heard the name Haygill before. Rupert said no.'

'Oh God . . .' Kathy whispered. The sense of foreboding that had been lurking in her mind throughout the previous night came lurching back with a vengeance, making her feel physically sick. She had to concentrate to hear what Brock was saying.

'. . . always believed that lightning never strikes twice in the same place . . .'

She didn't follow at first, then realised he was referring to an earlier case of theirs in which Leon had been held hostage for almost twenty-four hours by a gunman. She recalled the state he was in at the end of it. What the hell had been thinking of to do this?

'. . . probably sitting in some bloody strip-club guzzling champagne, but we've put out an alert for Darr's car just to be on the safe side. Unfortunately both Leon and Darr have got their mobiles switched off. Any ideas?'

'Could they have gone back to the lab?'

'From the West End? Unlikely, I should think, but I can get the UCLE security people to check for us.'

'I think I'll head down there myself,' Kathy said. She couldn't have offered a rational argument for her choice, but she had to move, to do something, and some obscure corner of her brain, a corner that specialised in ironic references at inappropriate moments, had flashed up a phrase – *This is a Springer Nightmare.*

As she pulled on her coat and headed for the lift, another thought came into her head, a visual one this time, of the black river which flowed past the university, past the end of the steps on which Springer had died, past the building in which Darr worked, the river now in spate after the recent rain, sucking its debris through the city and out past the Thames Barrage to the great emptiness of the North Sea.

It was an inspired image, and one which Leon Desai also had before him at that same moment, but with a terrifying reality, the boiling swell of black water swirling against the stones of the wall on top of which he was teetering, and though it was not the same place that Kathy had imagined, it was the same river.

He had joined Darr at the bar, breathing deeply like an actor to control his nerves. Darr had seemed pleased to see him, but also surprised, and had explained that Rupert had passed on a message about him not being able to keep their meeting. Leon had immediately realised what had happened, and made up a story about being able to postpone his departure until morning.

Darr had then said that he was bored with Thoroughbreds, and suggested that they go to another place he knew, and Leon found himself agreeing with hardly a qualm, in fact quite pleased with the proposal because he hadn't liked the idea of Rupert reporting on his unexpected presence to O'Brien.

They had collected their coats and walked a couple of blocks to where Darr's car was parked in a dark side street. Almost immediately he got in, Leon began to sense that something was badly wrong.

'Fasten your seatbelt, please,' Darr had said to him, with a strange tautness in his voice, and of course he had complied, and then seen Darr twist in his seat and press the door lock button that simultaneously locked all the passenger doors, before he started the ignition and set off. Then Leon became aware of a stir of movement from the back seat, and with a nauseating sense of disappointment with himself, of having been through something so very like this before and still not seen it coming, he knew that there were others in the car, so that when the cold blade of a knife was pressed to his neck and a sudden pungent gust of someone else's bad breath filled his nostrils, he almost said aloud, 'So lightning can strike the same bloody place twice, if you're fool enough to stand in it'.

'My friends are very dangerous men,' Darr said, without taking his eyes off the road. 'Please don't do anything to cause them alarm. I don't want the inconvenience of your blood on my car seat.'

Leon felt he should protest, play his role of the DNA-test salesman, but somehow he couldn't bring any conviction to it. He knew from experience that once men had embarked on a course such as this they weren't going to be put off by any play-acting he could summon up. For a moment he felt an enormous envy for Wayne O'Brien's smooth way with words. He'd be able to talk his way out of this, he was sure.

There were two of them in the back, he guessed, as hands began to rummage through the pockets of his suit, working down from his jacket to his trousers, pulling everything out. To compound his folly he had removed every indication that he was a police officer – his warrant card, his Federation membership card, his entry card to the gym and pool, his pass for the forensic labs. All they would learn from the contents of his wallet was that he lived in Barnet, not Liverpool. And then they found the tape recorder.

'Shit!' one of them said, and they began whispering urgently together. Not in English, he realised, and probably not Hindi, of which he knew a little, but something similar. Maybe Urdu.

Finally, after removing the tape and batteries and testing all the buttons they seemed satisfied, that it wasn't a transmitter probably, and they moved on to pull his mobile phone apart.

They were heading east, through the West End to the City, then on through light traffic. He caught a glimpse of the Monument, then the silhouette of the Tower, and still they continued eastward, in the general direction of UCLE. But before they got as far as that Darr turned off the main road and into a maze of small lanes hemmed in by tall unlit blocks. He brought the car to an abrupt halt and switched off the engine, opened his door and stuck his head out. There seemed to be no sound at all. Satisfied, Darr and one of the men in the back got out while the third held his knife at Leon's throat. His door was jerked open and he moved carefully, thinking that this was probably his best chance to run for it, but the thought had barely formed when both his wrists were seized and jerked vertically up his back. He cried at the sudden, excruciating pain in his shoulder blades as the two men pushed him forward to follow Darr who was striding ahead towards a low wall. Out of the corner of his vision, his eyes still unused to the darkness after the car's headlights had been turned off, Leon thought he made out a cement mixer and scaffolding behind a wire fence. Then they were at the wall and forcing him to stumble up onto it, and in a sudden sickening heave of vertigo he found himself swaying forward over a void. He seesawed back and forward crazily, trying to balance, feeling as if only the burning pain itself was holding him back from flying into the empty dark. And then his vision cleared, and he made out, far below, the sheen of the writhing current.

Darr began shouting at him. He was very angry about something, but Leon couldn't take in half of what he said; by now he was focused on his certain impending death. As the shouting became more furious he was certain that he had only moments left. The knife would slide in, burning into his kidneys, he would be pitched forward into the swirling black current, and another anonymous corpse would be carried out to sea. With a teetering detachment he considered what his last thoughts should be. He thought regretfully of his mother and her ambition to become a perfect middle-class English lady, and of Kathy, with whom, had he been stronger and more honest, he could have been very happy.

He became aware that Darr was repeating something, again and again.

'You are a spy! Confess you are a spy!'

Leon sucked in a lungful of freezing air laced with diesel fumes and gasped, 'Yes, yes.'

'You're a detective!' Darr yelled, and again Leon agreed, yes, it was true, waiting for the blade. Would it be very painful? Was it better to die by stabbing or to drown?

There was a tremendous wrench on his arms and he found himself sprawled on the gravel on the landward side of the wall. The other two men – he thought he recognised them now from the pictures he'd been shown of the two Iraqis from CAB-Tech – hauled him up onto his knees and held his arms while Darr grabbed hold of his tie and began to slap his face, hard enough to make his head spin and his nose bleed. At the same time Darr was talking again, bitter and spitting, though at first Leon couldn't make out what he was going on about.

'You want to know about his wife, do you? Well, I'll tell you about his wife! She pesters me, she rings me up, she wants me to show her where I take our foreign guests. That's why she was at the club last night, pestering me, wanting me to buy her drinks, then take her somewhere discreet. . .'

Darr stopped slapping Leon and looked with disgust at the blood on his hands, giving his victim a moment to ponder this strange diatribe. Darr pulled a white handkerchief from his pocket and wiped his hands fastidiously, then raised a finger and waggled it in front of Leon's nose.

'But you can tell him that I haven't touched that drunken English bitch! I haven't laid a finger on her! You tell him that!'

Into Leon's mind came the image in the mirror behind the bar at Thoroughbreds, of the distant figures of Darr and a blonde woman. Haygill's wife he thought, his mind suddenly clear. He thinks I'm spying on him for Haygill, a *detective*.

'And you can tell him something else, too. You can tell him that I won't work for a man who treats me like a peasant, who sets spies on me! Eh? Eh?'

Leon mumbled, 'Yes, yes.'

'Eh?' Darr repeated, leaning down, his face close.

'Yes,' Leon nodded, and a tremendous blow between his shoulder blades sent him sprawling forward onto his face. He lay stunned on the gravel and heard the crunch of their footsteps receding into the night, the growl of the car engine, then silence.

Kathy had reached Poplar, and was beginning to wonder what she could reasonably expect to do when she got to UCLE, when her phone went. She pressed the button and a voice she barely recognised whispered, 'Kathy . . . Kathy . . .'

'Leon!' She skidded the car to the kerb and pressed the phone harder to her ear. 'Is it you?'

'Kathy . . . yes, I'm sorry . . .'

'Are you all right?' she demanded, hearing the panic in her voice.

216

His sounded unnatural, as if he were being strangled, and there were sounds of other people in the background. 'Where are you?'

'Kathy . . . I'm sorry . . .'

'For God's sake, Leon!' she almost yelled. 'Never mind about being sorry! Are you all right?'

'I've had a bit of bother. I was wondering if you could come and pick me up.'

He was on Commercial Road in Limehouse he said. She told him not to move and rammed the car into gear. At the next red light she rang Brock and told him she'd made contact and would ring back when she knew more.

Within five minutes she spotted him outside the pub he'd described, leaning in a patch of shadow against the wall. Her headlights caught him as she swerved to the kerb, and he jerked upright, looking dishevelled like a tramp. The lights seemed to alarm him and he stumbled as he turned to run.

'Leon!' She raced across the pavement and caught him.

'Kathy! How . . . how did you get here so fast?' He seemed astonished, disoriented.

'Are you hurt?' His nose was bloody she could see, and he was moving stiffly, but he was moving, and on his feet.

He shook his head and she threw her arms round him, laughing with relief. Her laughter seemed to drain the remaining tension out of him and he leaned back against the pub wall, holding onto her. They clung together in the shadow like that for a while until she whispered, 'You'd better tell me what happened, you stupid bastard.'

They went into the pub where Leon had told the landlord that he'd been mugged and had persuaded him to give him coins for the phone. Kathy repaid the money and bought the barman a beer and Leon a brandy while he went to the gents and tried to clean himself up. The bar was glaringly bright and crowded, the music from a jukebox deafening, and she found a small formica table as far from the machine as possible. She watched Leon weave slowly through the beer drinkers towards her and remembered the government scientist's words, 'We're all vulnerable'. Leon was looking very vulnerable at that moment, his hair and clothes more in order but his usual poise gone, his pride a major casualty. He sat opposite her and

217

muttered a thanks and took a gulp of the drink and told her the story.

When he reached the end he paused for another sip of the brandy, his hand trembling as he raised it to his mouth. He choked and coughed, and said, 'I'm sorry. You must think this is pathetic. I'm still . . . rattled.'

'I know,' Kathy said, and put her hand on his. 'I know exactly how you feel.'

'You?' He smiled doubtfully, disbelieving. 'Not you, Kathy. And the thing was that although I'd been through something like that before, the Sammy Starling thing, it didn't help. I thought to myself how ridiculous it was, this happening twice, and me even more helpless and terrified the second time.'

'It's the same for everyone, Leon,' Kathy said gently.

'No.' Leon shook his head adamantly. 'Look at Brock and Bren, fighting those skinheads off in Shadwell Road, and you taking on those blokes at the cemetery the other day . . . I'm not like that. I was afraid.'

She wanted to explain to him that in the cemetery she had reacted without having time to feel afraid, and that afterwards she had suffered for it. She wanted to tell him that she had self-doubts every bit as severe as his own, and that they were more crippling for her, in her position, than for him. But she held back, not sure that she wanted to make a confession to him. And there were things to be done. Later, perhaps, she would decide to tell him 'So Darr thought you were a private detective hired by Haygill to find out if he was screwing his wife?'

Leon nodded, gulping down the last of the brandy. 'She is a blonde, isn't she? I remembered that Darr was with a blonde woman when I arrived at the club yesterday. He put her in a taxi and came to the bar and there I was. When I started asking him questions about her he must have put two and two together and made five.'

Leon shook his head glumly while Kathy smiled.

'I'm sorry, Leon, but that really takes the biscuit. I wonder what Brock will say?'

'Oh, we can't tell him! That's why I rang you.'

'Rupert saw you at the club, leaving with Darr. He phoned Wayne, and Brock mobilised the troops. I phoned him on my way here to let him know you were safe. He's going to need an explanation.'

Leon groaned.

She leaned forward and gently straightened his tie. 'It hasn't been your night, has it?'

'No. But I'll tell you what, Kathy. You and Brock should be careful. I was lucky, but those blokes, the Iraqis, they're tough. I'm convinced that they'd have finished me off with one word from Darr. I'd hate to think what they'd do to anyone who really got on the wrong side of them.'

She nodded. 'Did they keep all your stuff?'

'Yeah. Probably threw it in the river.'

But in that, at least, he was wrong, for when Kathy finally delivered him to his parents' house in Barnet, after he had made his explanations on her phone to Brock and silently endured Brock's scathing assessment of his judgement and prospects, his mother opened the door to him with the news that a terribly nice Asian man had called with his possessions and a message that he must be much more careful in future.

19

The following morning everyone in the office seemed to be reading the *Herald* when Kathy arrived. Bren tossed her his copy as she walked in and asked what was going on.

'This should stir the pot,' he said. 'Does Brock know the editor or something?'

Kathy caught the front page headline, 'POLICE PROBE UNIVERSITY STAFF', and thought oh-oh. But the front page was only a sampler for what lay inside. It reported that Scotland Yard detectives had begun reinterviewing staff at UCLE in connection with the murder of Max Springer, and in particular those staff in the Division of Science and Technology with international and Islamic connections, with the unstated implication that they were hunting for accomplices of the assumed murderer Abu Khadra. It ended with references to further articles inside; *Academic strife*, page 3; *Science feature*, page 7; *Editorial*, page 10. It seemed as if Clare Hancock had managed to take over the whole issue with her story.

It was her name against the *Academic strife* report, which gave a detailed account of the long-running and increasingly savage feud between Max Springer and Richard Haygill, including Springer's 'Dr Mengele' jibe in the University Senate and culminating in quotations taken from his letter to the paper before he died. The article described these as coming from a document that had come into the hands of the newspaper that it had passed on to the police, and Kathy guessed that it was a measure of Clare Hancock's faith that there was a bigger story behind all this that she'd been able to persuade her editor to use it. The quotes included Springer's descriptions of UCLE as 'an outstanding leader in whoredom', and of Haygill as 'Svengali-like', as well as the prophetic final sentence, 'Those who speak out against tyranny must offer their very lives to the cause'. Against these tirades, the repeated 'no comment' responses of both UCLE and Haygill were made to sound evasive and guilty, and allowed the reporter to come to the conclusion that the whole débâcle must point to a deeper malaise at UCLE, to the failure of its administration to manage the affair properly, and to the possibility that both the university and CAB-Tech's director had something to hide.

The *Science feature* on page 7, titled 'STRUGGLING TO CONTROL THE GENETIC GENIE' and written by the paper's science correspondent, took a different approach. This focused on Max Springer's accusations that CAB-Tech's research work was unethical and beyond the control of the university or any other responsible body. It gave the familiar discussion of fears about the implications of genetic engineering a particular slant by looking at the way research companies operating in more than one country might evade ethical controls on their experiments and procedures. As a possible illustration of this, it named CAB-Tech's BRCA4 protocol as one that had raised concerns among UK regulators. Kathy wondered where they had got that from.

The editorial pulled together these different themes by proposing a Royal Commission into the regulation of multi-national genetic research organisations, as well as an inquiry into the management of UCLE.

Kathy put down the paper and wondered if Clare Hancock had spoken to her the previous day just to gloat.

The first reaction to the *Herald* edition came at ten that morning, with a call to Brock from the UCLE President, Roderick Young, requesting a meeting. He arrived at Queen Anne's Gate an hour later, and was shown into one of the ground floor meeting rooms. He shook Brock's hand with a sombre nod, looked around with distaste at the spartan furniture, the unshaded fluorescent light tubes, the green moss staining the brickwork of the tiny courtyard beyond the window, then took off his coat and threw it across the back of a chair and sat down. He had arrived alone, telling his driver to call for him again in half an hour, and he began by asking that their conversation be off the record and not recorded. Brock agreed.

'You'll have seen the *Herald* this morning,' he began, his voice a low growl as if he suspected people of listening at the door. 'As you might imagine, it's caused a good deal of consternation among my colleagues, particularly in Professor Haygill's area. Haygill will be getting his own legal advice, as will the university. The articles are potentially extremely damaging to both UCLE and CAB-Tech, as well as to the individuals concerned, as you can well imagine. Haygill's Principal Research Scientist handed in his notice this morning—'

'That's Dr Darr, is it?' Brock interrupted, making a note on his pad. 'Is he proposing to leave the country?'

'I don't know. Haygill's trying to persuade him to change his mind. But that's just a hint of the possible repercussions. Apart from the staff, the damage to CAB-Tech's reputation and the confidence of its investors could be immense.'

The words were there, Brock sensed, but not the feelings. There was no anger, no outrage in Young's voice. He spoke in a monotone, giving the impression of a chess player moving his pieces forward, one by one, to establish a position.

'Professor Haygill is understandably incensed. He feels that he always behaved with total propriety towards Max Springer, despite outrageous provocation, and he is now being pilloried by the words of a dead man against which he can't defend himself. He is in a mood to lash out, to defend himself, against anyone he perceives as an enemy. You understand?'

'Of course.'

'He even suggested to me that the *Herald* reports may have been deliberately inspired by the police.'

He paused and looked balefully at Brock for comment.

Brock said, 'Really?'

Young gave the briefest of smiles, as if he hadn't really expected to provoke a reaction.

'Naturally I will attempt to counsel him to avoid entangling us all in unnecessary complications. But at some point his interests and ours — that is, the university's — may diverge. May indeed have already diverged.'

'Is that so? I seem to recall you describing CAB-Tech as the flagship of your university's research effort, Professor,' Brock said mildly.

'Sometimes even the flagship must be sacrificed for the sake of the whole fleet. I'm thinking that it may become prudent, necessary, for the university to review the whole operation and management of CAB-Tech. Some kind of high-powered, external committee of review, with unimpeachable credibility. A senior judge, a retired vice-chancellor, a past president of the Royal Society . . . that sort of level. My dilemma is, that I don't want to set up a sledgehammer to crack a nut, you see.'

'No, I don't.'

'Well, if the problem is endemic, and the whole body is tainted, then clearly some powerful surgery is necessary. But if it's localised to one or two misguided junior staff who can be isolated and removed without damaging the integrity of the whole, well, that's a different matter. To be candid, Chief Inspector,' and here Young fixed Brock with a frank, almost intimate little smile, 'it would help me a great deal if I could have some guidance from you as to how deep, or should I say, how far up the CAB-Tech hierarchy your current investigations are reaching.'

'I'm afraid I can't comment on our inquiries.'

'You see,' Young went on as if he hadn't heard, 'we're both basically the same. We're both servants of the public. Just like you, my primary concern has to be the well being of the members of the public I serve, the students and their parents – you might be one of them – whose investment in their education at UCLE depends upon the good standing of the institution. I cannot permit any individual or group, no matter how prestigious, to undermine the value of the degrees our students leave us with, and which are the foundation of their future.'

Brock wondered if Young really believed he was making any impression with this appeal, for once again, although the words were said, there was no emotional force behind them. Yet somehow he seemed to feel he'd made his point, for after Brock repeated that he could say nothing about his investigation, Young nodded, promised his full cooperation, and got to his feet. When he'd gone, Brock decided that Young's sole objective had been damage limitation – to

223

persuade Brock that he at least lay outside whatever circle of guilt the police might be defining. He was probably on his way back to tell Haygill to stay calm, while he prepared the means to sacrifice him.

Brock's secretary Dot put her head round the door. 'I heard he'd gone. I've had another request for an urgent meeting. Mrs Haygill phoned. She wants to meet to speak to you personally. Shall I get back to her?'

Sheila Haygill was shown into the meeting room half an hour later. She was expensively dressed, with several large precious stones on her fingers, and carefully groomed. She moved into the room and sat down in the offered chair with deliberate care, and Brock thought at first that this was because the circumstances made her nervous. He thought she must have been stunning when she was young, but the buxomness had become over-ripe, and the natural beauty of youth had become formalised by make-up and hair styling into a kind of stiff counterfeit that matched her movements and also, when she began to speak, her speech.

'I am not a genius, Chief Inspector,' she began, 'like my husband. In fact I'm not very bright, as most people know.'

He detected a Manchester accent, and as she went on he decided that the stiffness came from a sense of inherent insecurity, despite her looks and possessions.

'But I know right from wrong, and I've tried, in my own way, to support my husband over the years to the best of my ability. However, he's away a great deal, and he's been under a lot of pressure recently, as you may know, and especially in the past months, and perhaps due to that, he hasn't always been fair to me. In fact, there have been times when he's shown . . .' her voice dropped to a whisper, 'his contempt.'

She paused and opened her handbag for a tissue, and dabbed her nose, then drew herself up straight. 'This morning I got a call from a friend, who told me that my husband has been employing a private detective to spy on me.' Her eyes narrowed in anger. 'I don't consider that the action of a loving husband.'

Brock shifted uncomfortably in his seat and cleared his throat. 'Are you absolutely sure, Mrs Haygill? Sometimes people can jump to conclusions . . .'

'Oh, there's no doubt. The man was confronted. He confessed.

But anyway, that's only the latest and final straw. It's a private matter between me and my husband. I only mention it to explain that I'm leaving him, and I don't feel bound to lie for him any more.'

'Have you been lying for him?'

'I . . . I've kept silent when I would have spoken out if it had been anyone else. Tell me, this report in the paper this morning, is it true that you suspect my husband of being involved in the murder of Max Springer?'

Brock didn't reply for a moment. He saw the tension in her eyes as she waited for his reply, and felt on a cusp, one of those moments where everything shifts.

'Mrs Haygill,' he replied softly, trying to sound very calm and reassuring, 'I'll answer that to the best of my ability, but first I'd like to tell you that I would like to record this conversation, and also invite one of my colleagues to join us. Will you agree to that?'

She hesitated, then nodded, and Brock lifted the phone and asked for Kathy. When they were ready Brock explained the caution to Mrs Haygill and went on, 'You asked me just now if we suspect your husband of involvement in the murder of Max Springer. All I can tell you is that we believe that Abu Khadra, a member of your husband's staff, pulled the trigger that killed Professor Springer, but we are not entirely satisfied that he acted alone. The report in the paper that we have been interviewing your husband and his staff at CAB-Tech once again is correct. Now, you also said just now that you have been keeping silent about something to protect your husband, is that correct?'

'Yes.'

'Please tell us what it is.'

Her carefully plucked eyebrows creased together in a frown. 'He came to see me, you see. About three weeks ago. The twelfth of January it was. I made a note in my diary at the time. Richard was at a meeting in York that day.'

'Who came to see you?'

'Max Springer. He came to our house. I was amazed at the nerve of the man. He'd never been there before, and of course he knew he wouldn't be welcome. I was just so astonished to see him standing at the front door, this untidy little man in his shabby mackintosh with his hair blown all over the place, that he was able to speak to me before I slammed the door on him.

'He said that he had something he wanted to tell me, something important for me to hear. He seemed so, well, *humble* in his manner, not at all the monster I'd heard of from Richard's accounts, that I let him in. We sat in our lounge room, and I remember noticing that he was wearing odd socks, and the collar of his shirt was dreadfully frayed. He said he'd come to warn me about something. He said he had some information about Richard's work which he was planning to make public, and when he did it might well ruin Richard.'

'He wasn't more specific about what kind of information it was? What it related to?'

'No. I wouldn't have understood anyway. It was just something to do with his work. Well, I thought it was very odd him coming to our house to tell me this, so I asked him why, and he said that one of the things he regretted about the fight he'd been having with Richard was the pain it might have caused innocent parties, especially myself. He explained that he had heard gossip at the university that our marriage had been running into difficulties, and he hoped he hadn't contributed to that. Only now he felt obliged to warn me that things would get worse for my husband, and I might like to consider how I could protect myself from the consequences, financially.'

'"Financially"? He said that? What did you understand him to mean?'

'I really wasn't sure, when I thought about it afterwards. I mean, Richard handles all our finances, and I hadn't a clue what our assets might be, or whose name they might be in. Short of divorcing Richard, I wasn't sure that I could "protect myself", but I did take some steps. I went through the records Richard keeps at home, and went to speak to an accountant.'

'What else did Springer say?'

'Nothing. He said that was all he'd come to say and got up and left.'

'Did he indicate when he was going to make the information public?'

'No.'

'And you told your husband about this visit, did you?'

Sheila Haygill lowered her eyes. 'No. I intended to at first, of course, but then I imagined the terrible fuss Richard was bound to make about it, him coming to our home and speaking to me while Richard was away, and me letting him in and listening to him. And . . . I wasn't sure that I wanted to tell Richard about Max Springer's advice to me. It would make him very angry, I was sure, and there again, maybe . . . maybe it was good advice. So in the end I just kept quiet.'

'You didn't warn him that Springer was planning to ruin him?'

'I didn't see how I could, without telling him the whole thing.'

'Maybe you could have given the warning to a third party to pass on to Richard. Someone like Dr Darr, for instance.'

He watched the reaction, the blink of surprise, the flush of the cheeks beneath her make-up, then she stared defiantly at him and said, 'I may have mentioned something to Dr Darr, yes. Sometimes, when Richard and I aren't . . . when he forgets to tell me things, about his movements and so on, I talk to Tahir – Dr Darr.'

'Rather than Richard's secretary?'

'She . . . she's very efficient and devoted to Richard. Unfortunately she doesn't like me very much. The feeling is mutual.'

'So what exactly did you tell Tahir?'

'I told him about Max Springer's visit and his threat to Richard. Tahir wasn't really concerned. He said that Springer was mad and always trying to cause trouble, that there wasn't any way he could damage Richard and that I shouldn't worry about it. I was reassured by his reaction . . . at the time.'

She hesitated and lapsed into silence as if running out of momentum, and Brock glanced anxiously at her. Knowing that she couldn't be compelled to give evidence against her husband he didn't want to lose her. 'Can I get you something, Mrs Haygill? A cup of tea, coffee?'

She roused herself. 'No, no, thank you. I'd just like to get this over.'

'Of course. There's something about Richard that you want to tell me?'

She nodded. 'I didn't think too much about Springer's visit after I spoke to Tahir, until I opened my paper on that Friday morning and saw the report of his murder. I was very shocked, of course, but I didn't connect it with his visit to me until later that night. Richard had been away on business again that day – he'd flown up to Glasgow for some meeting, and he didn't get home until late. I was in bed when I heard him open the front door, and I expected him to come straight upstairs to have a bath as he usually did after a long day. Only he didn't come upstairs, and I began to wonder if he'd missed his evening meal and was making himself something in the kitchen. I put on my dressing gown and went downstairs, but there was no light on in the kitchen. Then I noticed a light coming from his study. The door wasn't quite shut, and I pushed it gently, because sometimes he's quite irritable when he's tired, and I was about to say something when I caught sight of him. He was sitting with his back to the door, at his desk, taken up with something he was holding under the desk light, examining it. I saw straight away what it was. It was a gun.'

She came to a stop, staring down at her handbag as if seeing the scene again.

'What sort of gun, Mrs Haygill?' Brock prompted gently. 'Can you describe it for me?'

'Er . . . it was black, not very large – about the same size as his hand. Not like the kind of thing you see in Westerns. More modern, flat.'

'A pistol rather than a revolver then. And you weren't aware of your husband owning such a thing?'

'Good heavens, no! Why ever would he possess something like that?'

'Go on then, what did you do?'

'Well, I just froze. I didn't dare even breathe. My first thought was that he was going to shoot himself. I thought, maybe Max Springer was right and Richard is in some kind of terrible trouble and wants to end it all. But when I thought of Springer I remembered the newspaper report of that morning, how he had been shot at the university by an unknown gunman, and there was Richard holding a gun.'

'Examining it, you say?'

'Yes, I think so. Then he sort of shook his head, as if he'd come to a decision about something, opened the drawer of his desk, and put the gun inside. I stepped back from the door and returned to the foot of the stairs. I didn't dare try to get up them again without him hearing, so I called out his name, as if I'd just come down. He answered and came out of the study. He looked very tired and I asked him if he was all right. He said he was, then started to switch off the lights, and we went upstairs.

'The next day he was due to fly to the Gulf, and I was to drive him to the airport at midday. After breakfast he did some packing, then said that he was going to go for a walk to clear his head. I was surprised, because he never does that. I offered to go too, but he said he had some things to work out for his trip and he needed to think. He put on his old coat and I heard him go into his study before he left. Once I was sure he was gone I went in there and opened the desk drawer. The gun wasn't there any more. I searched all through the desk, and the suitcase he'd packed, but I couldn't find it. I began to think I'd imagined seeing it.'

Brock exchanged a glance with Kathy. 'Why?' he said cautiously, imagining what a defence counsel might make of this. 'Had you been drinking before your husband got home that night?'

'I'd had one or two drinks, yes. But I wasn't anywhere near drunk. I know what I saw.'

'But you're absolutely sure it was a gun? It couldn't have been something else black? His wallet perhaps?'

'No, no, it was a gun. It was the last thing I expected to see in his hand. I looked at it so hard to be sure I wasn't making a mistake. He turned it over, directly under the light. It glinted like dark metal.'

'All right. So how long was he away the next morning?'

'Not very long. Twenty minutes.'

'Have you any idea where he might have gone?'

'He turned left outside our gate, and when he returned he had mud on his shoes. There's a small wood not far from our house, with a pond. I thought he might have gone there.'

Brock thought, simpler to have wrapped it up and put it in his dustbin, unless he was expecting his house to be searched while he was away.

'That's really all I know,' Sheila Haygill said. Some of the stiffness had gone out of her and she sounded subdued, as if realising what she had done in informing on her husband.

229

'Did you and Richard talk about Max Springer's murder on that Friday night or Saturday before he left?'

'Yes. I didn't want to bring it up, but it was front page in the morning newspaper again, and it would have been strange not to. Richard said he'd read about it the previous day.'

'Where was your husband on the Thursday, the day Springer was killed?'

'At the university as far as I know. I believe he came home at about eight that evening, and he didn't mention anything about a murder.'

'How did he seem?'

'I've thought about that, but I can't remember. I mean, I didn't know anything had happened and I had no special reason to remember that day. I suppose he must have been normal or I would have remembered something, wouldn't I?'

Brock turned his collar up against the wind, and stared morosely at the icy water. He had knocked his knee getting out of the car, and the pain which had eased over the past week had returned whenever he put weight on his left leg. The pond was almost precisely circular as if it had been deliberately constructed by a landscaper, although it had in fact been formed by a bomb crater during the war, at a time when the surrounding wood was much larger than the present copse. It wasn't deep, at its centre no more than waist high to the two divers in black wetsuits working across it, but the leafy silt of the bottom was treacherous to sift through, and there was a wealth of miscellaneous objects beneath the surface – bottles, cans, a bicycle frame, a milk crate – to confuse the search. Two other men in rubber boots were working around the edge, and behind him a line of uniforms was working through the copse. At least the wind and drizzle were keeping curious spectators away.

The four men working the pond were converging on the furthest quarter when one of the pair in the water gave a cry and held something up above his head. He turned and moved in slow motion through the sucking mud towards the bank, handing it to one of the men there who slipped it into a clear bag and hurried back to the path where Brock was standing.

'A gun, sir,' he grinned.

Through the mud smearing the pistol, Brock made out some of the letters cast into its side, CESKA. 'Good,' he muttered. 'Let's get some lunch.'

Haygill stumbled as he was led into the room. They had waited until the following day to arrest him while tests were done on the gun, a Czech-made service issue pistol, probably about twenty years old, and confirmation received that it had indeed fired the rounds that had killed Springer.

'Are you all right, Professor?' Brock asked. The man looked even greyer and more harried than when he'd last seen him.

'Am I all right?' Haygill repeated, as if he were giving the question serious consideration. 'Well, yesterday my wife left me, my principal assistant resigned, and my university president stabbed me in the back. This morning I woke up with toothache, then I was arrested for murder. But otherwise I'm fine, thank you.' He ran a hand distractedly through his hair, adjusted his glasses, and sat down.

As gallows humour went, Brock had heard better. He wondered how Haygill would cope with jail. Perhaps it would be a relief, the weight of all those frequent flier points lifted from his shoulders. More likely it would destroy him.

'Can we get you something for the toothache?'

Haygill shook his head wearily, the bravado gone. 'I took an aspirin, thanks.'

His solicitor came in with Bren. Brock started the recording equipment, stated the formalities, then said, 'When did you first hear of the murder of Max Springer, Professor Haygill?'

'First hear of it?' It didn't seem to be the question Haygill expected, and he frowned in thought. 'Well, er, it would have been that weekend, I think. Probably the Sunday, while I was in the Gulf.'

'Yes, that's what you told me when we first met, on the following Tuesday, the twenty-fifth. How did you hear about it?'

'Phone call, I think, or perhaps an e-mail. From my secretary perhaps, or Darr. I can't remember. Is it important? Yes, I think my secretary phoned, because of the fuss they were making in the Sunday papers.'

'She phoned on a Sunday?'

'Yes. She thought I should know.'

Brock paused, letting this hang in the air for a moment, then said quietly, 'Only your wife tells us that you discussed the murder with her on the Saturday morning, over breakfast.'

Haygill looked shocked. 'My wife? You've spoken to my wife?' He turned to his solicitor. 'I thought wives couldn't testify against husbands.'

The lawyer shook his head, looking very unhappy with the inference that could be drawn from this, which Brock duly pushed home. 'Oh, they're quite at liberty to testify against their husbands, Professor. So you're saying that causes you to change your story, are you?'

'No! I'm not saying that. I mean . . . yes, she may be right. We may have discussed it on the Saturday. I may be getting confused. Maybe my secretary phoned to tell me about the Sunday papers, but I'd already heard the news.'

'Let's try again, shall we? Think carefully please, and tell me when you first heard about Max Springer's murder.'

Haygill exhaled deeply, took his glasses off and rubbed his eyes. 'It's quite hot in here, isn't it?' His forehead was shiny, his face pale.

Bren got up and poured him a plastic cup of water.

'Thanks.' He gulped it and took off his jacket.

'Take your time,' Brock said. 'Tell us if you're not feeling well.'

'No, no, I'm all right. Er, I think it may have been on the Friday I first heard. I had to go up to Glasgow that morning, and I believe I read about it in the morning paper. I'm not absolutely sure . . . I had so much else on my mind . . .'

'But the spectacular murder of a colleague on the university steps, surely that must have registered? And a colleague who was such a bitter enemy of yours?'

Haygill took another deep breath but didn't reply, and Brock went on, 'Tell us your movements from the time you flew back from Glasgow on Friday up until you left for the Gulf on Saturday, please.'

In a halting voice Haygill said he'd picked up his car at Stansted airport and driven home on the Friday evening by way of UCLE, where he had to leave some papers for his staff following the Glasgow trip, and pick up others for the Gulf visit. The following

232

morning he had packed, done some work on his laptop, then left for Heathrow with his wife around midday.

'Did you take a walk on Saturday morning?'

'Er, yes, that's right, I did. Sorry, I forgot that. I had a headache and I had to do a bit of thinking about the trip, so I went out for a short walk, oh, about ten thirty. I dare say my wife told you.'

'Where did you go?'

'Just . . . just round the block.'

Again Brock let his words hang, while he sat in silence, staring morosely at his notepad. The solicitor shifted in his seat. Haygill cleared his throat but didn't speak.

Then Brock reached down to the briefcase by his feet and lifted out a clear plastic bag containing the gun, and laid it on the table in front of Haygill.

'I am showing Professor Haygill the handgun listed as evidence L4327/1010, a semi-automatic pistol of Czech manufacture, known as a Model 52. Have you ever seen this before, Professor?'

Haygill was transfixed, eyes wide, body rigid. He stared at the gun for a long moment of silence, then, eyes still abnormally wide, rose slowly to his feet and turned towards the door.

'I take it that means yes,' Brock said quietly. Then, for the benefit of the tape, 'Professor Haygill has got up to leave. I am suspending this interview at ten twenty-three hours.'

They reconvened an hour later, after Haygill had had time to recover and confer with his solicitor. To Brock it was like looking at a man in the ring, slowly registering with every blow that he was out of his weight. He wanted to apologise, he said, so softly that Brock had to ask him to speak up. He wanted to set the record straight. He had been very disturbed to read the newspaper reports of Max Springer's death, that morning on the flight up to Glasgow. The account of Springer being shot dead on the university steps had seemed utterly incredible, impossibly melodramatic, and yet it had actually happened. The people he met at the University of Strathclyde that day had heard the news too, and kept asking him about it. He couldn't get it out of his mind, and at some point an awful possibility had occurred to him, one that at first he dismissed, but gradually began to haunt him. Suppose Springer's death was connected to his feud with himself? Suppose someone on his side, on his team, had decided to put an end to Springer's slanders for his sake?

'So you considered that a definite possibility?' Brock said, just for the record, disappointed with the line Haygill was taking.

'Only because the prospect was so appalling. I have a tendency to imagine the worst. Anyone will tell you. When we look at a new experiment, my first question is, what's the worst that can happen? Well, this seemed to me the worst possibility. I would never have imagined it before that day, but then, I would never have imagined that Max Springer could die like that.'

'Yes, but you did think it a realistic possibility?'

'There have been times, over the past year, when some of my people have become very emotional, very angry, about racist and bigoted intolerance that they have encountered in certain quarters. You know some of it, I think. I wondered if perhaps Max Springer's outrageous attacks upon our work had finally provoked a reaction that had gone tragically too far.'

'I thought he was passionately opposed to bigotry and racism?'

'So he said. The irony had not escaped me.'

'So, what did you do?'

'As I said before, I drove to UCLE that evening when I returned to London. It was true what I said about the papers I needed, but I also hoped to see Darr there and find out about developments, and hopefully put my mind to rest. Unfortunately he wasn't there, and I wasn't able to get him on the phone. I went up to the labs. It's habit, I always do that, to get an idea of the progress of work. There was an *Evening Standard* on one of the benches, lying open at a spread on Springer's murder. They'd obviously been discussing it. I looked at it, and read that the police were still searching for the murder weapon, and the horrible thought occurred to me that, if one of the team really had been involved, it might even be there, in our building. I even thought, for a moment, that I might search for it, just to reassure myself, until I realised how impossible that would be. If somebody wanted to hide something in that building, I might search for weeks and never find it. And anyway, I was ashamed of the thought. Standing there in the familiar surroundings of our laboratories, the very idea of one of my team being involved just seemed ridiculous.

'I went back to my office to sign letters my secretary had left and sort out the papers I'd need for the next trip, and at some point I must have looked up and noticed that the volumes on the book shelves on the wall facing me were out of order.'

Haygill gave an apologetic little frown. 'Sorry. That must sound unlikely. It was my bound volumes of the *Journal of Medical Genetics*, for which I was editor for several years. I was staring at them, thinking about something else, when I suddenly thought, "Why is 1990 in front of 1989?" So I got up, still thinking about this other thing, and walked over and pulled out the two volumes to switch them round, and then I saw a white plastic carrier bag rolled up in the space behind them.'

He stopped and took a deep breath. His colour had faded again, the gleam of sweat returned to his forehead. 'I'm sorry. I realise this must all sound totally unlikely. It still seems like that to me, like a bad dream, but it is the truth you see.' Another deep breath. 'I picked up the bag . . . it obviously contained something solid. Inside I found a brown paper bag, and when I lifted that out . . .'

He came to a halt, and his solicitor looked at him in concern and half rose from his chair.

'No, no . . . it's all right.' Haygill raised his hand to reassure him. 'Inside was that gun.'

They waited while he took a gulp of water.

'What were your thoughts?' Brock said.

'What could I think? It seemed to confirm all my worst fears. But then I tried to reason my way out of it. I didn't know if it was the gun that had killed Springer – is it in fact?'

'Yes.'

'Oh. Oh, God . . . Well, I couldn't be sure. I thought, maybe if one of these characters owns a gun, and is afraid you might search their belongings after this murder, then they might want to find a hiding place for it. In fact, the more I thought about it, the more plausible that idea seemed, because surely the murderer would want to get rid of his gun completely – throw it in the Thames, for instance? Whereas whoever had hidden this gun obviously wanted to keep it, and recover it later.'

'By "one of these characters" you mean your staff, do you?'

Haygill nodded reluctantly.

'And why would they choose that place?'

'Yes, that's what I asked myself. I became quite angry thinking about how they had put me at risk. But then I reasoned that they had probably assumed that the boss's office, behind the volumes that nobody ever looks at, was just about the safest place in the whole building. But clearly I couldn't leave it there. I considered the options, and decided to dispose of it myself.'

'You didn't feel it your duty to bring it to us?'

'I'm sorry. The implications, the consequences, were too . . . expensive. I felt we had too much at stake to allow this to derail everything.'

'So what did you do?'

'I thought of the river, but then I remembered the cameras on campus, and the possibility of someone seeing me, so I put it into my bag, with the idea of taking it as far away as possible. Well, you know where I finally threw it, into the pond not far from our house. I thought I had been careful. I had no idea that anyone had seen me do it.'

'Did you discuss it with anyone? Dr Darr, for instance?'

'No, no one.'

'So you considered him as a possible culprit?'

Haygill opened his mouth as if to deny it, then changed his mind. He shrugged.

'You had no theories? No specific suspicions? Who were the principal hotheads in the previous troubles?'

'The two Iraqi chaps, probably, Sabri and Durak. Yes, I thought if anyone had smuggled a gun into the country it would probably have been them.'

'Not Abu Khadra?'

'To tell the truth, I never even considered him. He was the least militant, the least aggressive of them all. I was astounded when they said he'd been arrested.'

'And even then you didn't come forward and tell us where the gun was.'

'What good would it have done? And anyway, Abu was never tried, never found guilty, was he? There hasn't been an inquest yet, has there?'

'Perhaps it might have cleared him, Professor, did you think of that? If that gun ever had the killer's prints on it, your actions effectively removed them.'

Haygill looked stunned. 'No . . . I didn't think . . .'

'And then, of course there's the possibility that Abu didn't act alone. Did you consider that?'

He hesitated, then nodded. 'I considered it. But nothing anyone said after Abu was arrested gave me any indication that they had helped or encouraged him, nothing at all. I mean, who do you suspect?'

Brock stared at him balefully. 'The obvious candidate is yourself, Professor Haygill. You're the one who stood to benefit from Springer being silenced. You're the one who attempted to dispose of the weapon, which, as you said yourself just now, is exactly what the killer would have done. And you're the one who lied about it until you had no choice but to tell us the truth. Or a version of it, anyway.' Brock looked at his watch. 'I have to tell you that we have obtained warrants to search your home, your car and your offices. Is there anything else you want to tell me before I conclude this interview?'

Haygill, looking defeated, shook his head. Then Brock added, 'There is one other thing. I asked you before for your documenta-tion on the BRCA4 protocol, and you refused. Now I must insist.'

'There is a copy in the drawer of my desk in my office at the university. It's locked, but my secretary has a key. I would ask,' Haygill shrugged hopelessly, 'can it please be treated as a confidential document. As I told you, it is commercially sensitive. I would hate to think of it floating around your offices, being photocopied . . .'

'I propose to give it to an expert, to give us an independent professional assessment.'

'Who did you have in mind?'

'Dr R.T. Grice, Home Office.'

'I know him.' Haygill considered this, then reluctantly nodded. 'Very well.'

After they had gone, Brock turned to Bren. 'Well?'

'It's him,' Bren said flatly. 'I reckon he picked Abu as the most pliable and dependable of the bunch. Maybe the most disposable, too.'

'Maybe.' Brock rubbed his knee, sounding unhappy. 'But he could make that story stick.'

'Finding the gun on his bookshelf? Come on, chief, that was the most improbable thing I've ever heard. Why would Abu leave the gun there? How did he even get into Haygill's office?'

'Mm. All the same, we need another angle, Bren. The money, we've got to tie that firmly to him.'

'Yeah. No luck so far, but now we've got access to his records we may come up with something. Interesting to think, isn't it boss,' Bren added innocently as they made for the door, 'if Leon hadn't pulled that stunt the other night, we wouldn't know anything of this.' He hurried out before Brock could reply.

20

They found a parking space in the housing estate behind Shadwell Road and made their way through the rear lanes towards the cries of hawkers, the smell of roasting meat and the sound of amplified music throbbing on the crisp morning air. Market stalls had been erected down the centre of Shadwell Road, and the street was packed with visitors savouring the mixture of the exotic and the banal. A stall selling hijab headscarves stood next to one specialising in cowboy hats; the aromas of cumin and fennel from a spice stall competed with those of a hot dog barrow, saffron and purple silks with heavy metal T-shirts, sitar and koto with electric guitar.

Distracted by an illustrated wallchart of selected positions from the Kama Sutra, Kathy was saved from being run down by a burly child on a scooter by a tug on her arm from Leon Desai. She stumbled against him and laughed and they moved on, flushed by a sense of intimacy in the mass of the crowd.

'Did you ever see Chandler's Yard?' she asked, and when he shook his head she said, 'I'll buy you a cup of coffee at the Horria Café.'

'Just so long as we don't bump into Dr Darr and his mates,' he muttered, sounding genuinely worried, and she laughed again, feeling unexpectedly light and happy this morning, with the sun overhead at last, the buzz of the crowd, and him at her side. She caught a glimpse of Sanjeev Manzoor in the distance, standing in the doorway of his shop, surveying the passing throng with a scowl of disapproval on his face, and she almost felt inclined to say hello to him and offer to shake hands, but wisely thought better of it and they turned instead out of the crowd, past the door to The Three Crowns and into the sudden quiet of the lane.

The activity in the street hadn't reached the Horria. There was one family of very pale-skinned visitors, looking slightly bemused by the menu at a table decorated with two small crossed and faded flags of the People's Democratic Republic of Yemen and the Yemeni Arab Republic, and there were two of the old men playing cards on a table at the back, but that was all and Kathy wondered how Qasim Ali made a living from the place. He was on his knees in front of the jukebox, fiddling with the switches. He gave a snort of disgust and struggled to his feet, giving the machine a hefty thump. Immediately a high-pitched female voice broke into an Arabic pop-song at full volume, to the consternation of the English family.

Qasim welcomed Kathy as a great friend, and on her behalf accepted Leon. He seated them at a table at the front where they were only half deafened by the music and could look out onto the cobbled square, to a small printing works opposite on the right, and a tiny second-hand furniture store on the left.

'Abu lived here?' Leon murmured. 'No wonder he was driven to murder.'

'Oh, it's not so bad,' Kathy grinned. 'Qasim turns the music down when people are praying in the mosque upstairs. We could have a look later if you like. Brock told me that your family were Muslim once. You never told me.'

'It didn't seem important.' He looked at her. 'We had other things on our minds.'

She met his eyes, dark and intent, and she felt a familiar response stirring in her. No, she thought, I'm not falling for that look again. Leon's adventure had brought them together again, but as friends, they had tacitly agreed. She was determined this time to move at her own pace, to try to keep control of the direction of her life. She looked out of the window and said, 'Perhaps that's why Brock agreed with you meeting Darr the first time.'

Leon winced. 'Don't talk about that.'

'Oh, but it was a success. From that everything fell into place.'

'You mean Haygill's world fell to pieces. And it was all a mistake. Mrs Haygill thinks her husband was spying on him when he wasn't. I don't feel very proud about that.'

'She wouldn't have told us about the gun otherwise. And anyway, their marriage was obviously on its last legs.'

'We don't know that. We don't even know he's guilty. How's the money trail going?'

'Nothing yet. They haven't found any obvious withdrawals from Haygill's accounts to correspond to the thirty thousand, and they've had no luck so far tracing the notes themselves back to his bank.'

'Hm.' Leon was silent for a moment, then said abruptly, 'How's Wayne?'

'Wayne O'Brien? Didn't you know? He doesn't exist any more. They've changed his name, address and phone number, and he's become somebody else. He's working on another job.' Brock had told her two days before, and at first she hadn't believed it, thinking it was some kind of practical joke. But it was true. This happened in Special Branch, Brock had said, they come and they go. All the same, she would have liked to have said goodbye. She had felt an unexpected sadness, as if she'd just learned that Wayne had died rather than merely moved on.

'Really?' Leon's shoulders straightened a little, and Kathy thought it looked almost as if a weight had been removed. 'Hell, what a life.'

'I liked him, Leon.'

'Yes, I know.'

'He was what I needed at that moment. Nothing too serious.'

'And I was too serious?'

'Yes.'

'Sorry.' He looked disconsolate.

'Well, now, ladies and gents,' Qasim boomed and put their coffees down in front of them. 'Mind if I join you?' He offered them his cigarettes and when they refused, lit up himself. 'How's the detecting going? I see you caught another one.' He puffed and reached across to a newspaper lying on the next table and showed them the report – 'BOFFIN QUIZZED IN MURDER HUNT'.

'We're not sure yet, Qasim,' Kathy said.

'He was Abu's boss, right? Makes sense to me. Abu'd never 'ave done it on his own. Fact I still can't hardly believe he did it at all. This guy must be a Svengali, right? Made 'im do it?'

Kathy remembered Springer using that word too; Svengali the

241

sinister manipulator, the evil hypnotist. Was Haygill really such a character?

'The thing that blows me away is that those two actually met, here in this very place, before any of this happened.'

'Which two?'

'Abu and this bloke.'

'Haygill, his boss? He came here?'

'No, no, not him. Him.' Qasim pointed a fat finger further down the page at a picture of the victim, Springer.

'Abu met Springer here?' Kathy stared at Qasim in disbelief. 'Surely not.'

'Yeah, it's true. Briony brought that old geezer here one day. He was interested in the history of our family. We had quite a chat. Then Briony said she'd take him upstairs to see the mosque, and on their way up they met Abu coming down. Right there . . .' he pointed to the stairs at the back of the café, ' . . . halfway up, they met, and Briony introduced them and they shook hands. Spooky, init, yeah?'

'You never saw them meet again?'

'No. He didn't come here again.'

They had met twice, Kathy thought, both times on stairs, one going up, one down. The first time they had shaken hands, the second time one had shot the other dead. Very spooky.

'How is Nargis coping now?'

'Seems OK, on the surface at any rate. She's a well calm girl, yeah? She's moved back upstairs, and George and Fran are keeping an eye on her. Every day she gets a little bit bigger.'

'Her father hasn't tried to make trouble?'

'Nah. He wouldn't dare. And they're getting counselling now, the pair of them, from the imam and the social worker. It seems old Manzoor is very taken with the idea of a grandchild. Anyway, he'd be too scared you'd come after him again wiv your swizzle stick if he tried anything. You got it on you?'

Kathy patted her pocket. 'Of course, Qasim. I always carry it when I come to visit you.'

His appreciative roar turned into a coughing fit, and he had to take a deep draw on his cigarette to recover himself. 'Tell me though,' he said through the smoke, his voice become squeaky, 'that money Abu left her. Is she going to get it back?'

'Depends. We'd be a lot happier about a lot of things if we knew where it came from.'

Qasim studied his fingernails. 'She won't tell you?'

'She says she doesn't know. Do you?'

'Abu wouldn't have told me. He'd have known I'd start charging them rent.' He gave a wheezing chuckle, his jowls and belly wobbling. Then he added, 'The only one he might have told, apart from Nargis, would be Fran. They got on well, Abu and Fran, and Fran is good with money. She used to be a merchant banker, did you know that? Well, not exactly – she worked for one, in the City, while she was a student, before she converted to Islam. She's got her head screwed on, and if I was in Abu's shoes, and had come into a bit of cash, I might ask Fran where to invest it. Understand that I'm only telling you this because I want Nargis to keep the money. If it's legit, Fran may be able to set your minds at rest. Nargis is on her own now. She and the baby are really going to need that cash.'

Kathy nodded, thinking that of course that only strengthened Abu's motive in taking the money to kill Springer. 'Do you think Fran would tell us?'

'I could have a word in her ear, if you like. She's getting a few things down the supermarket right now, but she should be back soon. Why don't you finish your coffees, do a bit more shopping in the street market, and come back in an hour, eh? You might like to have lunch here. Lamb kebabs is our special today, specially for market day.'

'Fine. Do we need to book?'

Qasim Ali thought that was very funny.

The sky was darker when they left the café, and as they strolled through the market again big drops of rain began to fall. They sheltered under the awning of a second-hand bookstall and studied the titles. They had been talking about Fran, and her abandonment of her previous life to take up the Muslim way, and Leon suddenly said, 'Ah!' and reached for one of the books. He checked it, then handed it to Kathy. 'Here's something appropriate. Used to be one of my favourites.'

Kathy read the print on the front, *Lawrence of Arabia, Seven Pillars of Wisdom*. She turned the pages, maps of the Middle East to begin with, then an introductory poem, the first verse of which she read out loud.

> I loved you, so I drew these tides of men into my hands
> and wrote my will across the sky in stars
> To earn you Freedom, the seven-pillared worthy house,
> that your eyes might be shining for me
> When we came.

'That's what Max Springer seemed to want to do,' she pondered. 'To earn us freedom, even at the expense of truth.'

'That's absurd.' Leon sounded shocked. 'You can't have one without the other, surely.'

'Yes, that's what Brock said.'

She turned the pages over and noticed a passage describing the Arabs.

'*"They were a people of spasms, of upheavals, of ideas . . . Their largest manufacture was of creeds . . ."*'

'I think that's what Springer meant by truth – the absolute truth of creeds, whether religious or scientific.'

'But they're completely different, scientific truth and religious truth.'

'All the same, Springer saw them both as opposed to freedom. At least, according to Briony Kidd.'

Her eyes skipped down to another phrase, '"Dry souls ready to be set on fire." Not exactly how I'd describe Qasim Ali, but you never know, I suppose. Let's go back and see what he's got for us.'

They ran back through the drizzle and found Fran Said, head covered by a black scarf, waiting for them at the table where they had previously been, drinking a cup of tea. Kathy introduced Leon and they sat down. The pale family at the central table was still there, finishing off large helpings of burgers and chips, but no new customers had been lured in by the amplified voice of Umm Kalthoum.

'I was telling Leon about your background, Fran. I think it's really interesting.'

Fran shrugged. 'Not really. I'm not sure I want an interesting life, just one that I can feel certain about.'

'Well, I think it's interesting how you opted for an arranged marriage, for instance.'

'It worked for me.'

'But not for Nargis.'

'It wasn't the fault of the system,' Fran said defensively. 'Her life here and the ways of the old country were just too far apart.'

'Yet the marriage in Kashmir was valid? So what could Nargis do, if, say, she wanted to marry someone else, like Abu?'

'That would depend on her husband. Under Islamic law, the wife can't initiate a divorce. If she did that through a British civil court, and her husband in Kashmir didn't want the divorce and didn't pronounce the talaaq, that's the divorce formula, then in the eyes of Islamic law they would still be married. Nargis hoped . . . hopes that her husband will divorce her so that he can marry again, only . . . she doesn't want it to be to her sister Yasmin.' Fran's voice had dropped to a whisper.

'No, and she's only fourteen, isn't she? So Nargis is still married, and that means that she and Abu were living in adultery . . .' Kathy saw the look of alarm flare in Fran's eyes and added quickly, lowering her voice, 'I'm sorry, Fran. I just need to understand the situation that Nargis and Abu were in. Islamic law is very strong on adultery, isn't it?'

'"Surely, it is a foul thing and an evil way." That's what the Qur'an says.'

'So they were faced with the alternative of separating and Nargis remaining faithful to a husband she detested, or living together as outcasts from their faith, not to mention under threat of dire retribution from her father and his brothers. That's about it, is it?'

'Yes.'

'It must have been a terrible dilemma. They must have been tempted just to disappear, and start again somewhere else. But where could they go where they could rejoin the Muslim community without being found out? What sort of resources would they need to do that? And then Abu comes home one day with thirty thousand pounds.'

Fran glared at her. 'You think it was blood money, don't you? You think someone paid him that money to commit a murder.'

'What else can we think, Fran? When we spoke to Nargis a week ago she said he'd brought it home about two weeks before. Max Springer was shot exactly two weeks before.'

'No! The only reason I agreed to talk to you is to tell you that you're wrong. That money belongs to Nargis and her baby. You can't take it from her.'

'Convince me. What do you know to make you so sure?'

'Suppose . . . suppose the money was a genuine gift, but it'd come from abroad, and the person who gave it didn't want it known about, maybe for tax reasons or something, in their own country.'

'Which country?'

'Lebanon.'

'Go on.'

'When Nargis came back from Kashmir and took shelter here, her friendship with Abu began again. They loved each other, and after a little while they became lovers – they couldn't help themselves. But Nargis was now married to someone else, and carrying that other man's baby. They were frightened to go to the imam for advice, because they were afraid he would denounce them. They began to dream of going abroad, to the Lebanon perhaps, where Abu's family live, or the United States where he has a cousin. But meanwhile Nargis' father had taken out the warrant against her, and they were afraid that they would be arrested if they tried to leave the country under her own passport, or if they tried to marry here and leave under his name. And all the time the baby was growing.

'A couple of weeks ago – and yes, it was the time of the murder of Professor Springer, but that was a coincidence – Abu came to me for advice. He had been able to obtain a sum of money from his father to assist them. Thirty thousand pounds, in sterling notes. With some of it he was hoping to buy a false passport for Nargis. But he was worried at having so much cash, and didn't know what to do with it to avoid suspicion. He wanted the money to be in Nargis' name, and he asked my advice. Should he open a bank account for her, or buy travellers' cheques, or jewellery, or a bank draft? I suggested a range of things, but a few days later he was dead.'

Fran's sincerity was plain, as was her sympathy for the tragic circumstances of her friends, yet she didn't seem to realise how incriminating for Abu her story was. His desperation to save Nargis, and his insistence that the money should be held in her name only strengthened the case against him.

'He said the money came from his father? Those were his words?'

Fran frowned. 'Not exactly. Abu was adopted, you see. He said something like, the money has been given to me by the man who has been a father to me. Something like that.'

'Is Khadra his adopted name, do you know? Will that be the name of his adopted father in Beirut?'

'I think so.'

'Well, we can try to check.'

Fran heard the doubt in Kathy's voice and said dully, 'You don't believe me, do you?'

'I believe you've told me what you believe to be the truth, Fran, but it won't help Nargis unless we can find some documentary evidence of where the money came from. Have you any idea how it came into the country? There must be bank records somewhere.'

Fran shook her head glumly. 'No, that's what I meant earlier, about Abu's father not wanting the money traced. Abu told us once that his adopted dad is a bit of a crook, a dealer in the black market. When I asked him why he'd been given the money in cash, he said he thought that was so it couldn't be traced. I assume his dad got someone to bring it into the country by hand.'

'So the father isn't going to be keen to talk to us about it, even if we do track him down.'

'I suppose not.' She sighed. 'I haven't helped, have I?'

'I don't know, Fran. The more we can piece together the better. Maybe you'll think of something else. What about your husband? Would Abu have talked things over with George?'

'Don't think so. Abu was secretive, and only told me about the money because he needed advice. George is hopeless with money.'

Later, walking back to the car, Leon glanced at Kathy, deep in thought.

'She's bright. Too bad she's given up the merchant banking. But I suppose that must be a tricky occupation for a Muslim.'

'How do you mean?'

'Well, they don't believe in interest. If they earn any, on bank accounts for instance, they're supposed to give it away to charity, as zakah.'

'What's zakah?'

'Alms. It's one of a Muslim's obligations. You can give zakah to

247

the poor, or the needy, or . . . there's a third category, with a funny name. I forget. What were you thinking so hard about?'

'The gun. The money was intact, thirty thousand exactly. So he didn't use it to buy the gun.'

'Maybe dad in Beirut sent it over with the cash.'

'Then why use it to kill Springer? If he was going to shoot anybody it'd be more likely to have been old man Manzoor.'

'Guns! That was the third category.'

'You can give alms to buy guns?'

'Sort of. Feesabeelillah, it's called. Money spent supporting the Muslim cause. Money for Jihad.'

The following day, Sunday, Kathy drove down to Battle to make her peace with Suzanne. They sat in the conservatory and drank coffee, just as she had done three weeks before, reading Max Springer's obituary.

'You're looking so much better, Kathy,' Suzanne said. 'Are you sleeping?'

'Yes, thanks.' Kathy smiled at hearing the brisk tone again that Suzanne adopted when discussing the health of one of them, her brood of grandchildren, Kathy, Brock − potential problem children all. 'I'm just sorry that I haven't been in touch more.'

'Oh, we're all busy. You were ready to go back, weren't you? I thought it was too soon, but you must have felt it was right.'

'I didn't think so at first, but, you know, you get caught up . . .'

'Mm. And David, he's very caught up at present too, I gather.'

'Yes. We've reached a point . . . it's hard to describe, where we seem to have most of the bits we need to wrap the thing up, but somehow it refuses to gel.'

'Sounds like my attempts to make plum jelly. And of course, this is David's moment, isn't it?'

'How do you mean?'

'The stage in the investigation where the great detective discovers the truth that's eluded everybody else.' She smiled mischievously. 'I'm not being sarcastic, but it is something like that, isn't it? The enlightenment. It's what David lives for, that moment . . . if you don't get there first.'

'Me?'

'Yes, you. He described you once as quick on your feet. I think that's what he meant. You've beaten him to it once or twice, haven't you?'

Kathy suddenly felt herself under examination, Suzanne looking at her over the rim of her coffee cup.

'You mean he resents it?'

'No, no. I'm sure he doesn't. I just think he's been surprised. That's good. You keep him on his toes. I know he was very worried that you might want to quit.'

All the same, Kathy had a vague sense that Suzanne was giving her a warning.

'I feel bad about letting Tina down after she went to all that trouble for me. Is she annoyed?'

'I honestly don't think she ever really saw you escorting old ladies round the pyramids, but give her a call. And how's your lovely Art Malik friend?'

'Leon?' Kathy laughed. 'He doesn't look like Art Malik, does he?'

'Brock says he does, a younger version. I'm dying to meet him. Did he contribute to your recovery?'

'He was part of the problem. You know we were, well, quite close, before Christmas.'

'I got that impression, yes. I never learned what went wrong.'

'A misunderstanding . . . no, a mistake, on my part. I missed an appointment. Only it was more complicated than that. There was a woman I was jealous about . . .'

'Freud said we don't really make mistakes like that. Maybe you missed the appointment on purpose, without realising it. Was he cross?'

'Yes. Everything fell apart after that. Probably just as well. Having a relationship with someone at work only complicates things.'

'Really? Only David happened to mention a Special Branch officer – oh, he didn't say anything, but it was the *way* he didn't say anything that made my ears prick up. Was I wrong?'

'Yes,' Kathy said firmly. 'That was a figment of Brock's imagination, I'm afraid.'

'Well . . .' Suzanne smiled quietly to herself. 'Figments can be fun sometimes.'

21

Despite newspaper reports that he was helping police with their inquiries, Haygill had been released on the evening of the Thursday on which he had first been interviewed following the discovery of the gun, pending further investigations. The searches of his premises had yielded plenty of documentary material, including bank statements and correspondence with backers in the Middle East, but nothing immediately incriminating. On the following Monday he was reinterviewed, this time by Bren and Kathy, with Brock observing from the adjoining room. Kathy's role was to look sceptical but say little, Bren's to be actively hostile and disbelieving. Brock was pleased to see that Haygill looked as if the weekend had not raised his spirits. He had dark circles under his eyes, and his speech had lost its former confidence and had become hesitant. Throughout the interview he looked frequently to his solicitor for guidance and, perhaps, reassurance.

'Tell us how you recruited Abu Khadra?' Bren asked, feeling more confident that Haygill's decline might throw up some mistake or inconsistency.

'It would have been about eighteen months ago, I think . . . umm, I can check the exact date . . .' Bren waved a hand dismissively and Haygill continued. 'I was on a visit to the University of Qatar. We'd recently lost our computer programmer, and the university provider wasn't giving us the sort of service we needed, so I was on the lookout for someone.'

'An Arab?'

'Well, not necessarily, but we're happy to recruit suitably qualified people from the region. Our sponsors like it, and we see it as part of our educational role. I think I explained to your Chief Inspector . . .'

'Yes, yes. Go on.'

'Well, Abu approached me. He'd heard of our project, and was very interested. He was just finishing a master's degree at Qatar, as it happened, and was looking for opportunities. He was highly recommended by his supervisor, and after meeting him a couple of times during my visit I offered him a job.'

'Just like that? No advertisements, interviews?'

'His position is funded by our external research income, so I have discretion.'

'So he owed his advancement entirely to you and to no one else.'

'If you like . . .'

'And this was the reason why he regarded you as a sort of father figure, is it? Or was there more to it?'

'Your Chief Inspector used that phrase, but really, that's putting it far too strongly. He was respectful, but no more than others.'

'Oh, come on, Professor! He hero-worshipped you! That's certainly the impression we've been getting.'

'Well, I don't—'

'You know his personal history, do you? He lost both his parents at an early age, and was taken in by a family in which, from all accounts, the father was a petty crook.'

'I didn't know that.'

'So when a man like you came along and changed his life, offering him a chance to work under you in Europe on a glamorous leading-edge research project, he obviously felt more beholden than an employee would normally do to his boss, don't you think?'

'I never was aware of any special sense of indebtedness,' Haygill said with a kind of tired persistence, sounding as if his stamina was giving out. 'He planned to do a Ph.D. at UCLE part-time while he was working for us, but . . . I don't think he ever enrolled. Probably we kept him too busy. He was very good at his work. We soon began to realise what an asset he was.'

'And naturally you praised him . . .'

'Yes.'

'And rewarded him. I see from his employment records that his salary was increased three times during the past fifteen months.'

'Yes. We didn't want to lose him, and salaries for such people have been going through the roof recently. Darr recommended, I agreed . . .'

This went on for some hours, Bren aggressively probing, Haygill fending him off with declining but stubborn energy. When they finally let him go he had given them nothing that changed anything.

On the following day Brock received two early phone calls. The first came from Haygill's solicitor, to say that his client was satisfied that he had done all that he reasonably could to assist the police, and that he had nothing more to say. If the police felt that they had grounds to charge him, they should go ahead and do so.

The second was from Mrs Haygill, requesting another meeting. When she arrived, she was wearing a new lime-green suit, her hair curled in a different style, and Brock guessed that the salons and boutiques of Cheadle Hulme had had a good weekend, for the purposes of morale. She sat very straight in her chair, holding an expensive new handbag in front of her like a shield.

Brock said, 'I thought you were up in Manchester, Mrs Haygill.'

'I decided to come back. I thought things over, and I decided that my place is by my husband's side. You should understand that we met yesterday afternoon, and we are reconciled.'

'Reconciled, I see.'

'And therefore I will refuse to give evidence against my husband, if he is charged with anything. My solicitor says you can't make me.'

'Well, that is true. But you did give us a voluntary statement before, which was properly witnessed and recorded. And we found the gun you spoke of, exactly where you told us we would.'

She flushed, pursed her lips. 'For which my husband has a perfectly reasonable explanation, which he has now related to me. He was trying to protect his staff out of loyalty. It was a mistake, but an understandable one.'

'To attempt to conceal a murder weapon, Mrs Haygill?' He looked at her curiously. 'Tell me, what brought about this change of heart?'

'I . . . I was too hasty. I reacted in anger to what I was told, when in fact it was incorrect. There was a misunderstanding.'

'About what?'

'It's really none of your business,' she snapped, then hesitated and seemed to decide that she shouldn't appear uncooperative. 'I mentioned the last time that I was led to believe that my husband had hired a private detective to spy on me. Well, it appears that was incorrect. The man who was mistaken for the detective heard what had happened and got in touch with me. He said it was all a misunderstanding and my informant had got it all wrong.'

'That was very decent of him. Did he say what his occupation really was?'

'Not in so many words, but I guessed, from something he said, that he was a reporter, sniffing around for a story about my husband and Max Springer. When he was confronted, he let it be understood that he was a private detective.'

'Why would he do that?'

'Tah . . . My informant accused him of being that, and he thought it simplest to agree.'

'And you're now convinced that your husband had no part in the murder of Max Springer?'

'I am.'

'Despite Springer coming to see you to warn you that he intended to ruin him?'

'I . . . I may have been mistaken about that.'

'About him coming to see you?'

'No, I mean, about him saying that he planned to ruin Richard. It may not have been as strong as that. Maybe . . . maybe it was more like, he wanted to have Richard and his research centre kicked out of the university.'

'Maybe . . .?' Brock looked at her with disbelief, and she lowered her eyes, embarrassed, but pressed on with the story she'd rehearsed, or been coached in.

'Though, of course, he'd have had no chance of doing that. So it was all nonsense really.'

Brock sat back in his chair and gave a deep sigh. 'And you've now told your husband about Springer's visit to you that day?'

'Yes. And I realise that I made too much of it when I talked to you. I'm sorry, but I was feeling quite . . . emotional, that day. Because of the story of the private detective, you see.'

After she left Brock sat alone in the room for a while, frowning, doodling a diagram of a ziggurat. He could imagine the regrouping that would have gone on in Haygill's camp after Bren had finished grilling him the previous afternoon, and with the return of his wife. He imagined the schooling of Mrs Haygill, the plans for damage limitation, and the dawning realisation that there might yet be a way out of what must have seemed an impossible situation. And Leon had played his part in Haygill's recovery, just as he had in his collapse. He reached for the phone and dialled Leon's number.

'I've just had a visit from Professor Haygill's wife, Leon,' he said, keeping his voice level. 'I would have appreciated hearing from you before you spoke to her.'

'I'm sorry, Brock.' Leon sounded suitably penitent. 'I just felt I had to do it on my own, without getting you involved, in case this ever comes out. After I heard about Mrs Haygill leaving her husband, I felt I had to do something to put things right with her. Apart from anything else, suppose I'd been called in court and Darr had recognised me?'

Brock had also thought of that. The whole thing had been misconceived from the beginning.

'I just thought this was the best way to get out of it.' Leon added, sounding very unhappy. 'Will it affect your case, her coming to see you?'

Somewhat mollified, Brock said, 'We'll have to wait and see. Don't worry about it. But Leon, the next time you decide to go undercover, speak to me first, will you?'

Brock's morning was made complete by a call from Reggie Grice to say that he had now read the document provided by Haygill, describing the BRCA4 protocol, and he thought it was brilliant.

'That wasn't the word I was hoping for, Reggie.'

'No, I know. I'm sorry.'

Everyone, it seemed, wanted to apologise this morning. 'What do you mean exactly?'

'It seems I may have misled you over this project. The whispers I'd heard aren't borne out by the document at all. There's nothing here that my committees would be likely to object to if the experiments were to be carried out in this country.'

'Nothing ethically dubious?'

'Not that I could see.'

'Could the document you've got have been sanitised, Reggie? It's easy enough to excise a few paragraphs or chapters on the word processor.'

'I took your warning to look out for that, but I honestly couldn't find any gaps in the process that's described here. It stands complete, and I have to say, it's bloody impressive. If they can get it to work the way it's set out here, it's potentially Nobel laureate standard. As good as that.'

'Oh, dear.' It seemed that Haygill's prospects were recovering as rapidly as they had earlier collapsed.

'Sorry.'

'Reggie, if Springer had got hold of a copy of that document, could he have misinterpreted it, do you think?'

'Did he have any scientific training? Biochemistry?'

'I don't think so.'

'Then I don't think he could have understood a word of it. It's a highly technical report, not written for the layman, or even for publication in a scientific journal. It's very specific to the discipline. More likely Springer got wind of the same misleading rumours that I'd heard, thought "no smoke without fire" and tried to fan the flames.'

Brock called a team conference later that day and they discussed their options. Bren was all for persisting with Haygill or failing that Darr, but, in the absence of any evidence of the source of Abu's money, it became clear that he was in a minority. Brock reported to Superintendent Russell that evening with his recommendation that Abu Khadra had acted alone, out of misguided loyalty, and without the knowledge of Richard Haygill. He also recommended that no charges be brought against Haygill for attempting to hide the murder weapon, in view of the fact that his wife had disclosed its whereabouts.

Russell read the single sheet of recommendations, then eyed Brock shrewdly. 'You're not satisfied, are you?'

'Is it that obvious?'

Russell smiled. 'What's bothering you?'

'Well, the money . . . But more than that . . . intangibles. The way Springer was murdered, so public, so theatrical. It doesn't seem to fit Khadra's purpose, or his character. Why not do it in some dark lane, miles away from the university, where there'd be nothing to immediately connect it with university politics?'

'But isn't that the way of the fanatic, Brock, to make a big public statement? To teach people a lesson? And Khadra was a fanatic, wasn't he? That passage in the Qur'an he left for you as good as said it.'

Brock shrugged.

'A negative result always seems less satisfactory, Brock, I know, but it is a result, nevertheless. I'm satisfied you couldn't come to any other conclusion. I'm sure the Crown Prosecution Service wouldn't support us pressing any further charges on the basis of what we've come up with.'

The following morning they gave a press conference at which they stated that the police had completed their investigations into the murder of Max Springer, and no further charges were being considered. This was widely reported in the news media that evening and on the following, Thursday, morning, when the *Herald* also carried an interview with Professor Roderick Young expressing his own and the university's complete confidence in Professor Richard Haygill and the hope that the tragic events of the previous weeks could now be laid to rest.

On Friday morning, while the team was dismantling the room they had been using for the Springer inquiry, Dot brought in a letter for Brock. It had been marked 'Personal' and addressed to him at New Scotland Yard. Inside he found a green printed pamphlet with an illustration of a clenched fist and a message in Arabic and English.

'Ruined are the liars who flounder about in ignorance. They ask: When will the Day of Judgement be? It will be on the day when they are afflicted with the Fire, and are told: Suffer your torment.' Sura 51 : 9

It caused a stir of concern, which Brock promptly dismissed. It was probably the tearaway Ahmed Sharif, not letting the opportunity for a bit of tub-thumping pass, he said. And in a way it seemed a rather appropriate footnote to the whole sorry business, which had begun with just such a letter to Max Springer.

They had a bit of a laugh about it in the office. Bren's theory was that it had been sent by the Inland Revenue. But Kathy didn't laugh.

She remembered Leon's warning about Darr and the Iraqis, and when she could get Brock on his own she said as much to him. He shrugged, an impassive, untroubled look on his face, and told her not to worry.

22

Brock woke suddenly, starting from the armchair in which he'd nodded off. A sound had woken him. He heard the plaintive horn of a train passing through the fog-bound cutting beyond his window, the bang of a fog-warning cap on the line. The warmth of the gas fire, the whisky at his elbow, the heavy book he'd been trying to read, the exhaustion of Friday night, had all sent him into a torpor. But he woke now clear-headed and alert, his mind filling with a conviction of remarkable clarity. His leg was aching and he stretched it slowly as if afraid of shattering the thought. In some odd way it seemed almost as if the pain in his injured knee and the idea in his head were connected, both equally sharp.

He gave a little shiver of excitement. Sometimes, rarely but sometimes, it happened this way. You have dug up all the information you're likely to get; you have struggled without success for a convincing solution; exhaustion sets in; you put it aside, have a bath, fall asleep, then, bang, it comes. The answer – complete, clear, inevitable, obvious.

He had fallen asleep thinking of Haygill and his wife, reconciled, tucked up now in bed together, but with what lingering doubts? And he knew that his own doubts about Haygill's guilt had been there from the start, and for the same reasons that he had expressed to Russell, that the extravagance of the assassination on the university steps would have been as out of character for the cautious Haygill as for the gentle Abu. But someone had choreographed the event, someone with an eye for theatre, who wanted to make a public statement. He thought of Darr again, the resentful lieutenant; might he have wanted to discredit Haygill in order to take over his position? Or the two Iraqis, jealous of Abu's standing with their boss. But what hold did any of them have over Abu to make him do such a desperate thing?

Brock had been trying to read Springer's autobiography, *A Man in Dark Times*, and had been finding it heavy going. The book was saturated with a mood of pessimism and despair, with mankind and its injustices, with fate and the death of his wife, and most of all, Brock suspected, with the author himself and his failure to quite fulfil the golden promise which his famous teachers had seen in him. On the whole, Brock felt, he could do without a bombastic mid-life-crisis confession masquerading as a humanist manifesto, especially at this stage of the week.

There was one chapter however which he had found gripping. It described a period when Springer had been caught up in events so powerful that his own ego had little chance to take over the story. In September of 1982 he had accompanied his wife Charlotte to Beirut, where she had been invited to perform in a series of concerts in aid of refugees. The timing could hardly have been worse, for on the morning after their arrival Israeli shells began to rain down on the city. Nevertheless Charlotte insisted on fulfilling her engagements, and they remained in Beirut under extremely difficult conditions. Their hotel was frequently hit by shell and sniper fire, and travelling to the concert venues, many of them changed at the last minute, was a nightmare.

Other Europeans were trapped in the hotel, and a sense of solidarity grew among them. Springer became particularly friendly with a group of French medical staff from Médecins Sans Frontières, and on the morning of Saturday, 18 September he came across them in the lobby of the hotel, hurriedly preparing to leave. They had been told of a major emergency in another part of the city, they explained, and their help was needed. On the spur of the moment he offered to join them. Afterwards he reflected that he had given it no thought at all, almost as if the decision was made for him.

They jumped into a couple of cars and sped off through the deserted streets and arrived eventually at the gates of the Shatila camp for Palestinian refugees. Nothing had prepared Springer for the horrors which he witnessed in the camp following the savage massacre which had begun on the evening of the sixteenth and continued through the seventeenth. After some hours he staggered out carrying a small boy survivor, whom he had found huddled in his ruined home with the bodies of his mother and sisters. Springer took the boy back to the hotel, uncertain what to do. The boy hadn't spoken a word since he had been found, and Springer had no idea of his name or whether he had any other family alive. For a time he had entertained the idea of adopting him and taking him back to England, but Charlotte had dissuaded him. She said that he was acting from a sense of guilt rather than love, and that the boy would be better remaining among his own people. Eventually they handed him over to a charity, and left the city. They never saw the boy again.

It was a dramatic story, one of the few in the book in which Springer wrote movingly of another single human being, rather than of humanity in the mass. And the description of the awful experience at Shatila was vivid, much more so than most of the writing. Brock turned the pages and found the passage.

I entered the camp on the Saturday morning with the French medical team. The scene was overwhelming, devastating. Survivors were still being discovered beneath the ruins of demolished shelters, and all of the effort was going into finding them. That and putting out the fires whose oily smoke hung heavy in the air, blotting out the sun.

Reading it again, he could almost smell the acrid smoke of the fires. He looked up suddenly and breathed in. He *could* smell the smoke of the fires. Sniffing the air in disbelief, he rose from his chair and went over to the door to the landing. As he pulled it open, a cloud of thick smoke billowed into the room. He backed away, coughing as the fumes caught his throat. Eyes streaming, he pulled out a handkerchief and covered his mouth and nose and pushed the door closed again, then scrambled for the phone.

An hour later Kathy ran up the lane and spotted him standing beneath the chestnut tree, watching the firemen rolling up their hoses.

260

'Kathy?' he said. 'How the hell did you get here?'

She was relieved to see that he seemed unhurt. 'The duty sergeant picked up your call and gave me a ring. Are you all right?'

'I'm fine. I was lucky that there wasn't much flammable in the bottom hallway inside the door. God knows what the smoke and water have done to my books upstairs on the landing though.'

'Was it a bomb?'

'No. I heard nothing. But you can smell the petrol, can't you? I reckon someone poured it through the letter box.'

'Your threatening letter . . . Didn't it say something about a fire?'

Brock nodded, taking it out of his pocket. 'It seems I should have taken it more seriously. "When will the Day of Judgement be? It will be on the day when they are afflicted with the Fire, and are told: Suffer your torment."'

'You think it's the Sharif kid and his mates?'

'I think it's his pamphlet . . . It was certainly a pretty amateurish attempt.' He frowned and rubbed the side of his beard. 'I hope it wasn't just a warning. Have you got your phone with you, Kathy? Mine's still inside.'

She handed it to him and he consulted his notebook which he had brought out with him and rang the number for the UCLE security office. When he'd identified himself he asked them if there had been any disturbance on campus that night. The duty guard said that there had been nothing.

'What about the CAB-Tech building?' Brock insisted. 'No attempted break-ins, nothing like that?'

'Absolutely not. The place is alarmed.'

'Good. Look, I think you should keep a special watch on it for the next few nights. Do me a favour and check it now will you?'

The guard agreed to do it and ring him back. Ten minutes later he reported that the doors were secure and the building in darkness. 'There's no way anyone could break in there without a swipe-card and the alarm code.'

'Do you have a record of who enters the building?'

'From their cards, yes. We get it here on the computer.'

'Check it now, will you? Who was the last one in?'

The line went silent while the man consulted his machine, then he came back, his voice doubtful. 'Funny. According to this someone went in ten minutes ago, and hasn't checked out.'

'What's the name?'

'A Mr Abu Khadra. You know him, sir?'

'Oh yes, I know him well. The trouble is, he's dead. Look, I want you to watch the door of the building, but don't try to enter it, OK? I'll be there as soon as I can, maybe twenty minutes.'

They ran towards Kathy's car, then saw a patrol car turning into the courtyard and chose it instead. They set off for the docklands, siren howling.

The security guard was waiting for them in the shadows at the entrance to the CAB-Tech ziggurat, which loomed massively overhead in the darkness. No one had attempted to leave the building, and there was no sign of activity inside. A fire engine had arrived, and an ARV, and Brock instructed Kathy to stay with them and keep people away from the perimeter of the building. She began to object as he turned to go in alone, but he raised his hand and said, 'If this is what I think it is, Kathy, one of us will be more than enough.'

The guard opened the front door and pointed to the lights of the alarm indicator just inside, which had been switched off. Otherwise there was no sign of an intruder. Brock sniffed the air in the lobby. It seemed temperate and fresh, the air-conditioning humming softly in the background, but his sense of smell had been badly impaired by the smoke he'd inhaled at his home.

'Can you smell anything? Petrol?'

'Don't think so.'

'Which floors are the laboratories on?' Brock whispered, and the man replied, levels three to five. He pointed the way to the stairs, then Brock told him to leave.

The darkness was even more intense inside the stair shaft, and Brock used the torch which one of the patrol officers had given him to find his way up to the third level. He switched off the light when he reached the door, gently eased it open, and, despite his scorched nostrils, was immediately struck by the pungent odour of petrol. He stood motionless in the doorway for some time, but could hear no sounds of movement, nor detect any stray light in the darkness, though there was a faint whistling noise that he couldn't decipher, that seemed to come from all around. The air-conditioning, presumably.

He went back into the stairway and moved up to the next level and repeated the manoeuvre. Again he heard the whistling sound, but nothing else, and was about to turn back when he caught a flash of light briefly reflected off a distant wall. He began to make his way carefully in that direction, weaving around laboratory benches and furniture by the faint green light of emergency exit signs. Gradually he began to make out the shuffling sounds of movement ahead, the raw, pungent smell of petrol, and perhaps another smell, more subtle and difficult to identify beneath it.

He came to a doorway to the next room and saw the figure with a small flashlight working its way along a line of benches. He felt along the wall at his shoulder for a light switch, found it, and turned it on. The hooded figure gave a little shriek and froze, pinned like a black incubus against the white dazzle of light from the bench lights. Then very slowly it turned, holding in one hand a metal can, and in the other a small, bright green object. A Bic lighter.

'It's me, DCI Brock, Briony. I'm on my own. I need to talk to you.'

Briony Kidd stared at him, then past him, checking, recovering from the shock of being discovered. She slowly laid the can on the bench beside her and lowered the cigarette lighter towards it, her thumb on the striker wheel.

'I will do it,' she said in a quiet, taut voice. Her face was very pale beneath the hood.

'Oh, yes, I don't doubt it. But I want you to do something else first.'

'What?'

He slowly reached across to one of the stools that stood nearby and pulled it over and sat on it, opening the front of his coat and taking a deep breath as if quite at ease, although the fumes almost made him gag. He realised now what the underlying smell was – gas. She had been working her way along the benches opening the gas taps. That's what the whistling sound had been. With a shudder he thought how catastrophic his action in switching on the lights might have been. One small spark ... Presumably the gas wasn't sufficiently concentrated. He forced his voice to sound calm, as if they had all the time in the world. 'I'd like a short tutorial with you, I the student, you the tutor.'

She curled her lip, the muscles tight across her face. 'Don't be stupid.'

'It won't take long. And I do feel stupid, it's true, for taking so long to understand what you and Max were doing. I take it this is your theory of action, is it? The highest form of human activity, taking events into your own hands?'

She said nothing.

'Only I'm just rather afraid that you can't repeat history, not really. That's what you're doing, isn't it? Trying to repeat what Max did. Someone said that history happens the first time as tragedy, the second time as farce.'

'Marx,' she whispered.

'Yes, I thought so. And I'm afraid this will be a farce, Briony. You'll burn yourself and cause a bit of damage, and it won't make the least bit of difference. Richard Haygill and his work won't be stopped.'

'That's what you were supposed to do,' she said bitterly. 'You arrested him, you had him in your hands, and you let him go.'

'I had no choice. The case against him was too weak. In the end, Max just hadn't done a good enough job. I think it was vanity that got in the way; he thought that the shock of his death would be enough to carry all before it. All the same, what he did was, in its own peculiar way, extraordinary, wasn't it?'

'Yes.'

'When did you first realise how he died?'

Briony shook her head with irritation and began to turn away.

'It's all right,' Brock said quickly. 'You have plenty of time. None of the people outside will interfere as long as I'm here.'

She hesitated, then shrugged and slumped onto a stool. 'All right.' She suddenly looked very tired, and he guessed she hadn't slept for some time. 'I didn't understand at first.'

'He hadn't confided in you?'

'No. He told me very little.' The faintest trace of bitterness. 'I was there, on the steps, the evening that he died.'

'Yes, I remember.'

'I was terribly shocked. I stayed for a while, then I left. I didn't want to go home. I needed to talk to someone, so I went to Chandler's Yard to see Fran and Nargis. Abu was there. He'd only just arrived, and it was obvious that something had happened to him. He was like a spring wound tight, pacing up and down, muttering to himself. The others were asking him what was wrong, but he wouldn't speak to them. Then I told them my news, about Max, and as I spoke I saw a terrible change come over Abu. He began trembling all over and staring at me with wide eyes. I asked him if he knew something about Max's death, but he just turned and ran out of the flat. Later Qasim said he'd found him praying downstairs in the mosque, and asked us if he was all right because he seemed to be acting so strange.'

'You knew Abu pretty well by that stage, did you, Briony?'

'Yes. When Nargis went to Kashmir to get married, Abu and I became closer friends. We. . . we talked a lot.'

Brock detected an edge in her voice as she said this, and said, 'He was a nice looking boy. Perhaps you hoped for more than friendship?'

'That would have been stupid, wouldn't it?' she snapped. 'He still loved Nargis, despite everything.' She said it too quickly, too angrily, and Brock recognised the jealousy behind the words.

'Well, anyway, you knew him well enough to see that he'd been profoundly affected by something that evening. Did you guess what it was?'

'Not at first. The idea of Abu being mixed up in Max's death would have been too awful. Even when I met you the next day and you asked me if Max had ever upset Muslims, I never connected it with Abu. When I thought about it afterwards I decided you must have had suspicions about the other Muslims working at CAB-Tech.'

'Did you decide to give us a nudge in that direction by telling the press that we were thinking along those lines?'

She flushed, 'Yes. I thought it would make it impossible for you not to follow that up. And I was sure it must be true. I thought Abu must have discovered something about what the others had done, and that was why he was behaving so strangely. I was in a state of shock over Max. Everyone was talking about him, the papers were full of stories, and I felt as if I'd lost, I don't know . . . a close relative or something. Then on Monday morning, when there was that speculation in the paper about an Islamic connection, they also reported that the police were saying that the killer had escaped on a motorbike, and suddenly I realised that it might have been Abu who killed Max. In fact, the more I thought about it, the more convinced I was that it must be true.

'I went to Chandler's Yard. I wanted to confront Abu and hear his denial with his own lips. But he wasn't there. When I went upstairs, no one was there. I went into Nargis' room and at first I thought I'd wait for them. My head was spinning. On the table was a packet of photographs and I looked through them. Most of them were of Nargis and Abu together. They looked so normal, so happy and untroubled by all the terrible things that had been happening around them. I felt I didn't understand them at all, and I began to feel this great anger. How could he have done such a thing? How could she protect him? Everything about their lives seemed to be a deception. They must both be fanatics, I thought, to do such a thing. And I thought that if only Nargis hadn't come back from Pakistan everything might have been different, and I might have saved Abu from ending up like this, a murderer. And suddenly I hated them both, Nargis as much as Abu, and I wanted to hurt them for what they'd done.'

She wiped the back of her free hand across her face, and Brock saw the glint of tears.

'So what did you do?' he urged softly.

She shook her head as if she wanted rid of something stuck inside. 'I took one of the photographs, and an envelope from the drawer, and I went out into Shadwell Road and posted it to Nargis' father. I betrayed them. I killed Abu.'

'Well, now, you couldn't have known that would be the result. Why didn't you come to us?'

'I had no evidence. I just wanted to hurt them . . .' Her tears were flowing freely. 'It was the most terrible, the most stupid thing I've ever done.'

'Until now, Briony. You can't put it right by doing this. When did you begin to suspect that it wasn't as simple as that?'

Briony sucked in a sobbing breath which turned into a choking cough. She recovered and gasped, 'On the day after Abu died, I went to Chandler's Yard again. I almost couldn't show my face, and yet I couldn't stay away. I had to hear for myself what had happened. I met Fran there, and she had been trying to console Nargis, who had told her something very strange. She had said that Abu had been very troubled, and had finally confessed to her that he'd been obliged to do something very terrible. There was a man he knew, to whom he owed a great debt. This man had once saved his life, and had given him an education, like a father. Now he wanted Abu to repay the debt with a single act. He wanted Abu to commit a murder.

'Suddenly I thought I understood. Haygill! Haygill had forced Abu to kill Max. I asked Fran if Nargis had named the man to whom Abu was indebted, and she said, yes, he was the man whose name had been in all the papers, Professor Springer. And I said, no, no, Springer was the name of the victim. What was the name of the other man? And she said, "There was no other man. Springer wanted Abu to kill *him*. It was the most terrible demand that anyone could make."'

There was silence apart from the gentle whistling sound. Brock cleared his throat, his saliva acid, then prompted her again. 'And you remembered the passage in Max's book, about the boy in the Shatila camp. The ages matched, didn't they? Was there anything else that convinced you he was Abu?'

'Little things. Once I took Max to Chandler's Yard. I'd spoken to him about Qasim and he was interested in the Islamic background. When we were in the Horria I took him up to see the mosque, and on the stairs we met Abu coming down. I introduced them, but, although they didn't say anything, I could see that they already knew each other. And not just as people who might have met once at a meeting or something, but as friends. As soon as they recognised each other they smiled, like friends. I asked Max afterwards, but he denied knowing Abu. There were other things too, like the child's drawing in his room, with the palm tree.'

'Yes, I remember. So you realised the truth.'

'I couldn't believe it at first, that Max had used Abu to commit suicide. I thought Fran must have got it all confused, yet she was quite adamant. Then I began to see the sense in it.' She looked suddenly puzzled at Brock. 'You aren't surprised? You knew?'

'I got there only this evening, Briony, just before you fire-bombed me, although I should have seen it earlier. In retrospect, Max wasn't very subtle about trying to frame Haygill. He'd warned the police, the press, even Mrs Haygill. And his clues! The one I should have picked up straight away was the green pamphlet, like the one you sent me this morning.'

'What was wrong with it?'

'He'd licked the gum on the envelope it was sent in, and we identified his DNA. When we discovered that, we assumed the pamphlet had come in a different envelope, when the obvious conclusion was that he'd sent it himself. Ironic that the science of DNA should trip him up, when he hated it so much. And he did hate it, and Richard Haygill, with a vengeance, didn't he?'

'He'd tried everything to stop him, and failed. No one was listening to him any more.'

'Yes,' he said, 'You pointed that out to me the first time we met, if I'd only realised. What was his favourite quote you had on your wall? About being overlooked?'

'"To be wholly overlooked, and to know it, are intolerable." Yes. That was how he felt. He'd laboured for so long, with his books, and they were no longer read, and he'd tried to act in the public arena, and he'd been excluded. But a free man can't be excluded. In the end, if he's desperate enough, he can make his voice heard. With his death he achieved what he had been denied in his life. People talked about his ideas again, and read his books and took notice of what he had to say. Only . . . only *you* failed.' The bitterness spilled out again. 'You failed in the important part, to stop Haygill. He escaped, and now I have to do this.' She lifted the lighter again in her trembling hand. 'If I don't then Max and Abu will have died for nothing. Don't you see? In a little while everyone will look back and think that their deaths were just some weird aberration, and they'll forget. But this way no one will forget. They will be remembered as martyrs.'

'But this is not the way, Briony. Max wouldn't want this. He killed only himself. You'll have to kill me.'

'Then get out, now!' she cried.

'But aren't you doing exactly what Max hated so much, what the enemies of freedom do? You're trying to turn a lie into the truth by

268

force!' He watched her frown as she considered her response to this, and he ploughed on, trying to keep his voice steady, although his throat felt on fire. 'Max spoke through his books, Briony. That's what you should do. Tell the truth, through your thesis.'

She snorted with disgust. 'No one reads Ph.D. theses.'

'I always thought the most powerful bombs in the world were books. I think Abu believed that too. He left his book for us. Have you seen it? Look . . .' He began to reach slowly to the pocket of his coat, Briony's eyes fixed on him, puzzled.

Kathy had waited with the security man in the lobby, straining to hear any sound from the building above. Brock knows what he's doing, she told herself, although the fire at his house had alarmed her, more than it had him, it seemed, just like the warning note in the mail, and he'd said nothing on the journey over about who he thought was behind all this.

'He told us to wait outside,' she said doubtfully.

'He reckons they've got some kind of accelerant, right?'

'Yes, petrol, probably.'

'Well, they picked the wrong building here. There's every kind of safety system in place against fire. I reckon the best we can do is watch the panels for the first sign of trouble, then direct the brigade to the right place.' He waved the beam of his flashlight over the control panels in the recess just inside the main door. There certainly did seem to be an impressive range of monitoring lights and dials. 'Most likely the worst they can do is burn themselves then get flooded by the sprinklers . . . Hang on.'

He was peering at a digital display in one corner. Kathy could see green numbers spinning fast, like the read-out on a VCR on fast-forward.

'What is that?'

The security man stepped back and said softly under his breath. 'God.' It sounded more like a prayer than an oath. 'The labs are piped with gas. That's the meter. All the bloody taps must be wide open.'

'What does that mean?'

'They're filling the labs with gas.' A note of panic had crept into

269

the man's voice. 'They're turning the building into a bloody great bomb, that's what it means. One spark, one pilot light. . .'

Kathy could hear the man's breathing, suddenly hoarse as if he could taste the gas already filling his lungs. 'Shit . . . We can turn the main off . . . Yeah, and throw the air-conditioning into exhaust . . .' He lunged towards a row of colour-coded metal wheels.

'Wait!' Kathy called out. 'Hang on. Will they know what you're doing?'

'How do you mean?' The man was shouting at her, almost hysterical.

'Will they know, when you shut down the gas?'

'Probably . . . yes. And they'll hear the extract fans go on.'

'Then wait! How long would it take to clear the gas?'

'Christ knows. Several minutes.'

Kathy stood motionless, thinking, then said, 'Don't touch it. Go outside and warn them. Make sure the neighbouring buildings are evacuated. Give me two minutes, then cut off the gas to the whole campus.'

The man stared blankly at her for a moment, as if half his mind was still struggling with the scale of the imminent catastrophe.

'Give me your torch,' she said. 'Where's the fire escape stair?'

He handed it over and pointed, still in a state of shock.

'Go!' she shouted at him, and he seemed to wake up, and turned and ran.

She was opening the door to the fire stair when she heard him call after her, 'I can see a light on at level four!'

The stairwell was bare concrete, and as soon as she smelled its sour smell, and heard the scuffling sounds of her progress in the half-light, she knew that her nightmare was in there, waiting for her if she allowed it. Her heart began to thump with panic, bile rose in her throat, and she came to a stop, halfway up a flight, forced to grip the handrail with trembling hands just to stay on her feet. She heard her own voice in her head, accusing herself. *You can't do this. You're going to fail. You can't even get up the stairs.*

'Stop it,' she said aloud. He isn't here. He's dead. This is a memory of a smell, that's all, an echo in the head. Move now or you and Brock and a million female cells will be blown into the night.

She stumbled on, upward, numbly watching her feet as they

climbed, step by step, level two, level three, level four. She hesitated in front of the door marked with a large red number four, then turned the handle and went in.

And there he was, waiting for her, a dark hooded figure, silhouetted against the bench lights, and hissing. She froze, and it took her a moment to realise that it was the gas taps hissing, and that he had his back to her, and in the shadows beyond him she could make out Brock, sitting on a stool. They were talking, though their voices were low and she couldn't make out what they said. She took a deep breath, and almost choked on the fumes of gas and petrol.

She inched silently towards the figure. His right hand was held out and she saw the top of the cigarette lighter held ready to spark. He seemed smaller than she had expected. Was it the wild boy Ahmed? Or one of the Iraqis? Maybe the other was somewhere nearby.

She remembered Leon's description of the knife one of them had carried in the car, perhaps in his other hand, which she couldn't see. She had her retractable baton in her coat pocket, but he would hear it snap open, and even if she struck his hand accurately, the flint might still spark. She would have to smother it with her hand, hang on to it long enough for Brock to get over and help. Meanwhile his other hand, with the knife, would be free.

She could hear Brock's voice now, calm and reasoned, as if pondering a question of law.

'I always thought the most powerful bombs in the world were books. I think Abu believed that too. He left his book for us. Have you seen it? Look . . .' He began to reach slowly to the pocket of his coat. The hooded figure seemed transfixed by what he was doing, then the all-pervasive hissing abruptly stopped, leaving a deafening silence in its place. The figure gave a cry and began to turn, and as Kathy threw herself at him she had a vision from her memory of him picking her bodily from the bed and throwing her against the wall. She yelled out, a wild cry of protest, and grabbed the hand that held the lighter. The figure wheeled round and Kathy forced herself to meet his face, and was astonished to see Briony Kidd gaping at her.

23

'But that was such a terrible thing to ask anybody to do!' Kathy said. 'Imagine how Abu must have felt when Springer put it to him, to help the man he worshipped to kill himself.'

'Oh, I think it was much worse than that,' Brock said, lifting the pint mug to his mouth.

They were in The Three Crowns, a dozen of the team that had been working on the case. It had seemed the most appropriate place to go to celebrate, and a mini-bus had been ordered for closing time to take them all home. Qasim Ali and his brother George had wandered in for a quiet beer during the course of the evening, and had been invited to join them. They and Bren and PC Greg Talbot from the local station were currently locked in a deadly serious struggle at the darts board.

'How do you mean?'

'I didn't say it to Briony, because I was worried how she'd react, but I think Springer intended all along for Abu to be caught. I think he was prepared to sacrifice Abu, and Briony's betrayal of him to Sanjeev Manzoor and his subsequent death suited his purposes very well.'

'But why? If he'd saved Abu, and helped him throughout his life. Why destroy him?'

'To make the case against Haygill stick. He needed to connect Haygill to the assassin, and to do that we had to discover who the killer was. The hints that he'd left us about an Islamic connection led us to Abu, and the gun he'd told Abu to plant in Haygill's room and the money should have done the rest. And when you think about it, he'd begun to manipulate Abu and use him for his own purposes for some time. If Abu was the child that Max had saved in the camp, then he must have kept in touch with him all those years while he lived with his adopted family, and sent them money for his education. And when Max learned that Haygill was working with people at the University of Qatar, where Abu was studying, he must have arranged for him to approach Haygill and ask for a job here at UCLE. He then used Abu as his spy inside CAB-Tech, to try to get something solid to attack Haygill with, like the BRCA4 protocol. Perhaps it was his failure to find this that drove him to the ultimate solution.'

A roar from the people clustered around the dartboard announced a winning bullseye from Greg Talbot, and Qasim and his brother were sent off to the bar to buy another round.

'He must have been obsessed with Haygill,' Kathy said. 'I could never follow why. I mean, that stuff about truth and freedom, and science being like a fundamentalist religion, I couldn't understand that.'

'I think most of the people who reviewed Springer's last book shared your opinion, Kathy.' Brock drained his glass in anticipation of the drinks which the barman was stacking on Qasim's tray. 'I don't know how it began, but I think his obsession ended up being purely personal. I think Haygill was right when he said that Springer hated him because he came to realise that what Haygill was doing mattered, and what Springer was doing didn't. Haygill had achieved everything that Max Springer might have aspired to, and he couldn't stand it.'

'Pure spite.'

'A total obsession. In the end Springer became a victim of the condition he despised. He lost his freedom to think straight because his mind turned a theory into an absolute truth.'

'I think Abu knew,' Kathy said suddenly. She was thinking of her first encounter with Abu, the look of recognition and resignation on his face. 'I think he must have realised the fate that Max had planned for him. Yet he still went through with it.'

'You may be right. Now that is tragedy, isn't it? I'd be intrigued to know where Springer got the gun though.'

'You don't think Abu got it?'

'I doubt it. Springer carefully stage-managed every detail of his death. I don't think he'd have left something as important as that to Abu. He might have messed it up, got caught trying to buy it, and that would have ruined everything.'

Greg Talbot wandered over, face flushed with his success at the dartboard. 'Here, Kathy,' he said, 'I still don't get it, that weird old bloke setting the whole thing up – setting me up, come to that. But you know what bothers me the most? That day when he came in to Shadwell Road to make his report about being threatened, he stood there for the best part of an hour listening to old man Manzoor ranting on about his missing daughter and how some bloke had abducted her.'

'Yes?'

'Well, did he know that the bloke was Abu?'

Kathy thought about that. 'It's possible,' she said, 'if not then, then later. Abu told him enough to know that they needed that money.'

'That's what I thought. He could have shown Springer a photo of his girlfriend, and Springer would have seen her picture on the missing persons poster in our front window.'

'What are you saying, exactly, Greg?'

'Well, he was such a devious old bugger, that if that student hadn't told you she did it, I'd have said that *he* was the one that sent that photo to Manzoor, and got Abu killed, so that he wouldn't be able to spill the beans after it was all over.'

It was a chilling thought, and Kathy had been pondering Abu's state of mind at the end, torn between two loyalties. How strongly had he felt about the work of his CAB-Tech colleagues, the generosity of Haygill, which Springer had forced him to betray? 'But Briony did admit that she was the one who sent the photo to Manzoor.'

'Oh yes, she *said* that, but could she be trying to cover up just what a totally ruthless old bastard her hero really was?'

'Greg, you have a truly devious mind yourself. You'll be a great loss to the Met.'

He grinned. 'Yeah, well, I made my choice, Kathy. I'm not going to put that uniform on again. But you? The lads were saying you're back on board again. I thought you were going to jack it in too?'

'Changed my mind. Found I couldn't do without it.'

She watched Qasim and George weaving back through the crowd, their hands full with the trays of pint glasses, when she noticed them abruptly stop. Across the bar the babble of conversation faded suddenly as everyone turned to stare at the man standing in the pub doorway. Sanjeev Manzoor was holding a brown cardboard box. The tension in his face was apparent to everyone as he stepped slowly forward towards the two men with the drinks. They seemed stunned and uncertain what to do, burdened as they were. At the last moment he glided past them and came to the table by which Kathy was standing, and placed the package in front of her, as carefully as if the slightest jolt might be fatal. A voice somewhere in the room broke the silence with a muttered 'Shit!' as Manzoor began to ease the lid of the box up.

He straightened upright with the box lid in his hand. Inside they could see something beneath a layer of green tissue paper. He addressed himself to Kathy.

'Sergeant,' he said, very tense and formal, 'I have completed your suit.' He drew back the tissue and lifted a hanger on which was draped a black jacket and skirt.

A roar of laughter filled the pub. Some joker called for a camera to get a picture for the front page of *The Job*, another for the phone number of the CIB.

Kathy took in a deep breath and said, 'Mr Manzoor, I don't know what to say.'

'It is not a gift, of course. That would be misconstrued. But it is a fair price, my best price. The invoice is in the pocket. When you have tried it on, I shall make final adjustments. And I would ask one favour. It concerns my daughter, Nargis.'

'Oh, yes?'

'Yes. I have a message for her, and I would beg you to deliver it for me. Since you are my enemy, she will believe it from you. Despite all that has happened between us, I want only what is good for my daughter. I hear that she is with child. I do not know if the child is of her husband, or of the other man, but I do not care. It is my grandchild, and I want to help her. If she wishes I shall instruct my nephew in Kashmir to divorce her. Please tell her this.'

'Very well.'

'Thank you. And to you, sir . . .' he gave a little bow to Brock,

275

then to Bren, '... and you, I offer my humble apologies for any discomfort my actions may have caused you.'

Bren nodded and offered his hand, but Brock, less forgiving and suspecting Manzoor's motives, did not. Someone told him to stay and have a drink, but he shook his head. 'That is not possible. I have done what I came for,' and he turned and left.

'Blimey!' Qasim marched forward and put his tray down on the next table. His face was red, whether from the excitement or the strain of holding the drinks Kathy wasn't sure. 'Never thought I'd ever see Manzoor inside a pub.' He passed drinks to Brock and Kathy and raised his glass in a toast. 'To old enemies.' He hesitated a moment with the glass almost at his lips as he saw the door open again and another Asian face appear, then he relaxed and smiled, recognising Leon Desai. He had been attending another crime scene, and he looked uncharacteristically tired and grimy as he came over.

'Get anyone a drink?'

Kathy said, 'We've just been refilled. I'll get you one. Sit down, you look beat.'

'Yeah. I'll have a wash first.'

They crossed the bar together, and when they were out of earshot of the others he said, 'I won't stay long. Can I give you a lift home?'

She hesitated, then said, 'I chipped in for the mini-bus. I'd better go with the others, Leon.'

He gave a resigned little smile and turned away.

The following day Kathy kept her promise to Sanjeev Manzoor and called on Nargis at Chandler's Yard. Alone in her room she wasn't wearing a headscarf, and Kathy saw again her beautiful, long, gleaming black hair.

'It's a shame you have to cover that up,' she said.

'I've thought about giving up the hijab often, but I never did. Not for the same reasons as Fran. While Abu was alive I did it for his sake, and now, with the baby, I feel I need my faith to hang on to. Qasim told me about Dad turning up at the pub last night, but he didn't say what he wanted.'

'He asked me to give you a message. Apparently he thought it would come better from me, since I'm what he described as his enemy.'

'That sounds like the way he thinks, yeah.' She listened expressionless as Kathy told her what her father had said. At the end she gave a quick shake of her head. 'That's easy for him to say, isn't it? He wasn't raped, was he? He didn't have his friend stabbed to death in the street . . .'

For the first time Kathy saw the turmoil beneath Nargis' extraordinary composure. Her mouth curled with the pain of grief and she covered her face with both hands and began to sob. Kathy put an arm round her and held her till the wave of despair passed.

'You know everything now, don't you?' Nargis whispered. 'Briony told you?'

'Yes, almost everything. If it's any comfort, I believe they will let you keep the money Abu gave you.'

'It's for the baby, you see. I don't need dad.'

'We'd still like to know where the gun came from. You wouldn't know anything about that, would you?'

'Qasim tried to find out. He thought he could prove Abu innocent if he tracked it down, but nothing came of it.'

On the way out, Kathy stopped at the counter of the Horria to speak to Qasim. For once the jukebox was silent. There were no customers and he was buttering bread slices, eyes narrowed against the smoke of the cigarette in his mouth.

'How is she?'

'It's going to take time, Qasim.'

'Sure, sure. Anyway, she'll always have a place here if she wants it.'

'You're a good friend. She tells me you tried to trace the gun Abu used, to help his case.'

She wondered exactly how he'd gone about it.

'Right. I just couldn't believe that Abu could shoot somebody in cold blood like that. Well, I was both wrong and right, wasn't I?'

'We all were. So you had no more luck than us then, with the gun.'

He squinted at her through the smoke. 'I didn't say that. Only it didn't help him, so I said nothing.'

'You found out where it came from?'

'Maybe. But I couldn't tell you if I did. My sources wouldn't appreciate it.'

'Really?' Kathy was filled with curiosity, and she thought she detected something teasing in Qasim's manner. 'Not even to the enemy of Sanjeev Manzoor?'

He gave a grin. 'Well, I might drop a hint to a friend, Kathy, but I couldn't go on the record, see?'

'I understand.' She leaned across the counter, all ears.

'Young PC Talbot told me what you'd found out about the gun from the slugs – 7.62 mill, probably Russian or the like, and used once before in a punch-up in North London, when a drug dealer got shot. Now it happens I may have an acquaintance who knows someone who knows someone who was mixed up in that. And through these contacts, I may have heard that someone else, a customer of one of these characters, had made inquiries about purchasing a certain item of hardware from them, and had in fact done so, round about last Christmas.'

'Go on.'

'Well, that's it.'

'No it's not. How did you know that this wouldn't help Abu?'

Qasim scowled with fake reluctance. 'Be-cause . . .' his voice dropping to a whisper, '. . . the party in question was at the same university as Abu, so it just made matters look worse.'

Kathy stared at him. 'The party? Male or female?'

Qasim spread his fat fingers. 'I've said enough.'

'Come on, Qasim! Male or female?'

'Male.'

'You said he was a *customer*. The man who bought the gun was a customer of this drug-dealer friend of yours.'

'Not a friend of mine, Kathy, no way!' Qasim protested, a look of determined innocence on his face. Kathy was wondering what sideline Qasim had developed to take the place of his grandfather's business in qat. But something else was itching in her mind.

'What was he buying?'

Qasim puffed his cigarette and looked vacantly at the motionless ceiling fan.

'Let me guess. It was coke.'

He looked at her in surprise. 'Good guess.'

'One of the teachers at the university acquired a taste for it when he had a spell at a university in California. He was caught trying to bring some home with him. His first name is Desmond. Am I getting warm?'

Qasim beamed. 'I think I'd better turn the bleedin' fans on, Kathy. You're practically on fire.'

As she walked across the cobbles of Chandler's Yard, Kathy recalled the little Welshman, Desmond Pettifer, Reader in Classics, mischief-maker and last remaining friend of Max Springer. She remembered his innocent inquiries about the calibre of the murder weapon, and wondered what story Springer had told him, and what had possessed him to help Springer buy a pistol. Did he imagine that Max was going to storm into Haygill's office and gun him down? Or the University President, perhaps, Roderick Young? Or had Max explained that it wasn't their lives that he wanted but their reputations, their place in history. And in a way he had succeeded, for he was now more widely discussed and read than he ever had been while he was alive, while they would probably remain tainted by what had happened.

It would depend on the coroner, she imagined, and what he would make of Brock's theory of elaborate suicide. For although both Brock and Briony had come by their separate ways to believe it, it still wasn't proved. The events could still be seen as consistent with Abu having acted alone, or with some other, unknown party.

She stepped out of the lane into the stream of shoppers on Shadwell Road. Someone was causing an obstruction ahead, and she recognised the youth Ahmed Sharif, thrusting green pamphlets into the hands of reluctant passers-by with a burning intensity in his eyes. She took one and read it.

'In effect you deny the Judgement. But there are guardians over you, honoured recorders, who know all that you do.' Sura 82 : 10

It was a reassuring thought. Leave it to the guardians. She moved on to the window of a travel agent, and looked for a moment at the notices of cut-price fares. Some things at least had become clear; the pensioners from Pontefract would not figure in her life. She was doing what she was best at, what she most wanted to do. Music was coming from the doorway of the shop, a bouncy number from

279

Bollywood Flashback, and she thought of Wayne O'Brien and wondered where he was now. He had helped her at a critical moment, in a way that perhaps no one else could have, not Brock, nor Suzanne, nor Leon. They had been too much tangled in what had happened to her, and now that she was free again she could return to them on her own terms.

She turned on her heel and strode off. There was a letter in a drawer of Brock's desk that she wanted to retrieve.